Poor Man's Summer

Pearlie Jenkins

Poor Man's Summer

A Novel

Copyright 2017 by Pearlie Jenkins

Published by Ginkgo Leaf Press, Kentucky
2017

ISBN-13: 978-1548894597
ISBN-10: 1548894591

Cover design by Nathan Paul Isaac

Such fine examples may not be the best to follow.
Hard to get away from all you've ever known.

Reverend John and the Backsliders
"Hand Me Down Lane"

Took it all and took the dirt road home
Dreaming of Jenny with the light brown hair
I'm gonna take the sins of my father
I'm gonna take the sins of my mother
I"m gonna take the sins of my brother
Down to the pond

Tom Waits
"Sins Of My Father"

"The world breaks every one and afterward many
are strong at the broken places."

Ernest Hemingway
A Farewell To Arms

for Lora Schwarz

Note:

If a traveler were to point down the shaded, tree-lined, two lane rural highway and inquire of a native, "Say, what town lies just down this stretch of road?" The stranger would most likely hear from the native, "Snorville. The town of Snorville lies just down this stretch of road." "How far might ya reckon?" the curious traveler might then inquire. "Ah, six, seven miles, I s'pose." His answer would come. A traveler might then genuinely express his gratitude and walk on the prescribed and reckoned six, seven miles, now knowing exactly where it is he is headed. A destination, though one might be hard pressed to find an authentic traveler type willing to admit it, is often just as comforting as none.

What precisely it might be that occupies the thoughts of general ramblers and self-proclaimed tramps one might be hard pressed to pin down. With his thoughts perhaps plural in nature, he might make his way, one light foot in front of the other and so on, hoping to find temporary work and opportunity in "Snorville." On the traveler would walk, towards sleepy "Snorville" perhaps in deep appreciation of the Appalachian foothills that surround the valley and the town. Perhaps smiling at the staccato _tea-kettle, tea-kettle, tea-kettle_ calling of the Carolina Wren. Perhaps not. He might saunter on, oblivious to calling birds, rolling pastures, occasional grazing Herefords, and dense forest. The hypothetical journeyman of question might find himself in a state of nervous apprehension, concerning how the attitudes and prejudices of the local constabulary and general populace of "Snorville" might be toward drifting stranger types. He might be well familiar with just how fickle small towns can be.

But that is all merely guesswork, that is to say, hyperbole and hypothetical. What is safe to assume in reference to the small but steadily growing town of "Snorville" and those who chance to vist it, is that many who have heard the name are surprised to see it on the white-lettered, green city sign. That's because the city sign reads, "Welcome to Sonoraville pop. 2116."

Part One: Of a Death Foretold

Chapter 1

S he waitin', now go on, and if she tell me y'all acted up, I'm a beat ya both blind. She waitin' now. Go on." Miss Jessie shooed the twin boys up the long dirt driveway toward the Lawford place.

Virginia Lawford waved a welcome from the porch of the large farmhouse. The twins stepped hesitantly toward her.

For reasons always mysterious to those outside the profession of education, the school year did not end on a convivial Friday, but on a recumbent Tuesday. On the Wednesday immediately following, Virginia Lawford began her employ as babysitter for Miss Jessie Simms, having allowed good will and steady income to interfere with untroubled summer idleness. She was now to earn two dollars a day babysitting the twins, Travis and Tobias, who had finished second grade, leaving Miss Jessie in need of child care between the hours of eight a.m. and five p.m. Miss Jessie worked first shift at the hosiery and though she was not the boys' mother, they often called her such. Their unwed mother, Netta Simms, had abandoned them, leaving her mother, Miss Jessie, alone to raise them.

"Mammaw?" One of the boys turned to Miss Jessie.

"Now go on."

"You sure you comin' back?" he asked with a suspicious squint of his eye.

"Child, you think I'd leave you? Let alone to be raised by white folks? I'm comin' back, Travis. And I toldja, ya mama comin' back, too. You just gotta give her time. Now y'all better act like you've had some raisin' while ya here."

Virginia called from the porch, "I got y'all scrambled eggs and ketchup all ready and a waitin'."

The twin boys winced at each other in disgust.

"They done ate, Virginia. Now, if they act up on ya, don't ya be shy about blisterin' they hind ends."

"They're fine," the girl called back to her.

"Naw, they ain't fine, they mean." Miss Jessie corrected Virginia and said to the boys, "I gotta get to work now, I can't stand here dilly dallyin' all the mornin'. You boys go on and behave yourselves. Be back this evenin'."

"This evenin'? You said three days, Mammaw."

"Naw, I said they was three days 'til the weekend. I didn't mean y'all was stayin here for three days. You boys don't listen. You stay here 'til I get off work, then I come getcha. Ya got three days of that 'til the weekend comes then you stay home. Then we do it all again next week. I'll be back this evenin' to getcha," she reassured them. "Now, go on."

"Swear it, Mammaw?" asked the boy named Travis.

"I ain't gotta swear nothin'," she said swiftly, "I tell ya I be back, then I be back."

"They got a teevee?" asked the boy called Toby.

"Don't matter what they got. Go on."

The boys turned and begrudgingly walked toward the house. The boy named Travis quietly muttered. "We don't need no damned babysitter."

At this, Miss Jessie seized the sulking boy by the elbow and gave him three hard swats on his behind. "Now," she said, pulling the teary eyed child around to face her, "Say it again. I dare ya. What about you?" She turned fiercely to Tobias, "You got anything to say?" Toby shook his head. "All right, then. Y'all mind her and y'all mind Mister Tom. Now go on. You makin' me late. I love y'all. Gimme a kiss. Y'all is good boys. Just sometimes ya ain't. Travis, why you make me whoop you like that?"

From the porch they waved back at Miss Jessie, then followed Virginia into the house.

"I ain't put the ketchup on the eggs," she said, "so if y'all don't like ketchup on your eggs you don't have to put ketchup on 'em. Me, I like ketchup on my eggs. I like ketchup on lots a stuff, especially on french fries. Do colored folks like french fries? Y'all a have to tell me stuff, 'cause I don't know much about coloreds."

"We done ate," said Travis.

"Well, they're cooked already if ya do want'em. Ketchup or no."

"Is you still in school?" he asked.

"Nobody's in school. School's out. For the summer. For everybody."

Travis looked curiously to Tobias then back to Virginia. "When it ain't out for the summer, is you still in it?"

"I am."

"What grade?"

"Eleventh. I'm in what they call my junior year."

13

"Why they call it that?"

"On account of twelfth grade bein' called senior year, I reckon."

"Why they call twelfth grade that?"

"I don't know."

"Why you don't know?"

"I don't know why."

"You don't know why they calls it that or you don't know why you don't know?"

"I just don't know." She laughed. "Ain't you boys a wonder? If'n ya don't wanna eat none, then what would you boys like to do?"

"Go back home."

"Besides go back home."

"Why's we a wonder?"

Virginia laughed and patted the boy's shoulder.

When the evening and the hour came, the trio met Miss Jessie at the end of the driveway. Exhausted from tag, hide and seek and storytelling, Virginia bade her goodbyes and tucked two dollar bills into her pocket. On the walk back up the long and unpaved driveway, she softly wept.

What joy it was to Virginia, to have an emptiness suddenly filled, a longing and lacking replaced with an abundance—this is the gift the children brought. Oh, they brought other things, certainly they did, but above all they brought joy, what joy.

After she had prepared supper for her father and placed it on the table, she sat with him and filled the usual silence with, "*And then Toby said—*" and "*And then Travis goes—*" until her father was obliged to remind her to eat.

She was saddened when Friday evening came. She offered to watch them Saturday.

Miss Jessie said, "Ain't no reason for that, Virginia."

"Well, if you can think of a reason, then you just let me know."

"I surely will, but—"

"You boys can sit with me on the Sunday School bus if y'all want to."

Before the boys could answer, Miss Jessie said, "I likes to keep'em close to me when we go to church."

"Oh, sure," said Virginia. "Sure, you do."

Chapter 2

On the bank of The Russell River, a wandering mutt of a dog sat low in the Saturday afternoon shade. Though he appeared relaxed, contented, and not particularly alert, he watched the teenaged boy closely with his sharp yellow-brown eyes, eager and ever ready for the boy to offer up something else to eat.

Li'l Roy Tucker had eaten the egg sandwiches he'd made the night before, feeding half of the last one to the yellow mutt that had followed him all the way to the river. The sandwiches now sat like stones in the boy's stomach and he wondered if perhaps they'd become tainted overnight. He winced slightly and with the palm of his right hand rubbed his bare abdomen. It would not occur to him that his current ailment was brought upon by what Sheriff Stearns, who also suffered a similar recurring malady, often referred to simply as "nerves."

Lean and shirtless, he stood in the afternoon sun, keeping a watchful eye on both his lines as he rose. Upstream, something broke the water, leaving concentric ripples rolling across the glassy surface of the eddy. His eye caught the movement too late to identify its cause, but he nonetheless cockily invited it to come his way. He walked to the edge of the water, his bare feet mud-caked and padded with thick callouses. At the shoreline he knelt, feeling the cool water seep through the faded and threadbare knees of his jeans. A school of shad darted through the shallows, silver in the sun. He studied them for a moment before scattering them with his cupped hands.

Here, a bend in the river created a deep and nearly still pool. Squatting, Li'l Roy studied the gentle, primeval water as it rolled lazily by. He regarded the broad bank at this point in the river with a reserved and unparalleled admiration. It was the fresh, earthy smell of the untamed water, the mineral smell of muddy banks, and there, just underneath it all, the unmistakable musty aroma of decay, somehow comforting with its scent reminding him of the circular nature of life ending and life beginning. He was drawn to the river's perpetual, timeless movement with a full understanding of the steadfast fact that the river had flowed through this bend since what he imagined might just as well be the beginning of everything in existence. Sometimes, it allowed him to be the last person on earth, or perhaps the first. He was content to be either. On the bank, he enjoyed exploring and musing on the infinite possibilities of whom or what had previously come to it with hook and line, with fish trap, with sharpened spear, with swift claw or hooked fang.

It shared with him one of the few memories he had of his father, before his father had to go away.He drank from his hands and splashed the remainder onto his face. He scrubbed rigorously, almost roughly around his eyes. He dipped again from the river and rubbed his wet hands around his neck, cooling his sunburned shoulders as the yellow dog watched on curiously.

Ever the hunter, he reached slowly into the water and carefully turned over a large flat rock. A crayfish was there just as the boy suspected it might be. Angered by the impolite intrusion, it kicked up a muddy cloud, tucked its segmented tail and darted backward, shadow boxing and challenging the boy with its large claw. Li'l Roy considered using his perfected technique of distracting the crawdad with his right hand while sneaking up behind it with the thumb and forefinger of his left, but decided against it. The yellow dog approached to investigate and the boy changed his mind yet again. Slowly, he submerged his left hand behind the freshwater crustacean. With his right, he entered the water just in front of it. The crayfish tucked tail and again bolted backward through the river bed. Its angled trajectory almost threw the boy, but instinctively, he moved with it and suddenly had it there just behind the claws. He pulled it from the water, its legs wriggling, its snappers snapping. He presented it to the dog, putting it just under the dog's nose in the playful hope that it might attach itself to the dog's snout. The dog snorted, retreated, then snorted again. The boy laughed. "I hear ya boy. I'm with ya. Ugly, ain't it?" the boy asked. He examined the crawdad, all whiskers, beady eyes and prehistoric armor. He gave it a tiny victory and let it pinch his thumb, holding the thing in the air and letting it slightly swing. He took it again with his thumb and forefinger and gently pulled until the crayfish lost its hold. He flipped it over, its spiny legs flailing, and he saw the eggs that it carried beneath it. He studied the eggs, thought they looked like half a blackberry, and then gently placed the crayfish back beneath the water and onto the floor of the muddy riverbed. It promptly shot backward and was soon out of sight. "You go on, little mama." Li'l Roy laughed to himself.

He stood upright and stretched. He was awake, fully awake and only now realizing how close he had come to falling asleep there on the bank waiting for a fish to strike. He would settle for a catfish, but was hoping for crappie or a bass. A good catch would mean that he could stay there on the bank all night, away from his brothers. By the position of the sun, he figured it to be somewhere after two o'clock, maybe even closer to three. They would already be well on their way to shitfaced.

16

To hell with them, both of them, Lenville and Ronny. The thought of them made him turn slowly and look up the steep bank that loomed behind him, up toward where the tracks met the trestle, as if with his dread he might have conjured them up. They were not there.

He reeled in his lines and was disappointed to see that both had empty hooks. He swore, spat and wondered how long they had been that way. Fish or no fish, he was spending the night on the bank. Summer had only just begun, but it flowed like the river and all too soon, the choice to sleep outside and away from home would be gone with the first frost of fall.

He retrieved the rusted metal pail. His fingers dug blindly into the black dirt that filled it until, feeling what they were looking for, they emerged holding a slimy, squirming night-crawler. He beamed at the Annelid. "This is the one," he explained to the disinterested dog. "I knew it when I pulled him outta the ground. This is the son of a bitch that'll land us some supper, boy." He hoped it would land him a bellyful and allow him to spend the night on the bank without hunger driving him back home where his older brothers would be—rowdy as all hell, all wound up from closing down Pudgy's Tavern. They would give him the business, harass him and provoke him for not going with them. He could go with them. Sometimes he did. But lately, it was ending badly more often than not, fights, near fights, and if his brothers couldn't find a fight, they would turn to him in their drunken violent but playful way. Tonight, he would skip the headlocks and the Indian burns.

There was also word around that Darryl Hickey was out for Lenville. Or was it Lenville who was out for Hickey? It didn't matter. Hickey was older and had a reputation for being some kind of a badass, but Lenville could handle himself in a fight better than any fella in Sonoraville and probably all of Whelan County.

The chubby worm squirmed when the prick of the hook pierced its flesh. Once it was secured and the boy was satisfied with its station, he kissed it for good luck like his father had always done. With a beautiful fluid motion, he gave it a fine cast out into the river. The line drew an arc and hit the water with a perfect amount of attention-getting splash. He flashed a proud and satisfied smile, shot a glance toward the dog as if the dog would congratulate him on such a fine cast. The dog was indifferent. Li'l Roy secured the pole to one of the Y-shaped branches he had staked into the broad beach of the bank.

From above and away came the first sounds of an approaching train. To the boy it was a siren's call, a seductive promise of something foreign and exotic. He had no doubt that one day he would split, jump aboard that rolling mechanical marvel of a dream and let it carry him away from this town to a place where he would not be Li'l Roy Tucker from those Tuckers out the way, but just another young man making his way in the world. He was sure it ran through Knoxville. He might like Knoxville. He might Like Chattanooga or Atlanta or even out west—way out west.

The engineer opened the horn valve and suddenly there was no sound in the world save for the sound of the air horn of the train. Countless times he had heard the horn, yet still he involuntarily jerked at its initial wailing. He cursed the engineer and laughed at himself as the all-consuming horn stopped and then started again, making him reflexively jump a second time.

The horn blowing was over now. The train rolled along. Li'l Roy sat to watch it go by and was charmed by its rhythmic roll as it crossed the train trestle above. He reclined there on the bank and was lost in the strangely lulling clatter and clamor of the thing. He closed his eyes.

Virginia Lawford had six dollars in her pocket. At the drug store, she picked up coloring books and candies, imagining the twins' delight in them as she did so. She spun the carousel of paperbacks around and around until finally deciding on *Beezus and Ramona* by Beverly Cleary to read to the boys. As a last minute decision, she picked up *We Have Always Lived in the Castle* by Shirley Jackson for herself.

Travis and Tobias, for all of their relentless curiosity, their rambunctiousness and their disobedient ways, had brought life back into the quiet Lawford home. Now, the weekend had arrived and the house was once again filled with quiet, so filled that she thought it might pop like an overinflated balloon. Virginia deposited her recent purchases in her bedroom, pocketed a handful of hard candy, took the book she had bought for herself and headed back outside.

In a rocking chair on the porch, she sat for a while, her book and Spots the cat on her lap. The boys were heavy on her mind and she realized that she missed them. Not as badly as she missed her mama, but still. Her father was in the field. She watched him tending first to this task and then to that.

She opened her book and upon reaching the last sentence of the first paragraph, she quickly closed it as if trying not to let any more of its words escape.

Everyone else in my family is dead.

She extended her arm, held the book out and let it fall from her hand. Spots jumped a bit when the book hit the floor of the porch. "Shhh," she said, stroking him. "It's okay." Gently, she picked the purring cat up from her lap and stood, holding it to her breast and slightly bouncing as a mother might do with a sleepy infant. "Shhh," she repeated. She placed the purring cat onto the smooth worn seat of the empty rocker and stroked his head and neck once more before heading down the front steps.

On the railroad tracks, Virginia Lawford had honed her talent for years and in the last summer of the 1960s, she harbored no doubt, and found great and sinful pride in the notion that no one anywhere in the world could walk the rails so well as she.

She marched on the rails, bringing her knees high, singing,
"I may never march in the infantry—"
She skipped along the rail singing,
"I may never ride in the cavalry—"
It was no longer even a balancing act. Her muscle memory had adapted an autonomic nature and she walked the rusted rails almost subconsciously. She walked them forward. She walked them backward. She walked them with a hopping sidestep. She leaped lightly across the ties and from rail to rail rarely having to hold out her arms to aid her balance. This is how she was spending the first Saturday of summer break.

It is easy to get lost in the ecstasy of early summer, with the final ringing of the school bell freshly faded and no longer lying in wait to rip apart daydreams and remind one that one's time is not one's own, to be beyond the have-tos and the must-dos of adolescent theater, public and awkward. Virginia was lost like that. School was out. Miss Jessie was off for the weekend from her shift at the hosiery. This day, this particular slice of summer belonged to Virginia alone.

She was headed nowhere in particular when, from the trestle, she spied the sleeping boy. Her soft voice trailed off, falling to a slightly out of key whisper, *"But I'm in the Lord's ar-my."* She immediately identified the boy as Li'l Roy Tucker, smasher of windows—the boy they had blamed for the fire at the school. Her body halted almost instinctively in a manner that served both fear and wonder. The Tucker boys, wild and dangerous, held her fascination like matinee idols held the affections of her female classmates. In coming across Li'l Roy Tucker from this unseen distance, it was to Virginia Lawford like coming upon an eagle or a mountain lion, or any of the most majestic and dangerous of wild, beautiful creatures.

On the bank, Li'l Roy Tucker's dream was light and new and of some endless summer. His father had been there, kissing worms and telling him what a good job he did casting lines out into the river. In that dream he had caught a fish, the finest of fish, a fish to be rejoiced over. He awoke and was immediately sideways with himself for both falling asleep and for waking up in the middle of a dream so swell. One pole lay forgotten and still unbaited and uncast. The other rested in the branch where he had left it. He looked to the sun and reckoned that he had slept for nearly an hour. He scrambled to the pole with the cast line and reeled it in. The chubby night-crawler was all but gone. Only chunky viscera remained there on the hook. Again he swore, disgusted with himself, the night-crawler, and whatever thieving bastard of a fish had stolen his bait yet again. He slung the pole to the ground and cursed its lack of loyalty. The fish were not biting and boredom had infected him. He scolded himself. He was going to have to stay awake if he planned on eating. He stood contemplative, his thoughts on his near future. Confident that a swim would wake him up, Li'l Roy Tucker looked to his left and then to his right and then to his left again as if preparing to cross Main Street rather than jump into the Russell River. It might run the fish off, too, but he could move upriver if that proved to be the case. He peered up the steep bank behind him, scanned the rocky, shimmering cliffs in front of him and, satisfied that he was alone, removed his dirty jeans and briefs.

Naked as a newborn, he took a few tenuous steps into the river and dove in. Breaking the surface, the cold water sent him into a sneezing fit. He pinched snot from his nostrils and flung it away, bouncing on the balls of his feet.

In the pool created by the bend in the river, the water was deep and still enough for him to swim in. He dove, pushed off the bottom and resurfaced, rolling over and over until floating lazily on his back. He let his lower body rise and fall in the water. Each time his parts broke the surface, he felt the stirring—his member swelling and stiffening. His midsection rose from the water and made him think of fuzzy floating sundials. He was considering giving himself a touch when he heard the yellow dog bark and his oldest brother Lenville's voice from the bank.

"Damn, boy, ain't you awful proud of that thing! Out here showin' it off to the whole damned world!" Startled, Li'l Roy lost the delicate balance of his floating position. His head went beneath the water and he came up on the balls of his feet, choking and coughing and hearing his brother say, "Now, that's the best arrowhead you'll find out here today, I guaran-damn-tee it."

His other brother, Ronny, was undressing. "I'm comin' in," he announced. "You keep that monster away from me."

Lenville Tucker laughed at his younger brothers. He took a moment to watch and to appreciate, to sear the image of this summer afternoon forever into prized memory—the silver ripples, the scent of the river, the laughter, the splash, the feeling, the goddamned feeling of it all. He took a long pull from a pint bottle, winced slightly, grinned to himself and hurriedly began to strip.

The summer air filled with intrusive merriment, jubilant shouts, curses and splashes, the imagined privacy and serenity of the bank and the river now dashed and shattered along with Li'l Roy's deluded hopes of avoiding his drunken older brothers this fine Saturday.

She watched him until he woke and then she ducked low and moved to the far side of the trestle and watched him from the other side. When the older brothers made their approach, she sought cover and concealment beneath the trestle itself, struggling to find steady footing in the large rolling rocks. A few rolled underfoot and continued down the bank. She held her breath until she was sure none of three brothers had taken notice. From her hidden position beneath the train trestle, Virginia Lawford watched the brothers climb the rocky cliffs on the far side so that they could dive into the river, skinny, sinewy, wet naked boys with furry thickets and what seemed like incredibly large 'things' dangling between their legs. 'Things,' 'ding-dongs,' 'peckers.' She had heard male genitalia called by all manner of names at school.

A ghostly voice from elementary school belonging to a girl named Tracy French reverberated in her head.

"Have you ever seen what boys have? I mean down there?"

Until this moment, these many years later, Virginia Lawford had not.

"I've seen what my little brother has. I've seen his *thingy*." A different girl had answered with a giggle. They had all been in the girl's bathroom at school. Virginia had sat eavesdropping from inside a stall.

"Well," began Tracy French, "boys put their 'thingy' into a girl's 'thingy' and then they both go crazy for a minute, and—"

"Eww, that's gross!" another girl protested and a chorus rose in affirmation.

"There may be more to it. I don't know. But that's how babies are made. I know that," Tracy French assured the gathering.

"I don't believe it." One of the anonymous girls had declared.

When the bell rang, Virginia had found herself suddenly alone in the girl's bathroom, feeling like she had been given a gift of understanding one of the great mysteries of the universe. She sat in the stall, on the toilet, contemplating this new information until the bell sounded again, informing her that she was now officially late for class.

There in the bathroom stall, a dark cloud of dread and panic had come over her, blotting out the wonder and the excitement of this new information. Being late to class meant she would be entering the class room after everyone was seated and facing the front where the door to the classroom was. Everyone would look at her. Everyone would stare. Mister Jackson would say something clever to her and they would all look at her and they would all laugh.

She had sat in the stall and she had not moved for the next hour, choosing to miss the whole class rather than endure the humiliation of everyone looking at her. Eventually, her legs fell asleep. Eventually, so did she until someone smacked the stall door very hard, startling her awake.

"Who's in there? Who's snorin' on the toilet?" A chorus of anonymous laughter came from the other side of the wall.

Virginia had slept through the break bell. From the next stall over, a curious head appeared over the short dividing wall.

21

"It's Virginia Lawford!" The girl had laughed. "She fell asleep while she was in there."

The girl had mocked her mercilessly and the others had joined her. That night the school had burned and everyone just knew Li'l Roy Tucker had started it. Virginia shook off the memory and focused her thoughts and eyes back onto the boys, and their nakedness.

that's how babies are made

Her adolescent heart picked up its pace and sweat bloomed in her soft palms. Virginia Lawford watched and she burned and she wanted, wanted so deeply, so desperately in that moment to go crazy for a minute, to make a baby, to feel a life growing, to hear the laughter and even the crying over the maddening silence of the quiet Hell that was home.

Having the Simms twins in her home with all of their noise and their laughter and their running and even their mischief had made the house even lonelier when they were gone.

Her mother's words found her.

"You take care of your daddy."

"I will, Mama."

"He's gonna need you."

"I know, Mama."

"Promise me, baby."

"I promise, Mama."

In the moments after her mother's passing, more than anything, Virginia Lawford wanted only to run, to find herself alone in the woods, on the railroad tracks, or at the river. But she did not run. She stayed and held onto her father.

And now, these many lonely months later, the cold reality of it all was upon her as heavy and as binding as the truth. Its weight reduced her shoulders, and in that period of time wherein youth blooms and blossoms, she only withered beneath the shadowy reality that she would not ever have a husband, a family. She could not. She would take care of her daddy and stay there forever in the quiet house and when her daddy left this world, leaving her even more alone in it, she would then be too old for anyone to want to marry.

Who would have her then?

She would find no husband. She would bear no children. She would die a spinster. She was certain of this.

Unless—

Netta Simms—

"Thought you said you was gonna go fishin' or huntin' arrowheads. Don't look like you was doin much of either to me." Lenville Tucker poked at his youngest brother.

"Damn, can't a sumbitch take a swim without runnin' it by you two?" Li'l Roy snapped back at his oldest brother.

"Sure a sumbitch can take a swim. You wanna swim?" Lenville took hold of Li'l Roy and held him beneath the surface of the water just long enough to totally infuriate the boy before releasing him.

"Goddammit, Len!" Li'l Roy cursed his oldest brother.

"Calm down, you little baby. Quit your cryin' and go get yourself a drink." Lenville pointed toward the bank.

"I don't feel like drinkin' none today," Li'l Roy said. "Got myself a gut ache," he added quickly.

"*Got myself a gut ache*," Lenville mocked. "Didn't look like you was achin' for nothin' but poon when we come up on ya." The eldest laughed.

"Only poontang he was thinkin' about was catfish." Ronny chimed in, pushing a large wave toward the younger boy. "He don't know poontang."

"Screw you guys."

"We're just messin' with ya, kiddo. Aw, come on."

Beneath the trestle, it was not the Tucker boys who held Virginia's thoughts, but Netta Simms. Netta Simms who had no husband, but had two boys. Well, she didn't have them now. Netta's mother, Miss Jessie had them. They had a father. Sure, they had a father, even if Netta was the only person who knew who their father was, though it was pretty clear given the boys' skin tone that their father was a white man. Netta Simms had left her bastard babies and gone on—out to California was the word. Virginia imagined that she could do as Netta Simms, except not go on. She could have herself a baby without having herself a husband, without leaving her daddy. She would be shamed like Netta. They would say things about her at school. Maybe she could try again to burn the school down. Her father would hate her. But he would come around. He had no choice really. She could have those things—a family of her own and still be there for her daddy just as she had promised her mother.

how babies are made

The Tucker boys were prime candidates, but which one? Did it matter? Not particularly. All three of them were beautiful. She preferred Li'l Roy, but— And then what? She had exasperated herself with the poorly thought out scheme until, somewhere deep within her longing thoughts, a near audible 'click' sounded and the answer to her dilemma became as clear as glass. She would lay with all three of

23

them. She would throw herself at each of them in turn, and when her belly began to swell, there would be no way of knowing which of the three had fathered the child. Not one of them would be able to lay claim to her baby. It was an out for them, and, for her, a way to have this thing she wanted so terribly without—

The boys' words brought the girl back.

"Aw, come on."

Li'l Roy Tucker waded his way back to the bank, put his ragged briefs on and sat on an old tree trunk beside the yellow mutt. "Couple a real assholes, right there," he said to the dog. The dog sat quietly and with little expression. Li'l Roy shivered with a chill. His wet flesh pimpled and begrudgingly, he reached for the pint bottle and took a long pull from it, letting the red whiskey warm him, and damn it felt good. He took another pull, spied Lenville's cigarette pack and reached for it. Inside the pack, along with a handful of Lucky Strikes, were two neatly rolled joints. Roy extracted one of the Lucky Strikes.

"Help yourself, little brother," laughed Lenville approaching from the river.

"I am," said Li'l Roy, flipping his brother's Zippo opened with a practiced move that sounded to him like swords crossing in battle and resulted in captive fire.

"Fire up one of those left handeds," Lenville offered.

"I'm good." Li'l Roy replied through a cloud of smoke.

Lenville Tucker brushed the water from his legs and bare buttocks with his large hands and put his underwear and jeans on. Li'l Roy studied his brother's hands as he did so, particularly his brother's nails and the line of grime that now deeply and permanently decorated them. To the younger boy, it was so much more than dirt, more than poor hygiene, more than grease, oil and grime. It was the mark of one who was making their way in the world, holding their own and content to do so.

For the past several months, since dropping out of school, Lenville Tucker was prone to use the words, "*the shop*." Down at *the shop*, out at *the shop*, yesterday at *the shop*. The more often the younger boy heard those two words, the more *the shop* became a mystical place, a place where work was done, where dirty jokes were told, where cold pops were consumed, cigarettes were smoked, where his big brother Lenville was lauded as the prodigy he was.

It was his ear. That is to say, his hearing, from which Lenville's talent as a mechanic sprung.

"Fire it up," Lenville would say and someone would turn a key or push a button, and a starter would roll over. Lenville would listen as the battery gave the jolt. He listened for valves tapping, pistons slapping. He listened for slippage, for belts that went *chirp chirp chirp chirp chirp* like baby chicks.

24

"How much change is rattlin' in the console, Len?"

"How many cherries been popped in that backseat, Len?"

His coworkers winked and nudged him, but they respected him and his uncanny ability as a diagnostician.

Len sat down on the old tree trunk beside Li'l Roy, shooing the yellow dog away. "Move over, ol' dog." Lenville lit a cigarette of his own. "Man, that water feels good." With squinted smoke filled eyes, he motioned toward the river

"It *was* good. For a while." Li'l Roy grinned a grin that was wiser than his years and then elbowed his big brother like how he imagined they did down at *the shop.*

Lenville elbowed him back and took the bottle from him. "Knocked the lead right outta your pencil, didn't we?"

"Shut up." Li'l Roy dragged out the last word and laughed. He blushed and turned his face away from his brother.

"Ya know, you really should go with us." Lenville sipped the whiskey and returned the bottle to his little brother. "What are ya gonna do? Hang out with mom and her new boyfriend all night?"

Li'l Roy took the bottle and drank. "Mr. Freeman ain't her boyfriend."

Out in the river, Ronny Tucker did a handstand leaving nothing but white and hairy buttocks facing the two on the bank.

Lenville laughed and shook his head. "Yeah, you just keep tellin' yourself that, kiddo. She can have a boyfriend, ya know. Even if it is a—a—an ol' bum like Freeman."

"Shit, I know. It's just weird seein' her like that. Mr. Freeman's okay. He ain't a bum, though. He's a hobo." Li'l Roy corrected Lenville.

Lenville asked, "Shit, what's the difference?"

Lenville Tucker's question to his little brother was rhetorical, but Li'l Roy answered anyway, saying, "They is a difference. You'd have to get him to tell ya. Hell, he can explain it better'n I can. Anyways, it ain't like they're plannin' on gettin' hitched or nothin'."

"You just let Mom and Freeman alone and come on with us."

"Shit, Len, I just don't feel like goin' down to Pudgy's."

"What's gotten into you, young'n? Lately, you're actin' like you don't want nothin' to do with us. You 'shamed of us or somethin'? Lay it on me," invited Lenville.

Li'l Roy offered, "I ain't ashamed, Len. I'm just tired."

"Geez, then take ya a damned nap. Gimme that."

Li'l Roy finished his cigarette and flicked it away in a manner that made him feel cool and nonchalant. He passed the bottle back to Lenville and said, "I had a nap. I'm just tired of all the trouble."

25

"Trouble? Hell, we ain't been in no trouble in a long time, Roy."

"Ya ain't gotta get locked up for it to feel like trouble, Len."

"I don't get you, young'n." Lenville Tucker shook his head. "Come to Pudgy's with us. No trouble. Swear it." The older boy promised.

"Unless Hickey shows up," said Li'l Roy.

"Ya got me there. That son of a bitch shows up, then there's gonna be trouble," Lenville admitted.

"Ya gonna fight him? Gonna stomp a mud hole in his ass?" Li'l Roy asked.

"Hell, no."

"Good."

"I'm gonna kill him," said Len, his words cold and absolutely unflinching.

Disturbed by his older brother's candor, the younger boy shot to his feet and took a step toward the river, suddenly wanting to put some distance between himself and his brother. He stepped a couple of measured paces away as if unable or unwilling to look at him. "Why's 'at, Len? Why ya gonna kill him?" he asked, slicking his lengthy wet hair back from his face and watching Ronny still in the river.

"Ain't no sense in— Sit down. Get back over here. Ain't no sense in layin' it at your feet, young'n. You let me worry about Darryl Hickey." Lenville drew from the pint. "Sit down. Come on, now."

"Hell, you don't worry 'bout nothin', Len," Li'l Roy countered and turned to his brother. "Just listen to ya, out here talkin' 'bout killin' fellas like it weren't nothin' to kill a fella—"

"See there, smart guy, you don't know everything. I worry about all sorts a shit. Now get back over here. I'm just carryin' on."

"Yeah?" probed Li'l Roy.

"Yeah."

"What are *you* worried about?" Li'l Roy asked, stepping back toward his brother.

"I'll tell ya what I'm worried about. One thing, I'm worried it's almost over for us. That's one thing I'm worried about. Ya ever get that feelin?"

"Don't know what ya mean." Li'l Roy sat back down.

"Sure you do. You know it is, right?" The older boy had picked up a short and narrow stick and now tapped it absently on a rock. He did not look at Li'l Roy. He waited as Li'l Roy sat in silent contemplation, but did not reply.

"What makes you say that?" Li'l Roy finally asked.

"Well, Viet Nam's been on my mind a lot here lately."

"Why you thinkin' 'bout that, Len? You thinkin' we're all about to get drafted or somethin'?"

"Oh, we're goin' all right. I guaran-damn-tee it. We're goin'. Poor folks. White trash. Ask some of 'em over at the V.F.W. how that goddamn draft works. It's comin' for all three of us. Any day now. So, we might as well be livin' it up while we can."

"We live out here in the middle of nowhere. The government don't even know there's such a shithole as Snorville."

"They know. Trust me. They don't know they's such a place as Snorville 'til they's a war on. Then they know, by hell." He paused then, exploring all of the ramifications of what he was about to reveal. "I got my notice to appear for a physical, Li'l Roy. Red brought it to me at the shop Thursday."

"What? What's 'at mean?" asked Li'l Roy.

"Means I go down and they have a doctor look at me, make sure I'm not flat footed or nothin', make sure I can still cough when someone's got my nuts in their hand. Shit, I ain't flat footed. I'm healthy as a horse."

"Then what?" asked the younger boy anxiously.

"Doc tells 'em I ain't flat footed and then they send me a notice of induction."

"Induction?"

"Jesus H., I'm tellin ya I'm drafted, Li'l Roy. They're sendin' my ass to Viet Nam."

"Shit," muttered Li'l Roy. "That goddamned Red shoulda lost that notice in the mail," Roy said, his stomach suddenly churning.

"Aw, he couldn't do that. He's the mailman. That's his job, deliverin' mail. It ain't on Red."

"Yeah, well," Li'l Roy swallowed hard, felt it come back and tried to swallow again, but could not. He suddenly vomited whiskey and egg sandwich.

"What the hell's up with him?" Ronny asked from the bank. "Hey, look at me, I'm Charlie Chaplin."

Virginia Lawford listened as the older boys goaded Little Roy into going with them to Pudgy's Tavern and she was pleased when he relented. She heard one of the brothers mention the train and she watched as the three of them looked down the tracks. She suffered a moment of panic. If she ran from beneath the trestle now, they would surely see her. She found herself with no option but to scoot closer underneath and into the corner where the trestle met the bank to avoid being seen for sure. She crawled slowly through the rocks and the dirt, up to where it was darkest and there she lay.

The train thundered above her and when the air horn sounded, it was nothing short of the end of everything she had ever known. It effortlessly swallowed whole her screams and straightaway drowned everything in its wake. The infernal assault of sound canceled out everything, the day, the month, the summer, the year, her home, her daddy and her dead mother. It invaded her body, pushing itself deeper into her, maddeningly vibrating her bones and her racing heart, filling her head with sound, sound, ravenous and wicked sound. She thought she would surely be torn apart by it.

The horn suddenly ceased and, as if it was only toying with her, came again in a giant merciless wave. The trestle itself buckled and bounced on top of her. She closed her eyes as tightly as she could and could do nothing else but wait for it to pass.

In the darkness when it was over, she heard only the sound of her racing heart above the ringing in her ears. She breathed heavily. She was exhausted. She was elated. She was alive and nearly hysterical, and she wanted, more than absolutely anything else in the world, to experience it all again.

Chapter 3

I t was an argued notion throughout the county that the Bailey Boarding House was the oldest house in Whelan County. If it wasn't the oldest, it did a great job of pretending to be, pretentiously dressing the part with its failing paint, its spired cupolas, protrusions, additions and many gabled roofs all decorated elaborately. The passing years had filled it with the stale air of forgotten stories, rumor, and dust covered whispers. When industry came to the area and the railroad tracks were stitched into the earth, the proud Victorian found itself on the side of the demarcation line that would forever doom it to stand "on the wrong side of the tracks."

Save for the Baileys and their single tenant, it stood all but empty. The top two floors had long been visited for the last time, and as the years rolled steadily and inevitably on, the house itself seemed to either have tired of its heyday or to have surrendered to its fate.

Hiram Bailey stepped out onto the grand porch, letting the screen door slam shut behind him. From inside the house, his wife's voice called after him, admonishing him for doing so. Bailey looked to Freeman who was sitting in an old porch chair. When he was sure he had Freeman's attention, he rolled his eyes at his wife's voice and offered a slight and dismissive shake of his head. Freeman grinned at the old man. Bailey stepped to the edge of the porch and surveyed the road and the nearing dusk, first one way and then the other, thumbing his suspenders as he did so. He did not speak directly to Freeman.

"I know what you're doin'," the lean old man said with a smile, his tone confident.

"'S'at so?" asked Freeman, amused. "Glad at least one of us does."

"Aw, don't get me wrong," Bailey waved a hand at Freeman and had himself a seat in a white wicker chair. "I ain't gettin' in your business or nothin', young man." Bailey addressed most men as 'young man.' Hiram Bailey would tell anyone who asked that he was eighty-two years old. Others would be quick to point out that Hiram Bailey had been eighty-two years old since possibly as far back as the

Eisenhower administration. "You're waitin' on them Tucker boys to come up that road so's you can run over to Mac's, pick up a bottle and go and visit their mama. Hell, I envy you. I don't envy her none, but I envy you."

"'S'at so?" asked Freeman for the second time. Bailey's words put Freeman slightly ill at ease, but Freeman was too good a card player to let it show. "Don't reckon I ever been envied before, Mister Bailey. Gotta say, I'm thinkin' it feels right nice to be envied."

"Glad I could help ya out, Freeman." Bailey looked toward the screen door, checking the proximity of Misses Bailey. "Yeah, she's way too pretty for you. She's too pretty for any of these ugly mutts around here. Too pretty to be walkin' 'round with her head down the way she does, too."

Freeman replied, "Then we're in agreement on at least three counts this evening, Mister Bailey, and I'll be sure to pass your kind words along."

"Naw, naw, don't do that," Bailey quickly retorted. He sat in thoughtful silence then, examining the idea for a moment before recanting. "I mean if you feel like you just gotta, then who am I to stop you?" Freeman's grin widened as did Bailey's. "Ya know, Freeman, this house used to be full of pretty women."

"Hadn't heard that," lied Freeman. Freeman had recently acquired employment at Smoky Mountain Millworks. From his coworkers, he had heard the sordid history of Bailey's Room and Board, but politeness and curiosity required he leave room for the old man to talk.

"Yeah," the elder man sighed, "it sure did. Long before your time." Bailey studied Freeman's face momentarily and Freeman stroked his graying beard. "Well, maybe not *so* long before your time." Bailey again cast a suspicious glance toward the screen door and turned back to Freeman. With his voice slightly lowered he said, "So full of pretty women that it was hard to find a room to fart in come the winter time."

The two men shared a laugh. "Sounds like a good problem to have, ya ask me," Freeman pointed out.

"Well," old Bailey sighed, "thank the Good Lord that them days is long over." Freeman sat, unsure of how to react to the old man's last sentence. Bailey again sighed dramatically. "Yea-up," he drew the word out, "thank the good lord." Freeman laughed and the old man laughed with him, looking sidewise again toward the screen door and saying, "You're gonna get me into trouble, Freeman."

The two men sat with their conversation as dusk approached and with it the Tucker boys.

Bailey said, "Looks like the coast is clear, young man."

Freeman said with a grin, "Looks like it."

"If ya ain't back on time, the missus won't let me let ya in."

"Yeah, I've slept outside a time or two in my life. I found me a spot out there in them woods. Cozy little spot." Freeman pointed with his chin. "I've found cozy spots all over the country. Got a talent for it, ya might say."

"I just bet you have, Freeman. Well, like I said, I envy ya."

"But not her?" Freeman joked.

"But not her. She's good people. She don't know it, but she is. Anyone tells ya otherwise, they're fulla shit." The old man winked at Freeman and nodded a salutation at the trio of Tucker boys as they passed. One of the boys raised a bottle toward the two men and old Bailey shook his head. "Lord, them boys is wild as bucks, though."

"So I hear," said Freeman, slowly standing.

"Hell," offered Bailey, "a fella pretty much has to envy them, too."

From behind the littered counter, Mac peered over his bifocals as Freeman entered the store. He folded the newspaper and removed the Chesterfield from between his teeth and said, "Evenin', Freeman. That Cold Duck came in today. Put it there in the cooler for ya."

"Great," said Freeman heading toward the cooler. Inside were twelve bottles. Freeman checked the stickered price tag, whistled and retrieved a bottle. "Thanks for keepin' it cool, Mac."

"No problem. That ain't gonna be it for ya, is it?"

Freeman said with a wink, "We ain't been knowin' each other that long, but still I figured you'd know me better'n that by now."

"Thunderbird or Rose?" Mac smiled, reaching for the bottles behind him.

"Hell, ring me up a half pint of each."

Mac rang up the sale, then dubiously stopped before giving Freeman the total.

"What? What is it, Mac?" asked Freeman.

"I ain't tryin' to get in your business—"

"Hell, Mac, it's okay, lot of folks lately not tryin' to be in my business. What's on your mind?"

"Well," Mac looked at Freeman over his bifocals. "Dollar to a dime says Jeannie's got no corkscrew."

"Now, ain't you good at what you do? You done found your callin', Mac." Freeman slapped the counter playfully and pointed, "Ain't a lot of men can say that."

"Lord, I pray that ain't true." Mac laughed.

"Ring me up a corkscrew, too."

Mac dropped a corkscrew into a bag and said, "On me, Freeman."

"Well, thank ya, Mac. I'll tell her the Cold Duck's from me and the corkscrew's from the swell fella behind the counter."

31

"You do that," smiled Mac.

"Thanks again."

"No problem."

"See you're readin' the paper there," observed Freeman, cocking his head to better see the print. "Reminds me. I got on a bus once, and the only seat open was beside a priest, but they was a newspaper in the seat, so's I ask him, 'Ya savin' this seat, Father?' 'No,' he says, so I lean over to pick up the paper and a half pint of Roses falls outta my coat pocket and onto the seat there. I see the priest fella sees it, kinda embarrasses me, but what can ya do, ya know? So's I pick it up, tuck it back into my pocket, pick up the paper and sit down and start to read it. The bus gets to rollin' and I get to readin'. I turn to the priest there and I ask him, 'Father, what causes arthritis?' and he says to me,'Too much hard livin'. Too much of the grape,' he says. 'Sin and wickedness,' he says."

"Yeah, that ain't true about the arthritis," said Mac, himself a mild sufferer of the condition. "Why that ain't true at all."

"Figured it must not be 'cause after a minute or two he musta got to feelin' bad about himself and the tone he'd done took with me, so he asks me all concerned-like, 'How long have you suffered with the arthritis, my son?' And I says, 'Oh, no, father, I don't suffer from the arthritis. Says here in the paper that the Pope does.'" Freeman laughed, but suddenly straightened up. "Shit, you ain't Catholic are ya, Mac?"

"Wouldn't matter if I was, Freeman. Wouldn't matter if I was," laughed Mac.

"Later, Mac." Freeman winked.

"Later." Mac returned the wink.

Freeman took his bag and went out into the falling night to spend what he could of it with Jeannie Tucker.

When the stillness returned to the store, it was different, heavier. Mac tried to return to his newspaper, but found he could not. His thoughts were stuck on Jeannie Tucker. Half-heartedly, he tried again with the newspaper, but the words came disjointedly and quickly lost their context. In surrender and acceptance of defeat, Mac stubbed out his Chesterfield, folded the newspaper and stared blankly out the window. Outside, night had barely fallen. Saturday nights were good nights for business, undoubtedly his best nights, but suddenly that fact was as pointless and as unimportant as everything else. He pulled a corkscrew from the rack and stepped from behind the counter and moved slowly toward the cooler where he retrieved a bottle of Cold Duck. He stood for a moment examining the label. At the front door, he twisted the sign to "Closed" and hit the switch, turning off the part of the neon sign that had survived the years and still glowed. He then turned off the interior lights, letting total darkness claim the place. With ease, he navigated his way through the dark store and headed up the creaking stairs with the bottle in hand to his empty apartment.

Out on the dirt road, Freeman walked on. Before reaching Jeannie Tucker's, he headed up the thorny bank and across the tracks and into the weeds on the far side. With a soft underhanded pitch, he tossed one of the half pint bottles into the tree line so that it would be there later when he came out to find himself a place to sleep.

Chapter 4

Tom Lawford and his daughter Virginia sit on their porch every Saturday evening and they watch the Tucker boys stumble up the road like a bunch of three legged dogs, staggering and weaving - young men with too much time on their hands, on their way to Pudgy's Tavern to get more liquored up than they already are. When the boys go past the Lawford place, "Quiet Tom" Lawford looks up, his eyes narrow as he catches his only daughter staring, bewitched. He admonishes her, "You stay away from them boys, Virginia." Like most adults around Sonoraville, Quiet Tom does not care for the Tucker boys.

Sometimes, the ruckus the boys make on their way back home jars Virginia Lawford awake and she lies in the heat of the summer darkness with the sheet pulled back, listening to them, just outside her window, slowly making their way home with abandon through the wild night, laughing, hooting and singing. She is warmed by them and their carryings on. Their presence in those dreaming hours has transferred them from average and earthly to spectral dream haunters haunting those rare and coveted types of dreams from which one wakes and immediately closes one's eyes and races desperately back toward, into the cruel and withholding darkness, only to find unsatisfying black.

Sunday mornings, she finds their discarded bottles along the road as she waits for the Sunday School bus. When she is absolutely sure that she is out of eyeshot, she picks one up, puts her nose to the neck of the bottle and deeply breathes it in. Something in the smell of whiskey makes the hair on her neck and arms stand up. Something inside those empty bottles wafts out and takes hold of her, sends her to some place dimly lit, smoky and absolutely savage where pretension is prohibited and punishable by public exposure and exile, and she knows she has no business being there, but cannot help herself but to desperately try and stay. She breathes it in and holds her breath for as long as she is able to. Her palms go dewy. Her head begins to swim and she understands well why some old-timers call the disparaged drink "*spirits*."

She catches the bus to Sunday School because after her mama died, her daddy quit going to church. She quit for a while, too until Miss Jessie, twins in tow, cornered her in the Cas Walker's and asked her when she was coming back. She shrugged her bony, adolescent shoulders and looked down at the ancient dirt in the cracks of the tiled store floor, wanting to sink down and join it.

"You know you need to be in church, now don't you?"

She nodded slowly and felt deeply ashamed. "Yes...yes, Ma'am."

"I'll see you there Sunday, then."

She nodded again, though Miss Jessie hadn't exactly been asking. The matter of her Sunday School attendance was therefore settled.

She stands dutifully waiting for that rusted blue bus to come bouncing down the dirt road and she passes the slowly moving morning studying the Tucker boys' footprints. She can tell who was the drunkest by the measure of their scattered steps. She knows Li'l Roy flanked his brothers on their right and either can't hold his liquor as well or drinks more of it. Li'l Roy's feet are the smallest. Ronny flanks the left and though his prints leave no specific pattern, they aren't as strewn as Li'l Roy's. Lenville belongs to the big prints in the middle and most times his are singularly successive and straight.

It is Lenville Tucker she hears over and above his younger brothers on those late Saturday nights. Sometimes she swears it could be the ghost of Hank Williams himself stumbling down the railroad tracks, howling his way through 'Kaw-Liga' or moaning 'Lovesick Blues.' Lenville's voice draws her from one dream into another. Sometimes she wakes herself softly singing along, her soft hushed voice floating out the opened window and entwining with his until the two voices become one thing, whole and complete and forbidden. It ends with a new silence and a sweaty exhausted sigh and she drifts again with a satisfied smile thinking how that boy sure can sing.

Sunday afternoons, she's awash with guilt coming home from church. She knows where her sinful thoughts will get her. She spends the entire Sunday morning ritual in a wicked kind of fog. Toward the end of the service, when the invitation is offered and the backsliders and the offenders of Christ slowly make their way to the altar, she sits with Preacher Sturgill's words tugging at her heart, her hands in a sinner's grip on the varnished pew, resisting the persuasive notion that the preacher is speaking directly to her, and knows all of her thoughts.

And so does Jesus.

She sits up in her bed, still as stone for what seems like hours in the pitch black and the pressing heat with her heart racing and her stomach full of flutters. She made sure the window was opened before it got too late, afraid that the slightest noise will wake her daddy. She wears breeches and sneakers beneath the sheet.

She must have fallen asleep, but only for a bit, because suddenly the boys are there, as if they just appeared out of the mist, the comforting and familiar sound of their laughter filling the night air with that intangible element they carry with them. She lets them get by for a ways as she lies questioning her assurance and confidence.

She slips out the window as softly and as silently as a shadow.

When her feet hit the ground out in the damp night air it is all she can do to stop herself from laughing out loud. She feels she has unearthed every phantom pole and post that hold the signs forbidding entry into a starlit and secret world, a world where the air is electric and something in the atmosphere makes her heart speed up and her conscience lighter and every No Trespassing sign in the universe topples from her sheer will.

She looks up at a night sky as immense as summer is short. She is lost for a stolen piece of time in the stars. It is as if freedom and willfulness have suddenly spread endlessly in all directions and blanketed life with wild possibility. The stars and constellations are so bold and numerous that they are now newly strange and unrecognizable.

She creeps along and follows the boys a ways, crouching and tiptoeing, not that they would notice if someone were to come through on a fire engine. She gets closer and cuts down the bank onto the dirt road and is past them. She keeps an ear out, trying to make sure she doesn't out run them by too far. She stumbles through the overgrowth, catching scratches on her face and her arms, and comes back up onto the railroad tracks where they now are. She sees them, black forms in the pale moonlight. Ronny Tucker bays at the moon to brotherly delight. She strides to meet them head on.

They are so dog drunk, so lost in their revelry that her approach goes unregistered. She lets all three of the drunken young men get right up on her. Being this close, close enough to reach out and actually touch, her mouth is suddenly sapped and goes dry. She fears she may throw up, but stands her ground, falling into the role that she has written for herself.

"Evenin," she nods, feigning confidence and trying to be as casual of the encounter as she possibly can. The younger boys go silent and their faces crumple in confusion. Lenville Tucker is not shaken. "One a y'all got a cigarette?" she asks.

Lenville Tucker laughs. "Well, well, what the hell we got here?"

She smiles sheepishly beneath the watching moon and she looks down at Lenville Tucker's large feet.

"You stay away from them boys, Virginia," she hears her daddy's voice in her head as she leans in for the cigarette. A grinning Lenville holds it high and upright in front of his shining eyes between his thumb and forefinger. She accepts it from him. He lights it for her, the sharp metal sound of the lighter flicking open gives her a start and then the flame is born.

There beneath the trestle, she smokes their cigarettes and drinks from their bottle.

They let Li'l Roy have her first. He's never been with a girl before.

Chapter 5

In his veins, Freeman carried both the blood of slaves and of slave owners. There were no written records upon which the existence of Freeman's ancestry depended, only years of hushed lantern lit tales of past generations, tales played out by shifting shadows on newspaper covered walls. Those whispered tales told of his great grandmother's irresistible beauty. A beauty in fact so irresistible that within an hour of purchasing her from the slave block for seven hundred and seventy six dollars, Freeman's great-grandfather, a sugar baron named J.C. Kenner, had mercilessly raped her along the road home. Kenner would continue assaulting her for the next thirteen years, where he would then turn his violence toward the oldest offspring of those abominable unions, his unacknowledged twelve year old daughter. From those incestuous molestations was born Freeman's father, thereby casting Kenner in the dual role of Freeman's great-grandfather and grandfather. Freeman's father, born free, would not take a wife until his mid-fifties, where he would then marry a woman who was herself, biracial. This lineage left Freeman, light skinned and carrying green eyes and dark wavy hair that time and neglect had left lengthy, matted and graying.

Upon introducing himself, he would put out his hand and with a cool lying smile say, "Freeman Fabbro. Most folks just call me Freeman." His first name was a fiction, a title invented and self-applied. The surname he borrowed from a swarthy fellow hobo who was called Smithy. Smithy wasn't Smithy's given name either. Smithy's given name was Fabian Fabbro. Fabbro, Smithy was quick to tell new acquaintances, was Italian for blacksmith, hence Smithy.

Li'l Roy Tucker called him "Mister Freeman." Most others had come to simply calling him "Freeman," with no preceding formality. Before she died, his wife, Mayrene, had called him *William*. After she died, she called him the same. Then came his time of wandering during which, for a brief spell, he had been called *San Jacinto*, or *The Hobo from San Jacinto*. Later, when he rode The NorthWestern rail and haunted the rails and the hobo camps of the Pacific Northwest he had gone by *Slow Dance Slim*. Along the way, some had called him *friend* and some had called him *son of a bitch*. Many had called him colorful racial epithets. In Fresno, the local constabulary had been the first to call him *Tramp* and *Vagrant* and then *Inmate*. Across the Midwest, some had called him *Smoke* or *Smokin' Willy*. He was again *Vagrant* and then again *Inmate* in Columbus. After his third incarceration, during which, his dead wife abandoned him, he christened himself *Free Man*. That was the moniker he wore during his relatively short stay in Sonoraville, Tennessee, which is where his dead wife found him.

The stolen surname, Fabbro, was a last minute, improvisational and intentional act of misdirection. It wasn't a sure bet, but If his last name was Jackson, he was a light skinned man of African descent, but if his last name was Fabbro, then in most cases, he was an olive skinned man of Italian descent.

He slept now in the growth beyond the tracks, beneath a great oak. He had fallen asleep in a sitting position, his back against the accommodating trunk, his bearded chin resting on his chest. He slept lightly even though he was by all accounts drunk, both on the wine and the carnal satisfaction of having recently bedded a woman. He slept through dreams, portentous and horrible. He slept through dreams pleasantly banal.

The howling woke him and when he opened his eyes he saw the ghost there in the darkness. He knew immediately that the ghost was not Mayrene, but thought he might ask just to be sure.

"Mayrene? 'S'at you?"

Brush crunched and cracked as the spectral figure floated on through the dark and the underbrush. Freeman rubbed the film of sleep from his eyes with his knuckles and squinted to better see through the moonlit darkness. He blinked a few times before letting his eyes close completely. When he again opened them, the howling turned to wanton revelry—ah, Jeannie's boys—and the ghost was just a girl, Quiet Tom Lawford's girl. Freeman had seen her dancing on the rails a handful of times, singing the old Sunday school song:

This train is bound for glory, this train
This train don't carry no gamblers, this train
This train don't carry no gamblers, this train
This train don't carry no gamblers,
No hypocrites, no midnight ramblers,
This train is bound for glory, this train

And now here she was, an ethereal presence out in the darkness and the late hour moving swiftly through the night and the brush. She had not seen him nor heard his whispered question. He watched her curiously through the fog of night and alcohol and mistakenly concluded that, like him, she must be running from something.

He shifted his weight, placed his hands on the ground and prepared to stand. Pain, electric and prohibitive, wrenched his spine. He retreated his effort and repositioned himself. He rolled his stiff neck from shoulder to shoulder, feeling the grinding and the grating, feeling muscles loosen as the pain lightened. Wincing, he paused in his effort and reminded himself that he was no longer a young man that he was no longer truly well enough to sleep out of doors.

He cursed the hour and the counting of hours. He was back in the land of unstoppable ticking clocks, pocket watches, wrist watches and general timekeeping, of schedules and of expectations, wait, too early, not now, okay, go, hurry, too late, now wait, now go. He cursed Ma Bailey and her damned boarding house rules. *"In by ten or don't come in."* That's what the wooden sign in front of the door said, but she did make exceptions for the nights that he worked. His shift at the pallet mill was over at ten o'clock. The Baileys expected him by fifteen minutes after ten. At twenty minutes after ten, too late, Ma Bailey locked the door. Saturday evenings, he spent with Jeannie Tucker and damned if he was leaving her place so early in the evening. He would not sleep at Jeannie Tucker's because of protocol and because of her boys. He would not tell Jeannie of the Bailey's curfew law, else she would insist he leave by half past nine. So, he let Jeannie believe he went on to Bailey's boarding house instead of telling her that he had found a soft spot in the trees and the brush to spend his Saturday nights.

He checked the half pint bottle of Four Roses in his lap and found it empty. Nonetheless, he put it to his lips, turned it up and waited for the single drop that was always there to creep like a condemned snail onto his tongue. To his right, he could hear the boys on the railroad tracks getting closer. To his left, he could hear the girl's steady rustling growing farther away. Freeman closed his eyes again and leaned back against the tree. He heard the hoot of a Great Horned Owl asking, *"Are you awake? Me, too."* He listened as the girl's noises grew more and more faint until he heard them no longer.

He drew his legs in. With his knees pointed toward the stars, he dug his heels into the soft earth and used the tree as a brace to help him stand. He winced through the pain and once he was on his feet, wobbled and swayed. His outstretched hand found the trunk of the tree and he anchored himself and reminded himself that he was still quite drunk. Cautiously, he stepped forward, stumbled slightly and caught himself on another tree. He shook off what he could of the alcohol and the clinging sleep and pushed himself onward after the girl.

The thick and thorny brush was not easily traversed by sober young men. It reached out for him, held him in places, slowed him in others, tried to prevent him, tried to tell him, *this, this has nothing to do with you, old man. Let the night have its way.*

Freeman stopped, struggled for breath and heard the voices from the railroad tracks.

"One a y'all got a cigarette?"

"Well, well, what the hell we got here?"

Through the darkness, Freeman curiously trailed them, sure they were headed for the broad bank of the river.

"Not the bank. Not the river." He heard the Lawford girl say, *"The trestle. Under the trestle."*

Chapter 6

Virginia Lawford has not slept. On the porch, she gazes eastward toward the dawn where the sun slowly rises above the foothills, setting ablaze and searing away the edge of night that clings there to the earth. To the west, night is still strong with stars still shining. Off in the distance, she hears "Gus" the Rooster crow, heralding the arrival of the light. She finds comfort in the fact that, like her father, the sun has no knowledge of what she has done. It will rise without judgement on this new day in the valley. She does take a moment to wonder what the moon and stars will say of her now that the night is over. But mostly, she surmises, they are strangers to her and do not know her as well as they may think they do. They do not know and could not possibly understand the joy, the light and the very life that a new baby will bring to the house, the hole that will be filled in her life and in her father's.

While she is considering these things, Sunday morning comes. Her father will spend the day in the fields tending what little livestock he is still able to keep while working full time at the pallet mill. She will do her allotted chores until it is time to ready herself for Sunday service.

Before beginning breakfast, she affords herself a worry. She does not know of this new thing she has done. She worries that those who have done it can see it on others who have done it. Will they see it on her? Will she see it on them now that she has done it? Will there be something different about her? Will there be some "tell" that she does not realize reveals her sinful secret to some? Will it be in her eyes? Her speech? In her walk? It could very possibly be there in her walk, she tells herself and as if on cue, she feels the ache. Will Preacher Sturgill know? Will he direct his sermon specifically at her even more so than she feels he may have done on Sunday mornings past?

He will know.

Jesus knows. An egg slips from her hand. The Lord in Heaven knows. She studies the mess on the floor. But, she reasons, Jesus and The Good Lord also know the why of it. She takes the dish rag from the sink and on her knees on the floor, she tends to the shattered egg.

She is startled by her father's voice behind her. "You's up awful early this mornin'. Up with Gus, wasn't ya?"

"Oh, Daddy, you spooked me," she confesses.

"Must not be livin' right." It is a joke, but her laugh is borne not of humor so much as apprehension. "But I'm one to talk." He sits at the kitchen table and puts his boots on.

She takes the opportunity. "You should join me this morning in church." She shifts her attention back to the ruined egg so not to pressure him.

"Maybe next week," he offers. "Too much to do 'round here today."

For the first time, she is relieved that he doesn't want to go.

Chapter 7

The yellow dog crossed the railroad tracks and headed northeast toward the dirt road to where the property values had long been lowered by the train, and the train smoke, the two factories and the southern breeze. He came to Pudgy's Tavern and sniffed around the gravel parking lot, found nothing to keep him there and moved on. Behind Mac's Package, he marked an empty trash can, sniffed it, and unsatisfied, marked it again before continuing his northeastern route. He did not linger outside of Bailey's Room and Board as old Ma Bailey had long since shooed him away for the last time with a hiss and a swift kick to his rear. He quickened his pace as he passed the hosiery and then the pallet mill. For a moment, he lingered at the head of the long driveway that led to the Lawford place until remembering that it was a sure thing that waited on down the dirt road.

Just past the Lawford place, the pavement ended and the dirt road began. It had never been christened with a proper name, but was generally referred to as Rural Route 3. On the dirt road, hardly a vehicle ever passed as the residents who lived along it rarely found themselves financially sound enough to count an automobile among their meager possessions. Rain often turned the dirt to mud and rendered the road impassable. The dirt road served more in the capacity of playground than it did thoroughfare. Children, nearly naked and perpetually barefoot, played marbles and hopscotch and wrote obscenities with sticks in the dirt of it. Cats and dogs lay in it equally stubbornly. A rooster named Gus patrolled it. Chickens pecked it. The dirt road led to an eventual narrow dead end where irritated, lost, or curious drivers were forced to pull off the trick of turning their vehicles around in the narrow space. On its western side were dilapidated, tin roofed houses and more lately, mobile homes lacking the underpinning to hide the concrete cinder blocks and even discarded tires that were their foundations. On its eastern side were fewer houses and a bank of mostly sycamores, blackberry thickets and various other thorny flora. Atop the bank, lay the railroad track and depending on where exactly one lived along the dirt road, the shortcut to town. On the far side of the tracks were cattle fields owned mostly by wealthy men who had long since left the duties to hired men and set up living quarters closer into town.

The yellow dog came to the Tucker place and sat and waited patiently in the yard until a smiling boy tossed him a slice of bologna from the kitchen window. The yellow dog gracefully leaped and snatched the meat slice from the air. He swallowed the meaty disc nearly whole and waited, curious if the boy would launch another treat from the window, though tradition and protocol had taught him that the possibility was not likely.

A smiling Li'l Roy Tucker sat back down in the chair at the littered kitchen table, beaming proudly at the dog and resisting the urge to sail yet another slice of pink meat through the window and out into the yard. He would have to see about getting his hands on what they called a "Frisbee." He'd seen dogs on television catch Frisbees and was sure this yellow mutt would put them all to shame. He pondered the possibility that dogs were trained to catch Frisbees by first using slices of bologna. He considered this further and decided that must indeed be the case and considered the matter solved. Silently, he congratulated himself for figuring this thing out.

The girl came to mind, her knees apart, bare and pale blue in the moonlight, his brothers' voices invading from behind him, cheering him on. Embarrassed, he pushed the thoughts away replacing them with thoughts of his oldest brother and a faraway place called Viet Nam.

Before they'd headed out to Pudgy's, Lenville told him again, "Don't mention me gettin' drafted to Ronny. I'll tell him and Mom when the time feels right. Keep it under your hat, kiddo." And so Li'l Roy had. He imagined Lenville in the jungles of Viet Nam, and found some comfort in the notion that Lenville would be just fine. Lenville was big, big and tough. Lenville was smart. Lenville would win the Viet Nam war all by himself and come home with a chest full of medals and ribbons. They would give him a parade.

Movement caught his eye, a slight movement at first, a flicker of a thing that he almost dismissed with a blink. When it came again, he flinched, slightly startled at the realization that it was a living thing so unidentified and not an axe handle's length away. The movement came from the fly strip that hung near the window like some absurd and perpetual decoration.

A menagerie of dead flying things littered both sides of the deadly trap. Among them, a furry white moth, far from dead, fluttered its one free wing pointlessly over the edge of the glue laden strip. Li'l Roy was taken in by the spectacle. He perhaps thought too deeply on the subject and when his eyes began to water, he shamed

45

himself. There was nothing to be done for the moth and this realization brought him an inexplicable sadness.

From across the street, voices drew his attention. He watched Miss Jessie and her grandsons as they gathered on the side of the dirt road to wait for the Sunday School bus. For Li'l Roy Tucker, it was ritual. He spent many Sunday mornings in the window watching the boys and their grandmother. They were black folks, but that fact was easy to forget out on the route. Miss Jessie was black. The twin boys were biracial, their unnamed father obviously white.

He laughed at the number of times Miss Jessie licked her hand and attempted last minute adjustments on the twin's stubborn hair. Each time she did, the boys scowled and ran their own hands behind hers, reclaiming their hair to its natural state. This particular morning, to Li'l Roy Tucker's amusement, the boys began licking their own fingers and wiping them on each other's hair. This exercise quickly escalated from licking their fingers to spitting into their hands, which in turn escalated to "hocking" long and drawn out "loogies" into their hands and then smearing that "loogie" into the other's hair. That particular exercise quickly escalated from wipes to swipes to slaps to pushes to shoves to a no holds barred wrestling match there in the middle of the dirt road. Miss Jessie revealed a switch, seemingly from out of thin air, and attempted to stripe the boy's into the submission she had failed to attain from their hair.

The fly strip vibrated as the white moth fluttered its wing.

The girl came to him again, her eyes deep and curious in the near dark. Again, he pushed her away.

Like alarmed crickets, the twin boys hopped around in a panic, unsuccessfully trying to evade the painful lashes of Miss Jessie's switch. *The switch dance*, Li'l Roy remembered it well. He watched as Miss Jessie caught one of the boys by the elbow (he could never tell which of the boys was which) and attempted to swat his corduroyed behind. The boy tried to pull away but Miss Jessie held on firmly and the two went around and around, both of them calling for the other to *stop it now, stop it*. Li'l Roy laughed as they danced circles around each other in an amusing recital that somehow reminded Li'l Roy more of the couples he had seen on American Bandstand than any square dancers at any barn dance. He laughed at the spectacle and tried to remember the last time his mother had taken a switch to him and his brothers. He concluded that it might well be as long as the last time they had all climbed aboard that same old smoke belching, gear grinding blue Sunday School bus and gone on to Sunday School to learn about Jesus and salvation with a hot penny for the offering plate in each of their pockets.

Those days now seemed long gone. Jesus and salvation now seemed long gone.

The girl came again, the girl who seemed to always be hiding herself from everyone, now ghostly, bare breasted. He focused his thoughts on Miss Jessie and the twins, diverting her image.

Eventually, the boys were whipped into shape and with their pouting bottom lips nearer the dirt road, they stood still and teary eyed while Miss Jessie dusted them off and attempted to wipe the phlegm from their heads with her handkerchief.

When the girl came back to his thoughts, he did not shake her off. He did not attempt to. She stayed mere seconds anyway as the flutter of the moth came again, a desperate call from a trapped and dying thing. He rose suddenly and without forethought, allowing the chair to bark across the floor. Hastily, he removed the trap from its tack. He had it now, but knew not what to do with it. Perhaps sensing movement, the moth fluttered its one free wing even more feverishly. The right thing to do would be to kill the thing. He wanted to kill it, to do it that last favor, but found he could not. Instead, he took it to the cupboard wherein was the trash can. He dropped the strip glue trap into the bagged can and shut the door.

He stood quiet, listening for any sound that the moth might make. He heard nothing, but still found that he was very unnerved by the thought of the innocent and furry thing starving to death, stuck in the deadly glue with no way to save itself there in the darkness of the cupboard.

He pushed his thoughts on to coffee. He considered making the coffee, but chose not to, knowing that the aroma might wake his brothers and where they were concerned, he hoped that they might sleep all day. Lately, he was finding the feeling that he was growing apart and away from them almost impossible to suppress.

He sat back at the table with his eyes on Miss Jessie and the twins, but his thoughts now away.

A sharp snore cracked and snapped him back into the morning and he realized that he had been drawn into a symphony—his mother from her bedroom, accompanied by his brothers from the room the boys all shared. As much as he enjoyed this time of morning, wherein he could sit in his own home in relative quiet and carry on as if he perhaps lived alone, he caught himself wishing that his mother might wake up, that together they might have a moment there in the Sunday morning stillness with understanding and hot coffee between them.

The distressed kitchen table was littered with remnants and debris from the evening before—ashes, empty cigarette packs, an empty bottle. Li'l Roy stared at the full ashtray. He studied the butts. The lipsticked Winston butts were his mother's. The filterless Luckys were Mr. Freeman's. He inspected the many butts, each in turn and separated them into two categories, smokeable and unsmokeable. To his excitement, the smokeable category stacked up quickly. Suspiciously, he listened for any sound of his brothers from down the hall. Hearing nothing but their snores, he rose from the table and crept down the hallway, past his mother's closed door and on to the room he shared with his brothers. He had left the door open earlier and he watched them now as they slept on floor bound mattresses. Content with their current state, he continued on to the back door at the end of the hall.

Quietly, he turned the knob and opened the door. The back screen door would be a problem. The spring always creaked. He spat in his hand and rubbed the spit into the old spring. He repeated the process several times until he was confident he had made a difference. He pushed it slowly, wincing at the noise it still made despite the amount of spit on the spring. His brothers snored peacefully. He stepped outside and guided the screen door closed, so that the spring did not cause it to slam.

He crawled behind the back steps where he kept hidden the occasional stash of returnable soda bottles. For a moment, he thought it was gone, but there it was, pushed up under the lowest step, an old and rusted Band-Aid tin. He retrieved it and crawled from beneath the steps.

Inside, he found a handful of marbles long since hidden away from his brothers and forgotten. He smiled at what was once his favorite shooter. He examined the "allies" and the "aggies" before putting them into his pocket and wondered where that slingshot had gotten off to. Inside the forgotten Band-Aid tin, he also found a length of leather string whose purpose and origin had long been forgotten. He smiled when he found two worn playing cards. He held them in his hand, bewildered that he had forgotten he was in possession of such a treasure. They were from a nudie deck that Ronny once had. Li'l Roy had secretly gone through the deck long ago and had been unable to part with the girl that was the ace of spades and the girl that was the eight of clubs. He had stolen them from his brother and tucked them inside the tin some years ago. Instantly, he was again in love. He felt warmth emanating from his center, but denied the urge and slid the cards back into the tin only to pull them out again for one long and last look.

Already, he was sweating. He took the rotting stick that his mother used to keep the back door open and wedged it between the big door and the steps. Once the front door was opened, this would create a cooling breeze through the house.

With the tin in hand, he crept back inside and sat at the kitchen table. He put the unsmokeable butts back into the ashtray and secured all but two of the smokeable butts inside the Band-Aid tin and stuffed the tin into the pocket of his jeans. He lit one of the butts from a book of matches that had been left on the table and dragged the stale tobacco smoke into his lungs.

The call of grinding gears drew his attention to the window. The Sunday school bus, pale blue and rusted, bounced and rocked its way down the dirt road. He watched through the opened kitchen window as it passed and then stopped, allowing Miss Jessie and her presently reformed grandsons to board.

At the end of the road, the blue bus performed a grinding and jerky three-point turn and headed back the way it had come, leaving a fog of thick blue smoke in its wake.

Virginia Lawford sat three rows up from the last seat. Her hair was tied back up now, like she wore it in school. She gave no sign, no smile, no wave as she passed by. By the time the bus had rumbled out of sight, he had convinced himself that she had looked squarely at him. It was even possible after further contemplation that she may well have even smiled at him, just as she had there beneath the trestle as he had come to her.

He envisioned her there in the darkness beneath the trestle, so different from the girl she was at school, her hair down, her eyes willful, confident and wise. She merely tried to help guide him into her, but when her hand touched him, he spasmed. When she gripped him, wrapping her hand around him fully, he trembled and ejaculated. She continued to guide him until he pushed himself into her and came again.

It happened so quickly that he wasn't even sure if it counted. In his doubt, he found a strange comfort.

He was again rattled from his thoughts as, from down the hall, came the sound of footsteps followed by the sound of the bathroom door being shut and pulled to. Before he had time to wonder if it was his mother or one of his brothers, faster footsteps and a sharp pounding followed.

"Hurry the hell up!" Ronny banged again.

"Go outside!" Lenville's muffled voice came from behind the bathroom door.

The back screen door opened with a screech and closed with a slam as Ronny headed outside to relieve himself.

The brothers congregated in the kitchen, swollen eyed and disheveled from their drunken sleep.

"Correct me if I'm wrong, boys, but wasn't that Quiet Tom Lawford's girl?" Lenville questioned. Li'l Roy's stomach fell. He had not considered the girl's father. "Li'l Roy, ain't she in your grade?" Li'l Roy nodded slightly. "She must have some kinda reputation, huh? Why ain't you started the coffee yet?"

"Naw. I mean, yeah. She's in my grade, but she ain't got no kind of reputation." Li'l Roy pondered the girl while absently scratching the peeling paint from the kitchen table top. He found he now had trouble making eye contact with his brothers. "I mean, not really. Not for that kinda stuff, anyways, not like some slut she ain't. I mean, she's got a reputation, but not that kind."

49

"Well, what kinda reputation she got, then?" Lenville asked, fumbling with the percolator.

"For bein'—" staring now at the worn and broken linoleum floor, Li'l Roy felt an odd surge of guilt, but never the less continued, "for bein' kinda—" he searched for the right word and could not find it. He gave up the search and instead, with his index finger, drew a circle in the air around his right ear. "Toys in the attic, man."

"She *retarded*?" Lenville asked accusingly, dropping the percolator. "You knew she was retarded and you didn't—"

Li'l Roy shot back, "No. Hell no, she ain't retarded. She's just different. A little on the shit house rat side. I don't know. Weird, man. Quiet. I mean, I reckon she makes good grades and all, but like, she takes a zero if she has to get up in front of the class and read or somethin'. And she ain't never played no games at recess or nothin'. But she ain't retarded. She gets picked on a lot, mostly by girls—that bunch a bitches. Y'all know who I'm talkin' about." Uncomfortable with it all, Li'l Roy attempted to steer the conversation elsewhere, quickly adding, "Hey, you guys know they teach dogs to catch Frisbees using slices of baloney?"

The two boys stared at their brother for a second.

"Well, I don't care if she is retarded." Ronny boasted, ignoring Li'l Roy's unsubstantiated claim. "And by hell, she's gonna have a different reputation now," he laughed, his eyes brimming with steadfast by-God resolve.

Li'l Roy felt a burn in his belly.

"No." Lenville commanded flatly, still working on the coffee. He shook his head to signal to his subordinate younger brothers that this matter was not up for debate. "No, she ain't ' 'cause we ain't gonna say a damn word about it to nobody."

"What?" Ronny protested, thrusting his chest, flaring his nostrils, shocked at the prospect of silence concerning their exploit. "What's the sense in gougin' some chick, if you can't go braggin' about gougin' her?"

Lenville raised his index finger to his lips and cast his eyes down the hallway. The boys sat silently listening. When the sound of their mother's light snore drifted down the hallway, Lenville continued in a hushed tone, "You go runnin' your stupid mouth and it's gonna get back to Quiet Tom."

"Pfft— That's what you're worried about? To hell with Quiet Tom. What the hell's he gonna do to the three of us?" Ronny tried to whisper, but the boy really did not know how.

Lenville hissed back at him, "Listen, dumbass, it ain't about what he's gonna do to the three of us. Whattaya think he's gonna do to her? I can see I got all the brains in this damned family. Hell, he'd lock her the hell up and never let her out again. Probably send her to some convent or something."

"Shit, they ain't Catholic. And what do you care what he does with her?" asked Ronny.

"I don't give a shit what they are. Listen to what I'm tellin' ya. It'll be a bunch of shit hittin' the fan if he gets wind of it. It'll be over. I guaran-damn-tee it. I don't know about you two, but I kinda like random, surprise pussy showin' up, and from what I seen, you boys could sure as hell use some practice. Now, if her daddy ever gets wind of what we did, then it's over." Lenville gave up the whisper, "So, keep your damned mouth shut about it, Ronny. Li'l Roy, you too. Ya hear me?"

Li'l Roy nodded, thought again how his oldest brother would fare in the war and changed the subject again, this time saying, "You shoulda seen Miss Jessie whippin' the shit outta Toby and Travis this morning." He laughed. "Funniest damned thing I seen in a long time. Man, she beats the hell outta them boys."

"What?" Ronny was baited. "Why the hell didn't you wake me up?" His mouth hung open in outright disbelief, as though his brother had let him sleep through the second coming or perhaps even the ice cream truck. "Dammit, Li'l Roy."

Chapter 8

The sun shone through the dense thicket in near tangible beams that warmed the forest floor, bringing to life those creeping, crawling things that wait through the night and the darkness for the return of the warmth and the light. A line of ants soon soldiered their way onto Freeman's bare forearm. In his sleep, he brushed them away. Eventually, the tenacious invaders came again, tickling, itching, and waking him fully this time. He lay on the ground on his left side with his bearded cheek resting on the inside of his shoulder, his forearm stretched out before him. Slowly and with blink after blink, his eyes opened. Without alarm nor any semblance of apprehension, he maintained his sleeping position and watched the ants explore his flesh for a while, until lightly, carefully, he brushed them away using only the edge of his nails. When he was free of the infestation, he groaned and rolled slowly to a sitting position, pushing himself up on weak and shaking arms. Some of the leaf litter fell from his bare forearms. He brushed away the clinging bits that lingered, leaving indentations in his flesh as they fell away. With slumped shoulders, still tired and in much need of more sleep, he sat and squinted in the harsh light of Sunday morning.

Out on the rural route, Gus the rooster crowed. Freeman checked the skies above for circling buzzards and to his relief, found none and so, smiling to himself, concluded that he must still be among the living. He rolled his creaking neck across his shoulders and cursed his landlords, Ma and Pa Bailey, for their puritanical rules. He blessed them for the thought of breakfast, though. Ma Bailey laid out quite a spread on Sunday mornings and that spread was calling to him through the trees and the morning.

With great effort, he found his feet and relieved himself with a seemingly endless stream. He stumbled through the overgrowth toward the railroad tracks, stopping twice to oblige a deep and productive coughing fit. He was well on his way to the boarding house before memories of what he had witnessed the previous night caught up with him. A familiar throb bloomed in the back of his mouth. With his tongue, he explored the molar that lately was becoming more and more worrisome. He thought again of the scene the night before. With no one but himself to hear, he cursed and shook the memory of the Tucker boys and the Lawford girl away. He was unable to do likewise with the toothache pain, though he did make several attempts.

In the kitchen, Ma Bailey jumped with a start when the screen door slammed shut. She called her curses out to Freeman as he followed his nose to the kitchen.

"Mornin', Misses Bailey, Mister Bailey."

Mister Bailey nodded from behind his newspaper. Ma Bailey said bitterly with her back to him, "You two gonna give me a heart attack with that damned door. Glad you could join us, Mister *Fabbro*. Clean towel's in the washroom."

"Thank ya, ma'm."

"Oh, don't go thankin' me. You oughta thank the Good Lord for my patience. That's who you oughta be thankin'."

To Mister Bailey's perilous amusement, Freeman clasped his hands together there in the sunlit kitchen, bowed his head and beseeched the Lord saying, "Lord, thank ya for givin' Miss Bailey the patience to put up with the low down, sorry likes of—"

"That'll do, Mister Fabbro," interrupted Ma Bailey, her back still to him as she tended to the work at hand. "You make light of the Lord again under this roof," she turned to him now,"and I'll put ya out on your black ass." Ma Bailey accentuated her point by wagging the kitchen knife she held in her shiny, red-raw hands.

"Now, ain't no needs to go cuttin' on no fellas." Freeman hammed it up. "I wasn't makin' light, Miss Bailey. I swears I wasn't."

"You better not be." Ma Bailey turned back to the work of slicing the potatoes for frying.

"Miz Bailey?" Freeman asked the old woman's backside.

"You still in my kitchen?" she asked, never ceasing the work.

"Am I black?" Freeman continued his performance.

"Black enough. Now cut the shit and go get yourself clean whilst ya still can."

The washroom was large. The plumbing ran along the outside of the wall. Freeman scrubbed the sleep from his face and washed his mouth with water and baking soda. In the mrror he investigated the wretched state of his teeth. There in the back was the current offender, black, jagged and throbbing. He pushed at it with his index finger and found it had no discernible effect on the dull throb.

black ass

Ma Bailey's words had wounded him more than he'd expected. He considered her, considered where he believed her heart to be, and dismissed her misguided playfulness.

He attempted to do something with the mess that was his hair and quickly surrendered. There were biscuits to be had.

Freeman sopped the last of the red-eye gravy and egg yolk from the plate with a split buttermilk biscuit.

"Lawdy, Miz Bailey," he said, "reckon I'm full as a tick and 'bout to pop. Don't you jes' cook up the finest breakfast a fella ever had? I do believe so. Why just look a here," he held up the plate. "I done cleaned this plate so good, why you ain't even gonna have to go washin' it. Why, you cook up the kinda breakfast men'd go to war fightin' to protect. I do believe—"

"That's quite enough, Mister Fabbro," Ma Bailey interrupted. "And your Uncle Tom act is gettin' old."

"You knows my Uncle Tom? Small world, ain't it now?"

Mister Bailey laughed and Miss Bailey scolded him, "Don't encourage him, Hiram."

"Fine fixin's Miss Bailey. Now, if you fine folks have no objections, I think I might retire to my quarters."

"You get no objections from me," Ma Bailey poked at him.

Hiram Bailey said, "Come see me later and I'll give ya a chance to redeem yourself on that checkerboard."

"Will do, Mister Bailey." Freeman rose from the table and made his leave. On his way out, he could not resist the temptation, and so said with a thick accent as he exited, "Yessa! Bestest vittles I done had in a long time. Make me wanna slap my own mama for never knowin' how to do it right. Yessa!" Behind him, he heard the sound of silverware abruptly falling onto china followed by Mister Bailey's laughter.

With his belly now filled with breakfast, Freeman slept Sunday away as had become his custom over the past few weeks. When early evening drew, he awoke and met Mister Bailey across the red and black checkerboard, and, as had also become his custom, let Mister Bailey beat him three out of five.

Chapter 9

When Moday morning arrived, Virginia was waiting, not on the porch, but at the road. She had begun her wait on the porch, but sweet anticipation had driven her to the end of the driveway. On the walk to the house she told the boys how she'd missed them and all about the coloring books and crayons she had bought for them. All the while absently holding her hand to her stomach.

"You sick or something?"

"No, I ain't sick. Do I look sick?"

"You keep rubbin' your belly like you need to poop."

"I don't need to poop. Ain't y'all somethin'?"

"I guess we is. We must be, else you wouldn't say it so much."

Mondays were slow at Mac's Package Store. Mac had a slight rush in the morning when the workers at the pallet mill and the hosiery came in for cigarettes and coffees before the start of first shift. A lull then followed until the kids began to stir. With school out now for summer, the kids would trickle in and out throughout the day for Nehis and penny candy, all on credit, promising to pay when their dad got paid or when the check came. Most never did, and Mac spent all spring stoning up his resolve to issue no more credit to them, only to cut his losses when fall eventually and inevitably came.

The second rush of the day was nearing with the shift change at the plants and Mac had long put down his paper and taken up the broom in preparation. He swept the porch free of the dirt the children brought with them from the dirt road. He wiped the sweat from his brow. Summer was yet to hit its height and the Orange Crush thermometer that had long been nailed to the porch read ninety two degrees. He tapped the glass of the thermometer lightly with his finger nail, but the red line did not budge. Mac shook his head in disgust at the heat and walked toward the road. In the distance he saw the mail truck approaching, which answered his question and reason for walking to the road. When he turned back toward the store, he stopped for a moment and entertained the crazy notion of throwing rocks at the neon sign above the porch. He resisted the idea with a cool and knowing smile as if he and the old sign had an understanding that the day was coming. Back on the porch, he glanced again at the thermometer and waved at Red as Red passed in the mail truck.

RR3 was the last leg of Red's route. Red had long ago plotted it out this way, arranging his weekday delivery schedule so that late afternoon found him out beyond the tracks and far from home. It was his custom to park the mail Jeep, a right hand drive DJ-5 Dispatcher 100, in the parking lot of the pallet mill, back in the corner and out of sight so as not to encourage any would be mail thieves. There, he would satchel the meager bits of mail for the half dozen or so addresses out on the route, lock up the DJ and head out for his walk down the dirt road. The walk was arduous, but between the rutted road and the children, the cats and the dogs and the chickens, it was much easier and much more tolerable for Red to simply park the Jeep and walk the last leg. And sometimes, on weekdays, if luck and timing and all of the other agents that sometimes, though rarely, conspire to give a man good fortune were on his side, he was allowed to end his day with a walk in the company of the prettiest woman he had seen in all of his near sixty years on earth.

"Why, Jeannie Tucker, we gotta stop meeting like this." The joke was old, but over the years, it had not occurred to Red to say anything else as he caught up with Jeannie Tucker on her walk to work.

"Hey there, Red. Any sweepstakes winners today?" Her joke was also old, but so long as Red kept laughing, she'd keep asking.

It is a thing of great pleasure and importance for a man of Red's age, for any man really, to walk a ways down a road with a pretty woman, and though it could be argued otherwise, it is not an act iniquitous nor morally corrupt, depraved nor deserving of much scrutiny. It is a simple pleasure, not unlike a sudden honeysuckle breeze or the sighting of a rainbow.

It can be safely assumed that the previous thought never materialized in either subjects' head as they walked along the dirt road discussing the pressing heat, the nearing county fair and whatever else it may be that occupies conversations on unpaved roads on early summer afternoons.

"I'm gonna stop in and say hey to Mac, take him his mail and grab a cold pop. You want one? On me." Red offered as the two approached the end of the dirt road and stepped onto the asphalt.

"Makes me pee too much. I just hate to keep runnin' to the bathroom when I'm on the clock," Jeannie answered, smiling when she noticed how she'd made the old man blush.

"All right, maybe next time, then," Red offered hopefully.

"Maybe next time, Red. Thank you, though."

"Don't you work too hard," he said to her. "This heat's a killer."

"Ain't it, though. You either, Red."

At the edge of the parking lot, the two departed as Jeannie made her way toward one of the opened bay doors of the pallet mill.

Now, as per earlier mention of iniquity, moral corruption and depravity, that was in reference to the act of walking with a pretty woman. One should not be so foolish as to argue the same about the moment a man watches a pretty woman walking away. There is, indeed and doubtless, depravity involved in that simple act.

When Jeannie was out of sight, Red walked on, entertaining himself with perverse thoughts of Jeannie Tucker and her bathroom habits.

He stopped suddenly. "What in the Sam Hell?" he asked the summer heat.

Red quick-stepped it to the now battered Jeep. The windows were shattered, the mirrors were beaten to odd angles. Issues of the local penny saver were strewn all around the vehicle. Someone had urinated on them. Furious and confused, Red looked around, scanning the woods, the hills, the tracks, but saw no one.

Chapter 10

Wednesday came with money, cash money, working young man's money, money spent frivolously on a moment, money earned with sweat and time and traded for beers, smokes and the everlasting memory of, money folded up by dirty, oily hands and fingers with grease laden nails, money given for the causes of food and roof and utilities, money that proclaimed Citizen and a place in the world, money that meant *respectable young man not to be easily dismissed nor disregarded*, money that said "Through Our Labors, In This System We Trust" across the face of it.

It was Lenville's custom, much to his younger brothers' delight, to arrive home on Wednesdays with a cold twelve pack of beer and Lucky Strikes all around. He would take his meager payday from *the shop* to Mac's Package, congenially allow Mac to catch him up on current events, a subject Mac had proud and thoughtful opinions on. He would let Mac express himself on matters political and social without interruption, without argument and then he would collect his beers and his cigarettes. He would thank Mac and head down the dirt road, emptying two cans of Miller as he walked along, singing whatever Hank Williams tune came to mind.

On this particular Wednesday, he did not sing. In the cool breeze of the caged metal fan that blew across the counter of Mac's Package, he and Mac had discussed the reality of space travel.

"The moon, can you believe that?" Mac held up the newspaper, his Chesterfield between his lips.

"Guess it's Mars after that, huh, Mac?"

"Mars and beyond." Mac had said. "Space, the final frontier."

Lenville Tucker now passed the walk home with his thoughts not on "wooden Indians," nor "jambalaya and crawfish pie," and not, for the first time in days, on the war in Viet Nam, but on the television show Star Trek and how quickly he imagined the future was coming.

Summer was on Rural Route 3. It was in the middle of the dirt road with the half-naked children, heathen and dirty faced, exploring and more than likely getting up to no good. There were black children. There were white children. The country was in turmoil over civil rights, but there in the poorest places, they had long since figured it out. Where poverty lived, where it hung its worse for wear hat, where it put its sore and aching feet up, it made all men and women equal in a way no law ever could.

Summer was in the front yard with two brothers and a dog.

"Where'd you even get that dog?" Ronny asked Li'l Roy.

"I didn't *get* him. He ain't the kinda dog ya get. He's the kinda dog just shows up where they ain't one." Li'l Roy answered his brother with a shrug.

"That don't make no sense."

"Don't matter if it does or if it don't."

"Well, he's one dumb son of a bitch. I'll tell ya that."

"No, he ain't," Li'l Roy rejected his brother's evaluation. "He ain't dumb. I just ain't a good teacher."

"You know what they say about old dogs and new tricks, don't ya?" Ronny asked knowingly.

"Hell, he ain't that old, and he ain't dumb neither," the boy reiterated.

"Don't kid yourself. He ain't no pup. He's got some years on him, that one does," Ronny pointed out.

"So."

"So, sew a button, so nuttin'," said Ronny. "I'm just sayin'."

In his right hand, Li'l Roy held an opaque plastic Crisco lid. He was attempting, in vain, to teach the yellow dog to snatch it out of the air the way he had seen dogs on television catch Frisbees, but was having no luck. The yellow dog would only fetch it after Li'l Roy had sailed it wobbling through the air, across the yard and into the dirt road. The dog would then retrieve it and bring it dutifully back to the boy.

Li'l Roy cocked his arm, preparing to sail the plastic lid yet again. "Go, boy. Go!" Roy commanded, making a waving motion with his hand. With a flick of his wrist, the lid took flight and sailed loftily across the yard, landing in the dry dirt road. The yellow dog sprinted after it.

"Like I said," observed Ronny with a shaming smile and a discouraging shake of his head. "Dumb. He's just gonna do the same thing he did before."

"You just wait," said Li'l Roy. He moved quickly up the front steps and into the house, returning to the yard seconds later with three slices of bologna.

"Boy, Mom's gonna whip your ass, feedin' baloney to that dog," said Ronny, half laughing.

"She won't know if you don't tell her, and you won't tell her."

"I will. I'm a blabber mouth don't ya know?" Ronny confessed. "Gimme a piece and I won't."

"Shit, go get your own."

"I don't feel like it. Gimme half a piece."

Li'l Roy tore a slice of bologna in half saying, "Geez, here ya go." He handed the torn piece of bologna to his older brother. "Now look," he held up the other half. "It ain't gonna fly like a Frisbee now."

"Might as well gimme that half too, then."

With a smile in his eyes, Li'l Roy motioned out into the yard with his hand. Ronny looked toward the road then back at his brother. Li'l Roy gestured again. Ronny looked again.

"What? What is it?" Ronny asked confusedly.

Li'l Roy motioned yet again. Ronny grinned, clearly now understanding his little brother's idea. He laughed, shook his head and rose from the front steps. Halfway into the yard, he stopped, barked like a dog, stuck his tongue out and began to jump around. Li'l Roy, smiling ear to ear, sailed the piece of meat through the air. It flew straighter than he had thought it would. Ronny caught it with his mouth.

"Good boy!" Li'l Roy called after him. "That's a good boy!"

"Throw another one!" Ronny called. "Throw me another'n."

"Shit, I ain't wastin' no more on you. It's for the dog." Li'l Roy flung the next piece high over the dog's head. The dog leapt into the air, snatching the slice of meat and swallowing it whole. "Good boy!"

"You'd rather feed that dog than your own damned brother." Ronny joked.

"Shut up." Li'l Roy said, picking up the Crisco lid and sailing it toward the dog. Without a hint of enthusiasm, the dog watched the lid sail toward him and then over him, making no effort to leap and catch it. Once it landed, the dog retrieved it and brought it back to Li'l Roy.

"Like I keep tellin' ya," said Ronny, finding his seat back on the front steps. "Dumb."

Roy readied the last slice of meat, flicked his wrist and sailed it through the air. The dog ran after it, leaped clumsily to a height almost twice his length, and snatched it out of the air as it sailed.

Ronny rose from the steps and headed toward his little brother. "Gimme that," he said, snatching the Crisco lid from Li'l Roy and heading inside.

"Hey, what's the big idea? Whattaya?"

"Just wait. Stay right here." Ronny disappeared into the house and reappeared in the kitchen window. "Now watch." He sailed the plastic lid from the window and the dog sprang into motion, moving quickly fluidly through the yard before leaping and snatching the lid out of the air as it sailed.

"Ah!" exclaimed Li'l Roy. "I'll be goddamned." The yellow dog brought the chewed, saliva laden lid back to Li'l Roy. "Good boy!" Li'l Roy scratched the dog's head and repeated, "Good boy!"

"Guess you's right." Ronny said from the window.

"Yeah, I told ya he wasn't dumb."

"I mean about you not bein' a good teacher. Throw that here."

Li'l Roy launched the lid into the opened kitchen window. Ronny missed the catch and the lid landed inside on the kitchen table. He turned to see his mother.

"Is that the lid to my Crisco?" she asked. "What are you boy's doin'?"

"Hey, here comes Len!" Li'l Roy called from the steps.

"Getcha a beer, Mom," Lenville offered.

"I'm headed to work. You boys try not to burn the house down while I'm gone. Chicken's on the stove."

"Hold up," said Lenville and followed his mother to the dirt road. "Here," he said, holding out a small sweat-soaked roll of bills.

"We're okay this week," she said. "You keep it."

"Naw, now come on. It ain't much. Take it," he insisted.

Jeannie Tucker did not count the money, but stuffed it deep into the back pocket of her jeans. "Thank ya, Len," she said, wrapping an arm around his neck and pulling him down to her for a light kiss on his cheek.

"Don't mention it, and don't work too hard," he said and returned to the front steps to join his brothers.

"Get up and let me sit down," he said to Ronny.

"Why would I do that?" Ronny laughed.

"'Cause one of us worked all day and brought home beer and cigarettes."

"How come Li'l Roy ain't gotta get up? How come I do?"

"I like that side. Now get up." Lenville said and Ronny did so with a groan. Lenville sat on the step. "Boys, me and Mac was talkin' about—"

Ronny interrupted his older brother, saying to his younger, "Get up and let me sit down."

"Yeah, you can go piss up a rope," answered Li'l Roy, laughing and giving an elbow to Lenville.

"Anyways," Lenville began again, "me and Mac was talkin' about how we're headed to the moon," said Lenville, opening a beer. "Oh, and we was also talkin' about—"

"Make him get up, Len. It's only fair."

"Who said anything about shit being fair?" asked Lenville.

"Well, I'm older'n him."

"He can't help that. Doesn't sound fair to him, does it?" Lenville pointed out. He continued, "Me and Mac was also talkin' about how you boys need to pay y'alls bills out there. He's nice enough to let you boys have credit. Gotta pay your bills, boys, else people'll start sayin' bad shit about ya." A moment passed between the brothers. The trio laughed. "I am serious, though, fellas."

"So, we're gonna land a spaceship on the moon?" asked Li'l Roy avoiding the issue of his unpaid bill.

"Ah, they're fulla shit," said Ronny with a wave of his hand and a swallow of beer, his mood now contentious. "They ain't gonna build no damned spaceship."

"Yeah, that's what I'm thinkin', too. Sounds a li'l farfetched to me, Len," agreed Li'l Roy, sipping from his own can. It didn't really seem that farfetched to Li'l Roy, but he thought he might throw a bone to Ronny.

"Shit, they done built it," Lenville countered.

"Nuh uh," Li'l Roy protested and looked to Ronny.

"Don't you boys know nothin?" Lenville asked. "Shit, they done built it and before ya know it, folks'll be goin' to the moon on vacation instead of the beach. The moon, Mars—"

"You believe that, Len? Ya really believe we'll be spendin' weekends on Mars?" asked Li'l Roy.

"Shit, no," answered Lenville, much to his little brother's apparent disappointment. "Not us. Not folks like us. When you ever known us to go on vacation?" he asked. "Rich folks, though. Yeah. But naw, not folks like us."

"Still though," Li'l Roy seemed to have quickly recovered, "still pretty cool, though."

"Cool as the other side of the pillow," said Len. "Beam me up, Scotty."

"Damn, you guys are so fulla shit," Ronny interjected. "You're fulla shit. You're fulla shit." He pointed at each of his brothers in turn. "NASA's fulla shit. The government's fulla shit," he continued. "Did I mention you're fulla shit and you're fulla shit?" Ronny wasn't sure he meant it, but he was sure he had a good time saying it.

Lenville held up the case of beers. "You wouldn't believe snakes cawled til one bit ya. Knock it off and take them and put'em in the fridge 'fore this heat gets to 'em anymore. They're already piss warm." Lenville handed the crate of unopened beers to Ronny.

"Why me?" he asked. "Why not him?"

"'Cause you're fulla shit," said Len and the boys all laughed.

When he was sure that Ronny was out of earshot, he turned to Li'l Roy and asked with his voice slightly lowered, "You doin' okay?"

"Yeah, I'm okay. Why wouldn't I be?"

"I's just thinkin' I wish I hadn't laid that Viet Nam shit on ya."

Li'l Roy said, "Yeah. Pretty heavy."

"Ain't it, though?"

On the rickety front steps, the two sat with the secret between them.

"When you gonna tell'em, Len?" asked Li'l Roy.

"Hell, I ain't," said Lenville.

"Ya gotta tell'em some time."

"No, I don't. I decided I ain't goin', Li'l Roy." Lenville drained the Miller can and crushed it.

"But, ain't ya gotta?"

"Yeah, but I still ain't. Don't think they're gonna want me by the time I get done. If they do, they're gonna have to come and get me."

"What's 'at mean? By the time you get done with what?"

"Ain't worked it all out yet."

"Are you serious, Len?"

"As a heart attack," punctuated Lenville.

"Whattaya gonna do, Len?"

"Ain't got nothin' to do with you right now, kiddo. So, don't worry about it, and don't open your mouth about it. I got it. Trust me on this, Li'l Roy. Shit," he said slightly shaking the crushed can he held in his hand. He called into the house," Hey, bring me one when you come back."

"Whatcha gonna do, Len?" Li'l Roy felt a burn and an uneasiness deep in his stomach. "If it's got to do with you, then it's got to do with me. That's just how it works, sorry to tell ya."

"I ain't a goin,'' he said flatly.

"Whatcha gonna do, Len?" Li'l Roy demanded.

"You're soundin' a lot like a broken record this afternoon, ya know that? I said I'm not sure yet."

"Aintcha gotta go?"

"You asked me that already. Yeah, but I still ain't."

"Are you scared, Len? 'S'at it?" Li'l Roy asked, his voice carrying a tinge of confidentiality.

"Scared? Shit, you ever know me to be scared a anything?"

"Nope." Li'l Roy answered without having to think about the question. He shook his head. "Never."

Lenville said flatly, "I ain't scared, Roy."

63

"I done had it figgered, Len."

"What you had figgered? You figgered I's just scared?"

"Naw, I done figgered you'd go over there and win that war all by yourself. I done seen ya comin' home with all sorts a medals and shit," the younger boy was suddenly excited, "all kinds of scars and, and you'd have a cool story for ever one of 'em about how ya got'em and—"

"Well, I hate to take a piss all over the plans ya got for me, but I ain't a goin'."

"Red never shoulda brought you that notice of abduction, or whatever it is."

"*Induction*," Lenville corrected, "but you're closer than you think. And I done told ya, it ain't on Red."

"Yeah, well—" Li'l Roy did not finish his thought. He only studied his hand and the scraped knuckles he had received while smashing up Red's Jeep.

"What'd you do to your hand?"

"Nothin'," Li'l Roy said. "Ya know, Len, you looked like a grown man walkin' up that road in that work shirt. All respectable and everything. I mean with your name there on it and all."

Lenville grinned and said, "I am a grown ass man."

"Sometimes, I don't feel like I'm ever gonna be a grown ass man. How do you know what to do? I feel like I don't know nothin'."

"Ah, you're already twice the man that Ronny is." Lenville peered over his shoulder. "Don't go rushin' it and don't go wearin' yourself out."

Ronny stepped from the house, beers and bologna in hand. "Y'all think our girlfriend's gonna show back up Saturday?" He handed a beer to Lenville as he squeezed his way between his brothers and stepped back out into the yard.

Li'l Roy flushed. He rose quietly, and stepped into the house. "Where you goin'?" He heard Ronny ask. "I'm takin' your step."

For a moment, Li'l Roy feared he might not make it. He swallowed the rushing vomit, held his lips together tightly and ran to the bathroom.

Chapter 11

By the time Saturday rolled back around, Li'l Roy was feeling chronically spent and was severely calloused and raw on the softest parts of himself. It did not escape him that he was both embarrassed and aroused by thoughts of what had happened there beneath the trestle with the Lawford girl.

The cigarette butt sizzled and Li'l Roy shook the match as a fleck of fiery ash drifted down and landed on his forearm. He smacked at it, smearing soot across his skin, but soothing the slight burn. He dragged a deep drag from the butt until he could feel the fire at his lips. With his thumb and index finger, he pinched the butt and flipped it far into the overgrown yard. The yellow dog went after it, found it and blew his disappointment through his wet nostrils. The dog sneezed twice and Li'l Roy apologized.

"Here, boy. Come here," Roy called.

Happily, the yellow dog bounded toward the front steps. Li'l Roy scratched the dog's ears, lifted the dog's chin and examined his snout. He found no injury from the lit butt, but did discover a tick on the dog's ear. "Hold still just a second, boy," he instructed. The dog did so and Li'l Roy pinched the fattened tick from the dog's floppy ear and placed it on the step. He struck a match, enjoying the scent of the Sulfur and touched the flame to the tick until it popped.

His thoughts fell on Virginia Lawford.

With his elbows on his knees and the sun on his bare brown shoulders, Li'l Roy smiled and thought it must be love. In the days that followed the carnal tryst beneath the trestle, the image of Virginia Lawford haunted Li'l Roy Tucker like a lingering dream that he could not shake if he truly and wholeheartedly wanted to. He had been sweet on girls before, but never so consumed, so haunted by visions and dreams. This new fever strangely affected his memory and ultimately yet merely momentarily, changed the events that had occurred there in the darkness, both on the tracks and beneath the trestle. No longer did he think about standing aside afterwards while his brothers had taken their turns with her. In his preferred memory of the event, no longer did he hear their sensual and primal moans. It was only he and she there in the forbidden night with the forbidden hunger committing the forbidden act. He felt they were connected now, that they would be forever tethered to each other by hunger and need.

This, he repeatedly assured himself, must be love.

Li'l Roy had, in the week prior, decided he would not join his brothers on their weekly trip to Pudgy's Tavern. No matter what they said to him. Concerning the girl, it was not that he feared she might not show up again, out of the darkness and the fog. It was that he feared she would. It certainly wasn't that he didn't want to be with her again. The reality was, he came to reluctantly admit to himself, that he didn't want to see her with his brothers.

Her—

—with them

Panic gripped him. He looked to the sun, squinting, fearful. Saturday afternoon had begun to wane and the threat of Saturday evening loomed like the nearing and inevitable end of everything. The night would come and the night did not give a damn.

She would show up. He felt his pulse quicken and his stomach quake. She would appear again like a hungry ghost out of the fog. She would lie down there in the darkness and if he was there, she would welcome him inside of her and then she would open her legs for his brothers. If he was not there, then they would all do it again without him.

He convinced himself there was still time to stop it all. He found his sneakers inside the house. From beneath the back steps he retrieved the five empty bottles he had stolen, collected and hidden. From the cupboard, he stole eight more. His mother would be upset with him for taking the bottles, but her disappointment was a price he was willing to pay. He put them all in a Coca-Cola crate and began his run, convincing himself there was still time to get to the Lawford place and then to Cas Walker's before they locked the doors for the evening. He cursed his debt at Mac's. No credit left for the Tucker boys, not even for a cold Nehi. If he didn't owe Mac so much, he could cut his trip and his trouble in half. But, he had run up such a tab, he would likely never again find the courage to darken Mac's door. He did not allow that bit of financial regret to hinder his plan. He would take Virginia out. On a date. To the movies. The two of them in the darkness, holding hands, her face lit by the blue light of the screen. She would go with him, first to Cas Walker's to turn in the bottles for the deposit money and surely there would be enough for soda fountain drinks and a hot and buttery salted popcorn they could share between them.

Spots, a barn cat, black and white with two chewed ears, was nimble for his age and despite his lifelong daring carelessness. To the front porch of the Lawford house, he brought the occasional bird, mouse and mole. Not, as was suspected and supposed, for reasons of praise and adulation, but for reasons of instruction. Spots had never seen the girl, nor the man, track and hunt anything and had long since designated himself their teacher. But they were slow to catch on.

Directly in front of each of Spot's chewed ears, were nearly bald patches where pink flesh was visible. This element gave Spots more an air of trouble and trial than was probably deserved, but these matching bald spots in front of his ears were not borne of scar tissue nor old age. Spots was a refined killing machine, the lack of fur in front of his ears an evolutionary and genetic advantage which allowed only minimal interference to his hearing.

His pupils dilated as he stalked his prey from above. Beneath him, a scant swarm of peaceful and lovely yellow Clouded Sulfur butterflies, each with a wingspan of less than an inch, flitted, fluttered and fed, oblivious to the excited feline above them.

Virginia Lawford read a book in her rocking chair. The rockers squeaked and creaked as they rolled across the plank floor of the porch. She was oblivious to Spots as he peered over the edge of the porch, his rear end rocking enthusiastically, his tail flicking hither and fore as though it were an entity independent of the rest of him.

Spots sprang from the porch. The small swarm dispersed in all directions, save for the one now pinned beneath Spots' front paws. Cautiously, Spots inspected his prey, lifting his paw slightly and allowing the small and crippled butterfly a moment of limping freedom. Spots quickly swatted it back down. He worked his pink nose between his paws and took the flying thing cautiously between his tiny front teeth. It fluttered, panicked and helpless.

Spots brought the butterfly up the steps of the porch to the feet of Virginia Lawford.

"What ya got?" She asked the cat and was suddenly appalled. "Spots! Damn you!" Virginia shot to her feet, her book falling to the porch. She lost herself in a manner that was recurring more and more often of late. "Damn you! See what you've done! Drop it! Drop it, you bastard! You dirty, dirty, bastard. Damn you! Damn you! Damn you! Drop it!" She stomped the porch. Spots growled and retreated. "Damn you!" She felt as though she could not stop herself. "Damn you!" she tearfully repeated over and over, even after the feline was long gone.

Eventually, she retrieved her book and returned fuming to the rocking chair. Her condemnation of Spots echoing and bouncing through her head.

damn you

damn you

damn you

Her attention was drawn to the road and the driveway. A wave of panic shot through her and again she bolted from the rocking chair.

Li'l Roy watched her rise from her chair on the porch as he approached. She was suddenly the prettiest girl he had ever seen. She stood, shading her eyes. To his chagrin, Li'l Roy realized that in his haste, he had forgotten to put on a shirt. He stopped running, placed the crate of bottles on the ground and approached the porch.

"Dangit," he said stepping toward the girl, "I forgot my shirt." A goofy grin spread across the boy's tanned face. "I—I put my shoes on, but I forgot my shirt. Can you believe a person could get so," he considered his choice of words there and opted for honesty. "Excited, so excited as to forget they wasn't wearin' a shirt?"

Virginia Lawford looked nervously up the road, the episode with Spots now far from her thoughts. "Li'l Roy, you stop right there. What are you doin' here? You can't be here."

"Huh? I come to take ya out, Virginia." He blushed, stepping toward the porch.

"Stop! Just stop, Li'l Roy. You can't be here. Daddy'll be back any minute. He's just gone into town. You can't be here. You gotta go. Now, go on. "

Li'l Roy's shoulders fell. "I've come a callin'. Virginia, I'm a askin' ya to the movies. I got these here bottles. We can still make it to Cas Walker's and turn 'em in before they close if we run. We could take'em to Mac's, but I'd feel weird about it, seein' as how I owe him. I mean, I don't know what pictures are on, but it don't really matter does it? If it's already started, we can just head to the Tastee-Creem for a milkshake and fries. Whattaya say?" he asked hopefully.

She studied the boy, blushing herself. "I can't, Roy. That all sounds real nice and all, but I can't. Daddy'd never allow me—"

"But—" Li'l Roy protested.

"You can't be here, Li'l Roy. Please go. Please, just go. Maybe sometime we can. But not now, though. Now, please leave before Daddy comes home and sees you and has a fit and skins us both."

"You let me know when we can?" pressed Li'l Roy with a wink and a blush.

"I will, Li'l Roy."

"Promise?" he asked.

"Promise, I will."

He was disappointed, but found comfort in the prospect. "All right, then. I'm a hold ya to it." The boy took up his bottles and began to walk away. He turned back to her. "Promise me somethin' else?"

"You really gotta go."

"Promise me somethin'."

"Sure, Li'l Roy. What's 'at?"

"You won't come out no more at night." He squinted in the sun.

Again, she blushed. "What?"

"You won't come out no more. You know, like—"

"I think I got what I wanted. Bye, Li'l Roy."

"So, ya won't?" Li'l Roy pressed.

"I won't."

"Well good, then. Bye, Virginia."

"Li'l Roy?" she called, and against her better judgement said, "I think I got what I wanted from *you*, I mean."

He stopped then and began to walk back toward the porch holding the crate of bottles out from him like a serving tray. "How do you mean?"

"Nevermind." She laughed anxiously, shooing him away with her hands.

"No, really, I don't—"

"I think you gave me what I was wantin'. Now go."

"I still don't—"

"It don't matter if you do or if you don't, Li'l Roy Tucker. You just gotta go. Now, go."

With his pride unbowed, the boy went.

Li'l Roy raced full tilt with the bottles, careful not to trip on the cross ties. He ran with a smile even though it hadn't all gone the way he had hoped it would. He ran with an enchanted calm, with his thoughts on tomorrow and the day after that and so on and so on. The yellow mutt ran swiftly alongside him with his tongue wagging, clearly overjoyed at the opportunity to run with the boy. "Who's a good boy?" the boy asked breathlessly as the two ran along with the returnable bottles bouncing in the crate. "Who is?" The sun was nearing the western horizon and the rails were a glowing gold. The two ran on, hell bent for Cas Walker's, the bottles clinking and growing heavier and heavier until the crossing appeared in the distance and the boy and the dog slackened their run to an eventual walk. It would be all right to walk now. He was sure there was time and he was sure Ronny and Lenville were safely behind him. He imagined them searching for him again down on the bank. He hoped he had thrown them a curve by heading into town rather than down to the river.

They were not looking for him. Ronny had suggested it. Lenville had shut him down.

"Not tonight. Leave him be," Lenville commanded Ronny.

"Yeah," Ronny had concurred. "Screw him."

The two had headed off down the dirt road.

Once on Main Street, Li'l Roy made himself pass by the Starlite Theater with a promise that on his way back, he would linger and examine the posters, basking in promises of adventure and the heavy aroma of buttered popcorn and what a night it might have been.

To his great relief, he found Cas Walker's was still open. At the counter, a thin pimply clerk counted the empties and gave Li'l Roy his deposit.

"Thanks," Li'l Roy offered, stuffing the money into the pocket of his jeans. "Afraid I's too late and y'all'd be closed."

"We're closing now and you really need to be wearing a shirt when you come in here," the clerk informed him.

"I wore shoes." Li'l Roy nodded as if this negated the clerk's rule.

"One's got nothin' to do with the other. Come on, I gotta follow you out so's I can lock the door behind ya." The young clerk began to step around the counter.

"Wait one second." Li'l Roy prepped himself for a dash, bouncing slightly. The anxious clerk said nothing, but offered Li'l Roy a disdainful expression that clearly stated though he wasn't crazy about the idea, the boy could go ahead, so Li'l Roy raced away, up and down the aisles, the rubber soles of his sneakers squeaking periodically across the buffed floor.

"Hey!" The clerk called after him. "Hey, c'mon. We gotta close. We gotta lock the door." The boy called back from somewhere in the store, but the young clerk could not understand him.

Li'l Roy returned, dumping bottles of RC Cola and a bag of barbecue flavored potato chips onto the counter. The total rang up. A breathless Li'l Roy was six cents short, but the aggravated clerk forewent the deficit, taking what the boy had (just as Li'l Roy had expected him to) and waving him off. "Just go. Go."

"Hey, thanks."

"Shirt next time," the clerk said.

"Got it," Li'l Roy agreed.

He passed Pudgy's Tavern in the dark. The jukebox sang into the night and waves of idle chatter and raucous laughter rose into the night sky. After Pudgy's, Li'l Roy left the railroad tracks and climbed down the bank. He continued past Bailey's Boarding House, the hosiery and the pallet mill. Past that, came the dirt road and the dirt road was dark. Passing the Lawford place, he looked down the long worn driveway. The porch light was on and he could see the swirling swarm of insects that were drawn to it, but no one was outside, not Quiet Tom, not Virginia. Li'l Roy continued on the dirt road with his grocery sack in hand.

In the purple dusk, the fireflies were signaling their glowing codes. At the edge of his yard, he hesitated, put an ear out and could hear the Russell River upstream from the trestle and the beach, washing over rocks. Cicadas called. Bullfrogs croaked. He was relieved at his brothers' absence in the collection of sounds that filled the night. They were out for the evening. They would probably give him eight kinds of hell when they returned later, waking him with knuckles burning across his scalp, or playful slaps to his sleeping face. They would call him names and drunkenly wrestle rougher than they meant to, but he would survive.

Through the kitchen window Li'l Roy could see his mother in the dim light of the single kitchen bulb. She was seated at the kitchen table with her friend, not her *boy*friend, Mr. Freeman. Their laughter came through the kitchen window. Li'l Roy stepped eagerly up the few steps and into the house.

"Well, look who it is." Jeannie Tucker heralded the arrival of her youngest son, her face flushed from the wine.

"Hey, Mom." Li'l Roy entered the smoky kitchen and opened the icebox.

"Thought you were with your brothers," she said to him as he piled RC Colas into the freezer. "Now, them'll freeze and bust and I'll be the one cleanin' 'em up. Why'd you go and buy pop? I got you boys some pop."

"I'm plannin' on drinkin' 'em all and I didn't wanna drink all the ones that you got for everybody."

"Roy Tucker, you better not drink all them pops tonight." She shared a smile with her friend.

"They's my pops. I bought'em. Hey, Mister Freeman."

"Hey there, Roy." Freeman nodded and jokingly pointed a pint bottle toward the boy. Li'l Roy stepped toward the man with his hand out to receive it.

"Li'l Roy, I wish you wouldn't. And you—" she shook her head and pointed at Freeman. "And Li'l Roy, why you wantin' to drink all them pops tonight?" Jeannie Tucker pressed her youngest, swirling the ice in her glass and taking a drink of her own.

"I just do." Li'l Roy shrugged while taking the church key that hung on a string tied to the handle of the refrigerator. He popped the metal cap with a whispering hiss and drained the sweet drink into his throat.

"You're gonna get a belly ache, Li'l Roy. You know your stomach." Jeannie warned, but the boy kept chugging. With the bottle now empty, Li'l Roy belched long and deep. "Roy Tucker." His mother laughed.

"Whew! That burned. Made my eyes water." Li'l Roy laughed. "Not tonight." He shook his head and examined the glass bottle making sure he had completely drained it. "Ain't plannin' on no gut aches tonight."

He belched another thunderous, gassy, eye-watering belch and when it was over, proudly smiled. Jeannie Tucker shook her head and her friend, not her *boy*friend, smiled at her and her boy.

Li'l Roy took another bottle from the freezer. "Li'l Roy, don't do that one like that. Just drink it normal like."

"I'm gonna. I'm gonna drink it in there and watch teevee."

"Ooh, see if Lawrence Welk is on," said Jeannie.

"Aww—" the boy protested.

"You heard me, now."

"You wasn't even watchin'—" the boy fought on.

"You heard me," she said again and watched as Li'l Roy carried his pop and the Cas Walker bag from the kitchen into the living room.."Whatcha got in that bag, son?" Jeannie asked after him.

"Potato Chips. Barbecue. Y'all want some?"

"You been takin' my bottles?" Jeannie Tucker asked suspiciously.

The television bloomed to life and he quickly worked the knob. "Looky there, Lawrence Welk is on."

Before sitting on the sofa, he moved one of the cushions from the far end and doubled it up on one end. He had trained himself to do this. A spring had sprung, but doubling up the cushions made short work of it.

Li'l Roy spent the night camped out on the threadbare sofa in front of the small black and white television where he drank too many bottles of RC Cola, ate an entire bag of barbecue flavored potato chips and enjoyed two banana moon pies he had shoplifted. Virginia Lawford's words repeatedly came to him. *I think you gave me what I was wantin'.*

The Lawrence Welk show was a Stephen Foster themed show. He watched until a lady came on and played a very honkytonk piano version of "The Suwanee River." After that, the show went downhill, the commercial with the caveman with indigestion was pretty funny, though. He called to his mother and asked if he could change it now and she agreed. He tuned the knob to NBC and caught the end of Adam-12 while he waited for the NBC Saturday Night Movie, in the middle of which he fell asleep.

It was not a knuckle burn that woke him, nor was it a series of playful slaps. It was a violent and tremendous shaking that woke him. He bolted upright, mumbling in dreamspeak, "I gave her what she was wantin'."

"Wake up, goddammit! Wake up!" Li'l Roy opened his eyes. Ronny was there in the blue glow of the off the air network, looming over Li'l Roy as large and as immediate as the future.

72

"Get up. Len's done killed Darryl Hickey."

"What? Where's Lenville?"

"He went to turn himself in. I'm gettin' Mom. Get up. We're goin' down there."

He sat on the edge of the sofa in the melancholy glow of the television, and rubbed his face with his hands. From down the hall came the muffled voices of his mother and his brother.

"Whattaya mean you ain't goin?"

"What does it sound like it means, Ronny?" Li'l Roy heard his mother ask.

"Sounds like you ain't goin'."

"Smart boy. You must get that from your daddy."

A door slammed. Ronny stomped into the kitchen. Li'l Roy watched as his brother opened the refrigerator. "Dammit, they's busted pop bottles all over the inside of the fridge."

Jeannie Tucker sat in darkness at the kitchen table, her glowing cigarette an angry firefly.

It had come. This was the moment that had loomed on the horizon for nearly a decade. It had come, justifying her fear and her worry, her anxiety and her dread. It was her secret and unspoken prophecy. It was the product of the bargains she had made, the pot for which she had long ago anted up. It was the spectre that lingered even once the dawn had come full and bright. It was her failure.

Li'l Roy sat silently on the couch. When he heard the sounds of his mother's weeping, his sinuses began to burn and he wept with her. He wept for her.

From down the hall came the sound of the toilet flushing. The bathroom door opened, its light spilling into the perimeter of the kitchen and the living room. Ronny came from down the hall and interrupted the quiet.

"Mom—" he said to his mother's silhouette in the kitchen window.

"Don't talk to me," she said. "Not right now. I don't even want to look at you."

Ronny offered no response. He went back down the hallway and into his room.

On the couch, Li'l Roy wept even harder.

Chapter 12

Technically, Gus was more than simply a rooster. He was a Bantam Ameraucana Wheaton cockerel, and this weighty mouthful of technicality seemed not to have escaped him. He strutted proudly, as if well aware of the fact that he was directly descended from great and terrible dinosaurs, and as though he was just as aware of the fact that most of the other nearby inhabitants were not. His tail was a full fountain of fire, ash and smoldering black embers, all the colors of Hell.

Gus the Bantam Ameraucana Wheaton cockerel wasn't picky when it came to excuses to crow. He crowed before the sunrise. He crowed as the sun rose. He crowed to say, "Here I am." He crowed as if to say, "Here I still am." He crowed as if to say, "I am Gus, Bantam Ameraucana Wheaton cockerel, and you can all go and shit in your hats."

Gus, proud and dutiful, stepped into the dusty dirt road and stood surveying his surroundings before calling out to the local residents.

Sunday morning came again, not with hope and newness, but with reality stark and bright.

Li'l Roy sat back in the chair at the kitchen table, smiling at the dog that stood in the yard just outside the kitchen window. Above him was a new fly strip already with quite a collection of specimens. He took the insect trap from the nail and deposited it into the trashcan in the cupboard. On his way back to the kitchen table, he retrieved a piece of bologna from the refrigerator. Once he was again seated in front of the window, he smiled at the dog and sailed the slice out the window. The eager mutt snatched it from the air and the proud boy smiled.

"Did I just see you throw a piece of baloney out the window?" His mother's voice startled him.

"I made the coffee." Li'l Roy admitted nothing.

Ronny Tucker slept. Jeannie Tucker sat with her youngest at the kitchen table.

"What the hell am I gonna do with you boys, Li'l Roy?" she asked. "That boy's poor mama."

Li'l Roy watched his mother drink her coffee. His mother's question was not the kidding around kind of question it had been so many times in the past. He did not have an answer for her, so he said, "I don't know how you can drink that without milk or sugar. I like coffee, but—"

"You don't like coffee. You like milk and sugar with coffee on top," she said.

"Yeah, I guess," Li'l Roy admitted.

"The day's comin' when you ain't gonna be able to cover the bitterness with sugar. You're just gonna have to swallow it down. Go wake your brother up. Johnny's gonna want to talk to him. Suppose he's at church now. Ronny needs to be at that courthouse when he gets out. I don't want him comin' out here."

"Johnny? You talkin' 'bout Sheriff Stearns?"

"The same," said Jeannie Tucker.

"Why you call him Johnny?" Li'l Roy asked.

"Habit, I guess. I grew up with Johnny Stearns, ya know," she answered.

"You did? You grew up with the fuzz?" asked Li'l Roy.

"Yep. So'd your dad, and don't call him that," she added.

"Y'all was friends? How come I never knew that?" Li'l Roy entertained visions of his mother and father as strange youngsters, palling around with Sheriff Stearns. He saw her there fixed in a place and time, just a girl, a girl who rolled the dice with a boy and wound up here.

"I didn't say nothin' about nobody bein' friends, now did I?" Jeannie Tucker corrected.

"No." Li'l Roy reflected. "I never really thought about you growin' up."

"You think I was always your mama?" she asked.

"Naw, not really, just never thought about it," confessed the boy.

"Go tell Ronny I said to get up."

"You goin' down there with him?" Li'l Roy asked.

"No, Li'l Roy. No, I'm not." She stubbed out her cigarette as if physically putting a period on the end of her answer.

"He's just gonna argue with you some more when he does get up, then."

"Yep," she confirmed. "Reckon he will."

"You want me to go with him?" Li'l Roy asked.

"You do what ya want, but first I want you to clean that mess outta the icebox. I told you that was gonna happen."

"Why's Stearns gonna want to talk to Ronny for?" Li'l Roy asked. "Ronny ain't killed nobody."

"He just is, Li'l Roy."

"Is Ronny in trouble?" the boy asked fearfully.

"Not if Johnny believes him."

"You believe him?" Lil Roy asked.

"Yeah. Yeah I do."

"You think Johnny—"

"Sheriff Stearns to you, kiddo." Jeannie corrected.

"You think Sheriff Stearns thinks Ronny might a been in on it?"

"Now, how am I supposed to know what Johnny Stearns is thinkin'?" she asked, and to cool the sting added, "No, Roy, I don't, but I'm sure he's gonna wanna talk to him."

Hesitantly, Li'l Roy asked his next question. "If Ronny knew Len was gonna kill Hickey, would Ronny be in trouble? Would that mean he was in on it?"

"I don't think Ronny knew what Len was gonna do. Hell, I don't even think Lenville knew what he was gonna do."

"What if he did?" Li'l Roy looked away from his mother, out the window.

"Then it was premeditated. You better not be tellin' me—"

"I ain't tellin' nothin, Mama, I'm just askin'."

"Go wake up your brother."

Li'l Roy stood. He had himself a look out the window as he did so. Miss Jessie and the twins were at it again. "Miss Jessie's out there whippin' the hell outta Toby and Travis." He laughed slightly and shook his head. "Them young'ns."

"You're one to talk about them young'ns," his mother replied sharply. Jeannie Tucker watched her youngest son as he stepped from behind the table. She suddenly regretted her spiteful comment. "You remember she used to hide you when you got in trouble? Her and Netta."

"I remember," Li'l Roy smiled.

"Remember what she'd say?"

"She'd say, *'Don't whip him, Miss Jeannie. He just a baby.'*"

"She'd say you's too pretty to be whippin' on." She was suddenly struck by her son's beauty, his way, his laugh. "Come here," she motioned.

"What?"

"Just come here."

The boy stepped toward his mother and leaned in. She pulled him to her and kissed his cheek.

"What was 'at for?" he asked.

"You're mine," she said, "I'll kiss ya when I want to. Now, go and get your brother."

Li'l Roy left his mother with her thoughts there at the kitchen window.

She had long been an early riser, though this had not been so since Freeman's appearance, and that was exactly how she had come to view Freeman's presence in her life, as an *appearance*, like a sudden and mysterious mark in the sky, or a new song on an old radio. She now slept in on Sunday mornings, and it was nice to sleep in on a Sunday morning, to lie there beneath the blowing and the whirring of the box fan, holding off the world and the worry with a restful but fleeting contentedness.

Many mornings, Jeannie Tucker sat and watched Miss Jessie and her grandsons. She considered the odd little family, the fatherless boys who despite their African features, bore a striking and damning resemblance to her youngest and to Johnny Stearns. She had spent much time considering their runaway mother, out in California last she heard, and old Miss Jessie getting older by the minute. She wondered if Miss Jessie had what it took to raise boys alone. She wished her luck as she drank from her coffee cup and watched the trio board the Sunday school bus.

Li'l Roy stood down the hallway. It was not beyond him to appreciate and recognize poignancy. At fifteen, he possessed those typical flashes of maturity that are not uncommon in adolescents. That is to say, he possessed the presence of mind to appreciate the juxtaposition of his sleeping brother against the horrendous act his brother had witnessed only hours before. He took notice of his sleeping brother's button nose, a trait Ronny shared with Lenville which gave them both a boyish and innocent aspect. Their hair was also darker. They had their father's size and were all around bigger boys than he. Their lashes were longer. Li'l Roy was mature enough to recognize the inherent sadness into which he was to wake his brother. He was not mature enough to resist the temptation of breaking his balls.

Walking on the tips of his toes, he crept slowly across the room. When he reached his sleeping brother, he leaned in and called to him, "Ho-ly shit!"

Ronny bolted upright, eyes suddenly wide.

"The house is on fire, Ronny! The sumbitchin' house is on fire! Get up! Get up!"

Ronny sprung from the bed. Li'l Roy jumped around maniacally, "Move your ass, Ronny! We're all gonna die!" Ronny Tucker was wild-eyed. "Get those stroke books from under your mattress!"

Ronny tossed the mattress, and before he could grab the pornographic magazines, his little brother's laughter caught his ear.

"I'm just messin' with ya. Man, you shoulda seen the look on your face." Li'l Roy cackled with delight. "Mom wants ya to get down to the courthouse before the fuzz comes out here lookin' for ya."

"Damn you."

"Couldn't help it, man. Ya looked so damned peaceful I just had to."

Ronny blinked his sleep swollen eyes. "Shitass." he said and wiped his face. "You think it's a good time to be playin' around like that?"

Li'l Roy had never seen a time when Ronny Tucker didn't think it was a good time to be playin' around. The weight of that thought broke him a little. "Sorry, Ronny," Li'l Roy offered.

"'S'allright." Ronny offered his hand to his little brother and to his surprise, the gullible kid took it. Ronny pulled Li'l Roy to him and quickly put the smaller boy in a headlock. "This is gonna hurt you more than it hurts me, young'n," Ronny laughed and quickly ground his knuckles across the boy's scalp.

"Ah, aah, ow, oww!" cried Li'l Roy, unable to free himself.

"What in the world?" Jeannie Marie stood in the doorway.

In the days that followed, Jeannie Tucker imagined the rumors spreading like kudzu, covering everything.

The whispers would be back. The ones that were so loud after her husband shot and killed Sheriff Bill. The ones that came after Li'l Roy had been taken in for setting the elementary school on fire. She knew they would be, the ones that she could hear and the ones that she could not. She would hear them from the kitchen table. She would hear them in the silence and above the radio. She would hear them on her walk to work. She would hear them at work, above the screaming saws and the pounding hammers. She would hear them in the night as she walked back home. She would hear them sober and she would hear them with a few drinks in her. She would hear them in her sleep, in whatever dreams she had left to dream.

"That bunch is just no good."

"They never will be."

Part Two:
In the Wash

Chapter 13

At Pudgy's Tavern, Freeman, Marty and Earl sat at the bar. Freeman entertained. "I got another'n for ya. A hotdog walks into a bar, orders a beer and the bartender says, 'Hey you, we don't serve *food* here.'"

"A regular Redd Foxx we got here," Slakey said from behind the bar. The men laughed. He placed the mug he'd been drying back on the rack.

"Red what?" asked Freeman genuinely.

"You mean you never—" Slakey started to ask.

They turned their heads in unison when the door opened.

On the floor of Pudgy's Tavern, a stain lay dark and stubborn, refusing to be removed, forgotten or ignored. It had settled itself deep into the grain and would now forever be a part of the wood. Sheriff Stearns cut a wide berth around the stain, very aware of the quiet and the sound of his heavy boots on the wooden floor as he did so. He nodded to Freeman, Marty and Earl as he approached the bar. The trio nodded in return. To his left, around the corner of the bar, sat two men in military uniforms. Stearns nodded a hello to them and turned his attention back to Marty, Earl and Freeman. Stearns singled out Freeman as he was the closest of the three.

"Quiet in here this time of day, huh, Freeman?"

"Yup. It is now." Freeman nodded in agreement.

Stearns nodded at Earl and then at Marty. "Marty, how's your dad?"

"Strong as Flander's mare one day, weak as water the next," said Marty.

"Tell him I said hey."

"Will do, Sheriff."

"You doin' all right, Freeman?" Stearns removed his hat and placed it on the bar, nodding a hello to Slakey as he did so.

"No complaints here, Constable," Freeman answered.

"Still holdin' it down over at the pallet mill for Ol' Ed?" Stearns seated himself on a stool.

"I reckon." Freeman nodded. "Ol' Ed went and made me the pilot."

"How's that?" asked Stearns.

"After they cut the wood, I pile it." The trio of barflies enjoyed a laugh at the sheriff's expense.

"That's good, Freeman." Sheriff Stearns shook off the joke. "That's good. Ol' Ed's a good man."

"Yeah, he is. I laid out on him a day or two there. Toothache." Freeman unnecessarily explained. "Gonna make it today, though." He hooked a crooked finger into the corner of his mouth, turned to the Sheriff and mumbled, "Bad tooth. son of a bitch'll be the death of me." He released the hold on his mouth and shook his head. "Really started givin' me fits about a week or so ago. I was eatin' some a these ol' stale peanuts Slakey keeps out here on the bar and—"

"Coffee, Johnny?" Rudy Slakey asked Stearns from behind the bar.

"Hey, Slakey. Coffee sounds great," Stearns answered, turned and continued with Freeman, "Toothache'll stop a man dead on the tracks. Best to just get it pulled outta there."

"Yeah. That's what I'm plannin'. The way I got it figured, alls I gotta do is—"

"Go see Richard French. He does all my dental work."

"Ain't got no dental work money, Constable. Hell, you know how them guys do. He'll get to pokin' around in there and start tellin' me what all I need done in there and how much—"

"French does a good job." Stearns shifted the talk back to what he wanted to know. "Who's Ed got workin' out there with ya now, Freeman?"

Ever leery of the law, Freeman shot a hidden glance to Marty and Earl and then hedged his answer like an old pro. "Oh, I don't know. They's a few of us workin' out there now. Says he's finally got him a full crew. Put us on shifts."

"Jeannie Tucker still out there?"

"Not sure." Freeman lied. "Might ask Ol' Ed. Or might even ask Jeannie Tucker. Now, there's a thought." Marty and Earl shifted uncomfortably on their stools.

Stearns grinned, looked to Slakey and the two uniformed recruiters and made a gesture with his head that could only be interpreted as *"This guy."*

Rudy Slakey placed the coffee cup on the bar in front of Stearns. He was bored with the exchange between the two men and though he bore no ill will toward Johnny Stearns, he was anxious to get the lawman out of his bar. He nodded toward the dark stain on the floor and said to Stearns, "I get the feelin' you ain't here 'cause of the quality of my coffee, Johnny."

"No, Slake. You're right about that." Stearns took a moment and sipped from the coffee cup. "Just need to follow up with ya. See if you've remembered anything you mighta forgot. Just followin' up. Mainly, we're still lookin' for that pistol."

"You thinkin' I'm a holdin' somethin' back from ya, Johnny?"

"Not at all. Not at all. It's just good to follow up with folks once the smoke and the adrenaline and all have gone down. Freeman, any of you fellas in here the other night?" Stearns removed a small notebook from his uniform shirt pocket.

Marty and Earl shook their heads. Freeman said, "Nah. But, I'm gonna move on and let you fellas talk about it."

"Don't run off on account of me. You don't have to go, Freeman." Stearns assured him. "This isn't exactly confidential."

"Yeah, Constable, but I might just overhear somethin' I shouldn't be hearin', and well," Freeman paused, "Hell, I talk too damned much. Just as soon not know nothin' if it's all right with you. That way I can't tell it. Gotta get to work. It's bad stuff anyways. You fellas enjoy your afternoon." Freeman tipped an invisible hat. "Slakey, I'll see ya later."

"Later, Freeman. Don't forget to bring money next time." Slakey turned to Stearns as Freeman made his leave. "He's right, though."

"Yeah, it's pretty bad stuff." Stearns agreed.

"Naw, I mean the part about him talkin' too damned much." Slakey corrected Stearns and Marty and Earl laughed with him.

"How much he had to drink and him goin' to work?" Stearns asked in amusement.

"Two beers and a shot. Hell, it ain't like he's on the saws or any of the machinery over there. Reckon Ol' Ed just lets him sweep up the sawdust and stack the scrap. Like he said, he's the *pilot*."

With Freeman now gone, Marty was closest to the lawman and at the height of discomfort. He signaled to Earl with a nod toward a booth and the two men rose from their stools. "We're gonna go plant our asses right over there. Let you fellas talk, see." Marty said to Slakey.

Slakey shot a glance toward the two recruiters as if worried they might follow suit.

Someone started up the jukebox and Buck Owens now asked the weighty question, "*Who's gonna mow your grass*?" Stearns was pleased to have the background noise as he continued his talk with Rudy Slakey.

Slakey said, "Like I told ya the other night, it was the most cold blooded thing I ever saw. I hollered at him. We could all see he was really gonna do it, Johnny. I told him, I says, as calmly as I could, 'Now, Lenville Tucker, you just think about what you're about to do.' I says, 'Len, you don't really wanna do this.' That's what I said and anyone in here'll tell ya I did."

"Nobody's blamin' you, Slakey. 'Cept maybe for you."

Slakey leaned his thin frame slightly in and across the bar, took a suspicious look around at his few customers and lowered his voice, "I coulda shot him myself, Johnny. Before he shot Hickey. I got my own .38 here behind the bar, but the truth is," Slakey leaned in as to be beyond earshot of the two uniformed men, "I was scared shitless to draw on Lenville Tucker and him armed, locked and loaded like that."

Stearns shifted his weight in the stool. "Don't beat yourself up, Rudy. Better ya didn't draw on him. Ever point a gun at a man?" Stearns dismissively drank from the coffee cup.

"No. No, I ain't," admitted Slakey.

"He'd a shot you down dead if he'd thought you to be a real threat. That's the way it would've happened, Slakey. He'd have shot you and then still shot Hickey. No doubt in my mind at all."

Rudy Slakey straightened his back and was obviously mulling over the number of possible scenarios that accompanied what might have happened had he intervened. He noticed Stearns' cup was empty. "More coffee?"

"Sure," Stearns answered. "Looks like I might have a long day ahead of me. Think I'm gonna need it."

Slakey brought the pot over and filled Stearns' cup. "That Hickey boy was pleadin' for his life, Johnny. You can write that down in your little notebook." Slakey, thought for a minute, halting the pour. He leaned in again. "But don't write that shit about how I was too scared to draw on him."

Stearns nodded a reassuring smile. "Gotcha." He winked. He wrote neither.

Slakey went on, "He had him beat, Johnny. Hold on, you fellas doin' all right over there?" The two recruiters nodded in unison. Slakey turned back to Stearns. "Now, I get it that the Hickey boy was the one who pulled the gun, but after Lenville got it from him and pistol whipped the shit out of him, he shoulda just let it be. It was over. Hold on a second." Marty and Earl had seen their opening and were headed towards the door. "Y'all just go on. That's right. I got your tabs, boys. They'll be right here waitin' for ya." He turned his attention back to the sheriff. "Sonsabitches."

"Whattayagonnado?" Stearns laughed and lit a cigarette. "As for Lenville, I'm not sayin' Lenville had to kill that boy, but it really ain't that easy, Slakey." Stearns blew smoke and decided to go with the short version. "See, Lenville says if he'd let Hickey get outta here after beatin' him like that, then there he'd be worryin' about when Hickey was comin' back at him. He's got Ronny, Li'l Roy and his mama up there and says he couldn't be worryin' about what might be comin'. Again, I ain't excusin' it—"

"Yeah, I guess a man can see that. That Hickey clan ain't soft, though. Seems like he'd be worried about 'em comin' after Ronny and Li'l Roy even more so."

"Yeah, we talked about that. Said once it had gotten so far, he really felt like he had no choice. I told him I'd keep an eye on the place, but I really ain't worried."

"Why's 'at?" Slakey asked.

"Would you go messin' with Big Roy Tucker's people?"

Slakey shrugged at this.

"That's right," offered Stearns, "you fit in so well around here that I keep forgettin' you ain't from here." At this, Rudy Slakey privately beamed. "The answer is no, though. You wouldn't if you was from here."

"Big Roy Tucker's in Brushy, though, right?"

"Still got reach and folks know that. The Hickeys do for sure."

Once outside, Marty and Earl headed silently towards Mac's Package.

Earl spoke. "I told ya I wasn't ready to leave," he said, his expression a perpetual question regarding just exactly what it was he should do next.

"Me neither."

"We're goin' back, right?" Earl asked hopefully.

"Yeah, see, just give Johnny a minute to ask his questions and finish his business. Might go see if Mac'll front us a pint."

"Now, that's a plan, Marty. Now, that's a good plan. You always was good at plans."

"Got that from my old man, see. He was always plannin' somethin'."

"Hey, if Mac says our credit's run thin, tell him it's for your old man like you did before."

"Naw, I still give myself hell for that," Marty confessed. "Wasn't right. Shouldn't a done it."

"Hell, Marty, I weren't tryin' to make ya feel bad and all. We can just wait that damned sheriff out behind Mac's or somethin'."

"Johnny Stearns is all right, but it sure was like he was stinkin' up the place in that uniform."

"Ol' Freeman didn't care much for Johnny's questions, did he?"

"Kinda picked up on that myself. That's on account a me bein' what they call perceptive like that."

"Well, I picked up on it first, so I must be pretty perspective myself. Like how I really picked up on how Freeman didn't like Johnny askin' 'bout Jeannie Marie.

Made me nervous as all hell. That's on account a Freeman and Jeannie bein' a little sweet on each other and all."

"They are that, ain't they? Ya think Freeman knows the whole story?"

"What whole story is that, Marty?"

"You bein so perspective and all, why don't you tell me what whole story?"

"About Johnny shootin' Big Roy Tucker?"

"Damn, Earl, now that's perspective, see."

Behind the bar, Slakey poured himself his scheduled shot of sour mash and tossed it back. He took his time then, standing silently and waiting for the mash to infect him before speaking. "Johnny, I seen some shit go down in the bar I managed in Atlanta, brutal fights, and I seen a few get cut and stabbed and all, but I ain't never seen nobody get shot like that. You ever see anybody get shot like that?" He poured himself another before realizing he had done so.

"Not like that," answered the sheriff. "I've seen men get shot." He looked presumably at Slakey.

"Oh, oh yeah. Sorry, Johnny. I wasn't thinkin'," Slakey said having heard the story of how Stearns had put three bullets into Big Roy Tucker. He had heard it countless times in the three months since he had bought Pudgy's Tavern. It was the kind of story that lingered and hung around like smoke in a dimly lit room. Slakey studied the extra shot he had poured and offered it to Stearns. Stearns shook his head and in the spirit of waste not want not, Slakey forewent self prescribed protocol and tossed back the second shot. "Yeah, didn't mean to drag that up."

"It's all right." Stearns waved him off. "I haven't seen a man get shot like that. Not in the face and not beggin' and pleadin' for his life. Not murdered like that, in cold blood." Stearns craned his neck around and then turned completely in his stool and looked at the bloodstained floor. "Almost did." He shook his head as if he might actually be able to shake the image from it.

"How's that, Johnny?"

"Nothin'. Never mind."

"Ya gotta do a better job of cleanin' that up, Slakey."

"Shit, Johnny, it won't come out."

"You don't want any of them Hickeys comin in here and seein' that. Put a rug over it or something."

"Some drunk son of a bitch'll trip over it."

"Get a rug, Slakey."

"Hell," Slakey sighed in defeat. "Guess I should. Damn, it was somethin', Johnny," Slakey went on.

"All right, Slake, after Lenville shot him, what'd he do then?" Stearns went back to his notepad.

"Well," Slakey began,"just like I told ya Saturday. He kinda just stood there," Slakey motioned again toward the dark stain, "over Hickey's dead body like he was studyin' on it or somethin', or makin' sure he'd killed him and then he said, 'Now that's it, boys,' or somethin' like that and then he looks at me and says, 'Go on and call it in,' and him and Ronny walked out just as cool as a couple of cucumbers."

"Just him and Ronny? Little Roy wasn't here?"

"Not that night," said Slakey.

"I'm not lookin' to bust ya for serving minors, Slakey. I just need the whole truth."

"He wasn't here, Johnny. Swear it. If he was here, I'd tell ya, but he wasn't here."

"And he had that .38 in his hand when he went out that door?"

"I can't say one hundred per cent, Johnny, but I can say ninety-nine that he did."

"Okay. Anybody leave right after?"

"Nobody moved. Nobody was goin' anywhere. A few assholes even tried to order drinks after that. Like we were all just gonna stand around the dead kid and—"

"Folks did eventually leave, though, Slakey. Who was the first to leave once the smoke cleared?"

"Shit, I couldn't tell ya, Johnny. Seems like nobody left for a long while. Everybody hung around waitin' for you guys. You know how folks are. Everybody wanted to see it through, tell their side of it, see how it was all gonna play out. "

"And what did you do? After Len and Ronny left?"

"Hell, I called it in. I've done told ya this. I called you people."

"And you don't remember anybody leavin' before we showed up?"

"I don't, Johnny. Lenville give ya a hard time when you boys caught him?"

"Catch him? Hell, we didn't catch him." Stearns answered. "He left here, sent Ronny home, says he tossed that .38 up towards the tracks and went and turned himself in. Confessed to it all. Told it all pretty much like you did."

"And you ain't found the gun?" Slakey asked.

"No, we haven't."

"Think he's lyin'?" asked Slakey. "Ya think Ronny's got that gun? You do, don't ya?"

"No. No, I don't." Stearns sipped his coffee. "Not really. Hell, I don't know, but we sure can't find the damned thing."

A hot breeze blew and the midsummer sun beat mercilessly down. Stearns sat with his sunglasses on, sweating and smoking behind the wheel of the police cruiser in the gravel parking lot of Pudgy's Tavern. He watched the heat rise in a blur from the pavement of the road. The small notebook sat opened on his knee. He tapped it with his pen while Buck's words flowed through his head, *"And who's gonna be your puppy dog when I'm a thing of the past? Hey, who's gonna mow your grass?"* On the page he had written the name *Little Roy* and the two words *not present*. Little Roy Tucker—named after Big Roy Tucker who, it would now seem, was going to get to spend the rest of his life in Brushy Mountain Correctional with his oldest son, Lenville Tucker.

In the heat, he cursed Jeannie Tucker for allowing Big Roy to give the boy his name.

His stare appeared vacant as he gazed at the mountains surrounding the valley, but his thoughts were on Big Roy Tucker as he did so. Johnny Stearns did not know that the mountains at which he stared were formed some unfathomable number of years ago when two great land masses met each other. He did not know that those land masses butted each other for eons, each attempting to occupy the same space as the other, each changing the shape and description of the other.

Not even in the presence of God and the church was Johnny Stearns' ashamed of his hatred for Big Roy Tucker. Hatred, in its deepest and most true form, does not suddenly appear like some newly discovered crack in a wall. True and lasting hate comes gradually, like the darkness of evening. True hate begins with a seed, perhaps dropped somewhere unknowingly along the wayside. With the correct ratio of sunlight to rain, it begins to grow. Once it has taken root, it is nurtured and then conscientously pruned until it begins to bear fruit. If Johnny Stearns were to attempt to remember just when and where that seed had been dropped, it would prove to be a difficult task as there had been many opportunities throughout his life for such seeds to be planted.

Big Roy Tucker was Big Roy Tucker long before there was the symmetry of a "Little Roy" Tucker. It was not a title that referred at all to obesity. Big Roy was never *fat*. He was simply large. He always had been. In elementary school, Big Roy had been taller than the tallest and broader than the broadest. He had bullied Stearns back in school, but Stearns did not feel particularly special in this regard. Big Roy had picked on every kid and sometimes even the teacher. To Johnny Stearns' reckoning, Big Roy had early on fallen into the easy trap of believing size equaled power.

If the seed had been planted back in elementary school, it would not bear fruit until years later, when Big Roy Tucker and Jeannie Marie McRicken first began to go steady. That seed would then be watered by the rumor that Jeannie Marie had become pregnant and was therefore set to marry Big Roy.

Marty and Earl stepped into the gravel lot, having concluded their business at Mac's package. Johnny Stearns watched them for a moment as they walked and talked. He blew the cruiser's horn and called, "Fellas! Hey, fellas, come here for a second."

The two approached the police car visibly apprehensive.

"Somethin' wrong?" asked Marty.

"Well, somethin's not right. Let's put it that way." Stearns slowly removed his sunglasses.

"What's not right, Sheriff?" asked Earl. "Now, we ain't done nothin'."

"Not a thing, see," added Marty, slightly shaking his head.

"No. No, I'm sure ya haven't. You two's good fellas. I was actually needin' your help."

"How's that, Sheriff? You needin' deputies? I always wanted to get myself deputized," Earl confessed.

"Nothin' so big, Earl," said Stearns.

"Aww," Earl replied, dropping his head in disappointment.

"But still, pretty important."

"What ya needin', Sheriff?" asked Marty.

"Well, my boys are bustin' their hind ends out here in this heat every day since Lenville Tucker—Well, they're lookin' for that pistol, fellas. The .38 Lenville shot the Hickey boy with. Lenville says he tossed it up toward the tracks," the sheriff pointed with his smooth chin, "but we ain't found it and we can't have a loaded .38 just layin' around waitin' for some young'n to pick it up. There'd be a reward in it if one a you fellas should happen to find it." Stearns raised his eyebrows and waited for a response.

"Yeah? What kind of a reward, Sheriff?" Earl's eyes grew narrow.

"Well, let's just talk about that. What sounds fair to you, Earl? Marty?"

Marty spoke before Earl could. "We'd just have to put some thought into that, see. Since you're askin' and all."

"Okay, fair enough. You boys do that, Marty. You boys do that. We'd sure like to recover that firearm."

The word itself, 'firearm,' made it all sound so much heavier than it had. A pistol was a pistol, tucked away in a drawer, and a .38 was a .38, just a number, just another caliber, but a firearm sounded like official police business. In the hours and days that followed, Marty and Earl would heretofore use the word firearm when discussing the potential reward.

"We'll keep our eyes out for that firearm, and we'll be thinkin' about that reward," Marty assured Sheriff Stearns.

"Spread that around if ya would," said Stearns, replacing his sunglasses.

Marty and Earl agreed to spread the word around, though they had no intention of actually doing so. They weren't idiots.

Stearns watched the two men as they walked away and entered Pudgy's Tavern. For a moment, he regretted bringing the two into it at all. He shook his head as the door of Pudgy's closed behind them and he smiled, asking himself how much harm they could do. His eyes turned toward the dirt road. He could go and ask Jeannie about the gun. He could do that. There was always the the chance that Ronny Tucker wasn't being honest.

He was curious about how she might be towards him after all of these years. He allowed his mind to take a treacherous walk then, a walk a part of him had long begged for, if only to see just what might remain between them. A walk back into the early nineteen fifties, to sniff around in forgotten, forbidden corners and doors that screeched forebodingly when he nudged them on their rusted hinges. Doors that were clearly marked "PRIVATE" and "DO NOT ENTER." The memories flowed then and spread like a stain.

Stearns slowly put the notebook back into his shirt pocket. He felt a slight discomfort as his stomach rolled and he noticed his hand was shaking. He blamed the second cup of coffee. The tires of the cruiser crunched and ground the gravel as he drove slowly across the parking lot. When he reached the pavement, he took a left and pointed the patrol car northeast.

Chapter 14

Jeannie Marie Tucker, formerly Jeannie Marie McRicken, sat at her kitchen table and scratched the paint from it while she stared out the kitchen window at nothing. Behind her was a long week of whispers and secret pointing at the pallet mill. Just beyond her periphery, all week long she imagined them all saying, "It was her boy, her oldest, who shot that boy in the face in cold blood while he begged for his life. It was her boy, her flesh and blood. She birthed that heartless monster. Boy's his daddy made over." The great weight was back on her. She had not felt it for such a long while and now she wondered if she had been foolish to ever think it had actually gone away, foolish and naive enough to think that in a place so small as Sonoraville, people would ever be permitted to forget anything. She could not outlive the legacy, the sins of her husband, no matter how hard she worked nor how much time passed. And now this, this horrible and bloody thing that Lenville had done, and with Ronny right there beside him.

She had wept over what Lenville had done. It would surprise many to know that she had wept the hardest for Darryl Hickey's mama.

She had not gone down to the jail see Lenville.

She would not.

She dragged from a cigarette and silently, she cursed her first born. She cursed his father in the penitentiary. She cursed herself for ever being drawn to the dangerous ones. She cursed herself for ever enjoying the juvenile excitement of being pulled between the sheriff and the outlaw. She wiped her eyes with the side of her hand, found some comfort in the fact that it was finally Friday and extinguished the cigarette in the ashtray that rested on the scarred kitchen table.

She rose from her chair and headed out the door.

Jeannie Tucker had not ridden in a vehicle since selling her husband's '52 GMC pickup. No matter the weather, it was her custom to walk. To put one foot in front of the other and repeat the process until she was where she needed to be. When the weather was dry, she enjoyed the walk. When the weather was wet, she donned an umbrella and trudged on. She walked to her job at the pallet mill, leaving home in the afternoon light shortly before two p.m. She walked home in the darkness. On Saturdays, payday, she walked to the pallet mill to pick up her paycheck, then to town, to the bank to cash her paycheck, to Cas Walker's to buy the few groceries and her cigarettes, and sometimes by Mac's Package for a cold beer to drink on the way home.

She did not lock the door behind her. Most of the time she didn't even close it. The boys were around. Somewhere.

Stearns sat, idle and contemplative behind the wheel. Since putting three bullets into Big Roy Tucker, putting him first into ICU and then into Brushy Correctional, Stearns had ascended from Deputy to Sheriff to small town legend. The truth of what exactly had transpired out on RR3, had long vanished, replaced by guesses, conjecture and outright lies. In spite of himself, he smiled.

Through the years, the three Tucker boys found their share of trouble, petty things mostly, but it was no surprise to Stearns that Lenville had come to find the trouble he had. The handful of times Jeannie came to the jail to collect one of her boys, he had avoided her. He had forced himself to. Avoiding her had not been so easy in the beginning, but to his surprise, it gradually became more and more so. Longings turned slowly to memories and memories turned slowly to ghosts. He had learned that the best way, perhaps the only way, to force the ghosts to move on, to cross over from the present to the past where they rightfully belonged, was to quietly ignore them, to starve them, to give them absolutely no attention nor sustenance. The easiest way he had found to do this was to shift his desires to other women.

He had done just so, and as life does, it had seemingly gone on.

With the windows down, driving along the the dirt road, he wondered how she might look now. He had seen her, had watched her even on rare moments, from clandestine distances, but he had not faced her. He afforded himself a glance into the cruiser's rearview mirror. His sandy hair had thinned and was as much gray as blonde around the edges. His face had rounded and his eyes had darkened. Though he was ordinarily not a man given to vanity, he allowed himself the shortcoming and considered all of this on his approach.

Reaching the house, he mentally marked the spot on the road where Sheriff Bill had bled out and died. Jeannie Tucker stood in the road in front of her house, talking to Red. Stearns pulled into the bare patch that had once served as driveway. Seeing her, he broke suddenly from the past and he caught himself smiling a strange and familiar smile. Jeannie Tucker did not smile in return. Immediately, he cursed himself for doing so. He caught a twinge of undeniable jealousy toward Red and he cursed himself again.

He stepped from the vehicle and nodded to the two.

"Afternoon, Sheriff," the mailman nodded. "Any news on who busted up my Jeep?"

"Nothin' yet, Red. Sorry."

"I better get movin'," said Red. "I'll see ya later, Jeannie. Sheriff."

"Be careful, Red," said Jeannie as Red headed up the dirt road leaving the two alone.

Concerning happiness or joy, Stearns had always found Jeannie Marie hard to read, as if she believed happiness to be a thing so fragile that it would fall to ash or dust at the mere mention of its own name.

"Jeannie, how've you been?"

"Really?" she asked. "How've I been?"

He studied her, found her still beautiful with the same sparkling emerald eyes and her hair still full and thick, red and curly. Her breasts were still high and youthful. Not one thing about her had changed. Not one *goddamned* thing.

"Sorry, Jeannie, hell—"

"Thought I might be seein' you. Wondered if you were gonna get around to comin' out here after that, all that. But we're gonna have to do this later, Johnny. I gotta get to work."

That was her way—to give him a little something and then snatch it away. "Then jump in. I'll give ya a lift. We can talk on the way."

"Last thing I need. Bad enough ya gotta pull up here in the middle of the day. Just as soon not show up to work gettin' out of a police car, Johnny. Not after—"

"Since when did you start givin' a fiddler's fart what anyone thought?"

Her eyes went distant, wounded. She turned from him and walked on wordlessly up the dirt road.

He knew his mistake and was ashamed of himself. He searched frantically for something better, for something with which to put them both back a few steps and to begin the interaction over. "It's official business, Jeannie." He called to her as she walked on and cursed himself again for his adolescent fumbling.

"My ass."

Stearns grinned a fond grin. "Hey, I'm serious, Jeannie." He stood in her driveway, watching her as she walked away. "Jeannie. Jeannie, wait. I really am serious." He stepped after her.

She stopped and turned to him. "I'm serious, too, Johnny. I gotta get to work." She turned toward the road again, ignoring him and doing her best to altogether belittle his presence and presumed authority.

"Ten minutes. All I need is ten minutes." He sounded to himself as though he were pleading with her. "Then we're done"

She stopped then and turned, studied him for a moment and said, "Doubt it, but I'd give'em to ya if I had'em, Johnny, but I really don't. I gotta go. You got Len, what do you need to talk to me for?"

"After work then. I'll pick you up." He ignored her question and hoped he sounded authoritative.

"And then this is over?"

"It is." He agreed, though he knew it would never be over. They had imprinted themselves into each other's lives, no matter the years.

"I'm supposed to be off at ten. Sometimes it's a little later."

"I'll wait."

She was sure he would. She was sure he had been waiting for years. Stearns passed her in the patrol car. Ahead, Red had stopped and she knew he was stalling, looking for a reason to wait and see if she was going to be walking up the road. She quickened her pace.

Sawdust smelled, to her, like good men. It smelled like work, noble and true. It smelled like building something rather than tearing something down. it smelled like someone believed that the world was going to hold itself together for a while yet. It smelled warm and honest, forgiving and new. It smelled reliable and loyal, humble, aged and wise. Sawdust smelled, to her, like her father.

The electric saws screamed their high pitched banshee chorus. The men hammered and stapled in a steady tempo of well organized, primitive rhythm, occasionally calling out to each other orders and assurances, amiable insults and wisecrackery. Work was happening, the kind of work that presented useful, practical product and sent it out into the busy world beyond. The finished pallets were stacked and banded and moved to the railyard where they would be sent and scattered across the country and possibly the planet. Jeannie Tucker was enthralled by this idea that a piece of wood she had put her hand on there in Sonoraville might eventually, somehow find its way to some foreign world. Occasionally, she would write her initials in some odd corner of a pallet and tag it with, "Sonoraville Tn" and the date, entertaining notions that others along the way might do the same and that by the time the nails and staples were finally failing or the wooden slats were too broken to mend, the pallet would be as marked as the tattooed ticket taker at the Whelan County fair.

Outside the loading bay and away from the noise, Freeman said to Jeannie Tucker, "At a certain local waterin' hole this afternoon, a certain representative of the local constabulary was making inquiries concerning your livelihood."

"Johnny Stearns," she said.

"Just thought ya should know. Looks like ya know." Freeman winked and headed back inside to return to the task of sweeping. "Oh," he called to her, "Quiet Tom says the checks are in the office. Says if ya ask, Ed's boy'll give it to ya tonight. That way ya don't gotta come in tomorrow for it."

"Thanks," she called to him and asked, "You get yours?"

"Naw," Freeman waved the idea away. "Figure it'll give me somethin' to do tomorrow."

"You comin' by the house?"

"Wasn't sure if you were in any mood for company, but if you're askin, then yeah, yeah. Sure will. Want me to pick up a bottle of Cold Duck? Gotta go by there anyway." He winked.

"Or two," she laughed nervously. "Or just something stronger."

Second shift was done and cleaned up by ten o'clock. She slid her timecard into the slot and the stamp came down heavily and with authority. She hung around for an extra half hour, finding one meaningless task after the other to keep herself busy. If Johnny Stearns was out there, she wanted him to wait.

Ol' Ed's boy came down the metal staircase that led to his office.

"Tucker? Everything okay?"

She hated being called that, but most of the men in the shop referred to her likewise. "Yeah, just tidying up," she answered.

"Mind your overtime," he said with a wink.

"I'm off the clock."

"Good, then, let's go home," he said. "Weekend's a waitin'."

From the driver's side of the cruiser, Stearns watched as the shift filed out. He caught curious glances and snippets of conversations. He nodded his hello as they walked by his window. "Evenin', Sheriff, " they said and nodded in return. They loaded themselves into pickup trucks and cars, some foregoing their Friday night ritual of opening coolered beers in the parking lot. Some walked. Some congregated and discussed weekend plans. Jeannie Tucker was not to be found. She was prolonging their appointment. He knew this and used this knowledge to pad his patience. He also knew if he commented to her about making him wait so long she would use the same excuse she had used earlier about not wanting to be seen in a police car. He knew this was bullshit. He had never known Jeannie Marie to give a tinker's damn about what other's thought. It was one of her most attractive and infuriating personality traits.

With a slight grimace, he drank from the bottle of magnesia and chased the chalky, gritty swallow with a swallow from a soda can. He lit a cigarette and watched as the lights in the pallet mill were systematically turned off and darkness swallowed the parking lot.

From the darkness, Jeannie's unmistakable silhouette emerged from the front door and approached the patrol car. He watched her approach and heard her say her final goodnights and weekend well wishes to her lingering coworkers. She opened the passenger's side door and entered the vehicle wordlessly.

"Evenin', Jeannie."

"Johnny." She offered in return and retrieved a cigarette. "Some of the boys like to end Friday night shift with a few beers in the parking lot. Forgot about that. You ran 'em off."

Stearns sighed in the dark. "How was work?'

She raised the lighter to her cigarette and then lowered it. "Really?" She laughed. "Like an old married couple?" She raised the lighter again and split the darkness with the orange blaze. The end of the cigarette glowed and brightened as she inhaled. It was dark again inside the cruiser and she exhaled a cloud of smoke, never looking at Stearns. She said, "Work was fine, dear."

"Geez, Jeannie Marie," Stearns sighed again and asked, "Stop workin' on me. Don't you ever get tired?"

"Sure, I do. I get damned tired. How's Phyllis?" She asked taking another drag. "Does she get tired?"

"Phyllis is good, Jeannie."

"I'm just sure she is. Still wearin' that beehive? She still workin' at the hospital? And Dickie?"

Stearns felt a sting and ignored it. "Dickie's fine, too. Be headed to the academy soon."

"Well, good for him. Please, do be sure and tell'em I was askin' about 'em. You takin' me home or what?"

Stearns started the vehicle and drove silently down the dirt road toward Jeannie's. In the driveway, he killed the headlights and the engine. He waited, curious if she would speak and what she might say. She said nothing.

"Jeannie Marie, did Lenville tell you what started this feud between him and Darryl Hickey?" Stearns asked her there in the darkness of the front seat of the patrol car as they sat in her driveway.

"So this really is official business?" She rolled down the window and tossed the cigarette into the yard. "Them boys don't talk to me, Johnny. Not about real stuff. I quit tryin' a long time ago."

"Lenville says word got back to him that Darryl Hickey said the only reason Big Roy had waited so long to name one of the boys after him was because Little Roy was the only one he was sure was his."

95

"Shit," she said, lighting a fresh cigarette and sighing a blue plume of smoke. "This damned town. Big Roy didn't even name him, Johnny. I named him."

"I always thought as much," he said.

"Don't start with me, Johnny. You got Big Roy. Just like you always wanted. You got him ten years ago, but you still can't just let him be got."

"I don't know what the hell that's supposed to mean, but Big Roy's damned lucky he got what he got. What was I supposed to do, Jeannie?"

"Big Roy was crazy. *Is* crazy. Anyway, worked out pretty damned good for you though, didn't it? You got to be the hero and the new sheriff. Everything worked out just perfectly for Johnny Stearns."

"Goddammit, Jeannie Marie. What was I supposed to do? The road Big Roy was on, he knew—hell, Jeannie Marie, you knew—that was where and how it was bound to end. What was I supposed to do? Answer me. He killed Sheriff Bill. The son of a bitch shot me."

With a blazing gaze, she turned to him and unleashed years of pent up fury. "Y'all didn't have to make us sound like a bunch of animals out here, Johnny! You think I wouldn't read the papers, Johnny? Shit, did you forget we had to live in this town? And maybe, just maybe, you're supposed to be honest about it all. I saw you. You were going to shoot him when he was layin' there. You were going to murder him. I saw you. And you walk around here like it didn't just tickle you shitless to shoot Big Roy when we all—"

"You think I'm tickled shitless by all that? Damn you, Jeannie Marie. A good man died."

She sat quietly for a moment. "I don't think he ever meant to kill Bill Cooper. He was just shooting. And I know this won't make a lot of sense, but I think he'd rather say he shot Sheriff Bill on purpose rather than say he didn't mean to. I saw his face. I saw how he looked when he realized he'd shot Bill Cooper."

"Well, he sure as hell meant to kill me, Jeannie."

"That he did. But you're not Bill Cooper. You're Johnny Stearns."

"What the hell? You can't be defending him—"

She gave it up then, "I know, Johnny. I know. I just wish it hadn't been you that shot Big Roy. I hate that he killed Bill Cooper. I hate that he shot you. Sheriff Bill was such a good man. I wish none of it happened at all. I wish I wasn't the woman married to the man who killed Bill Cooper. You can't imagine what that's like. Damn, I wish y'all hadn't gone on so much about what bad people we were. I wish you weren't the man who shot my husband. It's all so damned— I wish if you ever loved me like you said you did you hadn't been so chickenshit that you waited until me and Big Roy got together before you said something. Damn you, Johnny."

"Ain't none of this on me, Jeannie Marie, and If wishes were horses—"

"Yeah, beggars would ride. And yeah, Johnny, some of it, might be some little part of it, but some of it is on you. Hell, I gotta go."

"Can we talk tomorrow?" he asked.

"Tomorrow's Saturday. I got my tradin' to do tomorrow."

"I can take you," Stearns offered.

"You just can't help your damned self, can you? Thanks, but no thanks."

"Tomorrow night, then?"

"I'm busy, Johnny." She opened the door.

"With Freeman?"

"With none of your business."

"Wait, Jeannie, wait. I do have a question. Official business."

"Then ask it so's I can go."

"I will."

"Then do it."

"Okay, then."

"Johnny— "

"All right, all right. Lenville says he tossed the .38 he shot Darryl Hickey with up onto the tracks. We can't find it."

"Doesn't surprise me."

"Jeannie Marie, dammit. Anyway, there's a chance Ronny might have it. You haven't seen it have you?"

"If I do he'll eat it," she answered and Johnny Stearns did not doubt the truth in her words.

"Just let me know. We have to keep looking for it 'til we find it. Can't have one of the kids out here findin' a loaded .38 Special."

"I'm guessin' you asked Ronny if he had it."

"Yeah, I did," answered Stearns. "He says he doesn't have it."

"Then he doesn't have it."

The heavy door rocked the cruiser when she swung it shut and Stearns sat watching her make her way through the yard and into the house. A light came on in the kitchen window, he waited in the darkness to see her in the light.

Stearns turned the key and the engine of the cruiser roared to life. He smiled for her, felt somehow gratified for her that after a decade, she was finally granted a moment to say all of those hurtful things he was sure she had been practicing these many years. He shifted the cruiser, rolled out of the driveway and onto the dirt road.

Inside, Li'l Roy slept on the couch as he often did. She stepped quietly to the television and turned it off. Down the hall, she peeked into the boy's room. Ronny snored in his bed. Her heart ached for Lenville and she quietly cursed him for what he had done.

At the kitchen table, she poured herself a drink. She lit a Winston and wondered just who the hell Johnny Stearns thought she was. Did he think she was still the battered woman? Did he think she was still confused about the difference between love and appreciation? Did he still think she associated his arrival, his very face with her safety and the safety of her children? She had news for him. She would make sure he got that news the next time she saw him.

He still wanted her, though. That was obvious. And as much as she might curse him, it felt good to be wanted.

Chapter 15

L uck or Providence had hung a face on Earl Rainwater that was somehow less than the sum of its parts. That is to say, by all descriptive accounts, Earl should have been a handsome man. He was tall. Nearing sixty years of age, his hair remained dark, even at the temples, and thick even at the crown. Some had accused him of regularly dying it jet black, but it somehow preternaturally resisted graying. Like many folks of the area, Earl Rainwater claimed Cherokee blood. Unlike many folks of the area, and despite his pale blue eyes, there was no doubt that this was indeed the case with Earl. His skin was deeply tanned. His profile was stoic. His appearance noble. But, despite these attributes, no one ever confused Earl Rainwater for a handsome man.

Years of wheeling and dealing, picking and dickering, and trading this for that had made of Earl an accidental collector of curious dusty miscellany. His house was littered with, among other things, taxidermied carcasses, various truck parts, countless rods and reels, animal traps, lures, collectible liquor bottles, hub caps, National Geographic magazines, at least three complete, moldy and unperused sets of The Encyclopedia Brittanica, campaign buttons, highway signs, license plates, and only the heavens knew what all else.

He sat watching Dragnet, draining a can of beer and contemplating the reward Stearns had offered for the missing firearm. A reward would be a nice thing to get. He'd never gotten a reward for anything. Even nicer, though, might be the feeling that came with it. He'd never cracked a case before either. Unless, of course, it was a case of beer. It would be a downright dandy of a thing, a hell of a headline, "Earl Rainwater Cracks Case Of Missing Firearm." He might even get his picture in the paper. Why, it wouldn't be that much of a stretch to call him a hero. Some folks might even ask him to autograph the paper. He made a mental note to remind himself to make sure that he still knew how to write his signature. Hell, he hadn't signed anything in years.

For the first time in many years, Earl Rainwater got an idea. With a burst of inspiration encouraging a speed and determination seldom seen from Earl, he ransacked his house, pulling out every drawer and emptying every cabinet shelf, flinging objects into the air and occasionally, when he found what he was looking for, exclaiming to the stillness of his home, "Ah! Knew it!"

From beneath the kitchen sink, a hollow gong sounded when the metal of one long forgotten pot met the metal of another. This continued until Earl's voice rang out, "Ah! Knew you were here!"

From the cellar came the crash of mason jars sealed and filled with green beans, tomatoes and jellies. Earl's voice came up the stairs, "Ah! Knew it!"

From the high shelf of the cupboard, the clack of a mousetrap sounded. Earl howled in pain, and then exclaimed, "Ah! There ya are!"

When he was satisfied he had found them all, he sat on his sofa and arranged the found objects across the coffee table. On the television, Jack Webb was doing his thing. A whirring box fan blew cigar ash in an effort to quell the summer humidity. Earl sat beaming. A broad smile lit his face fueled by the notion that Marty Shoemaker was going to absolutely love this idea. This would be his first idea in all of the years he had known Marty. There was never any question that Marty was the smart one. Marty always had great ideas. But this time, this time all of the credit would go to him.

Spread before him on the coffee table, Earl examined his collection of 'firearms.' The newest weapon in the collection was nearly fifteen years old. It was a Smith & Wesson Model 29, the first from Smith & Wesson built to fire a .44 Magnum round. Earl picked it up and examined it. He was deeply satisfied by the weight of the thing. He reflected and thought it might have been part of a trade involving two tires and a truck bed, but he could no longer be sure. He considered its value against the possible reward Sheriff Stearns had promised, and placed it back on the coffee table keeping it in mind as a possible candidate.

He perused the collection again, dismissing the next firearm in line, the strange looking Sp-45 single shot Liberator he'd drunkenly traded for two Coleman lanterns. He assured himself of the odd shaped weapon's worthlessness, cursed the trade and lamented the loss of the lanterns.

He moved on to a pair of mismatched Colts.

Through the night and in the increments between practicing his acceptance speech for Citizen of the Year and worrying over what he should wear when they took his photograph for the newspaper, Earl dreamed of waving to the crowd from his float in the homecoming parade, tossing candy to the children and generally just being a hero.

"Who knows how many lives you saved, Mister Rainwater," he imagined the mayor saying.

Earl's anticipation was indeed so great, he may well have shortened the period between today and tomorrow by strength of sheer will alone. He paced back and forth in front of the bar at Pudgy's until finally deciding to press his luck and head for the door, mug of beer in hand.

"I'd rather you not take my mug outside, Earl," said Slakey from behind the bar.

"Geez," said Earl, "I'm just gonna wait outside, right there, for Marty."

"Wait without my mug."

Earl approached the bar. "Aw, Slakey. Dammit. Well, well, here then," Earl placed the mug back onto the bar. "Pour it into a bottle." He slid the mug toward Slakey.

In flat refusal, Slakey slid the mug back across the bar and shook his head. "That's not what we do here, Earl. We don't fill bottles up, we empty 'em."

"Ya want me waitin' out in that heat without a cold drink? Why, I'd stroke right out on ya. Then what would ya do?"

"You really want me to answer that?"

"Slakey—"

"I still don't get why you gotta wait outside," Slakey pressed.

"I done told ya, I need to talk to Marty when he gets here." Earl raised the wadded up brown paper sack.

"Well, you're in luck, then, Earl. When Marty comes here, he usually comes on in and sits right here at this bar. Usually, right next to you, Earl. Whatcha got in that bag there anyways?"

"Slakey, I—"

"You know what? Changed my mind. I don't even wanna know." Slakey suddenly waved all concern away. "Tell ya what, drink that one down and I'll give ya a bottle, but you ain't takin' my mug outside. I'll never see it again if you do, and they ain't givin' them damn things away."

Making a show of it, Earl drained the mug of beer with audible gulps. Slakey did as promised, popping the top from a cold bottle of beer with a mildly irritated shake of his head. Gratefully, Earl took the cold brown bottle and his grocery bag and went outside to wait for Marty.

Slakey turned to the two men in military uniform sitting at what had lately become their usual spots. "You guys havin' any luck?" he asked.

"Too damned hot," said the one with three stripes and a rocker on his collar.

"Ain't that—"

The door opened and Earl stood, cradling the sweat soaked, disintegrating paper bag in the crook of his elbow and carrying the now empty bottle in his right hand. His face shone from sweat and his hair was wet around the edges.

"Another bottle, Slakey," he ordered.

"Geez, you pour that one over your head?" he asked and the recruiters laughed, embarrassing Earl Rainwater.

"No, I didn't pour it over my head. I poured it in my belly. It's goddamned hot out there." Earl approached the bar and slid the empty bottle toward Rudy Slakey. Slakey opened a new one and swapped it for Earl's empty. Earl rolled the cold bottle slowly across his sweaty forehead and made his way back outside.

Slakey turned back to the uniformed men. "They say this heat ain't gonna let up for a while. Where you fellas stayin'?"

"We're over at the—"

Earl Rainwater walked back through the door with the bottle emptied.

"Now, shit, Earl," Slakey protested.

"Hell, hold on. There's Marty." Earl meant to place the empty bottle on the nearest table, but in his excitement, he missed the edge. The bottle fell to the wood floor, but did not break.

"You're damned lucky, Earl." Slakey called to him, but Earl had already gone back outside.

When Earl showed Marty the Colt .45 "Peacemaker" and explained his intention, Marty Shoemaker did indeed love the idea. The two men went inside Pudgy's Tavern, ordered fresh beers and found a booth where they could privately discuss the finer points of their plan.

On the weedy, thorny bank of the railroad track, Marty explained to a pair of sunburned sweating deputies. "Thought we'd pitch in, boys. Help ya find that firearm, see."

"Hell, yeah. We'll take all the help we can get, Marty." The young deputy wiped his brow and asked, "How's your dad?"

"Ah, you know, standin' tall as a steeple one day, then' low as a horse's hoof the next."

"You tell him I asked after him."

"I'll do that. Damned hot out here, ain't it? Take yourselves a break, boys. Me and Earl'll take a shift."

"No can do," said the sweaty deputy. "Stearns comes around and catches us slackin'—"

"Well, suit yourselves, then. Me and Earl'll take this patch over here."

"We done went through that area, Marty. Hell, we done went through all of it."

"We'll just go back over it. Earl's got them keen eagle eyes."

"'On accounta me bein' Cherokee and all," Earl explained.

"Suit yourselves," the young deputy said and shrugged at his quiet partner. The other deputy shrugged back.

The older men sweated profusely. It was even hotter than they had anticipated. Too hot in fact for the duo to resist the temptation to accelerate their carefully thought out plan. Within two minutes of beating the bushes, Earl Rainwater dropped the Colt from his pocket and exclaimed, "Here! Got it! Got it over here, boys!"

"The hell you say!" exclaimed the deputy that had been quiet until now. He looked at the other with a suspicious expression.

"I got it right here." Earl held up the Colt, as if he were about to fire it into the air in celebration.

"Careful with that gun, old timer."

"I believe the correct word is firearm," Earl commented, lowering the weapon.

The deputy began to argue the validity of the find. "That ain't no .38," he said. "The sheriff says we's lookin' for a .38."

"Well, he got it wrong," said Marty. "Plain and simple. Great job, Earl."

"If they found it, then they found it. Search is over," declared the deputy who had earlier spoken to Marty. He moved down the bank.

"Now, you know they ain't just walked out here and—" the other deputy attempted to argue.

"Looks like they found it to me. Search is over. That means we can quit lookin'."

The young deputy's face lit up. "Gotcha. Gotcha. Great job, fellas." He moved toward Earl. "Give that here and we'll take it on over to the sheriff."

"I think we'll just take it in ourselves," explained Marty, intervening. "He's promised us a re-ward, see."

"Oh, I see, all right." The deputy grinned and shook his head. "You fellas is sure somethin'. You know that?"

The two men proudly climbed into Marty's truck and drove quickly to the courthouse.

"You found this?" asked Stearns.

"Yep," answered Marty.

"Out on the tracks?" Stearns scrutinized the dusty pistol.

"In the weeds just like Lenville Tucker said. Sure did. Me and Earl. We done cracked the case of the missin' firearm, Sheriff. Now, how's about that re-ward?"

"This ain't it." Stearns said flatly, handing the pistol back to Marty.

"Sure it is, see." Marty offered it back.

"Fellas, I told ya we were lookin' for a .38. This ain't no .38."

"Who said it was a .38? The Tucker kid? What's he know of .38s from .45s?" asked Marty.

"You got me there." Stearns confessed. "Okay, maybe it wasn't a .38. Maybe he got it wrong, but this don't match the description."

"He described it did he? Get a good look at it after drinkin' all of that liquor and before he squeezed the trigger and tossed it, did he? He studied it real good in that time, did he?"

"This ain't it, Marty," Stearns said flatly.

"How ain't it?" Marty pushed.

"It just ain't."

The following afternoon, Marty and Earl tried again, this time with the Smith & Wesson Model 29 and received the same resistance from the sheriff. By the end of the week, the determined duo would bring in a total of eleven pistols, four rifles, two shotguns, a defunct hand grenade Earl traded a truck battery for, and a broken bayonet. In all of that handling of firearms there were only two accidental discharges and only one of those came close to wounding anyone.

Chapter 16

J eannie Marie Tucker had long since stopped asking her boys to come with her to town on Saturdays, relinquishing the help with carrying the empty bottles to town and the groceries back. But in doing this, she spared herself the feeling of inadequacy that came with denying her sons' requests for frivolous desserts, potato chips and sugary breakfast cereals.

"Snorville" town square was a beehive of commerce and commencement on Saturday afternoons, a promenade of small town sorts with waving and hat tipping and congenial inquiry. For Jeannie, Saturdays were a lonely return to civilization. She studied her fellow townsfolk, envied them for how casually and without burden they carried themselves.

With polite enough salutations, she cashed her paycheck at First Guaranteed Deposit, stuffing the bills into the back pocket of her faded jeans and letting the change fall into her front pocket. Before proceeding to Cas Walker's for the groceries, she walked twice around the square, perhaps only to see if some would forget themselves and nod at her, or even dare to be so courteous as to wish her a good afternoon. Sometimes one or two did, usually men without their women close by. She had marked her progress in eighths of inches over the decade that had passed since her husband had shot and killed Sheriff Bill. Li'l Roy had set her back a bit pulling that stunt with the fire at the school house a couple of years ago. This Saturday not a single person offered her any politeness. Lenville killing the Hickey boy had set her back a few years in the 'Forgive and Forget' department as far as the citizens of Sonoraville and their sibilant whispers were concerned. Not only did they not speak nor even nod, she felt them intentionally avoiding eye contact as she approached. The hypocritical men whom she had come to count on to give her the slightest of boosts would not look at her until she passed by. She *felt* them looking then, and despite herself, added a slight swing to her hips.

Virginia Lawford looks up from her book and watches Jeannie Tucker walk up the dirt road. When Jeannie waves at her, she offers a wave in turn, slow and more of fingers than of hand.

"That's your mammaw," she says looking to her stomach.

That's how babies are made.

She had learned that those years ago. She had fallen asleep in the bathroom and the girls that found her laughed at her. Laughed at her so mercilessly that she had run home and cried the afternoon away, suffocating beneath the dread of the next day until—

Until night fell.

Until night fell and she dreamed of kerosene, of vengeful fire, of smoke black and billowing.

Morning came and with it news that the school had burned. She sat with the radio remembering how the flames danced like freed demons, orange, blue and yellow, unbound into the night and the darkness.

Jeannie Tucker managed to enjoy the afternoon window shopping the dress shops and even the Western Auto. She was always curious as to what movies were playing at The Starlite Theater, though she had been a teenager the last time she had been inside and felt the thrill that came when the lights first dimmed and the screen flickered as the film began to roll. The posters outside promised fun and intrigue. One advertised *The Love Bug*. The poster claimed, "You have been warned! *The Love Bug* will split your sides and steal your heart!" She smiled at this, studying the poster. The other feature currently playing was *Where Eagles Dare*. She didn't care for war pictures although she did like Richard Burton. The Eastwood kid was great as Rowdy Yates in *Rawhide*, but she wondered if he would ever actually make a career on the big screen.

Beneath the "Coming Attractions!" sign was a poster for a movie titled *The Wild Bunch*. It looked to her like a western. She didn't care much for westerns either, but for William Holden she might be persuaded to buy a ticket. She decided then and there that was what she was going to do. When *The Wild Bunch* came to The Starlite, she would go and watch the matinee with popcorn and a sweet fountain soda to boot. She promised herself this treat at least once a month, but never came through for herself. She took one long last whiff of the smell of the buttered popcorn that wafted onto the sidewalk. Somewhere a horn blew and she moved on toward Cas Walker's.

Out on the rural route, on the front steps of the Tucker house, the two brothers sat and argued away the Saturday afternoon. The yellow dog was not interested in their conversation.

There in the sun, Ronny Tucker playfully shoved his brother's bare shoulder. "I swear, Li'l Roy, sometimes I think you do this shit just so somebody'll beg ya."

"I don't." Li'l Roy contested, his flat tone relaying both truth and boredom.

"You didn't go last Saturday and look what happened."

"You can't put that on me. Don't even try it." Li'l Roy dismissively scratched the head of the yellow dog.

"Hell, Li'l Roy. You don't ever know. You bein' there mighta stopped it all from happenin'. I'm just sayin'. "

"You couldn't stop it. What makes you think I could?"

"You're right. Felt like Sheriff Stearns was blamin' me, too."

"Hell, I ain't a blamin' ya. That shit's on Len. What'd Stearns say to ya?"

"He just asked me why I didn't try to stop him. Why I just stood there. Hell, he thinks I got that gun."

"You got it?"

"Hell, no."

"Wish ya did."

"Why's 'at, Li'l Roy?"

"Why? In case any of them Hickey sonsabitches comes out here lookin' for revenge. That's why."

"Shit, they ain't comin' out here. This is Big Roy Tucker's place, don'tcha know. We're Big Roy Tucker's kids. Naw, they ain't comin' out here." Ronny Tucker shook his head.

"Big Roy Tucker's locked up," Li'l Roy reminded his brother.

"Don't matter," Ronny countered.

"Yeah, well I'd still feel better if you had that gun," said Roy.

"Yeah, me, too," admitted Ronny.

"I don't know why the hell Len tossed it."

"You should go see him and ask him." Ronny waited. No reply came from Li'l Roy. Ronny sighed. "Lenville knew what he was doin'. He says he knew the call had gone out. He said he knew they'd say he was armed and dangerous. He said he thought he could get to the cop shop before they found him, but he didn't want that gun on him if they did get to him. Shit, it don't matter. Listen, it's Saturday. We gotta go to Pudgy's tonight or else they'll all say we're too scared to show our faces out there."

"I really don't care what they say, Ronny. They say all sorts a shit anyway."

107

"Don't gimme no shit about not carin' what people say. By God, you'd care if they said you was hung like a horse." Ronny Tucker's eyes grew large and round, an affectionate grin bloomed. "By God, you'd care then. Why, you'd just love it. I guaran- damn-tee it."

Li'l Roy Tucker laughed at his brother, but despite his laughter, he heard himself say to Ronny, "Don't say that."

"It's true and you know it."

"I mean the *guaran-damn-tee it* thing. That's Lenville's."

"Bullshit. It's Dad's. Not Lenville's."

"I wouldn't know."

Ronny reclaimed his seat on the wooden step beside his little brother and the yellow dog. "How old was ya when he went up to Brushy? Seven?"

"Six. I remember some things, though."

"Yeah, I don't remember much, either. But I ain't forgettin' that we got a reputation to consider. You should remember that, too."

"How the hell could I forget? To hell with the reputation we got. That's what I say."

At this, Ronny stood again and suddenly broke into song. The yellow dog was suddenly very interested. "*People try to put us d-down.*" Ronny Tucker sang and waited for his little brother to come in with the refrain. Li'l Roy did not. The yellow dog did. The boys laughed together. Ronny went on. "*Just because we get around.*" He jumped around as he sang and now pointed to his mute brother.

"Don't quit your day job."

"*Things they do look awful c-cold.*" He sang melodramatically into his brother's face, the yellow dog issued a low growl and mumbled a worthwhile bark, but still nothing from Li'l Roy. "*I hope I die before I get old.*"

Li'l Roy shook his head, laughing again at his brother and the dog. He threw Ronny a bone with a lackadaisical, "*Talkin' 'bout my generation.*"

"That's it little brother. We're gonna show'em just who the hell we are tonight."

"I done told ya. I ain't a goin'."

"Geez, you sure you're even a Tucker?" Ronny laughed. "Reputation's 'bout all we got."

"We sure ain't got much, then, do we?" Li'l Roy questioned and quickly added, "Reckon that's 'cause of our reputation?"

"Just listen to you. You make my damned head hurt. Jesus Christ."

"Better holler at somebody ya know. Jesus Christ done quit us, Ronny." Roy's thoughts flashed to that old blue Sunday school bus. "He had to. We was killin' him."

"Man, oh, man! Damn, Li'l Roy! Sounds like you really do need to get good and drunk. You keep too much shit on your mind, little brother."

"If I did need to get good and drunk, Lenville ain't here to get us nothin' from Mac's. We owe him too much money."

"Let me worry about that."

Mac sat on a high stool behind his counter with his ever-present Chesterfield between his stubby fingers and his newspaper spread before him. In his aging and increasingly lonely bachelorhood, Mac had become a voracious consumer of news and information. Whether this voraciousness was born from a genuine desire to know and understand current world events or from a genuine desire to be able to discuss those events, thereby prolonging a customer's visit, is heretofore unclear.

A small radio played almost inaudibly.

Upon hearing the sound of footsteps on the store porch, Mac looked up from his paper, checked his watch and cursed himself for allowing himself to be distracted by all of the news concerning an impending trip to the moon.

The door opened and Red the mailman entered.

"Afternoon, Mac. Hot enough for ya?"

"Red, I suppose it is. Gonna get hotter, though."

"'S'at so?" asked Red.

"Gonna break a hundred next week they're sayin'." Mac looked nervously out the window and checked his watch.

Red placed several envelopes on the counter bound together with a rubber band. "Gonna get me a cold pop," he said and stepped to the cooler. "A hundred degrees? Whew, now that's hot."

Mac drummed his fingers across the counter and again stole a look out the window. "Sure is," he said absently, and in an effort to rush Red back out the door offered, "Tell ya what, you take that cold pop on me, it bein' so damned hot and all."

"Well, gee, thanks, Mac. Mighty kind of ya." Red closed the cooler and popped the cap from the bottle with the opener that had been screwed into the counter. He raised the bottle in a sort of salute to his merciful benefactor and brought it to his lips. Mac watched, growing more and more impatient as Red drank from the bottle. "Ah," said Red. "Now, that's the right stuff on a day like today."

"Yeah," Mac replied eagerly, "Ain't it, though?"

"See what some asshole did to my Jeep? Now I gotta drive down that road and them young'ns won't get outta the way for nothin'."

"Take some penny candy."

"Well that'll just make it worse."

"Only at the start. When they get to you, give 'em the candies and tell 'em that's all ya got for 'em and they'll leave ya alone and go eat it."

"Thanks, Mac. I'll try that."

"Still no idea who busted up the Jeep?"

"I got some ideas. Ya know, I'm thinkin' that Freeman fella."

"Why the hell ya thinkin' him, Red?"

"Ain't he her boyfriend?"

"Whose boyfriend, Red?"

"Jeannie's."

"What the hell's Jeannie got to do with this? Ain't she got enough shit to shovel without folks draggin' her into everything?" Mac stubbed out his forgotten Chesterfield in a nearby metal ashtray.

"Hell, Mac, I ain't a draggin' her into nothin'."

"Good then. Don't." Mac looked again out the window.

"Mac, somethin' wrong?"

"No. Nothin's wrong. Why ya ask?"

"You lookin' awfully worried 'bout somethin', and you ain't mentioned Nixon or the goin' to the moon, or Viet Nam."

"To be honest, Red, I'm worried I'm about to drop a load in my pants. Hit me all a sudden right as you was walkin' up." Mac lied.

"Oh, I'll get outta your hair, then, Mac. Hell, whyn't ya just say so? I know what that's like. Shit myself a time or two out there deliverin' the mail. Last winter, got stuck in that goddamned big snow—"

"Red, I really gotta go."

"Go ahead," said Red. "Tell ya what, I'll watch the store for ya. I'll tell anyone comes in you'll be right back. You go on upstairs."

"I couldn't ask ya to do that, Red."

"I don't mind, Mac. Really I don't."

"Ah, you got your job to do. I couldn't—"

"Mac, I got it," Red insisted.

"I appreciate it," Mac argued stealing yet another peek out the window. "I'm thinkin' I'll just shut her down for a minute. Flip the sign and everything. That way, I won't be up there feelin' like I gotta rush nothin'."

"I suppose I can understand that, too" said Red. "Well, thanks again for the cold pop." Red raised the bottle again and tipped it toward Mac.

"Don't mention it."

Red exited the store and Mac peered out the window and was relieved that he did not see Jeannie Tucker coming up the road, carrying her bags from town, making her way to his store. He closed the paper, neatly folded it and placed it on a shelf behind the counter before racing up the stairs that led to his living quarters.

The pressed shirt was there, hanging on the bathroom door where he'd left it. He stepped past it and into the bathroom where he hurriedly removed his glasses,

110

and his shirt. He turned on the sink tap and splashed cool water onto his face and into his armpits. He shaved again and applied a heavy dose of aftershave. A shot of Listerine left him comfortable with his breath. He swapped the sweaty shirt for the newly pressed one and put his glasses into his breast pocket. A final inspection in the bathroom mirror encouraged him to apply a bit more grease to his salt and pepper hair before heading back downstairs just in time to greet Jeannie Tucker with a smile.

"Then get us a bottle and we can get drunk here." Li'l Roy pointed out. "Or out on the river."

"Ah, that's it!" The older brother exclaimed. "You're just scared. You're scared one a them big bad Hickey's'll be there."

"You can call it scared if ya wanna, Ronny. I don't care whatcha call it. I just get so damned tired of this shit. It's always somethin'. I ain't been hauled in in a long damned time and ya know what? I kinda like not gettin' hauled in. I like not worryin' about trouble. I like doin' what I want when I want. I like not worryin' about Hickeys or any other sonsabitches. Gimme a damned cigarette."

"Mom says Freeman's comin' over." Ronny said.

"So."

"You know when you're here you just get between 'em."

"No, I don't. All they do is sit at the table and drink and laugh."

"When you're here that's all they do." Ronny gave Li'l Roy a slight nudge and a cigarette from the pack. "Hell, little brother, I gotta go. You know I gotta go. Even if I'm hopin' Slakey makes me leave, I gotta go. I gotta at least show my face. If them Hickeys are out there waitin' for me, you'll never forgive yourself. Hey, I'll tell ya what, come with me tonight and we'll go the movies tomorrow on me. Popcorn and everything. *The Love Bug*'s on. You know you want to see that. Come on, we'll laugh our asses off."

"That's a damned kid's movie."

"Shit, you sound like Lenville. I wanna see it, and he ain't here to make fun of us. C'mon you know you wanna see Herbie. We can get us a chocolate shake and some french fries at the Tastee-Creem. Tracy's workin' there."

"'So?'"

"Didn't you swap some spit with her for a while? Damn, man, she's fine as wine."

"Just the one time."

"Cool. Hey, Buddy Hackett's in *The Love Bug*."

"All right. All right, dammit." Li'l Roy relented as he often did.

"Right on."

"Gimme a damned light."

Ronny shook his head. "Ain't got nothin' but the habit. Hey, did Tracy let ya cop any feels?" Li'l Roy blushed at his big brother's question, but admitted nothing. "Man, you're a cat of another color. If I got my hands on Tracy French's titties, I'd a told everybody."

"Hey, there's Mama," Li'l Roy pointed up the dirt road and the two boys ran to her like they had for years, not so much as to help her carry the grocery bags as to see what she had bought.

She watched as they ran to her. They were little boys again, shirtless and barefooted, excited and curious. She smiled at them.

"Here, take this milk," she instructed.

"Moon pies? You get Moon Pies?" Li'l Roy peaked inside one of the bags.

"Not this time."

"Aww."

"Sorry. Get this bag before I drop it. Here. Careful, it's got eggs in it. I got a cake mix. How's that?" The cake was her private apology for the way that she had treated Ronny in the wake of Lenville's crime.

"All right!" exclaimed Ronny. "I call lickin' the bowl."

"And Mac says y'all still ain't paid what you owe him."

The boys ignored her. She watched them run ahead, arguing over who was going to get to lick the spoon, the bowl and whatever else when the cake was made. She walked on, her load now lightened.

Chapter 17

I t was a feeling foreign to Jeannie Tucker to wait, knowing that someone, someone good and kind and giving was coming. It was a feeling that she thought she could get used to. She caught herself smiling, feeling hopeful in the midst of all that had happened for a rare moment and she decided to go with it. And strangely, it seemed almost easy, so she let it be easy. She tidied up. She dusted. She swayed to the music from the radio. The curtains were opened as was the front door. The screen door no longer hung true but somehow still swung easily enough on its hinges. An old shoe string was tied to its interior handle and hooked to a bent nail that had been driven into the door frame. There was an ever increasing gap in the top outside corner, but for the most part, it kept the flies and the wasps out at least until she opened the kitchen window. The back door had been propped open and the screen allowed a breeze to flow through the house.

They were an odd couple but he had brought her around to him. She liked his sleepy voice—a comforting, raspy baritone built upon bathtub gin and the kind of cool confidence gained from hard years. She liked his stories, his tales, and his jokes. They colored her days, her nights, her life now with bona fide laughter and an inspired quiet contemplation. She liked his voice. She liked his stories and God help her she liked him.

It was always hard to tell who Freeman might be when he showed up on Saturday nights. He might show up with his light and his laughter and his stories ready to bed her down, or he might show up with a quiet distance and a feeble reticence, his brow low and heavy. She came to care deeply for them both.

They sat on the front steps for a while before moving inside to the kitchen table.

"I wish them boys hadn't gone out there tonight. Trying to stop them from doing something, well it's like I might as well be tryin' to stop the rain."

"I ain't tryin' to be about your business, Jeannie, but have you gone to see your oldest boy since—" Freeman stopped there suddenly unsure of how to finish.

"I ain't and I can't. He's had his hearing. I know that. I don't know if they've moved him yet, though. I worked so hard since his daddy pulled that shit. Then Li'l Roy went and burned down half the school. I never went to see his daddy, either. Bastard." Absently, almost out of habit now, she scratched at the green paint peeling from the kitchen tabletop.

"My daddy was a bastard," he told her. "A real dyed in the wool, top to bottom and all around kind of bastard. Drank himself to death. Just like I'm doin', I suppose." As if to accentuate the truth in and hasten the realization of this prophecy, Freeman paused his tale and took a long and deep pull from his bottle. "After he died, Mama felt safe enough to tell me—tell me all the time—every day, mind ya—not to grow up to be like him. Said she prayed I wouldn't." He sighed then, long and almost painfully. "Ain't nothin' worse than feelin' like you've disappointed ya mama."

"You're far from being a real bastard."

"Not so far as you might think. I been enough of a bastard to be haunted, to deserve to be haunted."

"We're all haunted." She placed her hand upon his hand on the table and gave him a slight rub.

"Yeah. S'pose so."

Gus the Rooster crowed from the street.

"Yeah, we see ya, Gus," Jeannie called out the window.

"Now that fella there knows way more than he let's on. He's got it all figured out."

"You haven't been around long enough to know him," Jeannie pointed out.

Gus crowed again.

"Who's he belong to?" asked Freeman.

"He look like he belongs to somebody?" Jeannie asked playfully. The pair laughed together.

"He's a good lookin' fella." Freeman studied Gus for a moment.

"For a rooster, I guess. Yeah, he's pretty, but he knows it, too."

"Reminds me. My mama came from those bayou folks who hold to the notion that one can divine omens and portents in the guts and innards of things and she used to tell me all about how her mama and her granny would cut open the guts of the critters they cooked up. She said you could read the signs in chicken guts."

"Signs?"

"Yeah, I don't put much stock in it, myself." He paused then and considered the possibility that he was lying through what was left of his teeth. He continued, "But she'd tell me about how her mama and her granny'd study over those guts

114

divinin' all sorts of shit. Said her granny once prognosticated a comin' flood from rabbit guts. Took the Bible from the sittin' room and put it upstairs on a high shelf and made 'em all sand bag the place. It was good clear weather, she says, clear as could be, but six days later sure enough, the rain came down.

"She said all the time that she really didn't put much stock in it herself or that she wasn't much good at it. Said there was a whole lot in her life that she wished she'd a seen comin'. When she killed a chicken or a rabbit she'd throw the guts to the cats that hung around the place, said it kept 'em hungry for blood—mice and moles and such.

"Told me about this one time. Said she was pregnant with my brother. She killed a chicken and tossed its guts out the back door, and later she went out and found one of the cats gnawin' on the stomach and something shiny, something sparklin' in the sun caught her eye. Said it was somethin' in the ripped up stomach of that chicken. She said it looked like a little star shinin' out of that chicken's stomach. Anyway, she made the mistake of movin' too quickly on that ol' cat and it growled a low growl at her and took off under the house with that chicken's guts in its mouth."

"So, she never found out what was sparklin' in those chicken guts?" Jeannie asked, disappointed.

"Oh, she said she crawled under the house on her swellin' belly through the dark and the dirt and finally cornered that damned cat. Thought she had it there, but it climbed right over her head. Scratched her up pretty good and ran out from under the house."

"Bless her heart."

"Said she had to look for it for a while, but finally found that ol' tom in a tree. Said she saw that sparkle again up on that limb and it was a good thing she did too 'cause she'd just about talked herself into believin' she'd imagined it. Well, she went to trying to shoo him outta that tree with a rake and 'course that only sent him up higher. So up she goes all in her dress and her apron. Now the thing about cats, as you well know, is cats like to be high up. Smug bastards that they are they like to look down on everybody and everything. But, the truth is at the end of the day, cats are scared of heights. They really are. So, she climbed up there and backed him down a limb and he was afraid to jump. So, she reaches out and gets a hold a that little bastard by the nape of the neck. Then she realizes she can't climb down outta that tree with just one free hand—"

"Freeman, you're a pullin' my leg," Jeannie accused him. "Ain't none of this the truth and you know it."

"Naw, naw I ain't. Now, I'm tellin' you what the truth is. Said she climbed down and went and got a hand saw from the shed and climbed back up."

"Now, Freeman—"

"That's the way she told it. Says she'd sawn about halfway through that limb and that ol' tom opened wide and hissed at her just like the devil himself would and them guts fell right outta his mouth."

"All right then, so she finally got him. What was makin' the sparkle?" Jeannie asked anxiously.

"Naw, they landed on a limb below her and that limb was too small to climb out to."

"Dammit, Freeman!"

"So she climbed down to that limb and sawed it off."

"What was in that chicken's gut? Just tell me," she pleaded.

"Well see, we had this ol' dog at the time. Hutch his name was and ol' Hutch had been watchin' her this whole time—"

"Hush it!" She shoved his shoulder playfully.

"All right, I'm pullin' your leg about the dog," Freeman confessed. "It was a dime."

"A dime?"

"All shiny and mercury. See, ya just never know where ya might find something bright and shiny."

"Now, how'd a dime get in a chicken's stomach?" asked Jeannie.

"Well, I got an idea about that, but that's another story for another time. Now, Mama said she didn't know what it might mean in the world of omens and portents to find a dime in a chicken's innards, but she didn't much care either. Said that was the first free and clear dime she ever had."

"Aww—"

"Said she washed it up real good and put it on the window sill to dry in the sun. A little while later my ol' man come in from the field, washed his hands, saw the dime and pocketed it like it wasn't nothin' for him to pick up a dime he didn't lay down. "

"Dammit."

"She didn't cuss him for it. He died six years after that. She found him dead in the rockin' chair on the front porch. Reckoned his liver had just plum give out on him. She said she cussed him then, but not before she said a prayer for him and a prayer for herself, too. A prayer that she could make it in this world without a husband and a prayer askin' forgiveness for the dime she was about to lift from that dead man's pocket." Freeman stopped there, took another drink and finished his tale saying, "Yeah, my daddy was a real bastard."

She took his hand in hers and gave it an affectionate squeeze. "We're empty," she observed, rose from the chair.

"You need a scraper, sandpaper and stripper," he said.

"What's that?" asked Jeannie.

"For your tabletop here, Jeannie. Take ya the rest a your life gettin' it off there with your fingernail."

"Don't know what I thought I was accomplishing with that. Liked the color though. Guess I'll get around to that when I'm good and ready." There were no barbs in her words.

"Yes, Ma'm."

Later, when he felt her breathing become steady and heard the slight wheeze of her delicate snore, he lifted himself quietly from the bed. Softly, he carried his wadded clothes into the kitchen where he dressed.

This was their routine. He always left before the boys came home, whether she was asleep or awake to kiss him goodbye.

In the darkness, he stumbled drunkenly across the yard, up the thorny bank and across the tracks. As had become routine, he was not able to immediately find the half pint of Four Roses he had tossed into the wood line. He cursed himself for not being more particular about where he stashed it. He walked up and down the tracks and the edge of the wooded overgrowth using his Zippo for light and wondering what he might find this time.

Chapter 18

Quiet Tom Lawford watched them from the porch as they headed up the road toward Pudgy's Tavern. The laughing little bastards had even had the nerve to look over and wave at him. His blood boiled. He ground his teeth until his jaw ached.

Quiet Tom paced the porch until night fell. When the hour was finally upon him, he went inside to prepare.

In the bathroom, beneath the naked light bulb, he positioned the dusty brown potato sack so that the two misshapen holes he'd cut in it lined up with his eyes. He made some last minute adjustments and when he was satisfied with his line of vision, he topped his sacked head with an old sweat stained hat. His vision now debilitated, he bumped the light on his way out of the bathroom, sending shadows swinging across the walls.

He headed out the front door with with his resolve high and the hat pulled low. Beneath the potato sack his face was now bearded and blackened with coal dust as a precaution against the sack perhaps being loosened and removed in the struggle that might be waiting out on the tracks.

The girl offered up wail upon wail at the newly secured window, watching as the man disappeared into the waiting, hungry darkness.

Providence had taken care of one of the brothers for him—a particularly bloody altercation at Pudgy's Tavern that had ended with Lenville Tucker in police custody. Word around was that Lenville was going to wind up doing a stretch at Brushy this time. There were only two now—the middle Tucker boy and the youngest.

He ambushed them. He'd crept through the ditches of stagnant sour water and through the brambles much like his only daughter had done—only he wasn't there to get 'gouged'. He was there to do some 'gouging'.

After tonight, he hoped to be able to look at her again without the churning in his gut.

She had given herself to them. They had gladly taken her.

Still, there was the issue of honor.

"He's gonna miss the fair and the fireworks," Ronny Tucker said, stumbling from the night-slick, moonlit rail.

"Yeah, he's gonna miss a lot of things," agreed Li'l Roy.

"He's gonna miss The Scrambler."

"Yep. Man, I love The Scrambler. Them frogs is loud ain't they?" Li'l Roy noted.

"Yep," agreed Ronny and moved on. "He's gonna miss the corn dogs and the funnel cakes and the freaks."

"Yep. Them, too. And the titty tent," Li'l Roy added, "He's gonna miss the titty tent."

"Ooh, I love the titty tent."

"Hey, they's a little left in this. You want it?" Li'l Roy held up a near empty pint bottle.

"Shit, no," Ronny waved away the offer. "Hell, I'm done. Just don't feel right, does it?"

Li'l Roy tossed the bottle high and away. It came to earth and shattered on the tracks somewhere out of sight in the darkness ahead. "Knew one of us was bound to say that 'fore the night was over."

"Yeah. Shit, I just wanna get home and get in the bed."

"Me, too. Let's get a move on."

The brothers quickened their pace and walked on in silence. Ronny Tucker hopped back upon a rail and again attempted to walk it in the blue moonlight that lit the night, but quickly missed his step.

"You're drunker'n ya—"

Quiet Tom came low and quickly from the darkness and the shadows of the overgrowth. He sank the knife into the boy's back with a force so great the boy was lifted off his feet and sent crashing down onto the ties with Tom Lawford on his back. Ronny Tucker screamed his pain into the night and tried clumsily to reach behind him to the wound. The long blade penetrated his back, ran through his lean torso until its tip poked from his chest.

Quiet Tom pulled the blade from the boy and sank it twice more in quick succession.

Li'l Roy Tucker stood paralyzed staring mutely at the masked murderer.

When the violence was done, Quiet Tom stood with the elder brother's blood on his hands and on his shirt. He'd hesitated too long, giving the younger brother time to wrap his drunken head around it.

The boy made a motion to charge and Tom wielded the dripping blade. "Hold on there, son. It's done." A silver sliver of moon was up and the man and the boy locked eyes like bull wolves beneath it.

"What'd ya go and kill my brother for you murderin' son of a bitch? Now, I gotta kill ya back."

"Not tonight. Kill me tomorrow, kid." Quiet Tom Lawford's muffled voice came through the sack he wore. He tried unsuccessfully to steady his trembling, outstretched arm as he backed away from the boys. "Tend to your brother. There might still be time."

"I know who you are!" The boy called to him.

This revelation stunned Lawford, but with the bloodied knife, he held the boy at a distance. It was all out of him, all of the energy and his fury. The act had taken it from him, the blood-lust, and the desire for vengeance. Quiet Tom's breath was heavy now, hot and labored beneath the sack that hid his face. His heart hammered at a dangerous pace. It had not happened quickly enough. His humanity was back on him and the weight of the deed cleared his muddled thoughts. He would not kill the other boy. He could not.

In the stifling heat beneath the brown potato sack, he attempted to blink the sweat from his eyes to no avail. He clenched them tightly and rubbed them with the back of his free hand. When he opened them again the burning salty sting instantly returned. He hoped the boy was not picking up on his state.

"You coward yella bastard! You stabbed a drunk man in the back! You're a dead man!"

Ronny Tucker lay along the cross ties. He made low bubbling noises. Somewhere in those noises was his brother's name. "Roy?"

"Yeah? I'm here. I'm here."

"It hurts, Roy. Damn, It hurts so bad."

Li'l Roy knelt on the tracks beside his brother. "I know it does. It's gotta. I know it does. I gotta go get some help. Ronny, I gotta."

"No," Ronny said. "Don't leave me."

Li'l Roy reached for his brother's hand, found it and held onto it firmly. He cried with his brother. "We, we gotta get you off the tracks, Ronny." Li'l Roy sobbed.

"Don't leave me. Roy? I'm gonna miss the fair, ain't I?"

"You ain't gonna miss nothin'. We're gonna raise hell at that fair, me and you."

"Yeah?"

"We're gonna get so goddamned drunk. Heard they got new girls in the peep show this year."

"You put in—put in a word for me—with Tracy French—"

"You wanna feel them titties, don'tcha?"

"Roy?"

"I'm right here, Ronny."

"Don't tell Len I cried, okay? Don't tell him."

"I won't."

"Swear it."

"I swear it."

"Stay with me, Li'l Roy." The fallen boy pleaded and began the last question he would ever ask anyone, "You think," he shivered in the summer night, coughed a long and painful cough of black blood, but was determined to finish his question. "You think Jesus really done quit us, Roy?"

"I know who you are, you yella son of a bitch!"

Quiet Tom listened to the boy curse him as he retreated back down the tracks and disappeared into the darkness and the wet weeds. A few yards in, he stopped, staggered, fell heavily to the ground, heaved violently and vomited into the potato sack that covered his sweat soaked head. Panic gripped him even tighter when he failed to catch his breath in the heavy stench of it. He struggled desperately at the trappings of the sack and ripped it from his head leaving bile and unidentifiable pieces and particles in his hair and on his blackened face. He collapsed, feeling the cool earth on his burning cheek and he breathed the precious night air of summer. Trembling and wobbly, he regained himself, first on all fours, then slowly stumbling to his feet. He took a few staggered steps before returning to his hands and knees where he vomited again until he was only retching in long and drawn out dry heaves, his body trying to purge itself of the night's bloody deed. Water rolled from his bloodshot eyes, cutting white trails through the sweaty mask of coal dust. Again he found his feet and ran, careening wildly through the cane break and the weeds.

Inside the safety of his home, Tom Lawford stood behind his closed front door. There he rested his back against it and closed his eyes. A piercing scream ripped them open. Before him, his daughter stood in her nightgown, her mouth askew. A piercing, ear splitting scream poured endlessly from her lungs. It filled the room and escaped through every crack into the darkness outside. Tom suddenly struck her. She struck back at him blindly, ineffectively. He removed his belt. In his blood-soaked, vomit caked clothing, he beat her until he feared he might well kill her, too.

She lay in a heap. He stepped toward the dining room table.

121

"For the life of me, Virginia, I'll never understand why you—why this—" He did not finish his thought, but draped his belt across the back of a wooden chair.

Hearing her laugh, he turned, reaching again for the belt.

Slowly, she rose from the floor, "For the life of you? For the life of you?"

"Go to bed, girl."

She stood now, found her wobbly footing and approached him slowly. "It was for the life of you. You. For you! This! For this! Listen! Don't ya hear it, Daddy? Don't ya hear it?"

"What? Don't I hear—"

"Shhh- listen!" she hissed, limping toward him.

"I don't hear nothin, girl."

"The quiet, Daddy, can't ya hear it? Can't ya feel it? In your head and in your bones? Makin' ya feel like, like you're underwater? Like you can't breathe? Smotherin' ya with its weight. Don't ya hear it, Daddy? Don't it smother you, Daddy? Don't it pull you down? Don't it make ya dread comin' through that door? I see it in your shoulders." She stood before him and put her hands on his arms just below his shoulders. "I see it in your walk, Daddy. I hear it in the way you talk—like you just ain't got the air in you to speak a complete sentence, like you're exhausted and you're just waitin', Daddy, waitin' to die. I see it in you. Why can't you see it in me? Why do you help it to break me, Daddy? I'm here. I'm here with you. Alone in this house, in this tomb, with you."

He looked into her eyes, studied the blood around her nose and mouth and said, "Go to bed, girl."

"It was for you, Daddy. It was for us I did what I did. I did it for a baby."

His hand snatched the belt from the back of the chair and he struck her again.

After washing, he deposited his soiled clothing into the burn barrel out back and set them ablaze with kerosene and a match. From the dancing flames came black smoke, unfamiliar scents and arresting thoughts. He would not see his wife again. Hell and eternal fire was now waiting and each day of torment would be as the first.

Christ's words came to him.

If thy right hand offend thee...

It was there suddenly, his right hand in the flame, his flesh boiling, burning, and melting away. He snatched his hand from the fire, examined his injury, and headed into the house.

Inside, he cleaned and dressed his wounded hand. He took to the beard he had grown for the occasion with a pair of scissors and then a razor, cursing himself for letting it happen the way it had. He had gone out to kill the both of them, leaving their pockets turned out to look like a robbery. For a week, he'd practiced telling them what they were dying for, but ultimately, he had lacked the constitution for both speech giving and for killing.

There was still the youngest. Quiet Tom Lawford didn't reckon the boy had it in him, but blood was blood and brothers were bound. He found some solace in the notion that he was pretty sure he'd killed the boy who had been bragging about "gouging" his daughter.

Morning finally came to the Lawford house, its light a promissory declaration of newness and reprieve. He dusted off his only suit and took to work on his nicest hat with a brush. He drove the pickup truck to the church with the girl beside him. He shook hands with his left hand, fending off questions about the injury to his right. Word had already spread about the dead Tucker boy, but details were sketchy.

When the invitation was issued, he stepped to the altar and rededicated his life to the Lord. After the service, he accepted embraces and shook more hands. With the pastor, he made arrangements to be baptized.

They ate lunch at The Tastee-Creem, a rare refreshment for the both of them. Quiet Tom wanted to put his ear to the ground. They sat quietly, a remote island among the sea of surrounding conversation, rarely sparing each other a look, let alone a word.

Quiet Tom tried to follow the many conversations over the noise level.

"That poor boy, though." Quiet Tom listened intently. The woman was Betty Sizemore. Tom had grown up with her and her husband. She was the graveyard shift police dispatcher. "I reckon the same one set the school on fire that time. He looked so—so broken. He was covered in blood and I mean covered in it. Said, one a them," Betty looked around and lowered her voice. "Said, one a' them Hickeys done killed my brother. Wild eyed. I never seen such wild eyes. We called Johnny in and Johnny says, 'That boys in shock,' and you know, I never seen anybody really in shock before, but I betcha I'll know it if I see it again. He was just as pale as— He was gray, that's what color he was. He was plum gray. Johnny tried to talk to him, but the boy could hardly even speak. Couldn't get a whole sentence from that boy once Johnny—"

"That bunch." Quiet Tom heard her husband say.

"Yeah I know, but Lee—"

"That bunch is just trouble," her husband chewed his chicken fried steak sandwich.

Though no one spoke the precise words, *good riddance* seemed to be the overall tone among the men of the crowd. Quiet Tom Lawford found himself curiously saddened by this. He found himself wondering what kind of world it might be if every son of a bitch in it got what some other son of a bitch thought they had coming.

Quiet Tom rose and signaled Virginia to do the same. He stepped over to the Sizemores. "Lee," Quiet Tom nodded. "Betty." He nodded again.

"Afternoon, Tom." Lee Sizemore offered.

"Well, look at you, girl! Ain't you just all grown up." Betty Sizemore fawned over Virginia. "And just as pretty as a picture. Bet you got all the boys after you." Betty Sizemore winked. Virginia reddened as did her father.

"Overheard. Didn't mean to be eavesdroppin' or nothin'. Say it was one a them Hickeys done it? That Tucker boy said it was one a them Hickeys?" Quiet Tom asked Betty Sizemore.

"Sure did. Johnny's got a couple of 'em in custody."

This news caught Quiet Tom off his guard. "Johnny moves fast, don't he?"

"Sure does. They got two of them Hickey boys. Hey, what'd ya do to your hand there, Tom?"

On the sidewalk in the Sunday afternoon sun, though he had sworn himself to keeping a closer eye on the girl, he instructed her to walk straight home. He stood and watched her as she walked, limping and in obvious pain. He shamed himself.

Slowly, he made his way to the Whelan County courthouse wherein was housed the Whelan County Sheriff's Department. Inside, he found the small station nearly empty. He was not surprised to learn that Johnny Stearns was not in his office. He stepped into the break room.

"Mornin', Caroline. Tell me where I can find Johnny?"

"Well, hi there, Tom." Caroline Rumpke was all smiles. "How've you been?" She rose from the small table. "How's Virginia?" A famous hugger, she approached Tom Lawford with her arms extended. He accepted her soft but firm embrace and for a brief moment, thought he might erupt into uncontrollable sobbing.

When the two broke their embrace, Quiet Tom nodded almost shyly, hesitantly. "We," he began, nodded more confidently, finding his footing, "We're doin' okay, Caroline. We'll be okay. Where's Johnny?"

"Oh, Tom, they's been another killin'. One a them Tucker boys."

He found his brother-in-law out on the tracks with the other officers on duty. He stood in a group of onlookers, the brim of his hat pulled lower than usual, his lunch threatening to boil over and pour his guilt upon the dusty road beside the railroad tracks.

He disregarded protocol and with a feigned confidence and authority, broke from the small gathering and stepped toward the uniformed personnel on the tracks. When his brother-in-law caught sight of him, he ceased his advance and with two fingers motioned his directive. Johnny Stearns approached. Quiet Tom said, "When you're done here, come on by the house. We're gonna need to talk."

"Somethin' wrong?" the lawman asked. "What'd ya do to your hand?"

"Hand'll be okay. Come by?"

"Will do, Tom. Shame ain't it?" Stearns turned to the tracks.

"Sure it is. It's all a damned shame."

Chapter 19

For Freeman, the walk From Bailey's Boarding House to Jeannie Tucker's place was always light and promising. This particular Sunday it was not so. He carried with him the weight of all he'd seen there on the tracks. He also carried with him his doubts about what exactly he had seen there. He carried with him the absolute assurance that the information he held was bound to further the pain and anguish his dear friend must already be enduring.

Before reaching the step, a disquieting thought came to Freeman. He suddenly wasn't sure if he wanted to see her, if he could stand to see her. On the step, Freeman stood slightly trembling and poised to knock. He brought with him his condolences and a sordid story of late night entanglements. He reluctantly thought he might be bringing a key to it all—a key he would place at the feet of, or in the hand of, Jeannie Tucker for her to do with as she wished. From inside, came the sound of shattering glass. Freeman stood captured by the noise from inside and listened to the argument that boiled on between Jeannie and Li'l Roy.

"Mama, I'll kill ever damned one a' them Hickey sonsabitches."

"Stop it! You're breakin' my heart, standin' there talkin' 'bout killin' folks like it wouldn't be nothin' for you to go off and kill folks. You know who you sound like?" Li'l Roy thought he knew what her answer was going to be. He thought she was going to say that he sounded like his dad, although he knew for a fact that he sounded just like his oldest brother. "You sound like those goddamned politicians and talkin' heads on television talkin' about 'offenses' and 'battles' and all that bloodshed like they ain't even talkin' about real people, like they just want us to be numb to it all, and damned if they ain't succeeding. You sound just like those people."

"Then I sound like I sound. They killed my brother. Now how do you think that sounds?"

"It sounds heartbreakin', but what choice did Lenville leave 'em? This is the life you boys want. Now, take a damned long hard look at it."

"Ronny," Li'l Roy rethought this and began again, "Your *son* bled out up there on the tracks like some gutted animal and you're tellin' me—"

"You need to sleep."

"Sleep?" Li'l Roy was incredulous. "How am I supposed to sleep? You're tellin' me—"

She spoke at him, as if trying to inject her words into him, "I'm tellin' you I love all my boys, but dammit to hell, Lenville killed that boy. You wanna talk about *'like an animal?'* Shootin' somebody when they're down on the floor and beggin' ya not to kill'em, that's—"

"I ain't believin' you!"

"Well, believe it," she cried.

"So, they're just gonna get away with it?"

"Johnny's got 'em, Roy."

"He ain't got 'em all! And you're fine with that?"

"Oh, don't you dare! You little— I ain't fine with none of this shit, Li'l Roy, but you boys and your damned daddy ain't left me with much of a choice but to be fine with all of it. Am I supposed to be fine with you goin' out and gettin' yourself killed or killin' somebody—and you don't even know who—"

"I ain't gotta know who. I'll—"

"You'll what?"

"Kill'em." Li'l Roy Tucker suffered a complete loss of bearing. "I'll kill ever goddamned one of 'em."

"Listen to you," she said. "I wish you'd lay down. In here talkin' like that about killin' folks like it wasn't nothin' to just go kill folks."

"I'll kill'em all." The boy was being stubborn for its own sake.

"Kill'em all, Li'l Roy? Kill innocent people even? How would that make you different from what they done? Ronny didn't kill that Hickey boy."

"Ain't a damned one of them Hickeys innocent of nothin' and you damned well know it. And I *ain't* no different. Ain't never claimed to be."

"You are. You are different, Roy. Don't you ever let me hear you say that again."

"I'ma kill'em."

"And then what? Huh? They come back and kill you and then what?"

"They ain't gonna be nobody left to kill me."

"Goddammit, Li'l Roy. You'll keep your ass close to this house and you'll stay the hell away from that shithole bar. It's you and me now. You're all I got now. It's you and me."

Freeman retreated quietly down the steps of the front porch. The yellow mutt was suddenly there with a potato sack clenched in its jaw. The dog curiously offered up the sack and looked toward the window where the boy usually waited with the bologna. With no discernible reason nor forthought, Freeman stomped the ground before the dog and shooed it away. The dog retrieved the filthy potato sack and made its way across the street to lie beneath the shade of the sycamores. Freeman noticed Miss Jessie across the street, offered a wave and began walking up the dirt road toward Pudgy's Tavern.

Where the asphalt met the dirt, he waved as Johnny Stearns drove by him in the police cruiser.

Passing Freeman on the road, Stearns tapped the horn, waved to Freeman and then had a second thought. He stopped the vehicle and put it in reverse until Freeman was at his window.

"Afternoon, Freeman. Giving your condolences?" he asked from inside the patrol car.

"Well, truth is, I was gonna. Got out there and changed my mind. Might come back later. Figured she might not be too up for company right now, Constable. Thing like that happens, sometimes too many well wishers just make it worse. Nobody really wants company at a time like that, Constable. They wants to grieve and to be left alone."

"I gotcha, Freeman. You're thinkin' I'd just be botherin' her. Well, it's good she's got somebody lookin' out for her."

"You don't know that woman too well if you think Jeannie Tucker needs somebody lookin' out for her." Freeman said and immediately regretted it.

Stearns bit his tongue and chose not to inform Freeman of just how well he did know Jeannie Tucker. He said instead, "I do have to ask her some questions, Freeman. If that's all right with you."

"Ain't we all got questions?" Freeman could not seem to help himself.

"What's that?"

"See, there's one right there. Nothin', Sheriff. I's just ramblin'. How's Quiet Tom? Looked a little peaked when I seen him earlier in that crowd of rubberneckers out there. He's your cousin or somethin' ain't he?"

"Brother-in-law, Freeman. Funny you should ask, though. I'm headed by his place, too. Of course, that is, if it's all right by you."

"No need to get ugly, Constable. Do what ya gotta do."

"Why, thank you, Freeman. Thank you very much. I'll catch up with you later with my schedule for next week and run it by you."

"I'm guessing we're done here, right, Sheriff?"

Stearns did not answer, but put the patrol car in gear and drove on toward Jeannie Tucker's, cursing Freeman *Fabbro* as he went. When he approached the Tucker place, he looked toward the kitchen window and suddenly decided against stopping. He drove on to the end of the road and turned around, headed now toward his brother-in-law's house. When he passed Freeman again on the road, he did not blow the horn, but did momentarily consider running him down.

Just before reaching the end of the dirt road, Stearns passed Miss Jessie and the twins. They had changed from their Sunday clothes and were now picking blackberries from the bank. Without forethought Miss Jessie narrowed her eyes at the lawman as he passed. One of the twins, Travis or Tobias, fashioned a handgun with his thumb and forefinger and pretended to fire repeatedly at the police cruiser as it rolled by. Miss Jessie slapped the shit out of him. To spook the boy, Stearns gave the blues a whirl and let the siren wail for a second, but rolled on.

Chapter 20

O w," said the boy called Toby, breaking the silence that had fallen upon the laboring threesome.

"Ow, ow," said the boy called Travis, not to be out done by his brother.

"Shit!" Declared the first boy.

"Fu—"

"Now, that's enough!" Miss Jessie commanded not looking up nor ceasing the work. "Now, what if Jesus was to come back while y'all out here talkin' like that?"

The lengthening shadows of the sycamores did little to stop the rising summer heat. Along the bank, in the overgrown thicket, the thorny blackberries were abundant, fat and ripe. Miss Jessie and her twin grandsons had come to gather the waiting berries and in the late afternoon heat, the trio set to work at filling the stained baskets.

"If Jesus was to come back right now, maybe he could help pick these berries."

"You watch it now, little man. You just better watch it."

"It's so damned hot, though," the little boy swore.

"Mammaw?" the other boy called.

"What is it, Baby?"

"Why's they thorns?"

"Because it's not supposed to be easy." Miss Jessie answered. Casually, she did then cease her laboring and she focused on some imaginary fixed point there on the bank, as if a more suitable reply were hanging there among the thorny fruit or perhaps as though a ghost, more thoughtful and poignant than she, was whispering a better answer softly into her ear. "Or, maybe it was supposed to be," she said slowly from her trance, "but we had to go and make a mess of it." She held the trance and let the words linger and slowly dissipate into the air before physically shivering, shaking off the thought and returning to the berries.

"Huh?" the curious seven year old asked, his small face dramatically screwed into confusion and curiosity.

"Never you mind that just now."

"What about this'n, Mammaw? Is it a good'n?" the other boy asked, holding up a berry, his freckled face squinting in the sun.

"Not the red 'ns, Honey. Red'ns ain't ripe. The black'ns. Mind them thorns, now," she instructed, then added, "And snakes, too. Watch out for snakes."

"Ah, piss on a snake," One of the boys said with a dismissive wave of his small hand, his casual vulgarity not registering with him.

"You boy's mouths is gettin plum terrible, and I'll tell ya what—"

"Look at this'n! It's big, Mammaw." The boy called Toby interrupted. He held up a large blackberry and smiled an incredibly wide jack o'lantern smile.

"'That's a good'n, Toby," Miss Jessie commended, and impossibly, the boy's smile grew even wider.

"And this'n?" The boy who had escaped the scolding held up another unripe red berry, impressively plump. "It's big, too, Mammaw." The proud boy flashed his own smile, identical to his toothless twin's, and waited for the flood of praise that he was sure would be heaped upon him.

"She told ya, *Doofus*. Not the red'ns." Toby shook his head in exaggerated dismay at his brother. "You just ain't no good at berry pickin'. He just ain't no good at this is he, Mammaw?" The boy looked to the woman and waited for her to agree with his assessment of his brother's complete lack of talent where blackberry picking was concerned.

"Yes, by hell, I am good at this." Spurned, Travis defiantly objected.

"Honey, the both of ya does a fine job." The aging woman sighed, removed her floppy sun hat and wiped away the veneer of sweat that covered her forehead. A slight breeze blew through the thicket as she did so and the woman smiled in appreciation of it. She said almost absently, "Travis, you mind that mouth of your'n, now, ya hear me?" The breeze passed and she replaced her hat pushing her graying hair back behind her ears.

The boy called Toby was not satisfied with his grandmother's assessment. "Nuh-uh," he stubbornly disagreed. "I does a fine job on account a I pick the ripe'ns, and he does a bad job on account a he don't." The boy's expression and tone were meant to signal to the others in company that the discussion was over, that his words were divine judgement questionable only under the charge of blasphemy.

At this, the insulted brother's cheeks and forehead flushed. He ground his teeth and growled, signalling to his grandmother a nearing fit.

"Nuh-uh, boy. Now, we ain't throwin' no fits today. You just go on and reel it in, now, ya hear me? I know right here on the route havin' *turrible, turrible* days, so we got nothin' to carry on about in our own lives."

The boy called Travis made little effort to temper his fit. He popped the plump red berry into his mouth with the intent to somehow prove them both wrong about the red ones. While fervently chewing the berry, he formulated a different, but just as poorly thought out response. His chewing slowed and he made an exaggerated grimace to show that he did not care for the taste. With the berry in his mouth he said almost unintelligibly, "Ugh. You're right, Mammaw. The red ones taste like, like dookie." He then spat the chewed berry onto his brother and punctuated the insult with loud and musical laughter. "Haha! You got poop on you!"

Miss Jessie caught the boy by his elbow and gave him a quick jerk, turning him violently around. "Now, why in the world, on a pretty day like today, you wanna go gettin' yourself a whippin' ? Now, you know better. You know better. You think I like givin' y'all whippin's?" Exasperated, she waited for an answer that would not come until suddenly noticing her other grandson had meanwhile filled his mouth to bursting with ripened blackberries. She carefully paced her admonishment in the hope that there would be no misunderstanding as to the serious and grave nature of her warning. "Boy—don't—you—even—think—?" The willful boy did not give her time to tell him what not to think. He spat the mouthful of juicy, chewed berries into his brother's face, having to actually spit twice before he was satisfied.

"Ah ha ha!" Toby pointed at his twin brother's blackberry speckled and disgusted expression, delighted with his retribution.

Miss Jessie released her hold on Travis and grabbed the other boy violently and swatted him two stinging swats on his backside. Toby howled.

It was then Travis' turn to laugh.

"Boy, I don't know why you're laughin'." She shook the sting from her hand, latched onto the boy's arm like a snapping turtle onto a stick, as if she would not release it until thunder struck, and gave Travis the same as she had given his brother. He howled the same note as had his twin.

Back at home, Miss Jessie surveyed the berries soaking in the sink. She soaked the berries in salt water to drive the worms away. They had picked more than she meant to. Many of them not yet ripe, but not so many that picking them out would be such a hard task.

Miss Jessie made a decision. She then made two blackberry cobblers, one for her grandsons and one for Jeannie Tucker.

She stationed her grandsons in the front yard and told them where she was going. She pointed to the kitchen window at the Tucker place. "Stay where I can see you from there. From that window. Don't make me holler for ya or have to come find ya, 'cause if I do have to come lookin' for ya, I'm bringin' a switch. Got it?" The two boys nodded in identical understanding.

"When do we get to eat the cobbler, Mammaw?" Toby asked.

"Yeah, Mammaw." Travis pulled on her arm, almost causing her to lose the cobbler she carried.

"Ours is coolin'. This one's for Miss Jeannie. We'll eat ours when I get back. Y'all stay where I can see ya."

"Aw, how long'll that be?" Travis asked.

"Depends."

"On what?" Toby asked.

"On Miss Jeannie," she said.

Li'l Roy slept on the couch. His dreams were not light nor were they of some endless summer. His hands jerked in odd fits and his moans drew his mother's attention to him. Reluctantly, she woke him and convinced him to leave the rough sofa for the mattress and pillow in his room. She hoped he might find deeper rest there.

She placed a sheet over him and retrieved the box fan and moved it into his room.

Back at the table she scratched at the peeling paint and wept until she spied Miss Jessie coming through the yard.

"Miss Jessie?" she called.

"Last I checked. I made ya a cobbler, Miss Jeannie. Don't mean to be imposin'."

Jeannie rose and met Miss Jessie at the door.

"Made ya cobbler." Miss Jessie smiled.

"I don't understand."

"Pains me to no end about your boy."

"Oh, Miss Jessie, you really shouldn't have."

"Ah, it's just a cobbler, Honey. Oh, it's blackberry. We picked too many berries anyway," she said, though the word sounded more like *burries*. "Oh, looks like I woke you, Miss Jeannie. I'm sorry. I knowed better than to come botherin' you right now, I just wanted to see ya to—"

"I wasn't sleepin'. You didn't wake me. It's okay. It's fine. Really."

"I justed wanted you to know I's still here. Still thinkin' aboutcha ever day."

"Come in, Miss Jessie. Please, come in."

"If'n you sure and all."

Jeannie Tucker accepted the dish from Miss Jessie and the women stepped into the house.

"Should we eat it?" asked Jeannie.

"Why yeah, Honey. That's what cobblers is for. Eatin. Now, why alla sudden you actin' like you never had no cobbler, Miss Jeannie? White folks don't eat no cobbler?"

Jeannie laughed. "Come with me." The two made their way to the kitchen and Jeannie placed the fresh blackberry cobbler on the kitchen table, suddenly embarrassed at the sad state the table top was in.

"That baby sleepin'?" Miss Jessie asked. Jeannie smiled at this and thought how nice it was to hear someone use that word regarding Li'l Roy.

"Finally."

"Bless his little heart."

"I've got milk," she said. "You want milk?"

"Oh, I bet milk would just be great with them blackberries, Miss Jeannie. You mind if I sit here in this chair? I need to keep an eye on them boys." Miss Jessie pointed out the window. "Don't mean to stay too long."

"Don't you worry none about it. It's good to see you." Jeannie set the plates and poured the milk. "Travis and Toby lookin' forward to the fair?" She pulled two servings from the cobbler and sat with her neighbor.

"They is, but if they don't straighten up they ain't a goin'. I done told 'em."

"Mmm. That's delicious, Miss Jessie. Thank you." Jeannie wiped the corner of her mouth with her bare knuckle.

"Miss Jeannie, can I ask you somethin'?"

Jeannie Tucker felt a wave of apprehension. "You ask me whatever you want to ask me," she said, lifting another bite of cobbler.

"Honey, do you blame me for it? Is it my fault?"

"Blame you for what, Miss Jessie? For Ronny?"

"For sendin' Netta down to get the sheriff on Big Roy? I's afraid he was gonna kill ya. But if'n I'd minded my own business, well, it woulda probably just blowed over."

"I, it never, no, no way, Miss Jessie. I never blamed you."

"Didn't seem like we was such friends after—"

"I thought you quit talkin' to me 'cause we turned out to be such trash."

"Miss Jeannie! Don't you ever let me hear you say nothin' like that again! You want a whippin'?"

Jeannie Tucker laughed. "No, Miss Jessie. I don't want no whippin'." She shrugged, "After Big Roy killed Sheriff Bill and everybody quit talkin' to us, quit lookin' at us, even, I just thought—I didn't blame ya."

Miss Jessie laughed. "You mean you ain't been mad at me all these years? All this time?"

"Not for a minute." Jeannie did not cry as she pushed the fork through the juicy cobbler, but she feared she might. "I thought you was ashamed to know us anymore."

"I shoulda made this cobbler and had this talk a long time ago, then. Maybe I'm the one needs a whippin'."

The two women laughed and enjoyed the warm cobbler and the cold milk.

Miss Jessie peaked out the kitchen window to check on her own boys. She saw them clearly, their mouths caked in blackberries. Between them sat the demolished blackberry cobbler. They scooped at it with their hands.

"I want you to look at somethin'." She motioned to Jeannie and Jeannie moved to the window and leaned in close with Miss Jessie. "Honey, them little heathens'll be the death of me. God knows I love'em, but damned if'n they won't. Oh, they gonna git it."

Jeannie smiled and sat back in her chair. "It's hard raisin' boys. It's so hard, Miss Jessie." She pushed the fork slowly through the cobbler. A tear escaped the corner of her eye. Miss Jessie rose from her chair and went to her.

She held Jeannie tightly against her breast and Jeannie bawled. Miss Jessie wept with her.

Chapter 21

V irginia Lawford sits on the edge of her bed. Her door is opened, but barely. Her window has been nailed shut and she sweats profusely in the stifling, still air. She has always referred to the man who has come calling as "Uncle Johnny." She has not seen him in a very long time.

He is Dickie Stearns' daddy and Dickie Stearns is almost as pretty as the Tucker boys. She thinks Dickie Stearns would have made a great candidate to father her baby, but then remembers he is her cousin.

In the sitting room, the men speak in low voices and though she cannot hear them very well, she knows well what they are discussing. Through the crack in her door, she cannot see them. The only thing she can see is the curio cabinet her daddy made for her mama to display the glass figurines she collected before she died. Some of the figurines are mail order. Some are gifts from family and friends from places so far away and exotic as Germany and Disneyland.

Among the figurines, she has two favorites and would be hard pressed to pick one between the two. Her first favorite, but not her most favorite is a lion family someone bought for her mama at the Jacksonville Zoo. There is the proud lion with his beautiful glass mane. There is the lioness, powerful and feminine. And between them, the lion cub that she is absolutely sure is a little girl cub, a lioness in waiting.

Her second favorite is the horse, a glass mare sculpted in full gallop, her mane wild and beautiful, her chin high and her spirit obviously unbreakable.

So that she might have a better view, she moves to be closer to the opening in the door. Her bed squeaks. The men stop talking. She does not dare breathe until their voices begin again.

Tom Lawford is a visible wreck. He shakes. His eyes are wide. His mouth has gone dry. "I've failed her, Johnny. I shoulda sent her to live with my sister in Indiana when Peggy died, but I just couldn't stand the thought of losin' 'em both. I was selfish. I was nothin' but selfish. When she first got her period, I shoulda put her on the bus, put her on a bus like you did Netta Simms."

At this, Johnny Stearns bristles but remains quiet, listening to his brother-in-law ramble on until finally deciding to quiet him.

"You killed that boy deader than yesterday, Tom. You should've seen Little Roy last night at the station. He'd run the whole way, wild eyed, covered in his brother's blood. He'd tried to carry him, Tom."

Quiet Tom Lawford puts his head in hands and begins to weep in jagged breaths. "I did." He sobs. "God help me, I did and I liked to beat the 'hind end off my girl, too."

"Wait a minute. You tellin' me—does Virginia know you did it? She know ya killed that boy?" Stearns motions slightly with his chin toward the girl's bedroom door.

Tom Lawford raises his head and looks at his brother-in-law. "Yeah, Johnny. She knows."

Johnny Stearns whispers,"Good God, Tom."

"I know. I know." Johnny Stearns has never seen Quiet Tom so shaken. "Now," Tom begins, "What are we gonna do? We gotta do somethin' about that last one. Lord help me, I don't mean kill him or nothin'. Hell, I don't know what I mean, Johnny. She ain't gonna have no life in this town, this gets out. Who's gonna want her for a wife?"

Stearns rubs his face with his hand and cradles his chin and jaw with his palm. "I don't know, either. But we damned sure ain't killin' Little Roy Tucker. He know you?"

"Don't think I ever talked to him before last night, but he told me he knew who I was."

"Goddammit, Tom." Johnny Stearns sits quietly trying to to grasp the reality of it all. "Let me chew on it for a while. I gotta cut them Hickeys loose. They had alibis anyway."

"We could put him on a bus, too, Johnny. Like I'm gonna do with her. Like you did with Netta Simms—"

"Goddammit, Tom, stop talkin' about Netta Simms. I said let me chew on it."

Once Uncle Johnny has gone, her father calls for her. "'Bout time to head out for services."

She has not been to a Sunday Evening service in many years. Much like the morning service, she worries that perhaps the Devil has a hold on her because she cannot stay with the preacher's words.

When it is over, with his left hand, her father receives many handshakes and receives many hugs.

It is evening and they have had their supper. "Uncle Johnny" has long since gone. In the air, she can smell the rain is coming.

Will it, can it wash these things away?

They live very differently now. They are back in the stillness that held them for too long before. It is, to Virginia, much like it was after her mama died. They are now, each of them, both of them, in their own quiet and private way, struggling to find their breath beneath the new and strange weight of it all.

Quiet Tom has told her if the blood comes, then she is not pregnant. If the blood comes, he reiterates, then there will be no baby.

"We should pray on it," he says, and on their knees, they do. Quiet Tom does. She listens.

She listens to him tell Jesus that she is ignorant and she wonders, *who was to be my teacher?*

She listens to him tell Jesus that she is dirty and she wonders, *who was to bathe me?*

She listens to him tell Jesus that she has strayed and she wonders, *who was to shepherd me?*

She listens to him pray that the blood will come.

She prays silently that it will not.

She prays for a baby, fresh, new and blameless to bring love, real love, the kind of love that died with her mama, back into the house. She prays for the baby that will love her. She prays for the baby that will need her.

She prays that in her belly she is growing a little boy, an as yet nameless self, blonde and beautiful like Li'l Roy.

She prays Sweet Lamb of Almighty God, give me this. Give us this.

Quiet Tom says, "In your blessed name, we pray. Amen." The two of them get up from the floor.

Afterward, in her bed, she lets the rain sing her to sleep and she wonders, *what will they do with you, Li'l Roy Tucker?*

Chapter 22

On the route, the rain came, at first a light sunshower, deceptively comforting, a break from the sweltering heat, pleasant and cooling. Fat drops left tiny craters in the dirt road. The unbridled children capered and danced primitive pagan dances in it, and when the craters disappeared along with the sun, and the rain fell in sheets and waves, they played in the new and sudden puddles of mud neverminding the lightning nor the shotgun crack of thunder that rolled and echoed off the ridges and the hilltops, until they were cursed at and commanded homeward. Ditches became flowing creeks. Creeks became rivers. The broad bank beneath the trestle disappeared as the Russell River swelled and threatened to invade the rural route, but ultimately held itself within its course.

There was nothing to be done about such forces, just as when the blizzard had visited Sonoraville the previous March.

For two days, the irregular rain came and went. On the day she buried her boy, Jeannie Tucker stepped warily out the front door. The weather had granted her a reprieve. She surveyed the road ahead and then looked to the portentous and dismal gray sky. From the distance, The Russell River roared. She tucked her umbrella beneath her arm and appealed to the heavens that she not need it on this, the longest of walks.

"Take your shoes off, Roy." She did not look to the boy behind her. She stopped on the steps and slipped her bare feet from from her flats, hooking them onto her fingers. She wore the nicest dress that she owned. It was not black, but green.

"What?" asked Li'l Roy, a bit taken aback by his mother's strange command.

"Take your shoes off and tie 'em together and throw 'em over your shoulder. Take your socks off, too and stuff 'em into your shoes."

"Why you want me to do that?"

She sighed, weakly. "You're barefooted every damned day, Li'l Roy. Now, I'm asking you to go barefooted and you wanna argue with me. Just 'til we get to the pavement. You can put 'em back on there." The boy, abashed, did as his mother told. "Now roll your pants up at the bottom," she directed him, still not sparing him a look, and added, "as high as you can."

"What?"

With her chin, she motioned silently toward the road where the rain had transformed the dirt and most of the yards into thick and squishy mud. "You're not showin' up at your brother's funeral lookin' like you've been wallerin' in a mud hole. I ain't a havin' it." She stepped out into the marshy yard, holding up the hem of her dress.

The boy sat on the step and rolled up the legs of what passed as his nicest pair of blue jeans. "We can walk the tracks, Mama. We could just walk the tracks."

"The thorns'll get my dress. I already look bad enough. You can walk the tracks. I'll meet ya down the road a ways."

He did not consider his response for even a moment. "I'm walkin' with you," he said.

"That's my boy."

"But, what about you, Mama? We both gonna get muddy as all hell, but I can roll my pants back down and cover it up. What're you gonna do, you in that dress and all?"

"We can wash off in the bathrooms at Pudgy's."

"I don't know if I wanna go in Pudgy's, Mama."

She sighed again. "You think I do? If you don't want to go in there, then you can just roll your pants back down when we get to the church."

"Is it just us, Mama?"

She knew well what her boy was asking. "Freeman's gonna meet up with us at the boardin' house. No point in him walkin' all the way down in this shit."

They walked the first quarter mile with great trepidation, slipping and sliding in the mire, struggling to keep their footing as rich mud squeezed up between their toes. Once, Jeannie Tucker slipped, but managed to somewhat save herself by splaying out her arms in an attempt to keep the dress out of the mud. The damage to the dress was minimal, with only a splotch at the knee. The shoes she held were caked and ruined. Her free hand came out of the mud with a thick and wet sucking sound that otherwise would have made Li'l Roy laugh. Her hands were covered with the mud and she could not wipe the smear from her dress. "See how hard it is to get out of here?" she asked the boy before realizing she had done so.

"Even to the grave," he said and her heart wept for him.

She walked on with her soiled hands out in front of her in a way that reminded Li'l Roy of The Mummy and Frankenstein's monster. In a futile attempt at levity, he put his own hands out in a similar fashion and moaned. He looked to his mother, hoping she would laugh with him, but saw she was crying.

From behind them a woman's voice called, "Miss Jeannie! Miss Jeannie, wait!" Miss Jessie and the twins, dressed in their Sunday School cordoroys, trekked through the muddy rutted road. Li'l Roy looked to his mother and caught her smile and wave. She wiped her high cheeks carefully with the back of her muddied hand.

Jeannie Tucker opened her umbrella as the rain came again. She attempted to usher the twin boys beneath it.

"They all right, Miss Jeannie. Don't you go frettin' over them, Honey. They like it."

The paved road appeared in the distance. A pickup truck was waiting. Freeman emerged from the passenger's side of the cab with an umbrella. The group quickened their step.

"Marty's gonna give us a ride," Freeman called as the band approached.

"Them boys can get in the back." Miss Jessie moved to the tailgate and opened it. Li'l Roy and the two boys climbed in. Miss Jessie shut the gate and latched it.

"Thank you, Freeman. I gotta wash off," Jeannie Tucker insisted. She held her hands up for Freeman to see and pointed out the muddy spots on her dress.

Freeman nodded his understanding and ushered the two women inside the cab of the truck.

Once Jeannie and Miss Jessie were inside the cab, Marty explained, "Woulda come all the way down and gotcha but see, Freeman only just told me, Miss Jeannie. Probably woulda got stuck anyways, but I'd a tried. Watch that hole in the floor board."

"Thank you so much, Marty. I do appreciate it more than I can say. Sorry to track all of this into your truck. How's your daddy?"

"Strong as whiskey some days, weak as water the next. And don't you worry about this truck, Jeannie Marie. Oh, and my condolences. Sorry about your loss." Marty said, suddenly somber, his thoughts on his father, on the March snowfall, on the night his father had passed away.

It was not for reasons nefarious nor financial that Marty Shoemaker withheld the grim truth concerning his father's current condition. A mere handful of months earlier, winter had dumped such a snowfall that the roads had become impassable for several days. It was beneath this blanket of snow on a post midnight trip to relieve himself, Marty discovered his father had given up the ghost and died. He had seen his father there in the strange darkness, in the recliner where he had long taken to sleeping, nestled in blankets, his eyes staring vacantly, his mouth opened slightly as if anxious to get one last word out before the final moment came.

"*Dad?*" Marty had whispered through the quiet, but his father had not replied.

Strangely unshaken, Marty had moved on to the stove, stoked the dying fire and added a log. "Still comin' down out there," he said over his shoulder.

Those damned mice hadn't helped things, either—twin field mice, fat and healthy as though winter had been easy for them, big ears, big black eyes hopeful and shining even in the darkness, and—*cute*—all right, goddammit they were cute little bastards, like out of that Cinderella cartoon or something, but mice didn't follow you when you were awake. They followed you in dreams, darting from corner to corner, fluidly, rolling like quick little balls from sight to out of sight and back again until curious enough and brave enough to stop and study with their big concerned eyes asking, *"What will you do, Marty? What will you do?"*

And the snow—

It was the kind of snowfall that speaks to that part of a man's heart that still belongs to his ancestors. It was the kind of snowfall that left the world pristine, primeval and unmolested, that left a man feeling ancient and unbridled, with a feeling that ran so deeply through him that he could not recognize it as simple nostalgia. But nostalgia it was, though many would deem it impossible to be nostalgic for a time, for a moment, that one could not actually remember, for a time before man had ravaged the land and left it scarred and scorched.

The deep drifts had brought with them a queer, ethereal glow and lay in a sound absorbing crystalline blanket that cast an otherworldly shroud over the house, nudging Marty over the fence and onto the side to which he was already heavily leaning—the side that said to him, *"You are still asleep. This, this is a dream."*

Beneath those heavy influential factors, Marty had left his dead father there in the night and returned to bed where, shivering in the teeth chattering cold, he had pulled the layered blankets up around his face until the uncomfortable heat of his own breath had forced him to pull them back down a bit, taking a moment to look for those damned mice as he did so. They were there in the doorway, asking Marty, *"That's it? You're just gonna go back to bed? With him in there like that?"*

"Shut up," Marty had commanded. "This is a dream, see. Don't you feel it?" Marty turned his head from them, rolled onto his side and closed his eyes. Almost immediately, he fell back to sleep.

Now, here he was in the cold gray morning light, offering coffee to the old man who was unarguably deceased.

"Oh, Dad." Marty backed away from the recliner and returned to the kitchen, coffee in hand.

At the kitchen table, he lit a Chesterfield and sat in silence watching the snow fall through the window above the sink. He drank both the coffees, lighting one cigarette with another again and again and tried to focus his thoughts on his dead father just on the other side of the wall. Strangely, he found he had trouble doing so. He refilled both cups and kept the practice going throughout the morning. As morning evaporated into afternoon, he filled the ashtray with cigarette butts. When the coffee hit his bladder, rather than walking past his father, he chose to piss in the sink. From that vantage, he could see the snow outside was well up to the bed of the truck and still falling. There would be no leaving the holler, not for a few days anyway. Nervously, he washed his hands and scoured the sink with Comet.

In the stove, the fire had all but died. Instinctively, he walked toward the stove, stopping abruptly when he spied the pair of field mice. They scurried across the stained linoleum, between Marty and the stove and there they stopped, looking anxiously at the man towering above them.

Confounded, Marty studied them for a moment before eventually conceding, "Yeah. S'pose you guys are right." He would need to leave the fire out. It would slow down the process. "Because we're not gettin' outta here and they ain't nobody gettin' up here. Not in this." The duo then fled, seeking refuge behind the aging ice box.

Marty sat back at the table, lit another cigarette and shivered again.

By evening, he'd traded the coffee for whiskey and had donned his coat. By nightfall, he'd dressed in layers beneath it. He shivered and shook in the cold and watched his breath waft through the air.

He could hear the mice from their hiding place. He sat and smoked while they chattered on, trying to ignore them until his patience wore thin.

"No, I'm not." He heard himself say. "I'm not gonna do that. You guys should know me better. I'm not gonna just set him outside, see. Leave him out there for the coyotes and whatever else. I wouldn't do that. What? Naw, I wouldn't." Marty dragged from the cigarette. "Whaddaya mean when I get cold, I will? I'm already cold. Yeah? Ya think I don't know it's gonna get colder? But I ain't gonna do that." Marty's eyes fell on the telephone hanging on the kitchen wall. "You guys are right," he said to the refrigerator. "I should at least call somebody. The sheriff? Yeah, that's what I was thinkin', too. I know they can't get up here in this but—"

Marty stood, approached the phone and contemplated the words he would have to say. When he placed the handset to his ear, there was no dial tone, only dead air. Marty was relieved. Reluctantly, and as if only for show, he clicked the hanger a few times, but the clicking brought no change. He hung up the phone and said, "Well, there's that."

From the living room his dead father farted and Marty pretended he did not hear. He turned on the radio on the kitchen counter and turned up the volume so that he would not have to pretend he did not hear if what he did not hear should not happen again.

"May the bird of paradise fly up your nose
May your wife be plagued with runners in her hose."

Marty drank.

Around three a.m., he woke, his neck stiff, his head throbbing. When he rose from the kitchen table and moved toward the stove, the mice did not come.

In the living room, he closed his father's dead eyes and covered his head with the blanket.

"In the mornin', Pop. I'll see you in the mornin'," he said and took himself to bed as the warmth began to spread through the small house.

At first light, Marty was in the backyard, up near the treeline, with a shovel. He struggled with the cold and the hard work, but knew there was indeed harder work to come. He cleared a circle of snow roughly five feet in diameter and at it center, he built a fire, feeding it gasoline and firewood until the frozen earth and the surrounding snow were no match for it. He fed it until lunch time when he reminded himself that he could not remember when last he had eaten.

In the kitchen, he heated up a can of chicken noodle soup and ate it over the sink, watching the large fire outside burn black and orange beneath the gray sky.

The roads would clear. The snow would melt. And when it did, he would drive down into town and let it be known that Sergeant Shoemaker, who had served in France under Pershing during what he always referred to as 'The Great War,' was dead. Mister Shoemaker, retired wood shop teacher, was dead. Orville, who, until emphysema took him down, loved to walk the roads with pennies and peppermints in his pockets calling everyone 'neighbor' as he trod along even if he found himself on the far end of the county, had left his earthly home. "Dad," last of the real good men, widower, best father a boy could hope for, who always smelled like sawdust and home, was dead.

When the sickness first took him down, his presence along the county roads was immediately missed.

"Marty, how's your dad?"

"Strong as Flander's mule, one day, weak as water the next."

At Pudgy's::

"Marty, how's your dad?"

"Strong as an oak one day, weak as smoke the next."

144

Marty Shoemaker labored through the day and into the evening, sweating beneath the newly falling snow and his winter coat. When the hole was dug to his satisfaction, he rested, plotting out his next steps as he did so. It would not be as his father had envisioned, but it would be as close as Marty could get it.

At the entrance of the shed, he shoveled the snow until the door swung freely. Inside, he stood before the large object covered in blankets held on by rope. Would it surprise anyone in Whelan County to learn that Orville Shoemaker had built his own coffin? It would not. It also would not surprise them to see how simple yet beautiful its construction was. Its design was a throwback to the days before coffins became caskets, an oblong box of choice cherry, sanded to silk perfection and finished with a light stain. The hinges were from the front door of the cabin he had grown up in. Inside, Orville Shoemaker had lined the vessel with beautiful, primitive patchwork quilts his deceased wife had made.

Back in the house, he carefully removed his father from the recliner and carried him to the bathroom where he stripped him down and bathed him in a warm bath. He shaved his father's face and neck, and applied a dose of aftershave. He then dressed him in his best Sunday suit, oiled his hair and parted it neatly on the left side the way the old man favored it.

Darkness had fallen, but the night was brightened by the snow.

He had to put the coffin in the hole first, without his father in it. This he managed to do by placing a sheet of unused plywood over half the grave, resting the coffin on top of it and then hammering and pulling at the sheet of wood until first one end of the coffin teetered into the hole and then the other, falling to the muddy earth with a wet *plunk*. When it was positioned, Marty climbed in and opened the box.

There was no way to put his father into the hole that would not be rough on the old man, but Marty took great pains to keep the bumping and roughness to a minimum. Marty knelt there on the closed lower section as again the snow began to fall. Before closing the top half, Marty crossed his father's arms as the snow quickly accumulated on the old man's cold face. He offered one last adjustment to his father's hair, kissed him on the forehead and was surprised to find that the old man still smelled of sawdust and home.

"Ya look good, Pop. Go rest. Give Mom my love when you see her," Marty closed the upper section.

Gray dawn was breaking by the time Marty had filled the hole back up with dirt, snow and mud. Every muscle in his body tensed and cramped. His joints ached. His stomach screamed for nourishment. His mind called for rest. But before he could tend to himself, he resolved that there was one more task at hand.

He dragged the soiled recliner out the back door, through the snow to the far edge of the property. There he doused it in gasoline and set it to blaze.

He fell asleep in the hot bath and woke to find himself freezing in the cold of the house. He rose from the water and winced in pain. He dressed, started the fire in the stove and cooked himself three eggs, toast and bacon and washed it down with three cups of coffee.

Almost a week would pass before the road out of Shoemaker Holler would be cleared. Marty, short on provisions and burning up with a raging onset of cabin fever had driven hell bent for glory to the grocery store. When Marty made it to Cas Walker's and Bobby the Butcher asked about the old man, it was merely habit that made him answer, "Strong as a bull one day, weak as a turd the next." He hadn't even realized he had lied about it until he was back in his truck and on the road. He liked the way it felt, though. It felt like suddenly the old man was alive again, still somehow in this world. With sadness, he realized that if he told it true, folks would say how sorry they were and what a good man Orville Shoemaker had been and how they had always thought a lot of him. They would offer their condolences and then they wouldn't think about him anymore. They wouldn't ask about him anymore. So Marty kept the old man alive for as long as he could.

Back at home, he put up the groceries and, out of the corner of his eye caught a flurry of movement. The cute little bastards were back behind the ice box. Marty stepped from the pantry.

"I will," he said. "I'll call the Sheriff. Of course, I will. What? When? When I'm damned good and ready."

Later that evening, feeling as though they had left him with no choice, Marty set the traps.

Freeman stood in the parking lot. "Marty? Marty?" Marty Shoemaker shook off his woeful thoughts and turned to Freeman. "I'm gonna climb in back with the boys. She's gonna run into Pudgy's and clean up a li'l bit, so stop there if ya would."

"Got it," said Marty.

"No," Jeannie protested, looking at Miss Jessie's soiled clothing. "I changed my mind. I'm fine. Really, I am."

Marty put the old truck in gear and it jerked to a roll.

"Wait, Mister Marty! Hold up, now." Miss Jessie pointed to the dirt road.

"Well, looky here, see," Marty said and tapped Jeannie's elbow with his own. He turned the steering wheel sharply and the old truck moaned and shook like a great tired beast.

More were coming through the muck to pay their respects. They slipped and slid and marched through the rain, some holding their hands up and calling to the truck. Marty stopped the truck and waited. Before climbing into the truck bed they each in turn peaked their heads into the cab to let Jeannie Tucker know that they were sorry about her loss. Miss Jessie counted heads and took attendance as they did so. She was relieved to find that everyone on the route had come and she would not have to skin anyone as she had threatened to do if they did not come to that boy's funeral. She silently beamed in her accomplishment.

When they had all climbed into the bed and settled themselves in, Marty ground the gears again and the truck lurched ahead.

Through the back window of the cab, Li'l Roy smiled at his mother as the new arrivals piled into the back of the truck. She smiled back a tearful smile.

"Sis Tucker, I know it's hard, honey. I know you're lookin' for comfort. I know it's gotta seem like they's no comfort to be found. I offer you—" Brother Sturgill's words drifted as he turned to watch the police cruiser.

"Might wanna hold up there, preacher," a voice suggested.

The small gathering of mourners and payers of respect watched as Stearns exited the vehicle. A deputy exited the other side and opened the rear door. Lenville Tucker emerged from the back seat. Many curious eyes turned to Jeannie Tucker and she felt them on her like so many crawling bugs. The deputy escorted Lenville around the vehicle. He was dressed in a gray detention center jumpsuit. He wore leg irons and around his waist, a large leather belt to which his wrists were shackled. The deputy held him by the elbow and the two lawmen and the prisoner approached the graveside service.

"You just wait right here for a minute." Jeannie Tucker commanded her youngest son and went to her oldest son. The deputy stopped.

"Minimal contact, Ma'm," said the deputy.

Jeannie acknowledged the deputy's words with a slight nod. Her lips curled into a furious snarl and her eyes welled with tears.

"Look at me," she commanded her eldest. Lenville Tucker lifted his head, but found that he could not. "I said look at me," she snarled. Lenville Tucker raised his head and looked into his mother's furious eyes. A slight rain began to fall. Jeannie Tucker did not blink. She slapped her oldest hard across the face. Lenville's head shot to the side, a hot rose bloomed on his cheek. Still, his expression remained neutral.

"This is on you," she hissed. "This is on you, and when you get to Brushy, you tell your goddamned daddy it's on him, too." Lenville said nothing. Again, Jeannie slapped him.

"Ma'm!" exclaimed the deputy. He stepped between the woman and her son and looked to the sheriff. Sheriff Stearns held up his hand in a silent command to the deputy. The deputy yielded his current position and resumed his former.

Jeannie Tucker stepped away from her oldest son and walked toward the graveside. She clasped her youngest son's hand in her own and said quietly to him, "Li'l Roy, I know what you're gonna say to your brother. Don't you do it. They's police here. Don't you say it." Li'l Roy nodded. She turned and said to Lenville, "Get your ass over here beside me." Lenville and the deputy did so.

Stearns stayed back, shaming himself for not being able to avert his eyes from Jeannie Tucker in that green dress.

The rain grew steadier. Freeman opened the umbrella and held it over Jeannie.

"Please, Brother," Jeannie said to Preacher Sturgill. "Get this over with."

"All right, Sis," he said and cleared his throat. "Sis Tucker, I know it's gotta seem like there is no comfort to be found. I offer you Paul's words to the Romans: *What shall we then say to these things? If God be for us, who can be against us? He that spared not his own Son, but delivered him up for us all, how shall he not with him also freely give us all things? Who shall lay any thing to the charge of God's elect? It is God that justifieth. Who is he that condemneth? It is Christ that died, yea rather, that is risen again, who is even at the right hand of God, who also maketh intercession for us. Who shall separate us from the love of Christ? Shall tribulation, or distress, or persecution, or famine, or nakedness, or peril, or sword? As it is written, For thy sake we are killed all the day long; we are accounted as sheep for the slaughter. Nay, in all these things we are more than conquerors through him that loved us. For I am persuaded, that neither death, nor life, nor angels, nor principalities, nor powers, nor things present, nor things to come, nor height, nor depth, nor any other creature, shall be able to separate us from the love of God, which is in Christ Jesus our Lord."*

Once it was over, and everyone was again loaded into Marty's pickup, Jeannie said to Miss Jessie and to Marty, "Just a minute." She dashed through the rain toward the patrol car just as it was leaving.

Stearns stopped the vehicle and rolled down the window. "Jeannie Marie?"

"I need to talk to you for a minute, Johnny. In private."

Stearns put the vehicle in park.

At the rear of the vehicle, in the pouring rain, Jeannie said to Stearns, "Do somethin', Johnny. Help me. Before I lose another one. Do something."

"I will, Jeannie. I will." Stearns studied her for a moment and then started back toward the driver's side door but stopped. "Jeannie?" She turned back to him. "I want

148

you to know that I tried to make arrangements for Big Roy to be brought down for this. He's locked down in solitairy confinement."

"Yeah," she said, blinking the rain from her eyes. "Aren't we all?"

Chapter 23

There is a hole in the summer where the Tucker boys used to be.
a song unsung in the night
a stillness in the river
a fade in the day

Tom Lawford and his daughter eat a silent lunch in a silent home, the only sound the occasional scrape of the spoon against the wall of the soup bowl.

He still cannot bear to look at her.

"Eat." She hears him say.

Virginia is on the porch when the rain brings him in from the field. She sits in the rocker wishing the rain would stop so that he could get back to his work, taking with him the heavy air he now carries. He does not sit. She studies him as he gazes out at the downpour. His hat is wet and dripping. Distraction has allowed the rain to catch him unprepared. His heavy boots are caked with mud. She feels for him. He stands gaunt and exhausted. He is suddenly so old, so broken. He has his shoulder to the post and he does not look at her when he asks about the blood. In a moment of mercy, she tells him it has come.

She watches a bit of life return to his lanky shoulders. He walks away from her, through the opened front door, and, lost in his relief, she can see he does not notice the mud and the filth he tracks into the house.

She listens for the sound of his heavy boots to tell her he is returning to the porch and for a wild and brief moment, she considers running. She can see herself sprinting across the field, defiant and determined. He is suddenly beside her with something in his hand. He offers it to her without a word and she receives it likewise. He returns to the post and resumes his distant position studying the rain. He stands taller now.

She studies the bus ticket.

"I promised Mama I'd stay with you," she says.

"You're already gone, girl," her father says. She is going to live with her Aunt Betty in Indiana. "It's not 'cause I don't love you, girl," he says, more to the rain than to her. "It's 'cause I do."

She is not saddened by this news, but still she cries. Not because she doesn't love him, but because she does.

When the rain breaks, he heads wordlessly back out into the field. She sits in the comfort she finds in knowing that unless the rain returns, he will not come back to the house until it is time to head out for the evening service.

More than absolutely anything else in the world, she wants to go and lie beneath the trestle and wait for the train to come.

Chapter 24

L i'l Roy's legs dangled over the edge of the trestle and nervously he swung them back and forth. He sat beneath rainless clouds, rolling and thunderous, that moved quickly across the sky like a great and ghostly spooked herd. The rains had ceased. He had never seen the Russell River this muddy nor this strange color. He had never seen it so high. He had never seen it flow at the fierce pace it now flowed. It flowed so strongly that the air it pushed along slightly blew his lengthy sun bleached bangs from his eyes. He had heard rumors that a couple of folks had died in the flood. His thoughts were heavily on them, helpless in the current of it, being pushed along by an unstoppable force, their calling mouths filling with muddy water, flailing their arms until they were too exhausted to fight the mighty current.

He watched as an old car hood sailed through the rough water, like an unsinkable ship on an angry sea. There were an infinite number of garbage bags and pop bottles and more trees than he could shake a stick at. The deadly river was filled with floating dead fish. A front car seat came rolling along and he wondered if it belonged to the same car as the hood. A dead calf came, bloated and eyeless and he was suddenly no longer interested in what else might be headed his way.

Back at home, he gathered up empty bottles, trying unsuccessfully to keep them from clinking together and waking his mother. He planned on carting them over to Cas Walker's and cashing them in for the deposit.

The small bell above the door of The Tastee-Creem sang its one note tune. Resisting the urge to sit on a stool at the counter and spin around and around all afternoon, Li'l Roy made his way to the booth in the corner where he could sit in the sun alone and observe most of the diner. It was nearing half past noon, the midsummer sun had warmed the booth nicely.

From his front pocket, he retrieved the Band-Aid tin. He popped the top, tilted the rusty tin and shook it slightly. The two nudie cards slipped out along with three half smoked cigarettes he had scavenged. He quickly secreted away the cards but not before stealing a good and solid look. He dipped two nail-bitten fingers into the tin and retrieved a book of matches.

"What can I getcha, Roy?" Tracy French was there.

"Hey, Tracy. Two chocolate shakes. Two fries, please."

Tracy French extended her hand. "I'm sorry about Ronny, Li'l Roy. He always made me laugh. He was so funny. You okay?" She touched his shoulder affectionately.

"Thanks, Tracy. I'm okay. Ronny said he thought you was fine as wine."

"Aw, that's sweet," she said, not knowing what else to say. "Have them fries right up for ya."

Li'l Roy sat in the sun and lit one of the cigarettes. Tracy was roughly his age, but had always seemed older, more mature. In morose reverie, he sat with his gaze fixed beyond the window, watching the automobiles slowly travel up and down Main Street until, just in front of him, on the other side of the glass, a pickup truck slid into a parking space and came to a jerky stop. Dickie Stearns' face glowed in sunlight behind the wheel. He caught Li'l Roy staring, smiled and nodded his hello. Coolly, Li'l Roy nodded back but suddenly inexplicably embarrassed, he quickly looked away and down at the Band-Aid tin.

Tracy suddenly appeared with the milkshakes and the fries and Roy was happy to be distracted by them. She placed a milkshake and an order of fries in front of Li'l Roy, and placed the other order on the other side of the table.

"Those fries are real hot," she warned him. "They just came up."

"Thanks." Li'l Roy reached for the ketchup bottle on the table.

"Who's joinin' ya, Roy?"

"Nobody."

"Who's the other order for?"

Tracy stood smiling, waiting for an answer. They looked for a moment into each other's eyes and Tracy understood. "Just let me know if you need anything else."

The bell sounded as Dickie Stearns entered, and Li'l Roy was glad it did. Tracy walked away and Li'l Roy squirted a hefty serving of ketchup onto his fries. He heard Tracy French coo at Dickie, "*Hellooo*, Dickie."

Mr. Maynard from the hardware store entered the diner. Liza and Katy from the drug store came in behind him and seated themselves on the spinning stools and immediately started twisting in them. Four uniformed recruiters came in. Davie Boy Lewis and Mike Sizemore soon followed. The pair directly spied Dickie Stearns and made their way to him. They argued with each other momentarily as to which one should have to get into the booth first and it sounded to Li'l Roy like Mike Sizemore lost the argument and entered the booth with a groan.

Some pulled into the parking lot. Some walked from their jobs in town. They came in couples. They came alone. Five from the bank came in together. Very quickly, the quiet diner had taken on the volume of the school cafeteria.

The guys from *the shop* talked about how Mr. Barkman must ride his brake all day long and the torture he performed on clutches was an outright sin. Coach Hendershot told Dickie that the football team line up was a great one this year, but he sure missed having Dickie there to get that ball down field.

Li'l Roy finished his fries and sucked down the last of his chocolate shake. The movie was about to start. He left Ronny's fries and shake untouched, left two dollars on the table and knew it would not matter if it wasn't enough.

He waited until the sidewalk traffic was clear before entering the alley and scaling the wall.

With a final push, Li'l Roy tumbled through the window and into the store room of the Starlite Theater. The walls were littered with movie posters and bills. There were life size cut outs of various movie characters frozen forever in promotional poses. When he found his feet, he took a moment and let his eyes wonder about the magical room.

He opened the door to the hallway just enough to have a peak and seeing no one, stepped out into the hall, closing the door behind him. He headed for the stairs and was startled by the man coming up them.

"You're not supposed to be up here, son," the red fire hydrant of a man said.

"Sorry." Li'l Roy offered.

"Whattaya lookin' for?"

Li'l Roy studied the man, his nose was red and bulbous and supported a pair of black horn rimmed glasses. His thinning hair was slicked and oiled in a fashion that was quickly fading. Li'l Roy answered the man. "The balcony. I's lookin' for the balcony."

"Don't you lie to me, son. You come up here lookin' to lift some movie posters?"

"Do I look like I stole some movie posters? Look like I got a life size cut out of Jerry Lewis stuck down my pants do I?"

The bull-necked man's face reddened. "Why you— Get your goddamned smart ass back downstairs before I put you out on your ear."

When *The Love Bug* was over and the credits began to roll, the small theater slowly emptied. Li'l Roy Tucker did not rise from his seat. He sat for a bit, allowing his eyes to dry there in the semi darkness before stepping out into the sunlight and the rest of the world.

He made his way to the alley and sat out of sight behind a group of trash cans. He thought of Buddy Hackett and of how Ronny would have laughed his ass off.

Ronny—

Li'l Roy made several attempts at plotting revenge for Ronny's murder, each scenario playing out on the silver screen of his teenaged mind, each scenario ending in brutal bloodshed. It was a hell of a place to be put in by circumstance, where a man sought the blood, the misery, the terror, the death of another man. In the end, his better angels won over. Li'l Roy didn't want to murder anyone. He wanted to live in a world where he didn't feel he needed to or was required to.

Johnny Stearns sat in the gravel parking lot of Pudgy's Tavern facing the road. He let the unsuspecting boy walk by him with a cool nod in the careless afternoon.

By the time June arrived and properly settled itself in, Stearns' left arm was a deep, dark brown up to his shirt sleeve. The years had left the flesh there now prematurely aged and leathery, heavily spotted and with ignored or unnoticed signs of festering skin cancer. This unbalanced skin tone was a product of years of spending the summer months with his arm resting on the cruiser door, cigarette in hand.

He flicked the cigarette, put the patrol car in gear and guided it slowly from the crunching shoulder and onto the county road. He drove slowly, crested the hill and spotted the boy. He hit the switch for the blues and let the siren call out a single jarring wail and watched the startled boy jump. Sheriff Stearns drifted the patrol car back onto the side of the road, put the vehicle in park and exited it.

"Roy."

"Yeah?"

"I ain't one of your buddies in the alley, son. Let's try '*yes sir*'." Stearns watched the boy's eyes narrow slightly.

"Where ya headed, Roy?"

"I ain't headed nowhere."

"I'm gonna need you to get in and come with me, son."

The boy tensed again. "Ya get the murderin, yella Hickey sonofabitchin' bastard that killed my brother?"

"Gonna need ya to come with me."

155

Li'l Roy Tucker measured the sheriff's expression. "Just tell me if ya got him."

"I'm gonna need ya to get in and come with me."

There was no clock in the small room and there were no windows through which a person might measure the light as time passed. This was by design.

This was about his brother. It had to be. It wasn't about Moon Pies. But, why were they keeping him in the holding cell? He'd been in there for a while now, but he didn't care much. Hell, what else did he have to do? He couldn't comfort his mama. It was just him and Mama now. The funeral had taken it out of her. A better assessment might be that it was just him. Mama wasn't conscious long enough to be comforted. With the licks she'd taken this past week, he couldn't blame her, not one bit. There was the food that Miss Jessie and some others on the route had brought by. Casseroles in the fridge and cakes on the counter and the table. But they weren't going anywhere. Mama wasn't going to eat. She wasn't going to eat anything for a good while. She was just going to drink—drink and smoke. A smoke would be nice. A good smoke when you had nothing to do but sit and stare out at something made all the difference in the goddamned world. He'd asked Sheriff Stearns for one, but Stearns had told him he was too young to smoke and had refused to give him one.

Now it was just a matter of time. So, he sat in the stillness of the slowly passing afternoon and he bit his nails to the quick until they smarted and bled.

If it wasn't about Ronny, then it was just another shakedown. It wouldn't be the first time they'd hauled him in for no reason. He hadn't broken any windows. He hadn't started any fires. He hadn't done a damned thing. Virginia Lawford came to mind. He felt a stir in his pants and he pushed her away, embarrassed.

This could be about Lenville. It could be. But he hadn't even been at Pudgy's Tavern that night and that case was what the television shows called 'closed.' Lenville had killed Darryl Hickey. Plain and simple and with Darryl Hickey's own gun. A lot of witnesses. A lot of blood. A lot of people saying it was over long before Lenville shot him. Every one of them saying Lenville didn't have to kill Darryl.

Ya want people to say you boys are just like your damned daddy? Is that what you want?

There were times when he had wanted that. He was sure there were times when his brothers had wanted that, too. The killing of Sheriff Bill was a tale told after the fact to boys who were almost too young to remember that dreadful night. The tale that was told often neglected the family of Bill Cooper, their loss, their mourning.

you boys are just like your damned daddy

Li'l Roy was sure that folks had already been saying that for years. He never answered his mother with that thought though and that thought had never felt so grave. Now, here it was, the reality of *being just like your daddy*. He cursed Lenville

156

there in the holding cell for turning out to be just like their daddy. In that cursing, came a calming, a clearing of the mist that had clouded his vision for these past years.

You are different, Roy. Don't you ever let me hear you say that again—

He wasn't like Big Roy Tucker. He was like his mama. He was more like his mama and the truth of that suited him just fine. Jeannie Tucker could be a force of nature, a fury to be reckoned with when her hackles were up, but she was not mean. He was not mean.

He stared at the wall of the cell and did the imaginary math. Lenville was like his daddy, but he was like his mama. That left Ronny caught lost somewhere in between, in the middle. Li'l Roy felt his sinuses begin to burn and he wiped the tears away. Ronny wasn't in the middle anymore. He was at the cemetery at the Holiness Church, his blood still on the tracks waiting to fade away or to be licked up by dogs or washed away by the rain.

It was a hell of a thing, to be here and then be gone—traceless in history, just another poor, dirt road dead boy lost to bumpkin vendetta.

He shook his thoughts away from his dead brother and returned them to his current situation. If it was just another shakedown, then he knew the drill. They'd let him sit in the holding cell for a while, trying to work his nerves and then they'd come and get him to fink on somebody, ask him about some bullshit some son of a bitch had pulled somewhere and he'd tell them he didn't know shit about it whether he did or he didn't. Eventually, they'd cut him loose.

Sometimes, he lucked out and they kept him over lunch or supper and they'd bring him a chuck wagon sandwich and a bag of chips or some meat loaf with mashed potatoes and green beans.

His stomach rumbled.

Down the hallway, Sheriff Stearns sat smoking at his desk, cursing Quiet Tom and his daughter. For his stomach, he drank the chalky magnesia straight from the bottle and debated the things he knew for certain to be absolute truth. Tom and Virginia were still family. Tom was in it now and needed help. Virginia was bat shit crazy.

He had given Jeannie Tucker his word.

He let the boy sit in the cooler alone for over an hour. The boy did not once call out or bang on the door.

Hickey son of a bitch. That's what the boy had said. *Hickey son of a bitch.* It stood to reason the kid would have his mind set on the Hickeys.

Stearns worked his own imaginary math. The day would come, Stearns understood this. The day would come when Li'l Roy and Tom Lawford would bump into each other and a light switch would be thrown and it would all become clear to Li'l Roy, and when it did, there would be no stopping the blood that was sure to come. Or one day, Tom Lawford will have chewed on it all so long that he felt the only logical thing to do was to rid himself of the liability of the boy. Outside of that, it was obvious that Li'l Roy believed his brother had been brutally murdered by vengeance seeking members of the Hickey clan. Li'l Roy would be plotting vengeance of his own. That day must not be allowed to come.

Removing Li'l Roy from the equation was, to Stearns, the only viable solution.

The bolt sounded, echoed slightly in the small cell and the door opened. Stearns was there, lit cigarette in hand. He did not speak, but made a motion for the boy to follow him. Stearns led him down the hallway and took notice that the boy gave no regard when they passed the plaque and memorial to the prior sheriff, Bill Cooper.

Quietly, they walked on until the boy said, "I really gotta take a leak."

"This won't take long."

"But, I really gotta go." The boy protested.

"Jesus, son, you tryin' to work on me?"

"Ain't tryin' to do nothin' but take a piss. Honest."

Stearns pointed to the bathroom door. "Go there," he said, "and then come here." Stearns pointed at his own office door.

The boy measured what it meant that Stearns let him go in alone. Whatever this was, he wasn't in any real trouble.

"Have a seat." A relaxed Stearns motioned across the desk.

"Won't ya let me get one a those?" Li'l Roy Tucker dipped his toe into the water.

Stearns sighed in surrender and slid the pack across the weathered desk. "Been a helluva long week for the Tucker clan ain't it?"

Li'l Roy Tucker sat in the chair, struck a match and lit the cigarette. He dragged deeply, taking his time. He avoided eye contact. He didn't answer Stearns' question, but instead casually asked one of his own. "You get the son of a bitch that stabbed my brother to death? It had to be one a them Hickeys. Had to be."

"What makes you so sure, Roy?"

"Geez, all my trainin' as a law man, I guess. Revenge for Darryl is the only thing that makes sense."

Stearns leaned back in his chair, sighed again in secret relief, a smile growing on his face. "No. No, Roy. We haven't. Brought a couple of 'em in. Had to cut 'em loose."

158

Li'l Roy leapt from the chair, sending it crashing sideways. "You what? Cut'em loose? Ho-lee shit. I don't believe it. Why in the—"

"They had alibis, Roy."

"Who cares what the hell they had? Them sonsabitches. They're lyin', Sheriff."

"For what it's worth, I think you're right. I don't believe them." Stearns spun the web.

"Then why—why'd ya—"

"Sit down, Roy."

"I'll sit down, but by God you'll have me in here again. I guaran-damn-tee it. You'll have me in here again for murder."

Li'l Roy picked up the chair. Stearns smiled at him. "I had to cut'em loose, Roy."

Li'l Roy sat. "Yeah? Well, don't look so damned disappointed about it."

"It's not that, Roy. It's just—" Sheriff Stearns now leaned back in towards the boy as if to study him more closely, "Damned if you ain't Jeannie Marie up and down. Not just looks mind ya, but that whole 'take no shit' thing you got. Damned if that ain't your mother up and down. If your hair was red and curly instead of...you'd be her spittin' image."

"Instead of blonde and straight," Li'l Roy said and then observed, "Like yours." He noticed the framed photograph on Stearn's desk and reached for it. "Like Dickie's." Li'l Roy held the framed picture and studied the photograph. "Spartans ain't never gonna get another QB like Dickie Stearns. He's bound for the pros. He gonna play for the Vols?"

"Goin' into law enforcement like his old man. How's Jeannie Marie doin', Roy?"

"Now, that there's a shame." Li'l Roy placed the framed photograph back onto Stearn's desk and ducked his cigarette casually in the ashtray. "Seems like I heard that." He *had* heard it—in a conversation between his two brothers. Lenville had said that Johnny Stearns wasn't taking any chances so far as Dickie was concerned. Dickie supposedly had developed a bad knee to make absolutely sure he didn't wind up drafted. It cost Dickie a likely career in the pros, but made sure he didn't wind up in Viet Nam.

"I'm askin' about your mother, son. How's Jeannie Marie?"

It had slipped by the boy the first time as he was lost in thought about Dickie Stearns. Dickie Stearns who was treated like royalty at Sonoraville High. Dickie Stearns was the smalltown quarterback destined for the pros. It was like looking at a picture of a famous person and feeling like you had some kind of personal connection to them. He'd caught it the second time. *Jeannie Marie*—he knew that was his mother's middle name, and that some folks around the route called her that, but hearing the sheriff address her as such irritated the hell out of him.

"Son?"

Stearns' voice pulled him back.

"Well now, how do you think *Jeannie Marie*'s a doin'? *Jeannie Marie* is who she is and *Jeannie Marie* does how she does."

Stearns took the boy's venom in stride and performed a minute adjustment on the position of the framed photograph of his son. "I can only imagine she's doin' pretty poorly right about now." Again, the Sheriff leaned back as if subconsciously putting himself out of arm's reach of the boy. "Her oldest son murders a man one Saturday. Her middle son gets himself murdered the next—"

"He didn't get himself murdered. Some Hickey son of a bitch murdered him."

"Well, Perry Mason, seems like I recall a couple of years ago when someone set the schoolhouse on fire and everyone said it was you. I couldn't put the match in your hand, so I couldn't charge you with it. So, likewise, I have to be able to put the knife in someone's hand before I can charge them with killing somebody. Knowing someone did something and being able to prove someone did something—"

"Aw, horseshit. I've been told so many times that I set that school on fire y'all almost got me believin' I did."

"Well, at any rate, we're not here to talk about that school fire. Now we got this."

"Now we got what?"

Stearns studied the boy closely now and watched worry wilt bravado. "This rape thing, son. Whattaya think that's gonna do to Jeannie Marie?"

"What? What rape thing?" Li'l Roy Tucker asked, and though a familiar ache crept into his gut, he drew himself up impressively.

"I think you know damned well what rape thing," said Stearns.

Li'l Roy Tucker was unphased by the sheriff's swear. He sat in quiet contemplative confusion until, "Ah," his eyes widened and to Stearns' disappointment, the boy relaxed and his cocky expression mocked outright the hand the Sheriff had played. "You're talkin' about that Virginia girl. Pfft, ain't nobody raped that girl." Li'l Roy laughed and dragged coolly on the cigarette.

"Yeah, well, that's not what she tells." Stearns reeled in his irritation at the boy. "Says each of you boys raped her—had a go at her a month ago Saturday."

"Hold on, now, Sheriff, now, that's a goddamned dirty lie."

"So you're sayin' you boys didn't each have a go at her? Look, kiddo, I was your age once. I was a teenage boy walkin' around all the time with a pecker so hard you could knock one over the fence with it. It's like walkin' around with a good throwin' rock, or a good stick. Eventually, you're gonna wanna take a shot at

160

something. Hell, the moment gets right, you get three teenage boys and a girl, hell who knows?"

Li'l Roy laughed. "Sheriff, I ain't gonna admit to rapin' a girl I ain't raped. And hey, 's'at work the same with guns?"

"What's that?"

"You walk around with a gun, you eventually just gotta take a shot at somethin'? Somebody even?"

"You got that gun, Roy Tucker?"

"What?"

Stearns spoke slowly, "Do you have the gun your brother shot Darryl Hickey with?"

"Oh," Li'l Roy realized what he'd done. "Hell no." Li'l Roy laughed. "I'm talkin' about you, Sheriff. I'm askin' you if walkin' 'round with a gun on your hip means eventually you're just gonna wanna take a shot at somebody. That's what I'm askin'. I don't know shit about no other gun your boys can't seem to find."

Stearns visibly flushed at this. "Tell ya what—we get to the bottom of this mess, then you can ask me the questions. Right now, we got a raped girl—"

"I told ya, Sheriff, ain't nobody raped her." Li'l Roy turned his attention away from the sheriff now and sat silently studying the sunlit afternoon beyond the office window. "And I wish you'd quit sayin' that. Hell I've been a firebug 'cause y'all said I was. Now, I'm gonna be a rapist." He could be fishing. He could be hunting for artifacts and arrowheads in the caves. He remembered the flood waters and thought of the dead calf. He then thought of the girl there in the night. That crazy girl. The girl who never wanted anyone to look at her. He thought of them each in turn on top of her. Shame and embarrasment washed over him. He put the cigarette out in the ashtray and leaned back in the chair. He had one expression and then another. He involuntarily dropped his head in shame.

"Well?" Stearns pushed.

Li'l Roy nodded his head. "It wasn't right what we did. I think I tried to make it right, some way, but—"

"What you did? What did you boys do, son? Rape that girl?"

"No."

"You did what, then?"

"We each had a go at her." The boy said, still hiding his face in his hands.

"Look at me, Roy Tucker. You each had a go at her but you boys didn't rape her?"

Li'l Roy looked up, defeated. "We didn't rape her, Sheriff. She showed up outta nowhere that night and asked—" The boy cut himself off.

"Asked you what? If you would each have a go at her?"

161

"Yeah—"

"Howdy, boys! Beautiful evenin' ain't it? You boys wanna screw me?"

"No."

"No, what?"

"She said, 'You boys wanna put it in me and go crazy?' That's what she said. Now, dammit, that's exactly what she said."

Stearns laughed in spite of himself, rubbed his face with his hand.

"That's the truth. That's exactly what she said word for damned word. Now, don't you go laughin' at me."

"Easy, son. I ain't sayin' it ain't true and I don't mean to laugh at you, but who in this world's gonna believe that? Who's gonna believe you boys didn't come across that girl, say sleepwalkin'. That's what she says and her dad says she does it all the time and—"

"Quiet Tom?"

This startled Stearns, "You know her daddy?"

Li'l Roy nodded. "Quiet Tom. I don't know him. I know who he is when I see him."

"You sure about that?"

"Sure I'm sure. Why?"

"Ah, they keep to themselves over there. Didn't realize you guys were so acquainted."

"I didn't say we was *acquainted*. We ain't *acquainted*, but I know who he is. Everybody knows who Quiet Tom is. Y'all related or somethin' ain't ya?"

"He was married to my sister."

"And she passed away," Li'l Roy said quietly.

"Rest her soul."

"And that makes Virginia your what? Your—"

"My niece, son. That makes her my niece."

"Shit—"

"When was the last time you saw him, son?"

"Who?"

"Tom."

"Hell, I don't know. We didn't rape your niece."

"Let's get to the bottom of it then."

"I see him around. Mighta seen him in town here and there. Shit, he thinks we raped his daughter? Jesus!" He felt the queer poisoned sting of what could only be identified as heartbreak and betrayal. His hands began to shake. "This ain't, this can't be, she sayin'— that's damned crazy— Man, I just knew that shit was gonna—"

162

"Hold it now, son. Crazy, huh?" Stearns now spoke to himself as much as he spoke to the boy. "Here's a little lesson for you about crazy. You call him 'Quiet Tom,' right? You even remember why folks call him that? No? Didn't think so. Tom Lawford's a good hard workin' man. He works his fields and he works a factory job on top of that. Now, Tom's wife, my dear sweet sister, died a slow, horrible death and Tom and Virginia were by her side night and day. Might as well have killed Tom, too. He didn't say a word to nobody for at least a couple of years after she died. And I do mean not a word to nobody. You call that girl crazy and you call him 'Quiet Tom' like you know a thing or two about him and her. If that girl's a little crazy, maybe it's because after her mama died, she had to spend years in that house with a daddy who wouldn't look at her or even talk to her."

Li'l Roy wept at the force of Stearn's words.

"Now, here's how it goes. He wants you put away, but he don't wanna go draggin' Virginia through this. Now, he will if he has to and you and me both know how that's gonna go down and it ain't gonna be good for you and it sure as hell ain't gonna be good for Jeannie Marie. The girl's leavin' town anyway. Movin' to her aunt's. He just don't wanna go bumpin' into you in town or nothin'."

"I ain't followin'. How the hell am I supposed to be in charge of what he goes bumpin' into? This is too much. It's all just too much."

"Let's just take a minute." Stearns lit a cigarette and slid the pack back across the desk to Li'l Roy. He waited quietly for the boy to light up. He watched the tobacco soothe the boy. After a few moments he asked, "You ever think about joinin' the service, son?"

"You mean the military? Not really. Never really thought about it."

"I think you should do that, Roy. That's what I think. Think it'd be good for you."

"I reckon I ain't old enough."

"You just let me worry about that part, son. I'll send the recruiters your way." Stearns said and added, "Ya ain't got no medical conditions do ya?"

"Like what?"

"Flat footed? Asthma? Ulcers?"

"I don't even know what none a that is."

"Then you ain't got none of it. I'll send some fellas your way, and for Christ's sake try to keep Jeannie Marie away from 'em when they come."

"So, I ain't supposed to tell her I'm leavin'? I'm just supposed to up and leave her?"

"Tell her when it's too late for her to stop you, or for anyone to go lookin' too deep into how you come to be eighteen so all of a sudden. You don't want this to come to court, Roy."

"So, join the Army or go up to Brushy for rapin' a girl I didn't even rape?"

"Army, Marines, whichever. Not sure you're Marine material, though. I was a Marine myself." Stearns sat back and studied the boy. "Listen, son, no matter what they're trying to sell us on the television, this Viet Nam thing ain't endin' no time soon. With the draft and all you can bet you're goin' anyway. Just a matter of time, really. Like I said, I think it'd be good for you. Come see me in a couple of days and I'll have somethin' for you to give to the recruiters. Okay?'

"Ain't none of this okay. So don't go feelin' like you doin' me no favors here. I didn't rape your niece. And I never started that goddamned fire either."

"See you day after tomorrow. You can go."

Li'l Roy stood to leave and then sat back down. "We at the bottom of it now?"

"I'd say that's right."

"So now I can ask the questions?"

"Ask your question, son."

"How'd it feel, Sheriff?"

"Not following you."

"How'd it feel to shoot my daddy?"

Stearns had his elbows on his desk and now clasped his hands together. "Son, drawing your service weapon on a man with the intent to fire it, well, it's not a feeling any good law man wants to experience. Afterwards, you doubt yourself, you blame yourself, and all the questions you have for yourself keep you up at night and affect you in ways I hope you never get the opportunity to fully understand. Especially, if this man had a family. So, I went through all of that and at the end of the day, son, Big Roy left me with absolutely no choice in the matter. He'd done killed Sheriff Bill and tried to kill me. He made every single decision that night. He made them for everybody. Clear?"

"No, Sheriff. Not really. I mean it's clear what you're sayin', but—but you still ain't told me how it felt to shoot my daddy."

"All right. Okay, kid, you bein' about to go into the service and all, I suppose you're old enough to not have anybody sugar coat the truth for you. You want it straight and let's say you've earned that. I'll tell you how it felt, son. It felt like shooting a wife beating, cop killing, murdering, low life, sorry excuse for a man." Stearns did not blink, but watched as blood rushed into the boy's cheeks. When the boy dropped his head, Stearns asked, "Any more questions, son? And I'll advise you here to keep this in mind—if you don't really want an honest answer, then don't ask."

Li'l Roy looked into his lap and shook his head. He raised his head slowly until his eyes met Stearns'. "No, Sheriff. I reckon that'll do it." He hesitated then and added, "I'm sorry my daddy put you in that spot. He killed Sheriff Bill. You shot him. Sure you meant to kill him. It just didn't work out that way. That's justice, I guess, him gettin' shot, gettin' locked up and never gettin' out."

"Don't go kiddin' yourself, kid. There's no justice."

"Sure there is. There has to be. Don't they?"

"Son, what do you think justice would look like to Sheriff Bill? To his widow? To his sons and daughters?"

"He was a lawman. He knew what justice was. Just like you. And all us, us regular folk gotta believe in that."

"Justice would have to be something close to making things right again. Once Bill Cooper bled out, he wasn't comin' back. Somebody gets murdered, you can murder somebody back, but it doesn't set anything anywhere near close to being back to right. A girl gets raped, you can lock the rapist up, you can hang him, you can cut his balls off, hell you can even have somebody rape him in turn, but it never sets anything right again."

"If it ain't justice, then what is it?"

"You tell me. You wanna kill the fella killed your brother, don't ya?"

"Hell, Sheriff—"

"When you think about killin' him, does it feel like justice to you?"

"Feels like—"

"Feels like what?"

"Like revenge."

"You're almost there."

"Feels like hate, Sheriff."

"Now you're gettin' it."

"Hell, I ain't never gonna get it." With that, Li'l Roy stood. "Guess I'll see ya in a couple a days, Sheriff."

"Roy?"

"Yeah?"

"Make no mistake. I'm pullin' for ya, son." The kid offered a slight nod acknowledging he'd heard the sheriff, but said nothing. Sherrif Stearns said, "Hey."

"Yeah?" Li'l Roy turned to Stearns.

"Ya wanna see your brother while you're here?"

"What?"

Stearns stood. "Got any knives or anything on ya?"

"No."

"Not even a pocket knife? Do I need to pat you down?"

"Broke the blade off in a tree. Why ya wanna pat me down now for?"

"Keep our conversation here to yourself 'til we know more about what we can do. Promise me that, and I'll bring him to you."

165

Li'l Roy Tucker sat at one of a handful of tables beneath a slowly turning ceiling fan in the break room/visiting room of the Whelan County jail. There was a refrigerator and a coffee maker beside a sink. Li'l Roy poured himself a cup and resisted the urge to add cream and sugar.

The break room door opened. A robust jailer with a flat top haircut escorted Lenville Tucker into the room. Lenville was not cuffed, but wore a gray jailhouse jumper that, to Li'l Roy, made him appear broken, weak and vulnerable. Li'l Roy dropped his coffee cup into the sink and went to his big brother. He buried his face in Lenville's chest and sobbed. "I didn't do anything to stop it, Len. I just stood there. I didn't do nothin'."

"It ain't on you, little brother. It's on me."

"I didn't do nothin' to stop it. He came at us so fast."

"It ain't on you." Lenville Tucker held his little brother.

"You boys are gonna have to break it up. Unless you want strip searched before goin' back. You boys need to have a seat." The large jailer pointed at the table.

The brothers broke their embrace.

"I'm sorry, little brother. I'm sorry I wasn't there."

"I shoulda done somethin'. I let 'em kill him."

"I killed him. I might as well have killed him myself."

"Have a seat, fellas," the turnkey commanded. The boys sat.

"You got any smokes?" asked Lenville.

"Naw," answered Li'l Roy, "been bummin' from the sheriff."

"Is 'at right?" Lenville laughed. "You guys big buddies now or somethin? You really bummed smokes from Sheriff Stearns?"

"Hell, why not?"

"Ain't you somethin'?" Lenvilled smiled and reached across the table and rubbed Li'l Roy's head playfully.

"Hell, ain't we both somethin'," Li'l Roy countered.

"Mom know you're here?"

"Naw. Don't think I'll tell her either."

"She's got every right to be—" Lenville began.

"Lenville, why'd you shoot Darryl? They're all a sayin' you never had to. Why, Lenville? You ain't really that mean are ya? You ain't so bad as all that, are ya?"

"Hell, I'm worse, Li'l Roy," said Lenville.

"Don't say that." Li'l Roy wiped his eyes.

"Okay, Roy, here it goes. One time and one time only. Explain it to Mom if ya want to. It ain't really gonna matter."

"Okay." Li'l Roy waited. "Tell me."

"You ever hear any stories about Darryl carryin' a pistol around?" asked Lenville.

"No," answered Roy.

"Me neither. So, why you reckon he was carryin' one that night?"

"Umm, in case he run into you?"

"Right, so in his head, he'd already killed me. See? He wasn't comin' back from that. He'd a took a shot at me eventually."

"Len, you don't—you don't know that."

"I know it like I know my own damned name. Standin' over him there, I saw it, I saw it just as clear as day. If he'd had any second thoughts before then, well, I took'em from him with that beatin' I give him. I saw it clear as day, Roy. I saw him comin' back for me with that pistol. I saw him comin' back for us. All of us. Shit, I seen other things, too right then, Roy. I saw Viet Nam and I saw 'em sendin' me halfway around the world to shoot and kill men they say are a threat to me. Now, let me ask ya somethin'. What's the difference in goin' over to some god forsaken foreign jungle and killin' a man who's a threat to ya and goin' down the road and killin' a man who' a threat to ya? It's all so much bullshit, and it's all so goddamned heavy, Li'l Roy. I saw a chance to put it all down right then and there, a chance to leave it all on the floor out there at Pudgy's. So –bang!" Lenville smacked the table. Li'l Roy jumped. The jailer took a half step toward the boys. "And it was over." Lenville waved a flattened hand through the air above the table. "No Hickey. No Viet Nam. No draft. No choice, and I never really had one. None of us do when they's killin' to be done."

Chapter 25

*D*o somethin', Johnny.

Johnny Stearns changed only one piece of official information on the boy's birth certificate. He moved Little Roy Tucker's birth year from 1953 to 1951.

In the stillness of the late hour, Johnny Stearns stared at the new documents and the new documents stared back. The old one was now reduced to ashes in the ashtray. He had forged a copy for Roy and a copy to return to County General. Feeding the documents into the old Underwood typewriter and entering the official information had not been difficult, police work was paperwork, but forging the signatures had taken some practice, especially Big Roy Tucker's nearly illegible scrawl. On a piece of scratch paper, he had practiced until he was confident his version would pass. He knew it would never get so far as to be an actual issue, but he also knew to cover all of his bases. He stared at the blank line beneath the word Father and for a moment considered the notion of writing his own name and being done with it.

Before I lose another one.

Before I—

She would never acknowledge the truth. Which had been a good thing. Unlike Netta who after years of silence had suddenly decided that it was time the truth came out.

Help me.

He lit a cigarette, propped his heavy boots upon his desk. His eyes rested on the framed photograph of Dickie. He studied the picture—the Spartan jersey, the blonde hair and the blue eyes.

His thoughts moved back to Little Roy Tucker and their agreement. From the desk, he picked up the new birth certificates, reviewed the false information again, and found he felt no pride in what he had done even though he had convinced himself that it was the best thing for Little Roy Tucker. It would, he assured himself,

168

take the option from Tom Lawford as far as later deciding Little Roy was a liability. It would, he also assured himself, keep Little Roy from killing any Hickeys. Still, he felt ill at ease with it all.

Do something.

The boy's question had thrown him. He had no way of knowing what the boy did or did not already know, or what the boy did or did not remember about the night he shot Big Roy. He did not know if the boy, or anyone else for that matter, knew it was Netta Simms who had run all the way to the station.

"Mister Roy's a killin' Miss Jeannie! Y'all gotta go do somethin'!" A breathless Netta exclaimed upon entering the sheriff's office.

Deputy Stearns scrambled to his feet from behind his desk, sending papers to the floor along with a mug that he used as a pen holder. "Where's Li'l Roy?" he asked. "Where are the boys, Netta?"

"They at my house, Mister Johnny," answered Netta. "Mama's got'em."

Caroline Rumpke sat at her dispatch desk, her mouth open, watching as Johnny Stearns checked his weapon. "Caroline, get Sheriff Bill on the radio and tell him I'm headed out to Roy Tucker's on Rural Route Three and I may need some assistance. That sonofabitch is comin' in this time." Caroline stared at a Deputy Stearns that she had never seen. "Caroline! Get Bill on the—"

"Ten four, Deputy. Sorry. Johnny. Johnny, you be careful."

Stearns offered no reply. He bolted past Netta and out into the darkness.

"Young lady, are you okay?" Caroline asked Netta Simms. Netta was silent, but for her heavy, labored breathing. "Miss?"

Netta shot for the door and began her long run through the night back to the route.

He would kill Big Roy Tucker. As sure as he knew morning would come, he knew death was also on its way. Blue lights split darkness and a siren called through the night. For Jeannie, he would kill Big Roy. For the boys, he would kill Big Roy. For the good of Whelan County and all of humanity, he would kill Big Roy. To set the world right again, he would kill him. The truth of the matter gave him no pause, caused him no stutter—he would kill Big Roy because he had wanted the man dead for years. Speeding across the tracks, he silently thanked Big Roy for allowing him the opportunity.

Pudgy's Tavern, Mac's Package and Bailey's Boarding house passed in a blur. He sped past the pallet mill and the hosiery and hit the dirt road with a jolt. He braked suddenly, sending the patrol car into a skid. Ahead in the darkness, he saw the strobing lights of Sheriff Bill's parked patrol car and cursed himself for directing Caroline to call him. He should have come alone. Sheriff Bill would handle this now in that cool and calm way he had. Sheriff Bill would lead Big Roy out by the hand, and with his way would have Big Roy calmed and as gentle as a lamb. He cursed himself again for his lack of forethought.

Stearns quickly shifted the cruiser into park there on the dirt road behind Sheriff Bill's patrol car and exited the vehicle.

A voice called his attention to the house. "You got no business here, Johnny!" Big Roy called from the kitchen window. Stearns studied the house, lowered himself and sought cover on the far side of the patrol car. "Neither did he."

Neither did he—

None of the implications of exactly what those words meant escaped Stearns. *Neither did he—*there was a past tense inferred. *Neither did he—*some part of this was already over. Stearns called into the night for Sheriff Bill but received no reply.

From the kitchen window, Big Roy continued, "You got no business here! Now get the hell outta here! This is between a man and his wife, Johnny. Got nothin' to do with you. I told Bill Cooper the same thing. I warned him."

With his position still low, Stearns crept around to the front of Sheriff Bill's patrol car. He forgot himself when he saw the sheriff. Bill Cooper's sightless eyes stared up at Orion's Belt. The beloved sheriff lay in a pool of blood. Stearns ran to him.

A single shot rang out. A searing pain ripped through Stearns' chest and sent him sprawling into the dirt of the road.

"Goddammit, I warned ya, ya son of a bitch!" Roy called.

Stearns found cover behind the patrol car and examined his wound. He would live. Maintaining a low profile, he entered his cruiser from the passenger's side, cutting the strobes and then the headlights. He then cautiously did the same with Sheriff Bill's vehicle.

In the darkness, he peeked cautiously over the hood. In the light of the kitchen window he could see Jeannie Marie and Big Roy Tucker. He trained his service weapon on Big Roy, but forced himself to hold his fire. Big Roy had the advantage of both high ground and being close to Jeannie Marie. Until he was sure the big man was out of ammunition, he had no way of getting Big Roy out of the house. Surely, Caroline would try to reach him on the radio and getting no reply, she would send back up. Possibly even state boys. He would just have to wait it out.

He could not accept that scenario. His mind raced. He heard himself call into the night, "Big Roy Tucker, you goddamned coward!" A shot rang out, but Stearns did not hear it meet a mark. "You big pile of shit!" Another shot. No mark. In the darkness he muttered a swear. This tactic would take too long and he reminded himself that for all he knew, Big Roy had half a million rounds at his disposal.

A different plan began to form. He would have to play the big man from a different angle. He had to draw the big man out.

"You're a coward! You ain't even a man! I'm twice the man you are, Roy Tucker. You chickenshit bastard." Another shot. Then another. The second shot planted itself somewhere in the patrol car. "You come from a long line of chicken shits, Roy! Nothin's ever gonna change that. No matter how this night ends, it ends with you being a big pile of shit just like your goddamned daddy."

"Ah, fuck you, Johnny." Three wild shots.

"Hell, I'm twice the man you are."

"Doesn't look like it from where I'm standing, asshole. You look kinda small from here."

"Ask Jeannie Marie how it looks from where she's standing."

A shot. "Don't you say her goddamned name. Don't you say her goddamned name, Johnny Stearns."

"Jeannie Marie? You okay?"

Two more shots.

"Don't you talk to her."

"I gotcha, Jeannie. You're safe now. You're safe with me."

Big Roy barreled through the screen door. "Don't you talk to her!" He fired shot after shot as he approached the deputy. When the pause came, Stearns did not think, only reacted, rising from behind the patrol car and emptying his revolver. Big Roy's shots had been wild. Stearns' were not. The big man went down.

Stearns reloaded, keeping an eye on the big man as he did so. Big Roy Tucker was stumbling to his feet. In his hand, he still held the pistol. "Stay down, Roy Tucker!" Defiantly, Roy stood. Stearns rose and fired, knocking the big man backward and onto his back. Stearns' had seen the pistol fly from the big man's hand. Sirens were approaching. Johnny Stearns approached the fallen man. He counted three holes in the big man's torso. Without a word, he raised his revolver, pointing it again at Big Roy.

"No! Don't shoot my daddy no more!" A six year old Li'l Roy Tucker, dressed only in his underwear, had broken away from Jessie and Netta Simms and was now charging Johnny Stearns. The deputy was caught off guard by the powerful little boy and almost lost his footing. He offered no resistance as the little boy delivered blow after blow, punching his thighs and kicking his shins.

In the ashtray on his desk, he snubbed out his cigarette and headed for home.

He slept restlessly in fits and starts until removing himself from the bed he shared with his wife so as not to keep her awake.

He checked Dickie's room and found him sleeping.

He spent the night in the dim light of the kitchen burning cigarettes and considering his mistakes.

Cold feet stand firm. The boy's resolve would fade once he was out of sight of authority. Stearns considered this and his options. Fearing Li'l Roy might have a change of heart, Stearns did not wait for the boy to come and see him.

The patrol car rocked like a ship on stormy waters through the ruts and the potholes of the dirt road. Li'l Roy sat on the front steps. Stearns did not pull into the drive. He shifted the cruiser into park and motioned for the boy to come to him.

"Sheriff," Li'l Roy nodded.

From behind his shades, Stearns asked, "Ya hangin' in there, son?"

"Hell, got no choice but to hang in there, Sheriff."

"I guess that's right, Roy. Guess that's right. Your mama? How's she doin'?"

"She got no choice, either."

"Here. Don't lose this." Stearns handed the boy the altered birth certificate. "I've set ya up to meet a fella for lunch tommorrow. Don't disappoint him," Stearns said and added, "Don't disappoint me, son. And don't keep him waiting." Stearns tossed a cigarette into the road.

Li'l Roy said, "Let me get one a those."

Stearns fished half of a pack of Winstons from his uniform shirt. "Just take those."

"You sure?"

"No, but take'em anyway."

Chapter 26

W hen the hour came the next day, Li'l Roy met with a Staff Sergeant Sweeney at The Tastee-Creem, a briefcase and smile wielding soldier who instantly inspired him with his crisp uniform and shiny boots. They sat in a booth. Outside the window, vehicles drove up and down Main Street, folks strolled the sidewalks and the world went on as it always had. Staff Sergeant Sweeney bought him two chili dogs, an order of french fries and a chocolate shake. Li'l Roy paid the young uniformed man back with a signature.

Sweeney sipped from a coffee cup and said, "You're doing a good thing here, Roy."

Li'l Roy suddenly wished he hadn't ordered the milkshake, but had instead ordered a coffee like the young man across the table from him. He scanned the restaurant, hoping to see Tracy French and was disappointed when he did not. The dining room was packed. In the booth behind him, Dickie Stearns, Mike Sizemore and Davie Boy Lewis yukked it up. The more they laughed, the more Li'l Roy felt the curious urge to hit Dickie in the mouth.

Sweeney asked, "Get enough to eat?" Li'l Roy nodded. "Let's get you tested then. Whaddaya say?"

Li'l Roy sighed and shrugged, "If we gotta. I really ain't that smart."

"I'll bet a dollar to a dime that you're smarter than you think, young man. Come on." Sweeney stood and Li'l Roy followed him out the door. On the sidewalk, Li'l Roy watched as the soldier donned his cap and adjusted it. Soon, he would be like that, neat, trimmed and respectable.

At the library, Li'l Roy took their tests and was surprised to learn that he did very well. At County General, he underwent his physical exam and was again surprised to learn that he could indeed cough while someone had his nuts in their hand.

Staff Sergeant Sweeney dropped him off in the parking lot of the pallet mill, heeding Li'l Roy's warning about driving down the dirt road. Li'l Roy himself heeding Stearns' warning about keeping his mother away from the recruiter until it was too late.

"Four days, Roy. I'll be back on Sunday. I'll pick you up at noon. We'll have some lunch and then head to Knoxville."

Roy said, "Yes, sir." He felt suddenly out of sorts, misplaced in time, as if he had been plucked from his life and dropped into some blurred version of it. The heat from the chili dogs burned in his chest and that fire spread to the back of his throat. He swallowed and then swallowed again.

"I told ya, I'm not a sir. I'm a Staff Sargent. You can call me Bernie for now. Now, listen carefully, Roy, okay?"

"Okay."

"Don't go gettin' cold feet on your country."

"Ain't plannin' on it."

"Most fellas don't plan on it, but it happens. This'll be good for you, Roy. It will."

"I ain't gonna chicken out on ya." Li'l Roy swallowed again to no effect.

"Don't go gettin' in no trouble between now and Sunday either. We're gonna get ya set up in a hotel Sunday evening and Monday morning you'll be processed at the MEPS."

"I ain't gonna get in no trouble."

"Fellas don't plan on that either, but sometimes that happens, too. This is a good thing you're doing."

"Yes, sir."

"Bernie."

"Bernie. I know it is."

"All you need to bring is a change of clothes and do not forgot that birth certificate, it being the only ID you have. Still can't believe a boy your age ain't got a driver's license. I was chomping at the bit to drive when I was your age."

"We ain't never had nothin' to drive. Wouldn't a mattered if I had'em or not."

"I see. I'll be here Sunday. Noon."

Lil Roy nodded wordlessly and opened the car door.

On the walk home, he saw Virginia on her porch with Travis and Toby Simms. She waved to him. Without a thought, he waved back.

Li'l Roy suffered the exhaustion of preoccupation. A slow and quiet four days passed and now Sunday morning crept maddeningly into Sunday afternoon. He had a queer feeling of being out in the world now, a feeling that he was in it, but

174

somehow not of it and that it would indeed have its way with him for not being so. His mother had slept the morning away, snoring from her place on the couch, and was apparently due to do the same with the afternoon. The stillness coupled with the worry made the air inside the house heavy and hard to breathe. He thought he might use the river to get him through the morning. The flood water was gone and he was curious as to what it might have left there on the bank. From the kitchen table, he stole two cigarettes from his mama's pack. He studied the wrecked tabletop for a moment, shaking his head in disapproval. He thought now that the round and painted kitchen table top with its odd splotches of cracked green paint set against the exposed light wood color beneath looked like some strange map of some other world—perhaps a world where his choices had not been whittled down to joining the military or going up to Brushy. He slid a cigarette behind each ear.

A hymn began to ring through the quiet mid morning.

Ere we reach the shining river,
Lay we every burden down;
Grace our spirits will deliver,
And provide a robe and crown.

He had seen this before. The broad bank of the river was ideal for baptisms. He could see the congregation now coming up the road, some in suits and dresses, some in white robes.

At the smiling of the river,
Mirror of the Savior's face,
Saints, whom death will never sever,
Lift their songs of saving grace.

He watched them, looked to his sleeping mother and saw that she was undisturbed by it all. Their voices grew louder and more beautiful with each step.

Soon we'll reach the silver river,
Soon our pilgrimage will cease;
Soon our happy hearts will quiver
With the melody of peace.

He let them get by him a ways before following their voices to the river.

He heard the singing long before he reached the trestle and instinctively, he crouched down as he approached the bank. Stealthily, he positioned himself on the far side of the trestle and witnessed the proceedings secretly. Speckled throughout the bank below, some in their Sunday best, some in plain white robes, was the entire church congregation. Someone was being baptized.

175

Among the white robed parishioners, he spied Virginia Lawford. He focused on her. He tried to hate her, but found he could not. To his own surprise he felt drawn to her.

He remembered himself inside her, warm and moist and he felt himself becoming aroused. He rubbed a hand across the front of his jeans, feeling the sudden rigid state of his penis. He began to rub himself until he could stand it no longer. He unzipped his jeans and began stroking himself. He shamed himself for committing such an act while hymns were being sung and a church service was going on, but he did not stop. Nearing release, his eyes fell upon the two men who were wading out into the river. One was the preacher, Brother Sturgill. The other was Quiet Tom Lawford. He was sure of it. He felt himself go limp in his hand.

He put himself away, crept softly back up the bank and ran home.

Inside, his mother was still sleeping, snoring gentle snores from the dilapidated couch. For that, he was grateful. The dread he felt about telling her he was leaving was so unbearable that he could not make himself prepare for the moment. No amount of preparation, no steeled nerves nor careful forethought would soften it anyway.

He settled himself on the front porch steps with the yellow dog and began the wait. He'd smoked the two cigarettes and now resorted to biting his nails and spitting them into the yard. From the back pocket of his jeans, he retrieved the document the Sheriff had given him. The yellow dog sat with him as he studied the new birth certificate. He was now eighteen years old. Officially.

A line from *The Love Bug* ran through his thoughts, *"It's not fair, I'm being muscled and I just want you to know that I know I know it and I don't like it."*

He sat daydreaming, Virginia Lawford was now gone from his thoughts which now alternated between jumping aboard the next train and reluctant curiosity concerning what military life might be like. Stearns had told him that it would be good for him. Good for him but not good for Stearns' *most honorable number one son*, Dickie. It struck him then that he was now the same age as Dickie Stearns.

Eighteen.

With a smile, he entertained the idea of heading over to Pudgy's Tavern, stepping coolly in, dropping a quarter into the jukebox and playing something for the old-timers like Lenville used to do. Ronny could have The Who. Li'l Roy preferred Hank Williams and Lefty Frizzell. He might then sidle up to the bar and order a beer in the hopes that Slakey might decide to refuse him. You never could tell with that skinny shit. He had enjoyed beers in Pudgy's Tavern many times before, but always with Lenville or Ronny. He had a suspicion that by himself, Slakey might tell him to buzz off. How much fun would it be to pull the birth certificate from his back pocket, put it on the bar and proclaim his sovereign maturity?

The yellow dog barked softly when it spotted Freeman coming up the dirt road. Little Roy watched the old man slowly make his way to the overgrown driveway.

Freeman nodded as he approached the steps. "Roy."

"Hey, Mister Freeman."

"Just come to check on Jeannie. How's she doin'?"

"She's sleepin'."

"Good. Good for her. I won't bother her, then."

"I'll tell her you come by. Hey, you got a smoke, Mr. Freeman?"

Li'l Roy gave the yellow dog a gentle push from the step and Freeman sat down slowly beside the boy. He fished a pack of Lucky's from his shirt pocket. Li'l Roy thanked him as the train whistle blew then customarily blew again. They smoked quietly as it passed. Both of them charmed into silence.

"And Juanita from Reseda says, 'Damn, Free Man, you sure are ugly in the mornin'. And I says, 'Juanita, you're ugly all damned day.'" Freeman told his tale with the smell of liquor already heavy on his breath. The boy found there was something very comforting in the scent of the liquor mingled with the sawdust smell that Freeman always seemed to carry with him.

The two laughed together before falling into an eventual silence.

"I'm gonna do that." Li'l Roy said to Freeman, breaking their reverie. "I'm just gonna climb onto some empty car and let that train get me the hell on outta here."

"Any destination in mind?"

"Nah. Just ride it 'til I feel like gettin' off."

"That's how it starts. You just get on. And then you wake up one day and realize you've done a whole lotta gettin' on and not much gettin' off. Sounds strange. I know. Them rails get hold of you and they won't let ya go. They had a hold of me for better than twenty years. Hell, who am I kiddin'? They still got me. I think about lightfootin' it everyday. But me, hell, my life was over when I started hoboin'. Kiddo, yours hasn't even gotten started. It's different out there now, too. And gettin' more different every day. Now, I ain't the kinda hypocrite that'd tell ya not to. I'm just sayin' get yourself a destination in mind. Else you'll never get off."

"I kinda do got a destination," said Li'l Roy.

"Well that's more than I had. Where ya eyein'?" asked Freeman.

"West."

"West, huh? Here's your first lesson in Hobo Speak, kiddo. When a brother or sister hobo passes on, we say they caught the West Bound. That's what we say.

Caught the West Bound to the Sweet Bye and Bye. Anyways, west ain't a destination, kid. It's a direction."

"Can't it be both?" asked Li'l Roy.

"No. Not in this game."

"Hell, I just wanna get the hell away from here. I just wanna be free of all this crap."

"Don't go thinkin' that runnin' from a thing makes you free from a thing." Freeman instructed, then added. "And here ain't so bad."

Li'l Roy wet his lips and said, "It is if you're a Tucker and your daddy killed the sheriff. Believe me. Why in the world would you choose to get off here?"

"It felt right," Freeman held back the truth. "Felt like it was time to get off. Sometimes it just does. Startin' to feel a little like it's time to get back on. And you are who you wanna be, kid. Ya wanna be a Tucker?"

"Well, yeah. I wanna be a Tucker. I guess. Wouldn't mind bein' somebody else either. Or maybe be a Tucker some place else. Hell, Mister Freeman, I don't know." Roy admitted.

"This place feel like it's kickin' your ass? Givin' ya a good beatin'?" Freeman smiled and lured the kid in.

"Yeah, Mr. Freeman. It sure does."

"There's beatin's out on the rails, too, kiddo. Life here sometimes make ya feel all alone in the world?"

"Sure." Li'l Roy said and instantly regretted his honesty.

"You ain't seen lonely 'til you're near frozen to death and gettin' run off from some place where you ain't hurtin' nobody by some bull goose paid to hate ya."

"Hell, I ain't never even been on no train. Them sonsabitches cut through here all night and all day, just rubbin' it in with their whistles and their screechin' wheels. I just want to climb on one and take me a little ride—or a big ride—to anywhere."

"Oh, you got it double bad, son. You got the wanderin' way and the love for the train. I met guys like you. They ain't gettin' off 'til somebody rolls 'em off or carries 'em off. That really what you want?"

"Maybe it is. I think maybe it is," said Roy.

Jeannie Tucker was awakened by the train horn. She spent twenty minutes there in the kitchen window eavesdropping on her son and her friend. She now watched as the late model Crown Vic pulled into the driveway. She listened as Freeman made his leave.

She could hear the nervous uncertainty in her son's voice as he spoke with the strange man in military uniform.

"Got here a little early. Thought I'd ride on down. You're right about that road. You ready?"

"Thought I'd just skip the change of clothes and just put these back on tommorrow."

"Up to you. You got that birth certificate?"

Jeannie Tucker burst through the broken screen door letting the rusted spring pull it shut with a slam behind her. "What is this? You're workin' awfully hard for a Sunday, aintcha?"

"Staff Sergeant Sweeney, ma'm. Recruiter for the U. S. Marine Corps."

"I got that. He ain't old enough for the service or for your goddamned war. Li'l Roy, don't say another damned word." Li'l Roy blushed, embarrassed by his mother's anger and language.

"Ma'm he has a copy of his birth certificate. You didn't forget it did ya, Roy?" Li'l Roy retrieved the folded paper from his back pocket.

His mother slapped it away. "I don't give a good goddamn what he's got," she informed Sweeney I know how old he is. I was there when he was born. Li'l Roy, what in the hell are you doin'? Where'd you get this? Why you doin' this?"

"Mama—" Li'l Roy muttered. Jeannie Tucker stared her son down, waiting for him to finish. "Mama, I gotta go."

She took a step back, tripping on the bottom step and falling to a sitting position upon them. Li'l Roy went to her. She waved him off. "This is Johnny's doin', ain't it? Johnny Stearns put you up to this? Of course he did. This ain't what I meant. That damned dumb son of a bitch. It's all gonna be okay, Li'l Roy. I'm gonna talk to Johnny. This ain't what I meant. I meant for him—" What exactly had she meant that day at the cemetery? "This ain't what I meant, Li'l Roy. You ain't gotta go nowhere—"

"Mama—" Li'l Roy went to her. "I do gotta go. I gotta."

"I'm gonna talk to Johnny—"

"Don't talk to Sherrif Stearns, Mama. I gotta—Mama, I gotta go."

Chapter 27

Virginia watches the world speed by. The bus is smoky, musty and absolutely fantastic. She is seated just behind the driver, a man who obviously takes pride in both his uniform and the smoothness of his chin. Everything speeds past the window so much faster than she could ever have imagined.

Before she left, from the curio she took the lion family and the running mare. She wrapped them in one of her mama's old blouses and hid them away in her pocket book. She holds the running mare up to the window so that sun might shine through her. Her mane becomes fire and the mare is suddenly alive in her hand.

She is on a road now, and on down it, a boy is waiting. She cannot see him, not clearly, but he is handsome and kind and when he meets her, he will see in her something that he likes. He will make his intentions known and they will go on a date, to see a picture, like the date Li' l Roy had asked her on. They will hold hands and strike a spark. He will try to kiss her and she will allow him. They will fall in love with each other. He will take her for a wife and together, they will raise a family.

She has traveled west, much of the length of Tennessee, making stops in Knoxville, and the many small towns between Knoxville and Nashville. In Nashville, she changes buses and there is an hour wait between her arrival and her departure time. She walks up and down the sidewalk outside the bus station staring at the wonder of the tall buildings, each time allowing herself to go further and further until fear and worry convince her to go back inside the station and wait. There are many people going many places.

She boards a different bus, checking with the man at the counter to be sure that she is not bound for parts unknown before she boards. The seat behind the driver is occupied. She takes a seat third from the back row like where she always sits on the Sunday school bus. A woman from a place in Texas called Angel City sits beside her. The woman is a talker and she goes on about Angel City, Texas and the girl is green with envy that the woman is from such an interesting place as Angel City, Texas. Virginia decides she will tell the people whom she meets in Muncie that she is from Angel City. She listens carefully to every detail.

When she sees the sign ahead that says, "Welcome to Kentucky," she feels the heaviness of home, the crushing weight of expectation, fade and disappear. In the new lightness, she catches her breath.

In Louisville, Kentucky, they cross the Ohio River and the girl is dumbstruck by the sight. She weeps for Toby and Travis and how she will never get to tell them of the curious things she sees.

In Indianapolis, her journey is almost complete.

Muncie is so very different than her home. She can tell this before the bus has even stopped.

Aunt Betty and Uncle Carl are waiting for her outside. Aunt Betty runs to her. She holds her so very tightly and Virginia hopes she never lets go. Virginia hopes she is correct in her expectation of how her aunt will react when she tells her of the lie that is growing in her belly.

Part Three:
Extraction

Chapter 28

A cross those fabled, proverbial tracks, the question of Freeman's absence did arise.

"Where's he been?" Marty asked Earl.

"Dunno. Haven't seen him." Earl drank his beer.

By dawn, the pain had faded with the stars, and as the morning light began to slowly fill his rented room, Freeman closed his eyes. Exhausted and sleep deprived, he found no difficulty slipping into sleep in the presence of the invasive morning light.

Many hours later, he woke with the confusion one suffers after a long bout of sleep—he did not know if it was dusk, or if it was dawn. He rose slowly, his muscles stiffened from his lengthy slumber, and he had himself a look out the east-facing window. There he learned from the rising, greeting glow that it was indeed dawn.

His current state of painlessness had him feeling particularly congenial. He offered a salutation. "Good morning." He lingered there in the window as if he might be curious whether or not the sun would reciprocate his greeting. Freeman smiled at the new light and suddenly realized that he no longer felt the pain that had lately haunted his mouth.

He had slept for almost twenty four hours. Over the course of the previous days, he had only been able to grab an occasional wink, drifting off only to have the angry tooth rudely drag him, kicking and screaming, back into bleary consciousness. But, here it was a new day and the pain was gone.

Cautiously, like a young boy might poke at a dead thing with a stick, Freeman probed his tongue around the broken molar. There was no swelling. There were no instant shocks of bright white pain. A near toothless grin spread across Freeman's weathered face. He ran a hand across his bearded jaw, rubbed, found no swelling there either, and then laughed out loud in the silence of the small room. In beautiful celebration, he slapped his knee, laughed again and offered up a "hot damn and hallelujah!" This was as just a cause for celebration as was any wedding or any divorce.

With a jubilant spirit, Freeman reached for the nearest empty brown bottle. He held it up in front of the east-facing window so that the morning sun might shine through it. He peered closely inside, tilting the bottle first this way and then that. There, rolling slowly, he saw the tiny drop that he was hoping for move across the bottom of the bottle.

It was quite a comical figure that Freeman cut there in the morning sunlight with his head held all the way back in a posture he was sure made him look like a dime store Pez dispenser. Above his opened mouth, he held the bottle straight up and upside down. In that pose, Freeman waited patiently for sweet gravity to coax the tiny droplet down the neck of the bottle and into his waiting dry throat. He did not hold the bottle to his mouth. He did not want even one tiny atom of that tiny drop to be wasted on his lips.

He continued this ritual with the many other empty bottles that littered the small room, shuddering in electric ecstasy each time the anticipated droplets met his longing tongue.

"Did he ever tell you the story about the time he found the dime?" Afternoon light poured through the dirty windows of Pudgy's Tavern. Marty took a drink while waiting for Earl's answer.

"No. No. I don't believe so. Don't think I heard that'n."

Marty reiterated the tale, tickled to tell it. "He had this little sister, see? Wound up dyin' of meningitis or somethin'. Anyhow," Marty continued, "he says he found this dime once when he was a kid—all shiny and mercury, he says—and he says he had all these ideas about this dime see. Penny candy, baseball cards, bubble gum. And along comes this little sister of his see—a real snot nosed, bratty, big brother hater of a little sister. He says she comes walkin' up holdin' a chicken in her arms— said she carried them chickens around pretendin' 'em to be babies—she comes walkin' up, 'Whatcha got there?' She asks him. Says he holds that dime up between his thumb and his finger like this here see and he says to her, 'Just looky for ya self.' Says she puts that chicken down all the while studyin' that dime between his thumb and finger then she hauls off and knocks it right outta his hand tryin to grab it. And that chicken, faster than a jack rabbit in a prairie fire, pecks it up. Now here's the part that plum tickles me every time I think about that story. He says him and his little sister followed that chicken around for days waitin' for it to shit out that dime, jumpin' and wrestlin' each other over every squirt, but it never did."

They laughed together, there with their drinks between them, and when Earl's laughter subsided he noted observantly, "Hell, he's still chasin' that chicken." The two friends again erupted into laughter loud and gut borne.

Fishing through his trouser pockets, Freeman managed to reel in seven crumpled dollar bills, a nickel and eight pennies. There was a voice, almost a whisper, loving and patient there in his head, reminding him of just how long that money had to last him. It was May's voice, always comforting, always cautious. He obliged her. He seated himself on the edge of the small rented bed and thought hard on the subject before realizing that he had no idea how long that money had to last him because he had no idea what the date was. For that matter, he realized, he also had no idea what day of the week it was.

Freeman set to calculating on his fingers. He confused himself and began the problem solving again. He confused himself once more and abandoned the tiresome exercise all together, telling himself that it did not matter what the date was anyway. Today, he would celebrate. He would celebrate his seperation from that nagging and poking, cold hearted companion of late, from that painful presence preventing him from enjoying his existence here on this earth. No, today was different than yesterday. Yesterday and for many days prior to yesterday, he drank to ease the pain of the infected tooth. And before the business with the tooth had come along? Well, he was sure he had good reason on all of those days, too.

But, today, today was his to do with what he pleased. Today, he would drink in celebration, and who in the name of all that is decent and good in this world would or could fault him for that?

May would. Yes, May would probably disagree with all of his loaded logic and his skewed reasoning. *Probably?* He called himself out on his hedging. There was no doubt to be entertained where what May would or would not agree or disagree with.

"I just can't stand to see you this way." Her voice, not condescending, but compassionate came to him.

"Then look shum place else." He had slurred at her countless times.

Was it not bad enough that he had disappointed her in life that he had to continue to do so as she watched over him from her heavenly home? She was definitely in Heaven, she had to be, because her life on earth with him, his drinking, and the cancer had been hell enough for anyone. And wasn't he some kind of special son of a bitch for letting her die like that? For leaving her withered with the cancer and racked with the pain?

He would have traded places with her. Yes, he would have. But, wasn't that just the easiest thing in the world to say in regard to love? The way Freeman now had it figured, that whole 'die for you thing' was proof positive that when it came to love, people were just full of shit. Folks saying things like how they would die for other folks they loved so much said that because it was easy to say and sounded like a whole helluva lot. But, it didn't really amount to any hills of any beans and they all knew it. They knew that they would never be called upon and actually asked to do it. No, Freeman had it figured this way from what few hard lessons he had actually had the smarts to learn in his life. If people really wanted to express their love for someone, then they shouldn't go around saying things like, "I love you so much that I would die for you." No. That was too easy. It seemed to Freeman that if someone really wanted to proclaim proof of their love for someone, then they should pick a task that was actually difficult and that they might actually be called upon to prove. They should swear their love on something like, "I love you so much that I will think twice before opening my mouth when I am upset."

Now, that would be hard. Hard like love could be.

Freeman sat, staring blankly at the wall of the small rented room. He shook off the chill that settled into him and reminded himself of what a glorious day this was going to be. His eyes dimmed and dulled while behind them his thoughts scurried and scampered like army ants tasked with the merry mission of engineering the logistics of what would be this beautiful pain-free day.

First, he would slip on down to Mac's Package Store for a pint of Four Roses. No. Not a whole pint, a half pint. Having a whole pint had a tendency to make a fella want to find a drinking buddy, and when a fella with a bottle sets out to find a buddy, well suddenly he's got more buddies than he does bottle. A half pint then, for starters. The sheer thought of a virgin bottle of vino made his mouth water. He would take that bottle and step around behind Mac's, there in the tree line. He would sit there, not drinking at first, only smelling it, letting the murky bouquet of the bottled spirit swim into him and become part of him until he could stand it no longer and then—he wouldn't drink it—no, not at first. He would sip it, slowly lifting the bottle to his mouth, forcing himself to purse and pucker his lips so that he was only allowing himself sips. He would sip it there in the trees, away from anyone who might try to con him into sharing. There, he would sit and sip until the numbing warmth settled in and then he would head over to Pudgy's Tavern to shoot shit with Marty and Earl. He would then head to Jeannie's.

Marty and Earl were good for a round of beer a piece. But, they sure did like to make him sing for it, didn't they? They wanted jokes. They wanted stories. Stories of youth and folly. What story would he tell them today? Sometimes, they let him get away with telling a story that they had already heard, but he wouldn't do that today. No, today he'd remember a great story for them, a real knee slapper and a belly hugger sure to pry two rounds a piece from them. He'd think of a great one once the wine warmed him up. They wanted to laugh so they made him sing for his supper a little bit. But, that was okay. The stories he told them made him laugh, too. They made him remember. They made him forget. They made him feel young and alive again—young and alive and damned handsome.

"I'll tell ya the one that I love to hear him tell," said Marty to Earl.

"Which one's that?" Earl asked.

"The one where he went tryin' to sneak into that ol' girl's window and fell through her porch."

"The girlfriend with the sister that wasn't right in the head? What'd he say they called her?"

"Dumpy." Marty laughed and shook his head. "Imagine that."

"Yeah, Dumpy." Earl said. "Poor girl."

The two men caught the ear of Rudy Slakey the barkeep and the two recruiters who sat around the corner of the bar. They were glad to have someone to share the tales with.

"That's a great story there, see. I mean geez what a great story. Said he showed up over there in the middle of the night hornier than a three balled tomcat and drunk as a top, creepin around in the dark like a mountain lion across that back porch and all of a sudden it cracked like thunder and next thing he knew, he was pickin' himself up off his ass and all hell was breakin' loose inside that house."

"And," Earl took the lead, "that crazy sister comes out a screamin', 'It's the Lord! It's the Lord! He done come back like a thief in the night!'"

Marty took it from there, "And ol' dad out there in his sleeping gown with a shotgun pumpin' lead all over the place, a hollerin', 'Goddammit, Dumpy it ain't the Lord! It's one a them assholes from town come to take a poke at your sister!'"

Marty allowed Earl to finish the tale. "Freeman says he woke up in a tree with a hard on, a hangover and a helluva crick in his back."

The three men laughed together and as Slakey placed two fresh mugs in front of them, Marty said to him still laughing, "*Goddammit, Dumpy, it ain't the Lord!* You gotta hear him tell it, see. It's the funniest goddamned thing."

Behind Mac's Package store, Freeman slowly and gently stripped the paper seal from the promising pristine bottle, the foretaste of his inevitable prospect already at the task of charming him into complete capitulation.

He did sip—just as he had told himself that he would—the first time. The second time that he raised the bottle to his lips he sipped again, only longer than the first sip. On the third sip, he had to swallow twice and by the fourth sip, the bottle was empty and Freeman was back into his pockets for the money to trade for another.

With the second bottle, he did not even attempt to fool himself.

Two more bottles later, Freeman was drunk, broke and very ashamed.

"I just can't stand to see you like this."

"Then look shum place else."

Upon his arrival at Pudgy's Tavern, Marty and Earl greeted him like a prodigal son and now he was on—

"Here's one for ya." Freeman slumped at the bar and slurred at his friends. "She couldn'ta weighed forty pounds sho-soakin' wet. She was just talkin' bones—bones, skin, skin and pain, and me cryin' like a baby. And I says to her, 'I just can't stand to shee ya like this', .and she says, 'then look some place else'. And I did. And I never looked at her again." Freeman looked down at the weathered bar and then up at Marty and Earl. "Now get me a drink, you shun," he tried again, "you sonsabitches."

Chapter 29

June came and with it, the Whelan County Fair, bringing all of the smells, the carnival music, the rickety rides, the gaming booths with their barkers, the peep show, and the freak show with all of its unfortunate celebrities.

It took three days for Freeman to convince Jeannie to go. She was drinking just as heavily as anyone he had ever known. Her weight had dropped. Her green eyes had hollowed. She was fading, weakening before his eyes.

"My boys loved this," Jeannie said to Freeman, pointing at the freak show tent. "I never would go in. Always seemed so cruel to me."

"That's 'cause it is," offered Freeman.

Jeannie studied the painted signs.

"COME AND SEE THE WORLD'S FATTEST WOMAN!"

"INSIDE! TINY! THE WORLD'S SMALLEST MAN!"

"CAPTURED IN THE WILDS OF THE EUROPEAN CONTINENT! LUCA THE WOLF BOY! WILD! DANGEROUS!"

She envisioned herself then as "THE AMAZING SHRINKING WOMAN."
Watch as she makes wrong decision after wrong decision reducing her life until she is nothing more than Jeannie Tucker, mother of THE INCREDIBLE UNBELIEVABLE DISAPPEARING BOYS!

She was suddenly done with it all. "Would I be too much of a party pooper if I said, let's just go?" she asked.

"No, ma'm. Not at all. But the fireworks are about to start." Freeman raised an encouraging eyebrow.

"We can see them pretty good from the front steps of the house. They do 'em again on the fourth, too. Hows about this? Hows about we get us some corn dogs and a funnel cake, some popcorn, stop by Mac's and get some beers, and watch the fireworks from the front steps while stuffin' our faces?"

"Jeannie Marie, I do believe that's the best idea I've heard in a long time. You have no idea how much money you just saved me. I was about to blow my whole payday winnin' you that stuffed bear." Freeman pointed at the shooting range booth.

"Hadn't pegged you as a sharpshooter," she said. "But it wouldn't surprise me. Not one bit."

"Ah, I ain't no good with guns. Never had it in me. We got most our food from the gulf and what chickens we raised. That's why it was gonna cost me so much money."

"That doesn't surprise me either." She began to laugh, but was suddenly distracted. She turned to her right. Three boys that could easily have been Lenville, Ronny and Li'l Roy were sneaking through the dark behind the peep show tent.

She watched them forlornly. "Will the world always be so haunted, Freeman?" she asked absently.

"Yes," said Freeman without a thought. "It will." He was watching her waste away in front of him, much as he had watched Mayrene. She was a fighter, she had been toughened and calloused by the licks of life, but from where he was standing, he could see she was on the ropes and whatever will to fight she was holding on to was leaving her with every blow.

"Why won't he write me?"

"He will."

They gathered their corn dogs, a bucket of popcorn and a funnel cake, resisting the hard sell delivered by the carnival barkers at every turn.

When they reached the gate, Jeannie said, "There's Miss Jessie and the boys."

"Hey, Miss Jeannie! Mister Freeman! Y'all leavin' already?"

"Yeah," Jeannie nodded almost apologetically. "I'm just a li'l tired."

"Mawmaw, come on," one of the twins pulled at Miss Jessie's arm.

"I's a comin'. Wish me luck," Miss Jessie laughed. "Don't y'all make me whoop your hind ends in front of all of Whelan County. Be a shame to catch a whoopin' at the fair, now."

"Good luck," Jeannie said with a smile.

As they walked on, Freeman said, "Boy, I don't envy her."

"I do," said Jeannie.

Mac had closed early and taken himself to the fair.

The two sat on the front steps drinking sloe gin from the cupboard with their funnel cakes and corn dogs.

"Ow!" Freeman put his hand on his jaw.

"What happened? What is it?" asked Jeannie.

"Broke my tooth on that popcorn."

"Aw."

The first white explosion split the darkness casting an electric web through the night sky. Jeannie looked to the heavens. Freeman looked at Jeannie. To Freeman, she looked like a child about to blow out candles on a birthday cake. He removed his hand from his jaw and felt for hers as the sky exploded again.

Chapter 30

R udy Slakey, as tall and well groomed as he was well-intentioned, had only months before acquired the place from his Uncle Pudge. Pudge took his savings and what he'd made in the deal and moved to Destin, Florida. Rudy had managed a couple of bars and had jumped at the opportunity to own his own place, even if it meant moving from Atlanta to the sticks to do so.

For months before sealing the deal, Slakey had labored over what to call the place, an entertaining if fruitless exercise. *Dick's Halfway Inn* lingered at the top of the list, but like most of his choices, it was unoriginal. He entertained *The Crow Bar*, *The Dew Drop Inn*, *Someplace Else*, *The Hole in the Wall*, *The Fuzzy Duck*, *Larry's* (even though he knew no one named Larry, just thought it would suit a bar well enough), which led him to *Rudy's*, which led him to *Slakey's*.

Slakey's suited Rudy Slakey just fine. Wasn't that just what he had always wanted? His own name on his own place? So, he resigned from the enjoyable exercise of entertaining various names for his new establishment and settled on *Slakey's*. In the weeks leading up to the takeover, Rudy Slakey's excitement grew to the level of expectant father. He would pass his name along to the establishment that would outlive him. This thought made him momentarily consider curiously naming the place *Junior's*, but he reckoned that name would lead to years of questions and the answers might lead to even more.

So how come you never married and had a boy to pass your name on to?
The question would come anyway. It always did.
He considered just calling the place *Dorothy's* and being done with it.

It was all for nothing anyway. It was likely that Rudy Slakey had not heard the Yiddish proverb: *Der mentsh trakht un Got lakht*. Man plans and God laughs. It is just as likely that he would not have heeded its warning at any rate. Renaming

Pudgy's Tavern turned out to be tantamount to renaming the town or even the state. In the end, Rudy Slakey could not bring himself to do it.

His Uncle Pudge was a good man. It was fitting that the place would continue to hold his name.

In the dim afternoon light of the near empty bar, Freeman probed the bleeding hole in his gum with his tongue. As he explored, a curious and perplexed expression began to slowly bloom on his narrow face. "Hey, now." He probed a bit more, his expression growing even more perplexed. "What the hell, Marty?"

"What?"

Freeman's brow was now impossibly low. "Aw, shit, Marty."

"What? What is it?" Marty demanded, the tightening tension mounting to an unbearable degree. Freeman leaned left in his bar stool, spat blood on the floor and stared at it as Marty seated himself two stools down. "What, Freeman? What's a matter?"

"What's the matter? What's the matter? You pulled the wrong goddamned tooth, you dumb sumbitch. That's what's the matter." A line of blood trickled from the corner of Freeman's mouth, staining his beard.

"Nah. No way, Freeman. I pulled the one you put your finger on, see." Marty contested, dismissing the accusation with a slight wave of his hand and drank from his glass of beer.

"If you weren't sure, then you shouldn'ta done it," Freeman argued.

"I was sure. Shit, Freeman. You had your finger on it. I got the right one. It just feels different to ya in there, see 'cause it's gone and all."

From behind the bar, Slakey shook his head in disapproval while pointing at the tool and the bloody mess. "Get that shit off my bar," he said firmly.

Freeman spat blood on the floor again before he retrieved the pliers from the bar where Marty had left them. "Gimme a towel, Slakey," he said, holding his jaw in his hand, massaging it slowly. "A clean one." His beard was now rust colored there in the area around his bottom lip. He shot a sideways glance at his friend and muttered, "Goddammit, Marty."

With the pliers now in his lap, he set to examining the extracted tooth, rotating it in the dim light, squinting at it as if it was a rare and priceless jewel. "Now, that there, that's a perfectly good tooth right there." He held it up so that the two men might see and acknowledge its perfectly good qualities and again he muttered, "Goddammit, Marty."

"Bring us another round, too, Slakey. On me." Marty ordered, turning to Freeman and nodding his head in a gesture he hoped would signify to his friend that a round was sure to make it good again between the two. Freeman returned the nod, signifying that indeed it did.

Marty moved apprehensively to the stool next to Freeman and put his hand on Freeman's shoulder. "Jesus, Freeman. Sorry. I swear that was the tooth you had your finger on. Hell, I ain't never pulled nobody's tooth before, see. How the hell'd I let you talk me into that?"

Freeman placed the tooth on the bar beside his mug of beer. From his lap, he retrieved the pliers and offered them to Marty. "Let's try this again." He directed. "Now, aim for the broke one behind the big bleedin' hole." Marty received the pliers and stood from his stool. Freeman leaned his head back, opened wide his bloody mouth and muttered something unintelligible, but was most likely yet another, "Goddammit, Marty."

Slakey brought the clean towel and began to pour the drinks. He stopped abruptly. "No. No. Hell, no. Don't even think about it, assholes. Fun's over. Marty, sit down. Freeman, you can thank me later."

"Wha—?" Freeman asked and spat out the blood again, this time to his other side.

"And quit that damned spittin'!" Slakey scolded him.

"Well," Freeman swallowed blood, "gimme a cup or somethin'."

Back on his stool, Marty absently placed the pliers on the bar and tossed back his shot. "Now, Slakey, you ain't gonna let him have gone through all a that for nothin' are ya? Hell, how ya think that's gonna leave me feelin' about this whole damned thing?"

"Better than how he's gonna feel about it. Bet on that." Slakey stuffed a dish towel into a coffee cup and slid it to Freeman. "And get those damned nasty pliers off my bar. Freeman, get that damned tooth outta my sight."

"Thanks." Freeman took the cup, spat into it and dropped the tooth into his shirt pocket.

The two men sat in silence like scolded children until Marty finally spoke saying, "Just wait 'til I tell Earl about this. Man, he's gonna be sorry and sore as hell he missed this. Hell, he ain't even gonna believe it. Pulled the wrong tooth." He laughed.

"See there!" Freeman whined to Slakey. "He did it on purpose! He pulled the wrong goddamned tooth on purpose!" In his agitation, Freeman knocked the coffee cup from the bar. It hit the floor and broke into pieces, spilling and splashing its bloody contents.

Slakey erupted, "You know what? How about both of you degenerates just get the hell outta here. Shit, now, I'm serious. Just get the hell outta here and I don't wanna see ya back in here today." He considered this for a second then continued,

195

"And I probably won't want to see you fellas tomorrow or the next day or the damned day after that, either. What the hell do you fellas think this place is? And goddammit, I went and let ya suck me right into this craziness. Just get the hell out. Both of ya. Pullin' teeth at the bar—"

"Gee, Slakey—"

"Just shut your mouth, Marty. Shut up, pay up and just get the hell out. Both of ya. Go play doctor someplace else. Now, I mean it. I bet you fellas never pulled a stunt like this on Pudge."

Wounded, the two men rose slowly from their stools.

"Slakey, I'm a little short, see. I'm gonna have to settle up next time."

"Goddammit, Marty." Slakey took his turn to mutter.

"Can I get one more for the road?" Freeman asked.

"Out!" Slakey pointed to the door and the waiting world beyond it.

Making their exits, Marty asked Freeman, "What the hell ya reckon got into him?"

"Hell, who knows?" Freeman shrugged and spat blood on the floor.

Chapter 31

P a Bailey was upset that Ma Bailey had drug him from the comfort of the fan.

"Just look at it, Pa. It's got to go. Just look at it." Ma Bailey pointed with both opened hands at a stack of lumber there on the corner of the boarding house property that had been cut into different widths and lengths.

"I know, Ma. I know. Ya think I ain't seen that pile? I've seen it like you have." Pa Bailey agreed, though dreaded the conversation he knew was sure to come.

The Bailey's stood on the back porch of their boarding house. Ma Bailey wasn't about to let the poorly stacked pile of lumber grow any larger. "Say somethin' to him."

"I will, Ma," Hiram Bailey assured his wife.

"When, Pa? When you gonna say somethin'? When we're overrun with rattlers and termites?"

"Today. I'll say somethin' to him today," Pa assured her.

"How 'bout now? He's up there now, ya know."

"I said I would," said Pa Bailey.

"Now?" Ma Bailey pushed.

"All right then, woman. Dammit. I'll go say somethin' to him. Now."

In his rented room, Freeman stared at the ceiling, rubbing his jaw.

You know that I don't care for the drinkin', William. I never did.

"I know." Freeman rolled over and faced the wall.

But she's good. She's a good woman.

"I know she is." Freeman curled himself into a fetal position.

She's made her mistakes and she's had the good sense to learn from 'em. She won't judge you. She don't judge you. It ain't in her. Not 'cause she's had her licks. It never was in her. You don't judge her either, and she can see that.

"I'm glad she can. I'm glad she knows I don't. May?"

Yes, dear?

"I'd do her the same way, ya know? If she was to get sick on me—I'd just do the same way with her as I did with you. I'd run. I'd run like hell 'cause I'm a coward. I'd run 'cause I ain't a good man."

Well, she's not exactly well right now.

She can still fight it. She still got time. She's bouncin' back some days.

You do love her.

"I'd still leave her. I'd still run."

You might. You might run. You might not. Even in the shape she's in, she's a lot prettier than I ever was.

"No. Don't, no, no. Don't you say that, Mayrene."

I'm just tellin' the truth. She's the kind of pretty men move mountains for. She's the kind of pretty that makes men crazy, too, though.

"Mayrene, when that cancer took hold of you, all I wanted was to put my hands around its black throat and throttle that murderin', evil thing until—and I woulda, Mayrene—"

I know you would have if you could.

"Watchin' somethin' like that hurt you like that, I wanted so bad to be able to, to just be able to reach into you, grab hold of that cold blooded and evil thing and yank it outta you and stomp on it 'til was just, just black mess beneath my heel, Mayrene, to shoot it right between its goddamned eyes—"

Now, you watch your language William.

"Sorry, May—to shoot it right between its eyes and watch it bleed out its black poison blood. I woulda killed it for hurtin' you. I woulda murdered it. I woulda stomped it. I woulda poked a pistol between its cold eyes and I'd a shot it for hurtin' you. Ain't a thing in this world got any business bringin' that kinda pain to folks and 'specially not to good folks. Not a thing in this world."

I don't care for that kind of talk. You loved me. I know that.

"I left you."

You get you some sleep, so's you'll be all rested up for her.

"May, don't go." Freeman felt the sting of rising tears.

Just for a little while. Hey, knock, knock.

"Who's there?"

Boo.

"Boo who?"

Sorry I made you cry, William.

Freeman smiled.

A knock. Freeman wiped his eyes, rose slowly from the bed and opened the door.

"Afternoon, Freeman."

"Mister Bailey." Freeman was momentarily taken aback by the sight of the old man.

"Wonder if you got a minute or two?" Pa Bailey asked.

"Why sure. Think I might. What's the matter?"

"Well, Freeman, you know I mostly mind my own business. So long as the rent's paid and all."

"My rent not paid, Mister Bailey?" Freeman asked.

"You're fine on that account. We're squared there," said Pa Bailey with a wave of his hand. "Square as dice."

"But not square on some other?" Freeman asked.

"It's not that you're not squared. Not exactly. It's just, well, I's a wonderin' what the situation is with that lumber you been stackin' up out back."

"Didn't think it was enough to cause no harm, Mister Bailey."

"A pile of wood like that, well ya know, it's a haven for things. Just didn't want no snake den out back there in the yard. You plannin' on buildin' somethin' with it?"

"Well yeah, I mean I ain't just collectin' it," said Freeman.

"I wish you'd go ahead then, Freeman. Ma's all over my ass about it. Get Ma off a my back about it, will ya?"

"I sure would like to, Mister Bailey, but I been waitin' for a good payday to get myself some tools. A saw, hammer and nails and such."

"Got all that in the shed. Got sawhorses, too," the old man offered.

"And you wouldn't mind, Mister Bailey?" Freeman asked.

"Naw. I wouldn't mind," said Pa Bailey.

"Well thank ya, Mister Bailey. I appreciate it. I surely do."

"Just clean up whatever mess you make. Don't leave my shed lookin' like this room." Pa Bailey pointed a crooked finger and waved it in a circle.

"Will do, Mister Bailey. Thank ya," offered Freeman.

"I'm an ol' carpenter," Bailey said. "What you gonna be buildin'?"

"A kitchen table."

"What you needin' with a kitchen table?"

"I'm gonna build it for somebody," Freeman explained.

"For Jeannie Marie?"

"Yeah."

"She got no kitchen table?"

"She needs a new kitchen table."

"Oh," Bailey said with a wink. "You need any help from an ol' carpenter you let me know."

"I surely will. Thanks again."

"Oh, Freeman—?"

"Yes, Mister Bailey?"

"You ain't stealin' that wood from the pallet mill are you?"

"No, sir. It's scraps. Ol' Ed's boy says I can take some of it."

"Sorry to ask, I just didn't want to be a part of nothin' if it wasn't on the up and up."

"Up and up it is, Mister Bailey."

"Well good, then. You let me know if you need an ol' hand like me. Give me a reason to get out from under the feet of Weknowwho."

"I'll keep that in mind. I surely will."

"Freeman?"

"Yes, Mister Bailey?"

"You all right?"

"Reckon so."

"What you bleedin' for?"

"What's 'at, Mister Bailey?"

"Your beard's all bloody. Freeman, you been cryin? You need me to get the doc?"

"No, sir, Mister Bailey. I don't need no doctor. Least I don't reckon."

Chapter 32

I f it was to be physical, she always made him bathe before. Freeman took no offense. It was a much welcomed part of the ritual of their intimacy   the steaming water, the fragrant soap, the cleansing. Invariably, he succumbed to the warmth and relaxation and she preened and perfumed herself as he slept in the tub, his deep rhythmic snores somehow comforting her as she studied herself in the mirror, brushed her fire colored hair and applied her make up.

She always had to wake him and she always watched as he rose from the tub, all hair and beard and bones, the murky water rolling from his emaciated body in sheets and taking with it, if only for the evening, the grainy residue of history.

"I fall asleep a lot of places. It just comes up on me, Jeannie. You get old overnight, ya know."

"Do ya now?" she absently humored him as she dried him with the towel.

"Hell, I heard somebody say that once. Don't rightly recall who, though. Mighta been my daddy. He was always sayin' shit to make himself look as smart as he thought he was, as smart as he'd convinced a lot of folks he was. Anyway, whoever it was I heard say it, I'd like to slap the shit out of 'em. It's one of them things. It's one of them goddamned things a man gets in his head and allows to be true. Allows it, I mean. See, here I've been thinkin' I got old overnight like I heard somebody say once, when I mighta just woke up feelin' bad and because I heard somebody say some ol' bullshit like, 'ya get old overnight,' well, hell, I let myself get old overnight, when if I never heard that, I might not be feelin' so old all these years."

"You ain't that old," she said, quickly adding, "Are ya?" She winked with a smile, trying to brighten his dark mood.

She was always softened by him. She finished drying his back and pushed her cheek to his bare skin. In her ear, she heard the muffled sound of his heart and the rattle in his lungs.

"Jeannie, I've, I've had May with me all day. Wouldn't seem right to—"

It wasn't always carnal. They gave only what the other needed and took only what the other offered.

"Wouldn't seem right at all," she agreed.

This night, she dressed him in a pair of Lenville's old and faded blue jeans. The length was right, but she had to cinch them up with a leather belt. Across his shoulders, she draped the towel she had used to dry him from the bath. She led him into the kitchen and seated him in a chair.

"Many years ago, I was in a barbershop—"

"You must mean *very* many years ago," Jeannie interjected.

"You got that right." Freeman smiled.

"I'm sorry. Go ahead." Jeannie sized up his head, pulling hair between her fingers.

"Louie the barber's about to cut my hair when through the window, he sees this kid comin' up the sidewalk. Louie says to me, 'That kid comes in here and I'll show ya how damned dumb he is,' and sure enough the kid comes in and takes a seat. Louie reaches into his pocket and puts down two quarters and a dollar bill and calls the kid over. Rufus, Rufus was that kid's name. Louie says, 'Hey, Rufus, come on over here for a second.' And the kid comes over. Louie says, 'Rufus, you can have the two quarters or you can have the one dollar bill.' That poor Rufus snatches up the two quarters and sits back down. Louie shoots me a look in the mirror ya know."

"You shoulda said somethin', Freeman. Lettin' him make a fool of that poor boy."

"You'll like this, Jeannie, now just wait. An hour or so later, I see that boy Rufus comin' outta the drug store with an ice cream cone and a comic book and I says to him, 'Ya know, Rufus, if you'd took the dollar bill you could buy more ice cream or more comic books, and Rufus says, 'Yeah, but then the game'd be over and I'd never get nothin' else.'"

"Ha! Good for Rufus." Jeannie laughed. "Is that true?"

"Well, sure it is, Jeannie. Whether it happened or not." Freeman answered.

She cut his matted hair there beneath the naked bulb in the kitchen, her fingers sending electric shocks through his damp scalp, her breasts bumping him, rubbing against his shoulders, his chest, his face. She then went to work on his beard—not shaving it, but first subduing it, then taming it with the sharp scissors. She made small talk as she went about the task.

"As a friend I'm telling you this. Just so you know. Word is, Ol' Ed says if you don't show up in the next couple of days, he's gonna have to quit ya for good." Jeannie said.

"Finally got my tooth out. Two of 'em." He leaned his head back to show her.

She pretended to look inside his mouth. "Good. Good for you," she said. "You can put 'em under the pillow."

"Might just do that. That's why I been missin' so much. Shew, thought it was going to kill me, Jeannie."

"Be still or I'm gonna gap ya," she warned and snipped the scissors.

"You gonna be okay, Jeannie?"

She stopped her task then only for a moment. He was her only friend. She considered herself an untouchable in Sonoraville. Big Roy had made sure of that. No one wanted to be associated with, let alone in a relationship with, the white trash wife of the worthless bastard who had killed Sheriff Bill. No one spoke to her when she ran her errands in town and all of these years later, given recent happenings, she imagined they were still talking about her, running down her name and those wild and good for nothing boys of hers, after she had passed earshot. She had grown accustomed to the loneliness. She had even fooled herself into believing that she had long since failed to notice it. But out of the blue, Freeman had come to Sonoraville and into her life. She had early on told him her story. He had dismissed it, and for that she had not yet found the words to thank him.

"I'm gonna be okay." She pulled a bit of his beard between her fingers, tugged it perhaps a bit too harshly and snipped at it. "Surprised Ol' Ed hasn't quit me. I'll be okay. Just wish that little shit would write me a letter or somethin'. Somethin' to let me know where he is and if he's okay." She stepped back like an artist from an easel. "There ya go, you handsome devil." She said and smiled at the explosion of color in his cheeks. "Took ten years off ya."

"Hell, keep cuttin' then."

Carefully, she removed the towel from his neck and his bony shoulders. She shook it out the back door and returned with a broom and a dust pan.

Freeman stood, "I can do that. Let me do that, Jeannie."

"I've got it." She moved his chair and swept up the hair from the worn linoleum floor, feeling his eyes on her backside as she went about the chore.

"You know how I said I fall asleep a lot of places?" Freeman asked. Jeannie smiled and confirmed. "I guess I shoulda said I wake up a lot of places. On the railroad tracks—well, not on the tracks, but you get it."

"Hold on a second," she said, putting away the broom and the dustpan. From the cabinet over the sink, she retrieved two glasses. "Went by Mac's earlier. Gin okay? And what are you talkin' about wakin' up on the tracks?"

"Gin's okay."

She placed the bottle on the worn kitchen table with two glasses.

"Sit down, you're makin' me nervous. That's what my mama used to say. And you're gonna get yourself killed sleepin' out there on the tracks or next to 'em or whatever. I know you won't spend the whole night here, but you've got your room. What are you thinkin'? Sleepin' outside'll be the death of ya."

"Habit. 'Specially in the warmer weather." He stopped momentarily and decided on a different path. "Truth is, they's curfew over at the Baileys. After ten, she locks the doors."

"Work ain't over til ten, Freeman."

"They make exceptions for the nights I work."

"You mean all this time you been sleepin' outside on Saturday nights?"

"I have, Jeannie, but I ain't complainin' about none a that."

"You'll stay here on Saturday nights from now on."

"Jeannie, I couldn't, that just don't look right."

"What? You afraid folks around here'll start gossipin'?" she laughed. "You can sneak out the back in the mornin'."

"Folk'll know I ain't left."

"So, leave out the front, then sneak back in the back, then sneak back out the back."

"Jeannie," Freeman sighed. "That ain't even why I brought it up."

"What are you tryin' to tell me?"

"Sometimes after I leave here, I go out up on the bank. Sometimes I go over the other side of them tracks in the yellow grass and park myself against a tree. Sometimes the sun wakes me. Sometimes the trains wake me. Sometimes the bugs or other things that scamper around in the night and the dark wake me. People. People wake me—" he paused, a reflective smile grew on his newly trimmed face. "Your boys made a lot a noise when they come back up on a Saturday night, Jeannie. Was a lot of nights I woke up to 'em hollerin' and carryin' on. Now, a couple a weeks before your boy got killed, one of 'em woke me up beltin' out a Hank Williams tune and I just sat there in the dark against the tree and listened. Boy could carry a tune."

"That was Lenville. You're talkin' about my Len. I could always tell when he'd been drinkin' 'cause he'd just sing and sing when he got to drinkin'. Bless his heart, Ronny, now Ronny sang drunk or sober, but whew, that boy was tone deaf." She laughed at the pleasant memory.

"That Lenville sang the good stuff, too, Jeannie. Not this loud nonsense ya hear nowadays."

"I know that's right."

"Jeannie," Freeman's face suddenly grew somber, "I woke up one night to hollerin', the kinda squawling that when ya hear it, ya know somethin' big and terrible done happened. A cussin' and a callin' out. People cussin' each other 'cause one of em done went and killed another."

Jeannie Tucker's smile abruptly faded. Her heart began to pound quickly, heavily. "What did you see, Freeman? What did you see?"

"I'm gonna tell ya, Jeannie. I'm gonna tell ya all of it. Not on account a I want to, but on account a I got to."

Part Four:
The Broken Places

Chapter 33

O ctober came and with it, the air turned cool and tender. The surrounding mountains transitioned from the blue side of green to yellow and the red side of brown. Aldrin and Armstrong had walked on the moon. The war in Viet Nam raged on. The Miracle Mets had won the World Series. Halloween was nearing and on its heels, Thanksgiving. Christmas would come. Soon, the decorations would be hung on the streetlamps down on the square. Marty Shoemaker considered this. There would be no fretting over what to buy the old man this year. October's arrival made it almost six months since he had buried his father.

Marty Shoemaker had heard the unseasonably warm period just after the first killing frost called by some, "Indian Summer." His own people had always referred to it as "Poor Man's Summer," and although he had never heard anyone explain it to him in such a way, he had always believed that it wasn't referred to as "poor" merely because it was found lacking, but also because "Poor Man's Summer" was meant to be endearingly derogative as it was a time of year that perhaps had put on airs and a brave face for a brief moment, and was allowed to pretend to be something that it was not. He could not justify this understanding, yet still it was the feeling the term gave him on some deep and unreachable level. It was a period that to him was the last of the fallen crumbs of summer. It was summer's last gasp, and It would not be long until the snows came again, blanketing the mountains and the valley, rendering the road into Shoemaker Hollow again impassable.

The impetus for Marty's decision was the want of a marker, a nice cut of marble that would remain standing once the house had long fallen and the woods and the undergrowth had crept back onto the cleared land. A tribute. A memorial. It bothered Marty to no end how quickly the earth had healed itself after he had taken the shovel to it, leaving Marty to second guess himself as to where exactly his deceased father now lay. He knew the spot, albeit roughly, but could no longer make out the perimeter of his father's grave. It was time for a stone, for something permanent and honorable. But Marty was no stone cutter. He would only muck it up and wind up settling for less than his father deserved.

He would have to get the stone in town. That would mean questions. Questions would mean more pretending, more lies.

It was time. This could no longer be denied.

It was Marty's intention to drive down to the courthouse, to find the sheriff and to finally tell it, reminding Sheriff Stearns of the heavy March snowfall and how it had stranded him with his dead father with no phone and no road out.

When Marty reached the mouth of the holler, he realized much to his amazement and embarrassment that he was all but ready to do this thing without a drop of alcohol to take the edge off. So, instead of heading into town to the courthouse, he turned the truck left toward the residence of Earl Rainwater, the only friend he felt he had left in this world.

At Earl's, he did not get out of the truck, but simply blew the horn in three short bursts. Earl opened the door dressed in a pair of long underwear. He held up one finger and disappeared back into the house. He reappeared momentarily wearing muck boots and a flannel coat over his johnnies now and approached the truck.

"Hey, Marty," he nodded. "Whatcha into this afternoon?"

"Dad's dead," said Marty and to his own surprise, he began to weep.

"Oh, Jesus, Marty. Sweet Jesus. I'm sorry, Marty. Where is he?"

"He's up at the house."

"And you're sure he's dead? Have you called an ambulance?"

"It's way too late for that," sobbed Marty. "I was going to see the sheriff, but damn Earl, I need a drink, see."

"Yeah, yeah, sure you do, you betcha. Hows about I drive? Scooch over. Earl opened the door and Marty slid across the seat. "Ain't that somethin'?" Earl said. "And him doin' so good just the other day. Geez, I'm sorry as hell for ya, Marty. Sorry as hell."

"On the house today, Marty. Your money's no good here today. Not that it's that good any other day." Slakey laughed and then apologized. "Hell of a thing to lose a dad. I know it is." Slakey reached a hand across the bar and placed it on Marty's shoulder, an act that caught both men surprised.

"Put one a them on me, Slakey," said Freeman. "Sorry for your loss, there Marty."

"Me, too," said Earl still in his long johns and boots. "I wanna buy my friend a drink." Earl wrapped his arm around his friend's shoulders.

"What's the occasion?" asked a lone drinker from the other end of the bar.

Slakey stepped over to the man and in a subdued tone informed him, "Man's dad passed away."

"In that case," the lone drinker took out his wallet. "A round on me. My condolences."

Marty tipped his mug toward the man and thanked him.

A trio of Army recruiters who had quickly become regulars overheard and each bought Marty a round.

Word soon spread throughout the hollers and down the dirt road that Orville Shoemaker, veteran of the First World War, cabinet maker extraordinaire and the sweetest old man you'd ever have the privilege of meeting had left his earthly home. Soon, Slakey had a full blown wake on his hands. The jukebox played. Food was brought in. Drinks were bought. A loss was mourned. A life was celebrated.

One of the uniformed men was just drunk enough to be just impolite enough to ask, "How'd he die? Lost my old man to a loggin' truck."

"Died in his sleep," Marty answered and began to drunkenly sob.

"Now, that's a good way to go, sorry to say, but it is." He put a hand on Marty's shoulder. "Last night?" the NCO pushed.

"Naw," Marty cried, "last March."

Earl choked on his beer.

The young recruiter moved his hand from Marty's shoulder as if he had placed it on something hot. He stood confused and looked to Slakey.

Slakey snatched the half full mug from its place in front of Marty and crashed it into the sink so hard it shattered. All eyes turned toward the bar.

"What ya go and do that for Slakey?" Marty asked.

Slakey spoke through clenched teeth. "Of all the low down— I mean you fellas have pulled some real shit in here, some real numbers I mean, but this here takes the cake. Ain't no redeemin' from this. You're gonna split hell wide open for a stunt like this, Marty. Now, get out." Slakey stood shaking his head at Marty, his disgust radiant and contagious.

"Slakey—"

"Just get out. Go on and get the hell outta here." Marty stood. "And you, too, you—" Slakey stumbled momentarily over his words until he straightened out his tongue with, "you underwear asshole!" Slakey looked to Earl.

"Slakey, I'm just as—" Earl attempted to defend himself.

"Don't look at me," said Freeman preemptively to Slakey. "I'm innocent on this one, Boss." Freeman sipped from his beer and watched as his friends exited the bar to a chorus of boos and hisses. They were legends now to be forever immortalized in story. Freeman lit a Lucky and was already working on how his version of the tale would begin.

Chapter 34

T he yellow dog crossed the railroad tracks and casually passed Pudgy's Tavern, his tail bobbing lightly. He approached Mac's Package Store and studied Mac as he passed, opting not to push his luck by examining the trash cans.

Byron "Mac" Lang swept the porch of the package store. He did not notice the dog. With the previous night's news of the death of Orville Shoemaker, he was especially distracted and feeling queerly nostalgic this morning. His own impending death was on his mind, and so far as bitter fodder for thought goes, worse than his own death, so was his own life on his mind. Mac shivered slightly though the late October morning air was unseasonably warm. He stepped from the shade of the covered porch and onto the parking lot to let the autumn sun warm him a bit.

He lit a Chesterfield and leaned upon his broom. He soon found himself studying the aging neon sign that hung above the porch. He frowned then as he contemplated whether the sign would last another winter.

That goddamned sign.

There in the warming October sun, Byron slowly shook his head and began to laugh.

When Byron Lang first bought the old feed building, a liquor store wasn't what he had in mind. If a person were to ask him, "How come a liquor store then?" Byron might shrug and tell the inquiring person it, "Just worked out that way." When he first bought the building, he reckoned he would stock his shelves with staples: bread and milk, eggs and sugar and flour. From behind the counter, he would cut deli meat, peddle chewing gum, chewing tobacco and cigarettes. On a shelf behind the counter, he initially and dubiously stocked a mere two dozen half-pint colored bottles of varying inebriants with the thought that he would likely be dusting them every week. His business plan was built solely and firmly upon the hope that the men working at the hosiery and the pallet mill would jump at the chance to purchase such staple

211

items on their way home from work, rather than drive into town to Cas Walker's place. He would accommodate the residents of the various hollers on this end of Whelan County, also sparing them the trip to town.

Byron Lang, for all of his entrepreneurial spirit, underestimated the lure and appeal of the overstocked shelves, the uniformed employees, and the fluorescent lights that drenched the grocery chain that had lately invaded the region. Cas Walker had put his name in large and white neon letters in front of the grocery store that he had constructed right in the middle of town. A set of white neon scissors towered beside his name. In the path of the scissor's blades was a green neon dollar sign. When the lights blinked and then lit up again, the scissors were closed, and the green dollar sign had been cut in half. They blinked again and again, cutting costs all evening long.

How could Byron compete with that?

As the loaves of bread molded on the shelf and the bottled milk soured in the cooler, he experimented with his own signage in an effort to draw in more customers—to no avail. The pretty colored bottles he stocked behind him disappeared quickly, though. So did the quarts of beer and the cold bottles of soda pop. Cigarettes did too. So, as Byron's grocery order dwindled, his liquor and beer order grew larger and the eyes of his fellow parishioners at First Methodist grew narrower. Against his wife's vehement wishes, his liquor stock soon spread from the shelf behind the counter to the shelf in front of the counter where he could keep an eye on it. It then spread from that shelf, to the next shelf over.

Byron continued to carry a few loaves of bread, some prepackaged lunch meat, a few dusty bags of flour and sugar and a few dozen eggs. For a while, the expensive and painted sign that Byron Lang had ordered all the way from Knoxville that read "Lang Grocery" towered above the porch awning. He initially held on to the meager grocery stock for his conscience, and perhaps so that his wife might be able to continue smiling and holding her head up.

Now, if a person were to ask Byron Lang, "Why does the sign out front now say 'Mac's Package?'" and "Who is Mac?" one might first want to make sure that one had a minute, or perhaps an afternoon, to spare.

But one might not get the whole truth from Byron. One just might not get it here, either.

But here it goes:

Most men who reinvent themselves, or begin to live under assumed names and aliases travel across the country, far and away from those who know them. Byron did it right at home. He didn't do it for shadowy reasons or haunting troubles or arrest warrants, nor even for romantic notions of actual reinvention. Byron did it for the most understandable reason of all. He did it to spite a woman, and possibly a church, and perhaps even a regional grocery chain. Though, like most acts committed out of spite, the persons on the receiving end of the spite truly did not give two shits what Byron did.

Byron's wife, Lucretia, found herself in white-hot love with Ty Maynard, a young man many years her junior and not in the liquor trade, but set to inherit the hardware store. His daddy, Bill Maynard, was languishing with TB. Ty Maynard was also a deacon and the boy's Sunday school teacher. Lucretia taught the girls. Apparently, as they compared classroom notes on temptation and sin, the two succumbed to temptation and sin. Eventually, the Sunday School lessons shifted their focus more onto Christ's forgiveness, planks in your own eyes, and the casting of first stones.

Lucretia left Byron and his would-be grocery store and promptly moved into Bailey's Boarding House. The papers were soon drawn up. The two were soon divorced. Lucretia and Ty were married. It was indeed scandalous, but the two somehow managed to survive with their social dignity intact.

Byron Lang quit the Methodist church and ordered yet another even more expensive sign, this time all the way from a neon sign manufacturer in Atlanta.

The sign arrived to much fanfare. A crowd gathered as the old "Lang Grocery" sign fell from the front of the store with a soft "foonf" and a puffy cloud of brown dust. A crane hoisted the new one into position. The new one read "MAC'S PACKAGE" in white letters set behind white neon tubes on a backdrop the color of dried blood. There was a bottle on the sign, outlined with neon filled tubes, and when the neon was charged and activated, the bottle floated up into the air and its contents comically drained from it. This it would do all evening long, Cas Walker be damned.

The group of onlookers craned their necks and gawked at the proceedings. This event would hold them until the fair came back to Whelan County.

Whitey Johnson, a county renowned wisecracker, approached Byron Lang who carried that same perpetual grin that new fathers carry the day their first child is born. "You sellin' the place, Byron?" Whitey asked..

Byron could not avert his eyes from the work at hand. "Careful, fellas," he called before answering Whitey's question. "No, Whitey, I ain't a sellin'." Byron answered, but did not look at Whitey.

"Then who the hell's Mac?" asked Whitey.

Still not looking at Whitey Johnson, with his thumb, Byron pointed at his own inflated chest. "Me. I'm Mac," he said, and then called again, "Now, easy, boys."

"You ain't 'Mac.' Hell, you're just Byron."

"I'm Mac *now*," Byron informed him, smiling still that new-father grin and watching the installation intensely. "Easy now, boys! Easy!" Byron called to the men.

Whitey Johnson had his teeth in it now, down to the gums, and he wasn't about to let it go. "Hell, you find out your daddy was a Scotsman and not a Kraut?" asked Whitey. A wave of laughter rolled from the men who had gathered. "Mac, that's Scottish, ain't it? You gonna take up the bagpipes or you just gonna go 'round whistlin' *Scotland the Brave* out yer *arse*?" The group of men laughed again.

Byron stopped smiling and now looked at Whitey. "Kraut's for wieners, asshole. I'm Mac now. Dammit, I always wanted to be called Mac."

"Hell, I always wanted to be called Well Hung, but tough shit for me, Byron. You can't just go around changing your name just 'causin' you feel like it. Ain't even legal." Whitey Johnson informed him.

"I just did." Byron's smile returned. He pointed up at the sign. "Were you wantin' somethin', Whitey?"

"Yeah, I was wantin' somethin', *Byron*."

"Whatcha wantin'?" asked Mac as the two headed toward the store.

"Um, a bottle of, let me see, um," Whitey readied his best Scottish brogue which wasn't very good and said, "*Scotch. Scotch whiskay.*" He then burst into an uncontrollable fit. Some of the men laughed along at the joke, some simply shook their heads.

"Git! Git on, now. I mean it, Whitey."

"Come on, *Mac*. I's just a funnin' ya. Come on, now."

"Mac." Byron liked the sound of it. He liked it very much. He looked up at his new sign as the two men stepped onto the porch. He liked the new sign just fine. He thought It would definitely do. He hoped Lucretia, Cas Walker and every-cursed-body at First Methodist liked it just fine, too.

He stood in the parking lot with his reminiscent smile and his broom. He could laugh at his foolish pride now. So, he did.

He ended the bout of laughter with a dramatic sigh and a wipe of his eyes. All of these years later, he still missed Lucretia, soft, warm Lucretia. Damn her to hell.

A late model sedan came up the road and with it a chilling autumn wind.

Byron "Mac" Lang, tossed his Chesterfield, picked up a hefty rock and threw it at the now weathered and defunct neon sign. A neon tube exploded, raining glass and powder down upon the rusted tin roof of the porch. Byron laughed wholeheartedly and looked around for another.

214

Chapter 35

T he yellow dog came to the Tucker place, found its usual spot in the yard in front of the kitchen window, sat and patiently waited. Jeannie Tucker rose from her chair and collected a slice of bologna from the refrigerator.

Saturday. Late October. No work. The radio played. Bill Anderson explained his obstinance, *"You don't understand the pattern of my life because my life has got no pattern. You don't see and you can't feel the wind that's blowing at my back and saying, 'move boy.' You think this burning fever in my heart is just a folly and I'm throwin' away my happiness by leaving you. Well, it's my life, throw it away if I want to."*

She had abandoned her old routine of walking into town on Saturdays, the need for supplies being not so frequent. She did not miss the window shopping nor the daydreaming outside the Starlite Theater. Mac cashed her paychecks at the package store when she bought her alcohol, having graduated to gin, and her cigarettes. Abandoning the practice had left her with more empty space to fill.

She sat for a while, in front of the kitchen window, smoking and slowly draining a bottle. She watched a train go by and recalled a conversation she had overheard between Freeman and Li'l Roy as it passed through, its heavy rhythm rattling the windows and the dirty dishes stacked in the sink. *"I just want to climb on one and take me a little ride—or a big ride—to anywhere."* She recalled her youngest son saying.

There was some comfort to be found in the *"tink"* of the bottle against the rim of the glass, the gurgle of the clear liquid as gravity pulled it from one container and into another. There was comfort in those things, if little else. With her glass refilled, she took up the task of scratching the paint from the table top with her fingernail. Patiently, she worked up a respectable start.

Jerry Lee Lewis was now on the radio trying to make love sweeter.

The table had long been an eyesore. She'd lately considered going at it with an ax. Fire would work, too. With her fingernail, she scratched again at the green paint that covered it, humming along with the radio. She had been at it for over an hour now, slowly scraping flecks and small patches to reveal the light original wood color beneath. She played the same game that most folks who have ever held an apple in one hand and a paring knife in the other have played. She peeled at the paint, curious as to how large a piece she could peel off before it broke.

She felt foolish over it now. She had just grown so tired of looking at it—the water stains, the cigarette burns, the worn places, the memories of the brutal fights she had with her old man at it, the low down dirty things they had said to each other at it. She hadn't used any kind of stripper or done any sanding on it, though. She hadn't even known that was how you were supposed to do it. Her house should be full of men who somehow innately knew these things. But they had all deserted her. She had birthed three sons. One was now in prison like his father. One was now in the cemetery and one was overseas in the service.

Almost six months had passed since his heated leaving and Li'l Roy had not once written her. He would. Soon. She was sure of it.

It was only just reaching twelve thirty and already she was riding high on an afternoon buzz. Soon, she would lay on the couch and settle in for an afternoon nap. She took another drink from her glass and studied the mess of a table top. She berated herself for being so stupid as to ever think that the past would allow itself be covered up so easily. She lit another cigarette, set her sights on a green-backed fly and reached slowly for the fly swatter. She smacked it flat and dead and flicked it from the table out the opened kitchen window, never minding the smudge of guts it left behind.

She watched them through the window and she thought they must be lost. A nice new car like that had no business out here. She thought they must be turning around when they pulled into her yard. She thought they were going to ask her for directions when the two men exited the vehicle. *More recruiters.* She thought they might be recruiters looking for recruits when she saw their uniforms. She quietly scoffed at them from her place at the table and considered saving them some time and calling out to them, "You've already got mine." But decided against it. Let them waste their time.

She watched them as they stepped slowly through the unmowed yard and she knew they were judging the squalor and the condition of the house. She muttered a swear and stood, turned the volume down on the radio and headed for the opened front door, cigarette in hand.

"Whattaya lookin' for?" She greeted them, her voice deep and smoky, her hair a red wildfire fueled by gin and sass.

"Miss Tucker?"

"Who's askin?"

The uniformed men looked at each other and then back to her. They removed their hats. "Lieutenant Colonel James, Ma'm. Are you Jean Tucker, mother of Private First Class Roy Tucker?"

She straightened her neck from the tilt she had given it. A lightheadedness settled on her as she felt the truth, merciless and damning, coming for her, but she denied it and in vain tried to change it. "Cut the shit," she said, feeling herself begin to tremble. "I'm Li'l Roy's mama. He done went and found some trouble? Lord," she laughed nervously, "what's that kid done now?" It would not be true until they said it. Li'l Roy would remain out there somewhere in the world until these two men pulled him out of it with their words. She removed a stray bit of tobacco from her tongue and with her lips made a "pthhh" sound, half spitting and half blowing. When one of the men began to speak, she hurriedly cut him off saying, "Li'l Roy's a good boy, ya know, he just gets up to some nonsense from time to time, but he really ain't nothin' but good. He's the best of this bunch. That's for sure. You tell him I said that, and you tell him I ain't mad at him, but I just can't help him right now. You tell him that and you tell him Mama loves him and you just be on your way now." The man who had not given his name listened patiently and then suggested that they go inside. For the first time, she noticed the small box and the large manila envelope he held in his hands. Her eyes welled up with tears. "Listen, fellas, I got no bail money and I sure as shit can't afford to get him a lawyer. Y'all don't be too hard on him. He's just a kid ya know." She glanced at the box again and continued, "So's y'all might as well go on and get back in that car and go on back where ya came from now and you tell Li'l Roy that I love him, but he's shit outta luck. Now go on." She felt the first tear break free and roll across her cheek. "Please, just go on now."

"Miss Tucker," Lieutenant Colonel James began, hesitated and with palpable doubt continued, "this is Captain Chase. He's a Marine Corps chaplain." He hesitated once again, giving Jeannie Tucker time to acknowledge the chaplain.

"Good for him." She wiped the tear away. Again her eyes were drawn to the metal box.

"Miss Tucker," The officer began and Jean Tucker suddenly felt the inescapable weight of the information that was about to be dropped on her.

"Please, just go. Go tell him what I said. Please. Hell, I'm beggin' here fellas." She wiped her runny nose with the back of her hand.

"Miss Tucker, the United States Marine Corps regrets to inform you that your son, Private First Class Roy Tucker, has been killed in action in the Con Thien

217

province of Viet Nam. These are his personal effects." He motioned toward the box the chaplain held. "The loss of a Marine—"

"Shut your mouth," she said softly to him, cutting him off. "Why couldn't you just go? You shut your mouth and just gimme Li'l Roy's things." She tossed her cigarette into the high grass and violently snatched the box from the officer's hands. "Now, just shut up. Just shut up and get the hell on outta here."

"Respectfully, ma'm, won't you please have us in?" the chaplain asked again.

"Get off of my property, you bastards! Now! Go on!"

"Again, respectfully, ma'm, we are here to help you with the arrangements. Private Tucker deserves a soldier's burial with full—"

"Don't. Don't you do it. Don't you tell me what that boy deserves. Don't you tell me what my son deserves. Don't you do it. You bastards have done enough, you and men like you. Now—" Jeannie Tucker trembled, felt the acid, the bile and the gin rising up from her stomach. She attempted to finish her statement, but instead heaved, vomited, reached for the wooden railing and missed. She went to her knees and heaved once more.

Somewhere she heard one of the men tell the other to find a wet towel. The man who had given the order was down with her now and she knew that the other had gone into her house. She raised her head and saw Travis and Toby Simms now staring at her from the road.

Inside, they sat at the kitchen table. Jeannie Tucker had washed her face and refused to lie down. She now poured herself a drink and offered one to each of the men. The officers declined. It did not occur to her to offer them something else.

They sat silently, letting her drink and get her head around it. Patiently, like the sentinels they were, they watched her for a long while, scrape at the paint on the table with the nail of her forefinger. Lieutenant Colonel James retrieved a pack of cigarettes from his pocket and lit a cigarette of his own adding a certain personable element to the current atmosphere.

"This is all on account of me." Jeannie Tucker said slowly and made no eye contact with either of the men. "I did this. I killed him. I stood right there in that graveyard and I told Johnny Stearns to do something and— I killed him. I told Johnny to— They lied about his age, ya know." She spoke directly to neither of the men. "They put his sixteen year old back against the wall and they drove him over to Knoxville and they sat in that recruitment office and they lied and they scared him into lyin', too. But, do ya think anybody gives a shit that he was only sixteen years old?" She began to scratch more fervently at the green paint. "Hell, that girl is fifteen. Think I don't know about that? You were all probably in on it. What the hell was he guilty of? It's not like she was a girl from town." She ceased her scratching

218

and lit another cigarette from the one she was smoking. She made eye contact briefly before returning to her nervous task at the table top. She did not look up when she questioned, "I thought you guys sent telegrams when this happens."

"Not anymore, Ma'm." One of the men answered, but she did not know which.

"You fellas already tell Roy's daddy or am I gonna have to do it?"

She looked up then. A confused glance passed between the officers. Captain Chase spoke. "Ma'm, our records indicated that Private Tucker's father was deceased. That's what Private Tucker told his recruiter."

"Hell, he might as well be. Shit. I'll tell him." She lied and refocused her attention to the table top.

She had closed the front door behind them. Particles of dust now swam through the wan quadrangles of light that poured through the three small rectangular windows on its top half. She was on the couch now and the small house was silent. The questions had been answered regarding her son's burial. He was to be buried beside his brother at the Holiness Cemetery. They had assured her they would make that happen and that they would get back to her with the details of the arrangements. She had not cried. She would not cry in front of them. She would not give them that not after she had puked in front of them. Now, she could not cry. She wanted only to sleep, to maybe find her baby boy in some dream of summer where she might hold him for a moment like she had before adolescence had driven its cruel wedge between them.

Sleep would not come.

The metal box on the kitchen table kept pulling her back from the darkness behind her eyes until finally, she surrendered and joined it there at the table. She studied it. She poked it. She ran her hand across its olive drab metal top and found it cold. *He's not in there. He's in a bigger box and that box is on a train on its way here now from Fort Knox.* She turned it, examining it from different angles. Suddenly, to her own surprise, she had it at her bosom, pushing its coolness into her skin, but she could not feel her son in it. *He's not in there.* With her eyes tightly shut, she pressed it harder and then harder against her until, if for only a moment, she felt his fleeting presence.

Mama, I gotta go.

Before going at the two latches on the box, she refilled her glass and lit a cigarette. Inside the box, she found his wallet with American money and what must be money from Viet Nam. There were two playing cards that upon their face bore naked women in varying states of undress. There was a wristwatch with a green band, some loose coins, an arrowhead and his dog tags. Beneath these articles were two white envelopes. She removed them and studied them. She placed them side by

219

side on the scarred table. The one on the left was addressed "To The Soldier Who Gets No Mail." It was sent by a woman named Abby Andersen with an Idaho address. The envelope on the right was blank, but it was not empty.

From the envelope on the left, she removed the letter and read:

Dear Soldier,

I hope this letter finds you safe under the protection of our Lord Jesus Christ.

We are doing an outreach program at our church, and it is so exciting to think that this letter that I am writing in Blanchard, Idaho (go Bulldogs!) will soon be in the hands of an American soldier in Viet Nam. Anyway, I am so grateful that I can write this letter and express my gratitude to you for fighting the communists over there now so that we won't have to fight them over here later. What you are doing is very brave and selfless, not unlike our savior was at Calvary.

Just a quick bit about me. I am a housewife. My husband is now the principal at Blanchard High School (go Bulldogs!). We have two little boys ages two and four. Their names are John Thomas and John Markus respectively. They are a handful (ha ha), but I love them with a love I did not know was possible. Sorry, I am just gushing and going on.

I would like to know about you. Also, I would like to put together a care package for you. I would like to know what items you need and also if there is anything you would like from the United States.

Know that my family and I are praying for your safe return. Thank you again, so very, very much.

God bless,
Hope to hear from you soon,
Abby Andersen

Jeannie Tucker studied the letter for a moment, noting the beautiful and loopy script. Carefully, she refolded the letter and placed it gently back into the envelope. She removed the letter from the blank envelope and read:

Dear Mrs. Andersen,

Thank you very much for your pen pal letter. My name is Captain Roy Tucker. First, I want to tell you that I opened this letter by mistake and even though I get plenty of mail from home sometimes so much that I have trouble finding the time to write back to my folks and all of the people from my home town who write to me I wanted to read your letter and write you back seeing as how I didn't want to give an opened letter to any of my soldiers. My folks and people back home send me care packages too with a whole lot of toilet paper, so we don't need no toilet paper. They send comic books and my guys just love to read them and pass them around. They

220

really like Sgt. Fury, Detective Comics, Action Comics, Strange Tales and Betty and Veronica. If you could send some of those, I'm sure the guys would aprishiate it. Oh and cigarettes. Some of my boys have the habit real bad. Oh, and banana moon pies if its not too much trouble.

A little bit about me is that I was born and raised in Sonoraville, Tennessee. I graduated third in my class and I was almost salutorian, but missed it by just a little bit. I was also quarterback and captain of the football team (go Spartans!). My daddy is the sheriff and my mama is a nurse and she helps with the music program down at the church. We are methodist but don't hold that against me (haha).

This war will be over soon and me and my boys will have rid the world of comunists.

Thanks for your letter
I hope to hear from you soon,
Captain Roy Tucker
PS I don't mind if you want to gush and go on about your boys.

Had they given her the wrong box? Was this a different Roy Tucker? She examined the dog tags. She ran it all through her head but couldn't seem to get a grasp of it. She reread the letter from Li'l Roy. And then suddenly, she did grasp it. She threw her head back, "Roy Tucker you little shit." She laughed belly laughs that came from the heart. She read the letter again, this time not distracted by its confusing content and she laughed at every bullshit sentence. Captain? Methodist? Where the hell did he come up with Methodist? Really? She laughed until she fell from the chair and then she laughed there on the floor. Goddamn, she loved that kid. She laughed until the tears came and her nose ran like a child's. She laughed until she let it break her and the laughter turned to moans and the moans to wails, until it was all sucked into the the silence of an opened mouth that wanted only to draw air but could not.

She found her feet and realized that the small explosion she heard was the sound the gin bottle made when it hit the wall. She then did the same with her glass before overturning the entire table.

Chapter 36

D amned shame," said Mister Bailey. "Heard he was over there. Wouldn't a thought him old enough. The youngest one, ya say? The little'n?"

"Yeah, and he wasn't old enough," said Freeman.

"Oh," said Bailey. "Ain't that poor woman had the licks? How's she doin' with it, Freeman?"

"She's down. Way down."

"'Spect she is. War and the shit we get up to," the old man fretted.

"The shit we get up to," repeated Freeman.

The question so often asked of Freeman was, "What brought you here to Snorville?"

The answer was without fail, "An eastbound L&N." That was the answer not solely because it was tinged with humor and humor was Freeman's natural way, but also because, within the brevity of that answer, Freeman escaped the boring and tiresome act of truth telling.

A truthful answer would involve a sort of confession, a professing of belief in a thing Freeman had long convinced himself he did not believe in. On a dusky Sunday evening, Freeman chose the truth when Mister Bailey said to him, "You know, young man, I never was clear on what exactly it was brought ya here to Snorville."

"An eastbound—"

"Yeah," the old man cut him off, "an eastbound L and N. You used that one before." Bailey waited and when Freeman didn't reply, Bailey said, "Ah, there I go again, bein' all about your business. Hell, I don't mean to be, but I ain't got no business of my own. Forget I asked. Ya done went and made me feel all shitty about it."

Freeman chuckled at the old man. "I don't care to tell it."

"So tell it then, or starve an old man to death. Up to you."

"You believe in signs, Mister Bailey?" Freeman asked, shaking a cigarette from the pack.

"What kinda signs?"

"Hell, I don't know," said Freeman, exhaustion suddenly creeping into his voice.

"Well, you asked."

"Signs like," Freeman paused, "signs like God, or, or the universe or somethin' or what the hell ever might be out there, is tryin' to tell ya somethin'?"

"'Or what the hell ever,' huh? You meanin' to tell me you ain't Christian, young man?" This question set Freeman ill at ease until he saw the old man's lips begin to curl.

Freeman spoke, his tone confessional. "Some days I am, Mister Bailey. Some days, I'm not sure what I am. But right here and right now, I am absolutely sure that I'm not. Now that might change here directly, but—"

"Hell, Freeman, don't piss all over yourself worryin' about what you're sayin' to me." Bailey leaned a bit in his chair and had a look through the screen door, when he was sure Miss Bailey was not within earshot, he continued. "I 'spect most folks is the same way. They won't admit it. But they are."

"I suspect as such myself," agreed Freeman.

"So you followed the signs here, eh?"

Freeman lit himself a Lucky Strike and told the truth.

The first time the information found him, it was a novelty, a curious discovery written on a piece of wood, a date, a town, a state, and two letters in pretty handwriting. He'd found this information scrawled onto a pallet in a citrus grove distribution warehouse in Tampa. The information then transferred itself in the same indelible way onto the wall of his mind. He would look at it from time to time, thinking about the hand that had written it. The handwriting was definitely feminine. Someone was trying to make their mark on the world in the only way available to them. Freeman could understand that. Hell, who couldn't. After a while, he left it there on the wall of his mind where it was all but forgotten and dust covered.

In a Louisville freight yard, far from warm and forgotten citrus groves, Freeman would wipe that dust away. The same information, written in the same warm and inviting handwriting, stared up at him from the dancing flames of a barrel fire. With a gloved hand, Freeman reached into the fire and retrieved the thin wooden slat that had been used for kindling. In the sparse snowfall, much to the bemusement and curiosity of his fellow transients, he smacked and swatted the fire from the burning piece of wood and studied the information. Save for the date, it was indeed the same. 6-15-67. Sonoraville TN JM.

In East St. Louis, mere months later, the information would inexplicably come to him again.

He did not believe in signs, omens and the like. But in considering this lack of belief, he thought he might make his way to Sonoraville, Tennessee in the unlikely case that he might later adopt a different posture regarding such things.

And so he had asked around, gathered information from fellow wanderers and hobos until he was confident he could find Sonoraville, Tennessee. With his itinerary and his curiosity, he had ridden the rails almost into the Carolinas.

In Sonoraville, he found Smoky Mountain Millworks. At Smoky Mountain Millworks, he found a different kind of sign—a HELP WANTED sign. With a shrug, he found employment.

When he finished his tale, he sat quietly, waiting for the old man to digest it.

"Young man?"

"Yes, Mister Bailey?"

"I liked your other answer better."

"Me, too, Mister Bailey. Me, too."

A pickup truck passed. The two men watched as Quiet Tom waved from behind the wheel. Mister Bailey returned the wave. Freeman did not.

"See Tom's still makin' it to church," observed the old man.

"Mister Bailey?" Freeman rose to his feet watching Tom Lawford disappear as he headed home.

"Yeah?"

"My account squared?"

"Square as dice, young man."

Freeman tugged at his belt loops, hitched up his pants and stepped from the porch.

On the route, it was as Freeman hoped. Quiet Tom sat on his porch. Freeman casually waved and stepped from the road onto the wide, worn path that was the Lawford driveway. A few steps in, he hiked his pants up, the weight of the heavy objects in his pocket immediately pulling them back down. He stepped toward Quiet Tom who was now rising from the rocking chair, squinting and shading his eyes from the sun with a raised right hand. To Freeman, it looked as though Quiet Tom had stood to salute his arrival. The thought of Tom facing death with such humility momentarily shook Freeman. Hesitantly, he stopped, his resolve suddenly weakened by the actual sight of the man, a man who was for all intents and purposes his friend and coworker, standing just ahead, living, breathing, being alive. For a moment, he abandoned the visit and turned back to the dirt road. Abruptly, he changed course again and headed toward Quiet Tom.

"Don't do this thing. Don't you do this thing you 'bout to do." May was in his head. Sweet Mayrene.

Freeman spoke softly aloud as he smiled and waved again at Tom Lawford. "Don't you watch me do this. You look some place else. You come back in a while, now, Mayrene. But Lord, don't you watch this."

Quiet Tom smiled from the porch and Freeman's heart sank further still. He looked back at the dirt road and again took a step back toward it, then again turned toward Tom Lawford who was now waving him on, welcoming him eagerly to his home. Freeman let his uneasy legs guide him as if leaving the entire business up to them, and they guided him onward toward the porch and Quiet Tom Lawford.

"Evenin', Freeman," greeted Tom.

"Tom." Freeman tipped an imaginary hat. Spots the barn cat was at his shins, bunting. Freeman bent and scratched the cat between the ears.

"What brings ya out here?" asked Tom.

"Well, I saw ya there—figured I'd— I ain't intrudin' am I?" Freeman asked. Spots put his front paws on Freeman's calf and began to knead. Freeman scratched the cat again.

"Heaven's no. Kick him away from ya. Spots!" Tom called to the feline. "Not at all. So lonely here since Virginia left, well I'll tell ya, I'm just glad you ain't a salesman 'cause I'd probably wind up buyin' everything in your catalogue just to keep ya here and have the company. Come on up here, Freeman. Have yourself a seat."

Freeman advanced up the steps and onto the covered porch.

"Weekend just goes by too fast don't it?" Tom offered.

"It all goes by too fast."

"Amen," said Tom. "Sit down. Got somewhere to be? I got lemonade, got some sweet tea made."

"Got some of this left." Freeman retrieved a half pint bottle from his front pocket and offered it to Tom.

"Never touch the stuff, but you go on ahead." Quiet Tom said and turned toward the front door. "I'm gonna run in and get me some lemonade. You want an empty glass or a cup or somethin'?"

"No, thank ya, Tom. Never touch the stuff." Freeman smiled.

Tom laughed. "That's a good one. 'Never touch the stuff.'" He laughed again. "Have a seat. I'll be right back."

Tom disappeared into the house. Freeman sat casually in a rocking chair and immediately began nervously rocking. Spots leapt into Freeman's lap. Freeman stroked the cat. On the horizon, the autumn sun was sinking quickly.

"Nice view from here this time of day, huh?" Tom was behind him now. His words startled Freeman. Freeman jumped and spooked the cat. "Sorry, didn't mean to spook ya there, Freeman. You must not be livin' right." Quiet Tom laughed and seated himself in his usual rocker. "Push him away if ya wanna."

"He's fine," Freeman assured Tom and continued to stroke Spots.

"I meant what I said about you goin' on ahead and all. Drink your liquor. Hell, it's fine by me."

Freeman uncapped his bottle and brought it to his lips. "Good stuff here. You sure?" Again Freeman offered the bottle to Tom.

"Never touch the stuff." Tom said and laughed at himself. Freeman laughed with him and an uncomfortable silence fell between the two men.

"I can't decide which I like better, Tom, a sunset over the mountains or a sunset over the ocean. The plains is nice, but a sunset on the plains is a third to the mountains and the ocean."

"I'm guessin' you're talkin' 'bout California sunsets? Now there's an odd lot of folks, I reckon. Californians." Quiet Tom offered his opinion.

"Yeah, odd folks, but beautiful sunsets. Knew of this goat farmer out there once used to climb up on a hill with his favorite goat and his dog and watch the sun set into the ocean. The sight of it put him in such a romantic mood that one evenin' he reaches over and puts his arm around the goat and that ol' dog goes to growlin' at him, showed that goat farmer all his teeth and all, so the goat farmer took his arm from around that goat."

"Odd folks," interjected Tom.

"Now, the night that fella got married, him and his new wife went up on that hill with the goat and the dog. He wanted to show her that sunset, see? That ol' boy got to feelin' all romantical again, so he leans over and says to his new wife, 'Hey, how's about you take that dog for a walk?'"

It took Quiet Tom just a second to realize Freeman had been having him on. He suddenly burst into laughter. "Now that's a good one! 'Take the dog for a walk.'" To Quiet Tom, it seemed even funnier hearing himself repeat the punch line. "Shoot, I think I will have a sip of that liquor, Freeman. Why I ain't had a drop since I couldn't tell ya. I could sure use it. If you're sure you got enough there."

"Oh, I think we got enough." Freeman passed the bottle to Quiet Tom.

Quiet Tom took a sip, not bothering to wipe the lip of the bottle with his shirt tail. "Oh, that's not bad," he said through pursed lips. "Couldn't tell ya how long it's been. The trouble it can lead to, though."

"Tell me about it," Freeman said. "I once got hauled in front of a judge and the judge says, 'You've been hauled in here for drinkin',' and I says, 'Well let's get started.'"

Quiet Tom erupted into laughter. "I just bet you did, Freeman. 'Let's get started.' Oh, that's funny stuff." Tom Lawford took another drink from the bottle. "You're a funny guy. Why you're a regular Redd Foxx."

"Red what?"

Spots purred loudly in Freeman's lap, his eyes narrowed slits.

From his shirt pocket, Freeman retrieved a pack of Lucky Strikes and a book of matches. "You don't mind do ya, Tom?"

"Not so long as you don't mind if I get one from ya. Might as well go all out."

"Might as well. Help yourself."

"Ya know, Freeman, I'm glad you come by. Really, I am." Quiet Tom traded Freeman the bottle for the cigarette. "I needed this. I needed this so bad. How come you never come up before? I see you on that road all the time." Quiet Tom struck the match and the air filled with the scent of Sulfur.

Freeman brought the bottle to his lips but did not drink from it. He passed it back to Tom and collected the pack of cigarettes."I really couldn't answer that. Only just occurred to me."

"You comin' back from Jeannie Tucker's?"

Freeman wet his lips, tasting the tiny amount of alcohol that his false drink had left on them. "Not directly," he answered. "Earlier. I went by there earlier. Her boy's dead. Li'l Roy. Barely got his feet on the ground. Hadn't been over there no time."

"Heard that. Ain't that some kind a shame?" Tom shook his head and gazed vacantly toward the sunset.

"It is," Freeman concurred.

"How's she doin'? I mean how's she takin' it and all?"

Freeman's face reddened, though he tried desperately not to show his hand. "Don't think she's gonna come back from it, Tom. She's down. Way, way down. She's hurtin'."

"Ah, she's a tough one. Damned tough. Trust me on that. That boy died a soldier. Beats any death he mighta found 'round here. There's comfort in that." Tom said.

Freeman's right hand involuntarily balled into a tight fist.

"Ma and Pa treatin' ya all right over't the boardin' house?" asked Tom.

Gus the Rooster crowed in the distance. Twilight came as Quiet Tom finished off the bottle. The heavy night air was suddenly filled with the high chirps of crickets and the atonal calls of bullfrogs.

227

"Still awful warm, ain't it?" asked Tom, fanning the front of his shirt.

Freeman wiped a film of sweat from his forehead. "It is. It is. Coolin' off, though." He wiped his sweat-soaked hands on his thighs. "Train should be comin'." Freeman looked out in the direction of the tracks.

"Say you rode a lot of trains? Bet you've seen it all, aintcha, Freeman?" Quiet Tom's speech was slurred now.

"Seen a lot. Sure have. I've even learned a thing or two in spite of myself."

"What have ya learned, Freeman?" asked Tom.

Freeman considered this. "Well," he began, "one thing I learned is I learned to tell a lot about a man by the way he walks. Hell, you kinda become some kinda expert at it when ya spend a lot a time bein' places that ya shouldn't be. You learn to tell long before a fella in a uniform with a stick on his belt gets to ya if ya need to say, 'Movin' on here, boss,' or if you can maybe grease him a little bit and convince him to forget he ever saw ya in the first place. You can tell that about a man by how he walks as sure as I'm sittin' here, Tom. You learn to. You have to." Freeman stroked the sleeping cat.

"'S'at right?" Quiet Tom slurred.

"That's right. Take you for instance, Tom. I bet I could tell it was you even in the dark. Not that you walk funny or nothin', just you got your walk and I got mine. I could tell it was you in the dark and I could tell it was you in a crowd a people millin' around the scene of, let's say some accident or somethin'. Hell, I ain't even got to be that close to do it."

Through the night the train whistle blew, exhausted itself and then blew again.

"There's your train," Quiet Tom said and laughed.

Freeman laughed with him, albeit weakly. He was suddenly very anxious. He would do this. For Jeannie, he would do this thing. He would do this and it would forever be a story he could not tell. He would do this. He would do this and then, when the train came closer with it's beckoning whistle, he would let it carry him away from what he had done. It would carry him away from Sonoraville and Whelan County, away from Jeannie Tucker, away from her in the night with her need and away from her in the sunlight with her proud independence. It would carry him away from a love he had long convinced himself that he did not deserve, away from playful bumping shoulders and from hungry bumping hips, from laughter and the looking forward and from the kisses deep and passionate. It would carry him from companionship to the haunted loneliness he knew was the wage of his sin. It would carry him closer to Mayrene and closer still with every passing day and with every passing mile until the final dusk where he would catch the Westbound and ride the high iron to the Sweet By and By.

Quiet Tom rose from the squeaking rocking chair and stumbled toward the edge of the porch to relieve himself, placing a hand upon the post in an attempt to steady himself.

"Knew this fella once had a daughter—" Freeman began.

"I got a daughter," Tom said, relieving himself off the edge of the porch.

Softly, Freeman lifted the sleeping cat from his lap and placed him on the porch. Spots immediately curled up beside the rocker and fell quickly back to sleep. Freeman rose slowly from the rocking chair. "I know ya do, Tom."

"Had me a wife, too. Got sick, though. Got the cancer."

Something electrical in nature crept up Freeman's spine and spread from the back of his neck through his shoulders, down his arms and out through his calloused finger tips. It caused his heart to stutter and skip and pimpled his knotty forearms. He stood still, momentarily paralyzed by this new information.

Tom continued as he zipped his fly, "We don't wanna talk about that, though. Nah, not right now. Maybe we could some other time if that'd be all right, Freeman."

"Yeah, Tom, yeah sure, maybe we could." Freeman's knees involuntarily jerked.

Quiet Tom turned to find Freeman now standing behind him. Tom was startled almost to the point of stumbling backward off the porch. "Whew! You spooked me, Freeman."

"Must not be— " Freeman began, but his breath had grown shallow. He tried again, "Must not be livin' right, Tom." With some effort, Freeman grinned and winked, but did not immediately yield the way.

"You okay, Freeman?"

Freeman nervously waved away the concern. "Far from it," he said and forced another laugh.

"Sit down, Freeman. You lookin' awfully puny all a sudden."

"I gotta take a leak myself. I'm okay. Hell, I'm fine as frog hair."

"If you say so. Hey, finish your story, Freeman," said Tom.

"What story's that, Tom?" Freeman asked now with his back to Tom.

"The one you was tellin' 'fore I went and got all sad sack on ya. About the fella with the daughter."

"Did it take her fast or did it take her slow, Tom?"

"What's 'at?" Tom asked the back of Freeman's head.

Freeman scanned the horizon and spoke as if to the growing darkness. "The cancer," he said solemnly. "Your wife, Tom. Did it take her fast or did it take her slow?"

"Took her slow," said Tom. "Took her damned slow. Let's talk about somethin' else, Freeman. Tell me your story."

Freeman stepped on to the edge of the porch just as Quiet Tom had done, unzipped his pants and began to relieve himself. "Knew a fella had a daughter. This fella's daughter was about to be married and her ol' man asked his future son-in-law, 'Now son, you sure you can give her the kind of life she's accustomed to?'"

"You can wait 'til you're done with your piss, Freeman." Quiet Tom laughed.

"Hell, I'm good," said Freeman his stream never wavering. "Anyways so ol' dad asked his future son-in-law, 'you sure you can keep her in the manner in which she's accustomed to?' And the future son-in-law says, 'Not sure I got it in me to be that much of a son of a bitch."

Tom laughed drunkenly, "Ah ha! Not sure I got it in me— That's funny stuff."

"Seemed funnier before," Freeman said almost to himself. He zipped his jeans and waited, listening until he heard the creak of the rocking chair and knew for certain that Tom was seated.

He turned and smiled curiously at Tom and stepped toward him. "Not sure I got it in me to be that much of a son of a bitch."

Quiet Tom laughed. "That much of a— Hey, wha—?"

The train horn sounded again and Freeman moved in on Quiet Tom, uncomfortably close. "Freeman, whattaya—?"

"William—" Mayrene's sweet voice came again.

Inside his pocket, his hand wrapped firmly around the grip of the .38. "Look some place else, Mayrene," he whispered.

But killing was not in him. It was not in his trembling hands. It was not in his somersaulting guts, not in his balls. It was not in his blood, warm and wanting. It was not in his heart, lonely, remorseful, broken. It was not in his spine, weary with the load. It was not in any of the countless cells of which he was composed. If it ever truly was in his tortured thoughts, then it had answered an invitation borne of anger and self deception. There at the threshold of the act, Freeman rescinded that invitation.

He was many of the things that he had been called. He was all of the things that he had called himself. He was a drunk, yes. He was a coward for sure. He was a liar even a bullshitter, sometimes a mooch and more than twice a thief, but he was not this. And what good would it do Jeannie anyway? One more sorry ass man killing another sorry ass man, as if that evened up some score of justice that wouldn't anymore be settled than his running tab at Pudgy's.

As if Quiet Tom had sensed a tension in the air, drunk as he was, and felt it go again, the chair eased forward on its rockers, Tom leaning inward this time and Freeman moving away. "Freeman? Hey, Freeman, you okay?"

In a visibly trembling daze, Freeman had stepped toward the edge of the porch.

"Careful, now, you 'bout to walk off that edge," Tom warned.

230

"Just realized I gotta go, Tom. Shoulda left a while ago."

Freeman removed his hand from his pocket and stepped from the porch in a giant step, his legs almost betraying him on the landing.

"Freeman?" Tom called after him.

He pumped his legs alongside the churning wheels of the train until his muscles burned and his bones threatened to turn to ash. From the darkness of the rail car, a hand reached for him. He pumped his legs impossibly harder, impossibly faster. He reached desperately. He was out of practice. He was old. He was sweat soaked and out of breath. Again, his arm shot out and he reached again for the strange and helping hand. He touched it, danced fingertips across a dry and weathered palm, lost it, touched it once again, grasped it, secured it, and like the old pro he was, swung himself up and into the rolling train car. With labored breath, he thanked the stranger for his assistance. The stranger said nothing, acknowledging Freeman's gratitude with only a silent and disregarding wave before seating himself at his spot in a darkened corner of the car. Freeman sat beside the opened door of the rail car. Almost absently, he wiped the sweat from his face and forehead and watched as Quiet Tom, "Snorville," Jeannie Tucker and the kitchen table he would never finish, never present to her, rolled away and became part of the past.

It was a familiar song that played in the night, a rolling mechanical rhythm that made him feel both lost and at home with the wind not at his back but at his face, and knowing no destination, only direction. West.

In the darkness of the boxcar he felt for his beloved Mayrene, but knew his search was in vain, that Mayrene had gone, gone to *look someplace else* if only for a while.

She would be back.

He hoped.

She would be back on down the track a ways, where strangers waited, strangers who had not heard his stories of found dimes and of romance interrupted by gunfire.

The helpful stranger approached from his darkened corner. In his hand he held out a bottle, inviting Freeman to partake.

"No, thanks," said Freeman reaching for the bottle. He had himself a long and soothing swallow. Returning the bottle to his benefactor, he said, "Never touch the stuff."

The stranger laughed, turned and walked back toward his darkened corner of the boxcar.

Hours later, crossing the Clinch River, Freeman let the firearm slip from his hand, down into the muddy water.

231

Chapter 37

M onday morning she was up with Gus. She bathed in a warm bath and readied herself.

She did not sit in her chair at the kitchen table in front of the window. She sat outside on the steps. There she waited for Red until she could not bring herself to wait a moment longer.

The yellow dog followed her to the railroad tracks where there it abandoned her, twice rethinking the notion before sniffing the ground and finally turning back the way they had come. Jeannie Tucker walked on into town. She walked with her chin up and her jaw strongly set against whatever obstacles may be waiting in Sonoraville or the world. She moved through the autumn sun with the late warmth on her freshly washed face and the slightest of breezes in her curly red hair. She walked to Main Street.

The first time it happened, she was almost too preoccupied to notice. A young, well dressed, familiar looking man, tipped his hat to her and bade her good morning. Reflexively, she did the same. Behind him, two older men, tipped their hats and offered their condolences. Word had spread of Li'l Roy.

"You need anything, you just come down to the VFW and let us know."

She thanked them and walked on to the post office where the two attending clerks told her how sorry they were for her loss. She thanked them and traded a nickel for a stamp. On the sidewalk, from her purse, she removed the envelope, now sealed and with Abby Andersen's Blanchard, Idaho adress written on the center of it. There was no return address and that was all right. Soon, a decent woman and a good mother would receive the letter and that good woman and decent mother would forever know and remember Li'l Roy Tucker as Captain Roy Tucker, whose mother was a nurse and whose father was the sheriff, Captain Tucker, who was a high school quarterback, who graduated third in his class. She licked the stamp and applied it to the corner, giving it a good press with her thumb, and she dropped it into the blue mailbox on the sidewalk. "I shoulda done more nice things for ya, Li'l Roy," she said out loud. There on the street, she let herself remember him—youthful and shirtless in the summer sun. Absently, but affectionately she ran her hand across the top of the mailbox.

"Sorry about your loss, Miss Tucker," a young man said lightly touching her shoulder as he passed.

"Thank you," she offered.

She scrubbed a tear from her cheek with the back of her hand and she walked on up Main Street in the the direction of Maynard's Hardware store. She planned on purchasing a scraper, sandpaper and stripper. Freeman had promised he would do this for her, sanding and scraping the old kitchen table, freeing it of all the scars of its past. But Freeman was gone.

Chapter 38

S tearns felt the dead boy with him in the cruiser. He fought the urge to speak out loud to the boy, to state his case, to ask for undeserved mercy or at least some sign that the boy understood it all.

For most of his life, Stearns had this notion, though its existence was never named nor even discussed in his thoughts, that death gifted the departed with omniscience and omnipresence.

Many years before, he had stood in the receiving line at his grandfather's funeral, his mother with his plump eight-year-old hand held tightly in her own, quietly commanding him to *quit fidgetin'*. A handsome man, tall, dark suited and somber and with the wisest of blue eyes approached, nodded slightly and said softly to his mother, "My condolences." The man then politely embraced her and said, just loud enough for young Johnny Stearns to hear, "He was a good man and he's gone to learn the answer to everything." His mother had smiled and in return had offered a diffident nod.

His mother had found the thought so pleasant that she repeated it to various payers of respect no less than half a dozen times when they expressed their mutual sorrow concerning the loss of her father.

"Sorry about your loss. He was a good man."

"Thank you," she would say and with a pride seldom expressed continue, "He's gone to learn the answer to everything."

When he thought of his grandfather, he thought of the funeral, of the strange man's words to his mother and how his mother repeated those words, used them as a cushion for her fall.

For years to follow, she used her dead father as a tool to help keep her son in line.

"Johnny, you know PawPaw Henry can see you, don't you?"

He was well into his teens before realizing his grandfather surely had better things to do in Paradise than to sit around spying on his chronically horny grandson. Still, every time death came to someone close to him, he felt their presence lingering near him for varying amounts of time. There were times he still caught himself speaking to his mother.

From the cruiser, he watched Jeannie Marie as she went about her business in the town. The secret act filled him with a reminiscent yearning. When she left the hardware store with a plain brown bag, he let his curiosity kill the time. Had the dead boy been in the cruiser, he could have told his father what was in the bag. But the dead boy was not in the cruiser. Why would he be? He was with his mother.

When her walk led her in the direction of home and out of sight, Stearns tossed his cigarette into the street and rolled the cruiser toward the intersection. He let his patience restrain him, waiting more than half an hour before heading across the tracks.

The yellow dog barked and Jeannie looked up from her work at the table. She stood and watched out the kitchen window as Stearns pulled the cruiser into the yard and killed the engine. Almost casually, she freed the curtains that had forever been parted and pushed them toward the center of the rod. They fell together in a dusty collision, leaving the kitchen suddenly dark. She pulled the string and the naked bulb above her glowed to life. In the living room she twisted the button on the door knob.

She was unphased by the first knock, intent on scraping and scraping away at the green paint. When he knocked again, she turned on the radio, twisted the volume knob up and returned to the task at hand.

He knocked a third time, calling her name. She scraped and scraped. Large pieces of paint peeled away, and she let them fall and break apart upon the linoleum floor.

He did not knock a fourth time.

Acknowledgements

In the early days of this novel, Jeff Wiles, Jason Foster, Chris Minton, Kenny Burton, Sandra Harris, and Andy Miranda were kind enough to read it and offer feedback. Their thoughts were instrumental in turning this into a work that I am proud of. Clara Babinski and Steven Terry worked tirelessly to help me clean and tighten this thing up. Their input was invaluable. Nathan Paul Isaacs created the cover and Amy Isaac's perceptive reading led to the brief description on the back cover. Without Wanda Fries, this book would not have happened. To all of you, I am eternally grateful. P.